SOMEONE
HAD TO DIE

SOMEONE HAD TO DIE

a James Butler mystery

JACK LUELLEN

Light Messages
Torchflame Books
Durham, NC

Someone Had to Die
Jack Luellen
luellenwriting@gmail.com
www.jackluellen.com

Published 2022, by Torchflame Books
an Imprint of Light Messages
www.lightmessages.com
Durham, NC 27713 USA
SAN: 920-9298

Paperback ISBN: 978-1-61153-450-4
E-book ISBN: 978-1-61153-451-1
Library of Congress Control Number: 2022901573

This is a work of fiction based on the author's recollection and documentation of actual events and people. Conversations have been recreated. The names and details of some individuals have been changed to respect their privacy.

For Isabelle Faith.

With your love,
anything is possible.

PREFACE

THIS IS A WORK OF FICTION based on the author's rec–ollection and documentation of actual events and people. Conversations have been recreated. The names and details of some individuals have been changed to respect their privacy. The major protagonists are entirely fictional. Any resemblance to actual persons living or dead is entirely coincidental.

The scenes describing the meeting with Félix Gallardo in prison and the kidnapping of Caro are entirely fictional. Those names, characters, places, events, and incidents are the product of the author's imagination, and are used in a fictitious manner. Any resemblance to persons, living or dead, or actual events, is entirely coincidental.

In Mexico, as in other nations of Hispanic or Latino culture, individuals usually have double surnames. A child is given a double surname composed of the "male part" of both the mother and the father's surnames. The male surname is the first of the two surnames.

If parents are of Hispanic or Latino descent, it is probable that each of them has a double surname composed in a similar fashion. Thus, if the mother is named Anna Pérez Garcia, and the father is named Servando Morales González, their son Fernando would be named Fernando Morales Pérez.

To Anglos unfamiliar with this naming system, the second surname looks like the person's last name, but is the mother's family name. The first surname, which looks like the person's middle name, is the father's family name.

ACKNOWLEDGMENTS

THIS BOOK would not have been possible without the support and encouragement of so many people. I particularly want to thank Jessica Vaisz, Jennifer Jaskolka, Mark Ulmer, Nathen Baalman, Rebecca Murray, Jesús Martinez, Carrie Donatelli, and Candace Kearns Read for enduring my earliest discussions about this project, and then indulging my various drafts and rapidly changing ideas. The research work done by Eli Polley was invaluable. Ahna Mee, Jackie Haney, and Reggie Robba are owed a huge thank you for enduring my yelling across the office whenever I'd unearthed a new fact or developed yet another theory.

In everything I do as a lawyer, and in every draft of this book, I try to honor what Edward Medvene taught me, much of which I failed to understand until years later. I have tried to respect the legacy of Agent Enrique "Kiki" Camarena.

I am indebted to everyone at Torchflame Books, and especially to Meghan Bowker for her invaluable editing. Jolene Rheault, Jori Hanna, and Cristina Deptula have done more than I could have ever hoped for in helping me market and publicize this book. Sonja and David Vaisz have supported and encouraged me in ways both big and small, spoken and unspoken, for years. Thank you for everything Corrie Luellen. Finally, Lori Krogel's support and encouragement have meant so much to me and made this project much more meaningful.

In honor of my dad, Howard Jack Luellen, and my mom, Judith Peters. I wish they could have seen this.

GLOSSARY OF REAL CHARACTERS

Alan Bachelier:	DEA agent stationed in Guadalajara
Albert Radelat:	American murdered in Guadalajara, at La Longosta
Alfredo Zavala Avelar:	Mexican government pilot; kidnapped and killed
Armando Pavon Reyes:	Primer Comandante, MFJP
Antonio Garate Bustamonte:	Former Mexican police officer turned US informant
Ben Mascarena:	Missionary killed in Guadalajara
Carlos Enrique Salazar :	"El Cholo," Cartel leader murdered March 19, 2021
Dale Stinson:	DEA agent in Mexico; identified Caro's voice on tapes
David Herrera:	DEA agent; translated Camarena interrogation tapes
Dennis Carlson :	Missionary killed in Guadalajara
Edward Rafeedie:	US federal judge; presided over Camarena cases
Elaine Shannon:	Journalist; author Desperados
Emilio Payan:	Drug leader Mexico
Enrique Alvarez del Castillo:	Governor of Jalisco, Secretary of the Interior, 1983–88
Enrique Camarena Salazar:	"Kiki," DEA agent kidnapped and killed in Guadalajara

Ernesto Fonseca:	"Don Neto," Mexican drug leader
Félix Ismael Rodríguez :	CIA Paramilitary Operations Officer
Gary Webb:	Reporter San Jose Mercury News
Hector Berrellez:	DEA agent; former head of Operation Leyenda
Hector Cervantes Santos:	Former Mexican police officer turned US informant
Humberto Alvarez Machain:	Mexican doctor; kidnapped and tried in the US
Ismael Zambada- Niebla:	"El Mayo," Mexican drug leader, Sinaloa Cartel
James "Jaime" Kuykendall :	DEA Agent, Resident Agent in Charge, Guadalajara
Javier Barba Hernandez:	Mexican lawyer turned drug lord
Joaquin Guzman Loera:	"El Chapo," Mexican drug lord, Sinaloa Cartel
John Walker:	American murdered in Guadalajara, at La Longosta
Jorge Godoy:	Former Mexican police officer turned US informant
Juan Arevalo de Gardoqui:	General; Mexico's Minister of Defense, 1983-88
Juan Matta Ballesteros:	Honduran drug lord; connected to Félix Gallardo
Lawrence Victor Harrison:	Alleged CIA operative; communications work for drug lords
Manuel Bartlett Diaz:	Mexico's Minister of Interior, 1983–88
Manuel Buendia:	Mexican reporter, murdered May 30, 1984
Manuel Ibarra Herrera:	Mexican Federal Judicial

	Police Director, 1982–85
Manuel Medrano:	Assistant United States Attorney
Miguel Aldana Ibarra:	Primer Comandante, MFJP, Interpol Director, 1982-85
Miguel Angel Félix Gallardo:	"El Padrino," Mexican drug boss
Paula Mascarena:	Missionary killed Guadalajara
Pedro Aviles Perez:	Mexican drug lord in Sinaloa in 1960s and 70s
Phil Jordan:	DEA Agent; Director of El Paso Intelligence Center
Rafael Caro Quintero:	"Rafa," drug lord in Guadalajara
Ramon Lira:	Former Mexican police officer turned US informant
Raul Lopez Avarez:	Former Mexican police officer; convicted in US
Rene Lopez Romero:	Former Mexican police officer turned US informant
Rene Verdugo Urquidez:	Former Mexican police officer; convicted in US
Robert "Bobby" Castillo:	DEA agent; identified Caro's voice on interrogation tapes
Robert "Tosh" Plumlee:	CIA operative
Rose Carlson:	Missionary killed in Guadalajara
Ruben Zuno Arce:	Mexican businessman; convicted of conspiracy in US
Sal Leyva:	DEA agent
Sara Cosio Martinez:	Socialite, girlfriend of Caro Quintero
Samuel Ramirez Razo:	"El Samy," MFJP officer working for drug lords
Sergio Espino Verdin:	MFJP commander working with drug lords

Susie Lozano:	Secretary, DEA office in Guadalajara
Tiller Russell:	Filmmaker; The Last Narc
Tomas Morlet Borquez:	DFS officer

CHAPTER ONE

"I DON'T WANT TO DIE," the man mutters over and over, his voice hoarse and faint. "Don't want to die. Don't want to die."

The afternoon sun slithers into the room through gaps in the partially closed shades. Silence lingers in the room, interrupted only by the muffled whir of a ceiling fan. The room is barren—no furniture, rugs, pictures—save for the lone wooden chair in the middle of the room.

The man is bound to the chair, new ropes tied into perfect knots harnessing his arms and legs. A red and blue bandana, new and pressed, is tied tight around his head, blinding him. His face is wounded and bruising already. The once-white t-shirt he wears is soaked in sweat and blood.

A tall, muscular man dressed in crisp new jeans and a white buttoned shirt, neat and well-pressed, opens the bedroom door and pauses to survey the surroundings. His rigid gait emits an aura of substance as he slowly enters the room and gently closes the door behind him. He approaches the bound man in the chair, then crouches in front of him, drawing close. With one finger, he raises the bound man's chin.

"You know, sir, this does not give me any pleasure. I would like to see you go home to your family."

"Please, I beg you. Please don't hurt my family."

"Don't worry. Your family will not be harmed." The man stands and takes a deep, controlled breath. "My friend, I can

1

end all of this—all of the pain and suffering—if you just tell me what I need to know."

His deep voice and polished Mexican accent echoes off the baren walls. He pronounces his words slowly, articulated for emphasis.

The bound man struggles to speak, his parched throat restricting the sounds from escaping.

"Comandante, how many times must I say it? I've told you everything I know. Everything."

The man's voice becomes a bit louder, but remains composed.

"I am the only one who can save you now. The only one who can help you."

The bound man strains under the burden of the ropes.

"Please, Comandante, I want to help you. Ask me anything. I'll tell you everything I know."

The interrogator carefully removes the blindfold and stuffs it into his back pocket as the bound man blinks uncontrollably in the light.

"Look at me." As the interrogator stares into the bound man's eyes, his voice becomes deeper and more forceful. "I am going to give you just one more chance. It really is quite simple. Just tell me who killed Special Agent Enrique Camarena."

Slowly shaking his head in distress, with tears pouring down his cheeks, the bound man's words seep like blood from his lips.

"I...I just don't know. You have to believe me."

The interrogator adjusts his stance, shaking his head, remaining emotionlessly aloof as he looks down upon the bound man.

"I do believe you. More's the pity." He reaches behind him, producing a pistol.

Without either a word or hesitation, a single shot rings out, the sound amplified within the sterile walls of the small room. The bullet strikes the bound man square in the forehead, knocking him over to his death on the floor. Without a glance back, the shooter casually turns and strides out of the room, leaving the door wide open.

James Butler jolts up in his bed, sweating profusely, his chest heaving. *Son of a bitch. Another night, another damn dream.*

The clock on the nightstand reads 4:19 a.m.

James struggles to rise, sitting on the edge of the bed for a moment to regain his bearings. He reaches for the glass on his nightstand before realizing it's empty.

After standing slowly, James presses the blue button on the remote on his nightstand to turn on the light on the ceiling fan above, the fan already spinning at medium speed.

Approaching forty, James has the lean and well-toned body of a runner whose metabolism has not yet succumbed to the wraths of age, and a head full of dark hair that further belies his age. The large bedroom is meagerly decorated but well-appointed with furniture, dominated by the king bed with a large cherry-wood headboard, matching nightstands, and two dressers—one upright, and the other with a large mirror.

James staggers down the circular stairs to the condo's main floor, and into the kitchen. After opening the refrigerator and gazing across the options, he reaches into the cabinet to the right to retrieve a small glass, and fills the glass with orange juice before downing it in a single drink. He sets the glass in the sink and runs water from the tap to cover the bottom of the glass, before shuffling back upstairs to his office across the hall from the bedroom.

The office is clean and well-organized. One could even characterize it as sterile. A large L-shaped mahogany desk sits aligned against one wall, with a large dual-screen computer configuration on top. Next to the desk, a color laser printer rests on a small but ornate mahogany stand. Other than the computer, the desk is clean save for three books: *Desperados*, Elaine Shannon's seminal examination of the kidnapping of Enrique "Kiki" Camarena, a former special agent with the United States Drug Enforcement Administration (DEA); *O Plato O Plomo?*, another examination of the Camarena murder by his former supervisor, James "Jaime" Kuykendall; and *Eats, Shoots, & Leaves*, an essential resource for any true grammar nerd.

On the other wall, just to the left of the desk, hangs a large cork board. Three photographs figure prominently among various knickknack items affixed to the board. The photo to the far left is a black and white picture of a man standing next to a very tall marijuana plant. The middle picture was taken at a gala—James flanked by a woman, a bit younger than him, and a gentleman somewhat older than both. The men are dressed in tuxedos, while the woman wears a black cocktail dress. The last picture on the right shows James at his law school graduation, shaking hands with a much older gentleman.

James stands in front of the cork board, his gaze fixed on the picture on the left. James's quiet but determined voice finally breaks the silence.

"Goddamn it, Kiki. I don't know who killed you. But I promise you, I am going to figure it out. Maybe then, you'll let me sleep."

CHAPTER TWO

THE RISING SUN HAS BARELY BEGUN TO SHINE on the Pacific Ocean as James enters the offices of Castle, Smyth & Palmer, a prominent boutique firm in the Spectrum area of Irvine, California. James joined the firm six years ago, recruited by named-partner Brian Castle. James became a full equity partner two years later, at a much younger age than is customary.

Castle, Smyth & Palmer, comprising nearly twenty partners, an equal number of associates, and a sizable support staff, maintains a sterling reputation as litigation specialists with specific expertise in entertainment law, antitrust, and white-collar criminal defense.

The firm occupies the twenty-third floor of a twenty-four-story building at the west edge of an office park near the intersection of Jamboree Road and MacArthur Boulevard, a half-mile west of the 405 Freeway. The main partners, including James, enjoy offices with spectacular views of the Pacific Ocean, even if occasionally interrupted by jet traffic in or out of neighboring Orange County Airport.

With a practice comprising a mix of civil and criminal litigation, James has garnered experience substantially greater than his years, and has developed a widespread reputation as a hard worker, a smart and creative thinker, and a skilled advocate in front of a judge or jury. An outstanding track record, even in difficult cases, and a personable demeanor make him highly sought-after, and as a result, highly respected and well-compensated.

The office will not open for about another hour. James is almost always the first lawyer in the office. He attributes the difference to his Midwestern upbringing and schooling, where sleeping in was regarded as a signaled weakness. James relishes these hours in the morning, when he is alone and can ease into the workday before others arrive and his day is interrupted by emails and the ringing of his office phone.

This morning, though, the usual peace and quiet is disrupted by the early appearance of Erica Walsh, the firm's head paralegal, de facto office manager, and part-time receptionist. Looking appreciably younger than her thirty-two years, Erica's long auburn hair, kind emerald eyes, and soft voice belie her incisive mind and fierce determination.

Long ago, she decided against law school, believing she could serve clients and her community equally well from her multi-faceted role with the firm. She often takes not-so-subtle joy in setting straight anyone who assumes she is just a pretty face and not as knowledgeable in her field as any of the lawyers in the firm.

Erica's seemingly ever-present high heels make a distinctive tap on the hard wood floors as she breezes into James's office and sits in the chair across from him. A few moments of silence pass before James looks up.

"You look like hell," Erica says, with a smile.

"Thanks," James deadpans.

"Trouble sleeping again?"

"This time was different. More real. Too real."

James shares with Erica the details of his early morning nightmare.

"Christ, dreaming about your own death is intense, even for you."

Erica is the only person in the office—or anywhere, for that matter—with whom he had shared his recurring nightmares, and he had given her the most basic elements of its background.

In the early to mid-1980s, the DEA had agents working in Mexico, doing some pretty incredible work in unearthing and disrupting major portions of the drug trade in Mexico. On February 7, 1985, a DEA agent in Guadalajara, Enrique "Kiki" Camarena, was kidnapped, interrogated, grotesquely tortured, and eventually murdered. Ostensibly, the murder was carried out by drug traffickers in Guadalajara, as retribution for successful interdiction efforts by the DEA.

"Ostensibly?" Erica had asked the first time he told her.

"I say that because more than thirty-five years later, there is still mystery and controversy surrounding the case, including some recent media attention and allegations that are both salacious and controversial."

Today, Erica inquires a bit deeper about the genesis of James's nighttime thoughts.

"Didn't you once say there were some pretty gruesome audio tapes of Camarena being tortured?" Erica surveys James out of genuine concern.

"There are. The whole case is a complex puzzle. Apparently, my subconscious is concerned about it."

"Apparently concerned? It seems to me you're tortured by it. You are practically reliving his torture in your mind. I'm sure there are reasons why it affects you so much. Care to share?

"I'm still working through that myself. When I understand it, I'll share."

"I don't believe you. Not even a little bit. But that's fine. I'll still be here for you. But you know, I can't even remember your last relationship, and you have no family. Don't you want more?"

"I'm happy. I have all of this. This firm, you, and Brian are my family."

"Sweet, but I just see so much going on inside you—all the time. I honestly believe that if you free yourself from some of that internal angst, you could be incredibly happy and even more amazing than you already are."

"Now you're just talking crazy. But thank you, Doctor Laura. Your sage counsel and concern are duly noted. It's just not that simple." James turns his gaze back to the brief on his computer screen.

"I know. Anyway, I just wanted to check on you. What's on the agenda this morning?" Erica stands and starts to leave the office.

"Prepping for Friday's hearing. You know Judge Campbell is not going to be happy to see me again after our appeal."

"No. No, he won't. I'll let you get to it, but be good to yourself, damn it." Erica doesn't wait for a response before turning and strutting down the hall toward her office.

"I love you, too," James shouts, as she escapes his view.

CHAPTER THREE

LATER THAT DAY, under the glow of city lights illuminating the night sky of Corona del Mar, across the Pacific Coast Highway from Crystal Cove, the ornate gate to the parking garage of the Ventana del Mar condominium tower begins its slow opening path. As the gate rises, security lights come to life, illuminating the path to the level below. A two-door, jet-black Audi convertible, top down, slowly descends. After gliding to a spot near the elevator, James pulls his leather briefcase from the back seat and waits for the elevator.

A green up arrow soon illuminates, and the elevator doors open. James enters the sleek and modern elevator, waives his wallet in front of the security panel, and the number 12 lights up. The elevator doors open on the building's top floor, consisting of only four condominium units, each with a corner and spectacular views. James purchased his unit as a pre-construction investment and was rewarded with one of the two units with stunning ocean views.

Using the key card in his wallet, eschewing his techier Apple watch link, James activates the remote lock below the numbers 1201, and the front door opens.

The condo is reminiscent of James's office: Stylish but not overdone. Neat and organized. Cool. Lacking personality.

The formal dining room to the left likely has never been used. To the right, the signature living room is distinguished by the breathtaking ocean views through floor-to-ceiling windows. An oversized leather couch and two chairs surround the enormous television on the wall. The walls are tastefully decorated with a variety of art pieces reflecting no particular style or theme.

James sets his briefcase down near his couch and moves to the designer kitchen. A large gas range is the focal point of the room, along with the marble island with built-in cutting boards. Pots and pans hang above the island but show little signs of use.

Past the refrigerator, James enters a large walk-in pantry, gently pushes on the upper left corner of the back wall, and steps back as a door slowly opens, revealing a temperature-controlled dual-zone wine vault holding around three hundred bottles. James peers in, quickly surveys the options, and chooses a perfectly serviceable red blend. Upon returning to the kitchen, James dexterously opens the bottle and pours the wine into one of the large wine glasses pulled from the built-in oak rack. He sets the bottle on a coaster on the island, the remainder of the wine sealed in by an Indiana-University-logoed wine stopper.

Carrying his glass of wine, James quietly ascends the open stairs spiraling to the loft style second floor. He turns to his right and goes into the office, turning on the light switch with his elbow as he enters. Placing the wine glass on a leather coaster on the large desk, he boots up his computer with purpose and determination.

Tonight, James's attitude is different than many nights when he would sit at his computer and troll the web for information on the case. Maybe it's last night's dream. Maybe it's the wine. Maybe, even, it's Erica. Whatever the source, James is more certain and clearer of focus.

He types quickly, and a Word document appears on the two screens. A title, in bold and large type, is centered at the top: ENRIQUE CAMARENA.

Enrique "Kiki" Camarena Salazar was born on July 26, 1947, in Mexicali, Mexico. He attended high school in Calexico, California, a town on the American side of the

Mexican border, directly tied to the much larger Mexican city of Mexicali, the capital of the Mexican state of Baja California. Calexico is a desert town located about 120 miles east of San Diego, and 60 miles west of Yuma, Arizona.

Camarena served in the United States Marine Corps from 1972 to 1974. After his discharge from the Marines, he joined the Calexico Police Department. While serving as a police officer, he served as a Special Agent on the original Imperial County Narcotic Task Force.

In 1975, Camarena joined the DEA at its Calexico office. In 1977, Camarena moved to the DEA's office in Fresno, California, before being assigned to its post in Guadalajara in 1981. By all accounts, Camarena was an excellent fit in Guadalajara. His personality and demeanor earned him the trust of both informants and Mexican police and officials.

During his time in Guadalajara, the DEA operated in Mexico with the permission of the Mexican government, and was subject to its rules and laws. DEA agents were not permitted to carry weapons, and they could not make arrests. Instead, they gathered information that they were expected to pass on to appropriate Mexican authorities. A significant problem faced by Camarena and his brethren was that the drug traffickers had bribed and operated in tandem with many of the police, as well as the Dirección Federal de Seguridad, or DFS, the Mexican counterpart to the CIA, and even some in the military. As a result, DEA agents operating in Mexico never knew if their information would be disclosed to the traffickers, and worse, were never sure who had their backs during the raids on which DEA agents sometimes accompanied Mexican officers.

From most reports, Camarena was a true believer in his mission, which made him committed. His fellow agents described Camarena as being deeply upset by the terrible consequences of the drug trade and narcotics trafficking in Mexico, while also disappointed by the ineffectiveness of the United States' efforts to solve the problem.

Kiki also was a devoted family man. His wife, Mika, and their two boys had joined Kiki in Guadalajara, and become a part of the tight-knit community of American agents working in the foreign country.

Typically, DEA agents are assigned to a foreign post for a five-year tour. Camarena, though, had asked to be transferred back to the States before his tour was completed. Tragically, Kiki was to have left Guadalajara for San Diego only a couple weeks after his abduction.

James leaves the Word document on one screen, but moves the second screen to the Microsoft Edge web browser and searches for the Department of Justice's Freedom of Information Act requests. FOIA is a federal law that mandates the disclosure, in whole or in part, of information or documents in the control of the United States government.

James had used the FOIA process many times over the course of his career, and had revisited the process recently while delving deeper into the Camarena case. He had surmised that maybe, just maybe, since Camarena's murder took place more than thirty-five years ago and the legal proceedings in the United States had been largely resolved, someone would respond to a well-crafted FOIA request without undue scrutiny. Maybe he could get something of interest—something that would shift his progress on the Camarena case in a new direction. It was wishful thinking, at best. Delusional, at worst. But James decided to run with it.

James stares at the FOIA request form, taking stock of obvious fact that the profound gravity of the request did not match the form's relative brevity.

He takes a deep breath. "In the immortal words of Tom Cruise, 'Sometimes you just have to say what the fuck.'"

James works quickly to complete most of the form, but pauses on the request for the precise description of the documents requested.

Recently, the case had received new attention through a drama series airing on Netflix, and a documentary from

Amazon Prime that purported to shed new light on the circumstances surrounding Camarena's murder. Most notable from the Amazon documentary are new and dramatic allegations that the United States Central Intelligence Agency had somehow been involved in the kidnapping, interrogation, and perhaps, even murder of Agent Camarena. The claims— which James found dubious, at best—asserted that Camarena had discovered that the CIA was aiding the Nicaraguan rebels, as part of the Iran-Contra affair, by cooperating with the Mexican cartel, and Camarena was silenced to keep the CIA's actions undercover.

James, like everyone else with an interest in the case, wants to know more about this CIA connection, but also fears that an FOIA request that focuses only on the CIA connection may well stick out too much. Plus, it could be too narrow and too easily dismissed. On the other hand, an overly broad request could be easily dismissed.

James pauses and thinks before finally inputting the information into the form: All documents, reports, interviews, or memoranda relating to the involvement or potential involvement of the United States Central Intelligence Agency (CIA), the Mexican Direccion Federal de Seguridad, or any other governmental agency in the United States or the Republic of Mexico, including, with particularity but not exclusion, any communications in any form between any employee or contractor of the CIA with anyone working for or on behalf of the United States Drug Enforcement Administration (DEA), relating in any manner or form, in whole or in part, to the kidnapping, interrogation, and murder of DEA Special Agent Enrique Camarena, on February 7 and/or February 8, 1985.

Because a FOIA request regarding a person other than the requesting party requires the request to either be made with the permission of the party about whom the information is sought, or be accompanied by evidence that the party is deceased, James uses a quick Google search to produce Agent

Camarena's official DEA obituary. James solemnly attaches the obituary to the FOIA, the gravity of the request and Camarena's sacrifice clear.

With the form now fully completed, James makes a quick review and hits submit, so as not to lose his nerve or have second thoughts.

Shortly thereafter, a form email confirmation appears: "Your Freedom of Information Act request has been received by the United State Drug Enforcement Administration."

A blast of dread shakes James's core. *Oh my God. What did you just do James? You'll never be able to put this genie back in the bottle.*

CHAPTER FOUR

NEARLY THREE WEEKS HAVE PASSED since James filed his FOIA request with the DOJ, and James had nearly stopped thinking about it daily. Instead, as he was inclined to do, he threw himself into his work, pouring his mind and energy into his cases with more than his normal zeal.

One early morning, James is again alone in the office, when his solitude is disrupted by the mechanical tone of his office phone ringing.

"James Butler."

"James, it's Steve. I suspected you'd be in the office already."

Stephen "Steve" Williams is an Assistant United States Attorney based in downtown Los Angeles. James and Williams met a half-decade ago, shortly after James joined Castle, Smyth & Palmer, when Steve was working at a criminal defense boutique in Newport Beach. The two played against one another in a lawyer's basketball league and had become friends.

Despite having a successful practice and being on partnership track at his firm, about four years ago, Williams decided he wanted to do more *good* for the world, left private practice, and joined the United States Attorney's Office in the Central District of California. Williams proved to be not only a good lawyer, but also astute to internal politics, and rose to a supervisory role in the Narcotics division. In the years since Williams became an AUSA, he and James maintained their friendship, even as they worked on opposite sides of a few cases—a tribute to both men, and to the nature of federal criminal practice.

The cases put together by the FBI or the DEA are almost always well-organized and complete, and rarely do defense attorneys find mistakes or effective strategies for defense. Perhaps counterintuitively, it makes the defense attorney's job easier, if less exciting. Not infrequently, the best defense becomes a good plea-bargained deal, and in that regard, being friendly with the prosecuting attorney never hurts. On the other hand, because the prosecuting AUSAs hold most of the cards, some of them can be sanctimonious and difficult.

Williams is one of the good ones. James thrives on the challenges of going up against good lawyers and investigators, like Williams.

"Per usual, I am the first one here," James replies. "What's up?"

"We're friends, right?" Williams says.

"I'm always more than a bit suspicious when someone asks a question like that, but I'll bite. Yes."

"No, I'm serious. We're friends, so can I be candid?"

"Like you've ever needed permission to speak your mind. Whatever it is, just say it."

"Then I have to know, what on earth are you thinking?"

"If only I knew what you were talking about."

"Your FOIA."

"Oh, that." James rubs his chin as he speaks.

"Yes that. Seriously, James. It nearly slipped through the cracks and was handled administratively with a simple denial, but then it got into the wrong hands, and it's become a giant mess. I *accidentally* got a copy of an internal memo, and let's just say, you got the attention of people whose attention you neither want or need."

"Crap. I really was hoping I could sneak it through since it's been so long," James replies.

"Good thought, but it didn't work. Especially not now.

Our office and the DEA are all twisted in knots about how to deal with the recent allegations."

"The allegations about the CIA?" James says.

"Yes. That, and the allegation that Camarena's supervisor was on the take. Not to mention that the witnesses being relied upon, whom the government relied upon in its prosecutions, came across looking batshit crazy. The angst at the DEA is real, and every new inquiry with any merit gets people more and more uptight, especially those who have something to lose if it turns out the facts were not as presented."

"So are they going to tell me to jump in the nearest convenient lake?" James says. "I mostly expected that to be the result."

"No. I think they've decided against trying to stonewall you. Apparently, your reputation, and Brian's, precedes you, and the powers to be assume you would fight a flat refusal, and that worries them, too. My guess is that they're going to try to jerk you around some. Let them. Play their game. I'll try to keep on top of it and give you a heads-up when I can."

Williams's words and tenor provide James with a small sense of encouragement.

"Thanks, man. I appreciate it. And I owe you."

"Just be careful, James. There's a not an insignificant amount of institutional anxiety around this case now, and we aren't the only ones interested."

"Who else?"

"I can't tell you that. But you can figure it out."

"The CIA?"

"I have to go," Williams says, before the call is disconnected.

The CIA. Great. Exactly who I do not need looking over my shoulder.

CHAPTER FIVE

JAMES WORKS LATE IN HIS OFFICE as the sun starts to fade into the western horizon. Gazing out over the Pacific Ocean, admiring the blended red and orange hues of the Southern California sunset, James loses himself in the moment, allowing himself a rare opportunity for reflection.

His tranquility is soon broken by an interoffice call from Erica.

"James, there's a retired DEA agent, Joe Aguilar, here to see you. He apologizes for not having an appointment. Do you want me to tell him you are unavailable?" she whispers.

"Thanks, but you can show him back."

James adjusts his tie, straightens some documents on his desk, and turns a file over so the case name will be out of view for his unexpected visitor.

Agent Aguilar enters James's office looking as if he had just walked out of central casting. He's a big man, tall and burly, wearing jeans and cowboy boots, a tan hiding the weathered skin on his face.

James shakes his hand, introduces himself. Aguilar's hands are large and rough, evidencing hard work over many years.

James offers Aguilar a seat in the visitor's chair across from his desk.

"How can I help you, Agent Aguilar?"

"I'm here to ask you to stop whatever it is you are doing relating to Kiki Camarena."

"What, no small talk?" James pauses for a moment, his effort at whimsy obviously falling on deaf ears.

James leans forward on his elbows, as he tries to be reassuring.

"Look, I'm not trying to make waves. I'm just poking around, trying to find a few answers. Call it personal curiosity. Certainly nothing that should cause you, or anyone else, a moment of concern."

"Did you know Kiki Camarena?" Aguilar says brusquely.

"Since you know full well that I didn't, I'll assume that was a purely rhetorical question, and that you have a point to make." James sits back up and leans into his leather chair.

"Well, I knew him. He was a friend and colleague. Good agent. Good man. He should be allowed to rest in peace. His family should be left alone. There's been enough attention and stupid crap recently. The family doesn't need that. No one does."

"Hold on." James's back stiffens. "I'm not looking to make any issues for his family. I'm curious, and I am fortunate enough to have both the resources and the ability to try to sate that curiosity. It's just for me. I have no intention of doing anything with the information."

"Mister Butler, there are books. There are movies. There are three seasons of mini-series, for goodness' sake. There's something calling itself a documentary. Buy a TV, hole up with a pretty secretary for a weekend, and satisfy your curiosity."

"If I really thought the official story told the truth, I wouldn't be looking behind the curtain, would I?" James stops abruptly, not wanting to give away too much.

"Others before you have looked. Investigations have been undertaken. Witnesses paid. Despite all of that, the story remains the same."

"Take a good look around the room, Agent Aguilar." James points to his diploma and more than a few awards scattered across the office. "This is what I do, and I'm good at it. Maybe

I have a mindset that's different? A fresh set of eyes? A unique perspective?"

"Maybe. But Kiki will still be dead. His family will still be missing a husband and a father. Nothing you do will change anything." Aguilar's face is flushed with anger. Or at least irritation.

"Maybe. But I find it very hard to believe there's nothing new to be discovered. No new connections to be made."

"No disrespect to you, Mister Butler. You seem like a decent guy. You really do. And I don't want to be condescending, but this is far beyond what you know or can know. There is so much here you don't want to touch."

"But I do, and that's the point, Agent Aguilar." James articulates his words to emphasize his strident determination.

"Which leads me back to wondering what the root of your interest is. It has to be more than curiosity."

"I have a personal connection to the case. Let's leave it at that." It's now James's turn to express irritation.

"That is curious, Mister Butler, because I can't see anything indicating even a tangential connection. Would you like to explain?"

"It is personal, and really none of your business."

"Well, it better be important, because you are walking into issues you cannot comprehend at this point. Do yourself a favor and turn away now. While you still can."

"That almost sounds like a threat." James barks, standing from his chair.

"Not from me. But if you really start digging, the threats will be real. No offense, but this is above your head," Aguilar replies with matched intensity.

"No offense taken, and I appreciate the thought," James retorts through clenched jaws. "But I think now is a real good time for you to get the hell out of my office."

Agent Aguilar rises without saying a word, and walks slowly toward the lobby. James watches until he turns the corner and is out of sight.

Damn, he was so cocksure. Have I gotten out over my skis?

Erica calls from the front desk. "He's gone, and he looked pissed. Are you okay?"

"I'm fine. I'm stupid, but fine."

CHAPTER SIX

AT 3:02 THE FOLLOWING AFTERNOON, James's work is interrupted by the ubiquitous ding of a new email notification. Normally, James has that feature turned off, preferring to work uninterrupted by minor distractions. But after Williams's call and the visit from Agent Aguilar, James wants to know when new emails appear in his inbox.

Noting that the email is from the Department of Justice, James takes a deep breath and opens the email. The DOJ informs him that it will release some documents, including some redacted documents, pursuant to his FOIA request, but only in paper form, and only if James pays the costs of retrieving and copying the documents—to the tune of a cool $3,700, plus $850 for *research*, and a $250 delivery charge.

James whistles on seeing the price tag. He does some quick math on the copying charges—$3,700 at $0.18 a page is about 21,000 pages. Guessing about 1,500 pages per box, that's about fourteen or fifteen banker's boxes of documents. Not too many, he concludes, but enough to try to hide something or to dissuade someone with only a fleeting interest.

James runs through the various scenarios of what the DOJ could be planning by agreeing to such a large production, when a call from Williams brings his attention back to the present.

"James, I only have a second. Did you get the email?"

"Yes, I did. And that's a hefty price tag."

"Pay it. They're going to try to test your resolve. Most

of what you'll get will be things that you could find on the Internet, mostly on Verdugo's website, which I assume you have reviewed in detail."

Rene Verdugo was a defendant in the first Camarena criminal trial in the United States. Verdugo had been convicted, but was later released when the forensic hair analysis testimony of an FBI investigator had been thrown out as unreliable. Verdugo returned to Mexico, but his attorneys constructed a website dedicated to his case and his claimed innocence. Until it was taken down when the domain was not renewed, the website was a treasure trove of documents presented at, or revealed in connection to, the three Camarena trials in US courts.

"I have. In detail," James replies.

In fact, he had spent many nights pouring over the documents that had been stored there.

"Good," Williams says. "I know digging through all the documents for the relevant ones will be a giant pain in the backside, but trust me here, it will be worth the effort."

"Okay, thanks."

Williams hangs up the phone without a goodbye.

James calls the number on the DOJ email and provides his credit card for payment and home address for delivery. The boxes, he's informed, will be delivered Friday afternoon—three long days away.

James's work on Friday is interrupted by a call from the concierge at his condo building, telling James the boxes have been delivered.

He packs up his briefcase to head home. On his way out, he passes the open door to Erica's office.

"Only working half a day, you slacker?"

James pauses to respond, sticking his head into the doorway to Erica's office.

"I have boxes, lots of boxes, waiting for me at home.

"Do you need any help?" Erica says.

"Thanks, but I don't even know what I have yet. It'd be a waste of your time at this point. Besides, I've assured Brian that my side project wouldn't be a burden on the office."

"Okay, but you know how to reach me if you need anything."

"I do. And as always, I appreciate it and you."

"Happy reading!"

Driving home, James tries to picture the mission ahead of him, and wonders where it will take him. At the same time, his short drive down Jamboree Road, past the hotels, shops, and restaurants, past Corona del Mar High School and the Newport Beach Country Club, where he is a member, reminds him of the many bountiful things he has in his life.

Maybe Aguilar is right. Why take the chance of looking under the wrong rock?

James knew some of the stories of witness intimidation and threats to journalists. He has heard stories that in the 1990s, a reporter in Las Vegas apparently got too close to the case, and his car mysteriously blew up in front of his house. A lawyer for one of the Camarena defendants had a home on the water in Santa Barbara that was destroyed in an explosion, allegedly because of the presence of fumes from the remodeling of a kitchen. Anecdotally, James has heard of lawyers and witnesses being followed, phones tapped, and other subtle and not-so-subtle acts of intimidation.

James has no real family to worry about, but he does worry about the firm and his career. And when he lets his mind go too far, he even worries about his own personal safety.

As James nears his complex, he reminds himself that self-doubt is not how he got to where he is today. Plus, he has put in a lot of time and effort into thinking about the case in ways he believed were unique, producing themes and ideas with promise. A big key to James's success, he asserts, is that he is confident but not cocky, and he truly has an ability to identify things others could not, or chose not to.

I have to see this through.

Upon opening his front door, James looks inside and sees four stacks, each four boxes high. *Not too bad.* James surveys the room. *I've dealt with worse.*

He approaches the first stack of boxes and notices each box is labeled "DOJ/DEA BUTLER FOIA REQUEST," with the number range of the Bates labeled pages inside. He pulls down the top box from the first pile, noting that it starts with "Bates Number 000001."

At least it isn't BUTT 000001. He smiles at his own joke.

James opens the box lid, looking for an index, but cannot locate one either on top—where one usually is found—or before the first page. He yanks down the second box and quickly determines that it, too, lacks any sort of index.

The volume of documents were not overwhelming. James had worked on document cases in his career that were massive—many, many times greater than the stacks in front of him. But if there is no order or system to the way the documents were put into the boxes, the task could be dauting.

There has to be a systematic way of processing this mess. After all, this is what you do, damn it.

James decides to segregate the boxes and their contents, not in the order they are labeled, and not by date, but as best he can, by topics. As he begins looking through boxes, it becomes apparent that, even though there is neither a rhyme nor a reason to the documents' placement in the boxes, files or groups of files had been heaped into the boxes together.

James stands back, surveying the task ahead. With a deep breath, he resolves, This is manageable. It's simply a matter of taking my time and identifying the method someone used to fill these.

As he moves files and papers into various piles, James comes across a Redweld containing witness statements relating to Camarena's kidnapping, and he stops to scan through the documents. James knows the story. He'd read it and seen it on screen. People he trusted with his life had described it with such an air of certainty, James would have sworn they had been there.

He reads the file meticulously, focusing on every detail. Everything is as expected. Nothing radically different—no one with a materially different point of view.

Despite this consensus, there is a pit in James's stomach. For reasons he cannot articulate, something just doesn't feel right.

One of the interesting aspects of the case, as it has been explained to James, was that there were no real witnesses to the kidnapping itself. Despite the belated and unsupported claim of one person, that there were *dozens* of witnesses, no one saw it happen. Not one of the witnesses or informants interviewed about that day described the series of events that led to Camarena being taken away. Not a single witness from the streets of Guadalajara described, with real specificity, any of the alleged kidnappers or the circumstances of the abduction. No one, other than the kidnappers themselves, heard anything being said to Camarena.

The closest James has ever seen to an actual witness statement was a driver for the Consul General who was walking down the street, in the opposite direction, who might have seen someone being forced into a small car, and might have seen that small car driving off around the time of Camarena's abduction.

James is also familiar with a confidential informant for the US government, Rene Lopez Romero, a former Mexican police officer who claimed to be part of the contingent that abducted Camarena. But James also knows that Lopez's credibility was suspect, and there were some material inconsistencies in his statements and versions of events.

While reading through the various statements and records, James starts to have more questions. There are more and more issues, and things that are simply not clear. He is struck by the fact that Camarena was not a rookie, but an experienced agent who knew tensions were high. He had to have been consciously concerned about his safety and the safety of those he worked with. James is also aware that, in the days following the abduction, some had surmised that prior to being taken, Camarena had reached his truck and opened the door. But if that were true, how was it that he wasn't able to get inside, or use the two-way radio in the truck's cab, or otherwise protect himself? On the other hand, why would Camarena's truck have been found unlocked in the middle of the day, with his radio inside?

There also was testimony at one of the US trials, that when Camarena was abducted outside the consulate, he was *fingered*, or *identified*, by a blonde consulate employee working with the cartel. Curiously, though, the government did not even try to find or identify this employee at trial. In the overall understanding of the abduction of Agent Camarena, does the absence of the identity of the *fingering* employee mean the witness was lying, or simply wrong, about this occurrence? Or if true, is it significant that Camarena's abductors needed to have him pointed out? Had he not previously been identified or known?

Slow down, Alice. Stay out of the rabbit hole, James chastises himself. None of these issues alone is overly significant. Heck, they may not even be material when tied together. You must be calculating and methodical. That is the only way you will have any chance to uncover the full story.

CHAPTER SEVEN

SUNDAY'S MIDDAY SUN shines through the bay window in James's living room—a room which now embodies organized chaos. Piles of documents dot the living room floor, each labeled with color-coded Post-its, and each with a yellow legal pad on top. Empty banker's boxes are stacked in the dining room, arranged in a manner to allow pathways to the kitchen and bathroom, as well as the stairs to the office and bedroom.

Empty bottles of water and Diet Coke line the kitchen counters, accompanied by more than one empty bottle of wine, and several food delivery containers.

James sits on the floor in front of one of the stacks of papers. Gone are the tailored slacks and Caporicci shoes, replaced by running shorts and shoes, and a Maurer School of Law at Indiana University Bloomington t-shirt.

James is taking notes from documents in the stack labeled "Lope de Vega," when he is startled by the ringing of the intercom from the lobby. After slowly rising, he stiff-legs his way to the intercom monitor, and replies without looking to see who's there.

"Yep?"

"It's Erica. I have treats for you."

"Come on up." He presses the intercom button, allowing her access to the elevator.

James checks his look in the hallway mirror, trying to fix

his hair a little, until his grooming is stopped by a light knock at the door.

When he opens the door, he finds Erica holding In-n-Out bags.

"Double-doubles, fries, and vanilla shakes. Enough for two!"

"You know me too well." James takes the bag and a cup from Erica.

"I'd love to take all the credit, but I can't." Erica enters the condo as James shuts the door behind her with his foot. "When I told Brian what you were up to this weekend, he said that sometimes, in situations like this, you can get a bit..."

"Focused?" James sets the food and drink on his coffee table.

"I think 'obsessive' was the word he used." Erica sets her shake next to James's.

"He knows me well." James smiles.

"In any event, when I told him I was going to check in on you, he thought you might need something to eat."

"Your dad is a good guy."

"Yes, he is."

Erica surveys the unit, walking among the piles, viewing the Post-its and notepads. Surveying the kitchen, she shakes her head.

"At least you're well-hydrated," she says. "Maybe I should have brought something healthier?"

"Heck no. This is perfect."

"Have you been at this all weekend?"

"More or less. Okay, more than less."

"You aren't going to go all Graysmith on me, are you? Erica retrieves plates and napkins from the kitchen.

James smirks at the reference to Robert Graysmith and his notorious hunt for The Zodiac Killer.

"No," he replies. "I'm doing just fine. I've slept, eaten, and even went for a run."

"Good. Now the question is whether you're finding anything?"

"Lots of stuff I already knew, and a few trees worth of useless information."

"What's the battle plan thus far?" Erica sits on her knees, on the floor across the coffee table from James.

"It took a bit, but I finally settled on trying to segregate documents and files between completely useless and potentially helpful, and then organizing the latter by topic, which are indexed on the whiteboard. As it turns out, the DOJ didn't give me quite as much of a mess as they might have thought they did. I've also made some copies, so some documents now are in more than one pile. The process has actually been helpful to force me to refine and focus my thoughts."

Erica puts James's burger and fries on a plate and places it in front of him before fixing her own plate and distributing a hefty supply of napkins.

"You know, we could have scanned these into a database at the office and made the work more efficient," Erica tells him.

"I know, but I didn't want to use firm resources any more than I have to. And you know me—I'm old school. I like to get my hands dirty."

"Jesus, you say that like you are eighty. You're thirty-nine. How old school can you be?"

"My mentor always thought there was an intangible value to a good attorney seeing and touching the documents, feeling how they are organized and fit together."

The two stop to eat for a moment, before continuing the conversation.

"Okay, grasshopper." Erica smirks, adjusting her position on the floor. "Where are you now?"

"I think I have my piles, with most of the totally irrelevant documents put to the side. Most of the key topics to drill down and try to understand better have been identified, and are noted on the Post-its and on the whiteboard. I've started going pile by pile, taking notes on the legal pads on each stack. There's also a place on the whiteboard for *critical* information. And I have maps of Guadalajara and Mexico, on the dining room table."

"Of course you do," Erica says. "Do you want some help?"

"How foolish would I be to turn that down?"

"Okay, I've been intrigued by the case every time you've brought it up. But if I'm going to help, I need to understand more. I know the basics, but..." Erica leans back onto her hands, anticipating a monologue from James.

"You know about the kidnapping, interrogation, and murder, right?"

"Like I said the basics. You've explained those."

James takes a few bites of his meal, sips from his shake, and looks around the room, mentally noting the vast amount of information in front of him, before turning to Erica.

"This weekend, I focused a lot on the statements taken shortly after the kidnapping, notes from interviews with some of the government's confidential informants that came forward a few years later. And then today, I was reading through notes on the interrogation transcripts, including from some trial transcripts and other documents generally available on the Internet. With each new document and each page, it gets less clear."

"What gets less clear?" Erica sits back up again.

"The why."

Erica shoots James a glance of stern disapproval.

"Why what? I'm gonna need a bit more explanation, please."

"Of course. Let's start with the fundamentals. Around this time, 1984 and 1985, the Mexican drug trade was largely dominated by a group of traffickers that later became known as the Guadalajara Drug Cartel, reputedly headed by three main narcos: Miguel Angel Félix Gallardo, Rafael

Caro Quintero, and Ernesto Fonseca Carrillo. The DEA had been successful in negatively impacting the marijuana side of the cartel's business, much to the dismay of the cartel, particularly Caro Quintero."

"Okay," Erica says, before James continues.

"The question I keep asking myself is, why? Why would the cartel kidnap, interrogate, and kill—intentionally or not—a DEA agent? Wouldn't anyone—even an uneducated drug addict like Caro Quintero—have known such actions would bring the full force of the US government down on the cartel? If the cartel was annoyed by the actions of the DEA before the kidnapping, they had to know that the level of interference post-kidnapping was likely to be exponentially worse. And if one was inclined to do so, why tape the interrogation?"

"I can't disagree with the logic there," Erica says. "But we know someone *did* pick up, interrogate, and murder a DEA agent. *And* they did tape the interrogation."

"Right," James replies. "There must be a thought process. A rationale. Even if not rational."

"I'll ruminate on the semantics of that later," Erica says. "For now, though, where do these questions lead?"

"We can start with the standard, time-worn answers," James says. "The customary answer is that the cartel, particularly Caro Quintero, was so distressed over the recent raids on their crops—especially a huge raid on a field at Rancho Búfalo in the Mexican state of Chihuahua—that it wanted revenge on Camarena personally, and information on how he and the DEA were able to find and raid its fields. Add to that Quintero's ability to bribe politicians, military, and police, and he felt invincible."

"The retaliation explanation is one I've heard before," Erica says. "Isn't that what the first mini-series said?"

James looks at her inquisitively. "The first mini-series?"

"I've been doing my homework." Erica smirks.

"So what I've been saying is old news to you?"

"A little. But I wanted to hear it from your perspective."

"Well, in answer to your question...it is. The Netflix series *Narcos: Mexico* also follows this logic. At least, in large part."

There are at least three significant programs about Agent Camarena's abduction and murder. The first came in 1990, and was a three-part NBC miniseries called *Drug Wars: The Camarena Story*. It was, in large part, based on Elaine Shannon's book *Desperados,* generally regarded as the definitive examination of the development of the cartel and the Camarena abduction. But the mini-series was highly stylized in keeping with primetime mode on network television.

The second program was on Netflix, which followed the successful and popular *Narcos* three-season series depicting the rise and fall of the Medellin and Calli cartels of Colombia. Thus far, *Narcos: Mexico* has had three seasons. It uses dramatic license, as would be expected, but starts from a decent factual foundation. Notably, it places Félix Gallardo at the top of Cartel leadership, and depicts him as the CEO of the early 1980s Mexican drug trade.

Finally, in late July 2020, Amazon Prime aired a docuseries, *The Last Narc*, which purports to be a documentary pointing to alternative theories on the Camarena case, and is almost totally based on the allegations of a former DEA agent and three former confidential informants.

"But I sense you're not satisfied," Erica says.

"The simple problem is that, as I see it thus far, none of these theories adequately account for the alleged presence of several high-ranking Mexican officials at the interrogation. Or the audio tapes. Or the multiple planning meetings that the government alleged took place prior to the abduction."

"I get it," Erica says. "The standard story, for lack of a better term, has holes. But does that mean it's wrong, or not what happened?"

"No, it doesn't." James pauses, running his fingers through his hair. "But even if it's not wholly incorrect, I think it has to be incomplete. Other people have had some other alternative—or perhaps, complementary—theories."

"Do any of them make more sense to you?" Erica says.

"Not alone. For example, one alternative secondary explanation posits that members of the Mexican government had become sufficiently concerned about what the US government knew about their involvement with the cartel. This concern allegedly grew worse after investigators with a committee of the US House of Representatives, met with Mexican officials and DEA agents in Mexico shortly before the abduction. This was a key point in *Narcos: Mexico*."

"But that argument does not assuage your concerns?" Erica stands, walking again between the piles and boxes, focused on James's notes.

"Not really," he says. "If we assume that Caro Quintero would have been wary of kidnapping a DEA agent, wouldn't Mexican officials, who dealt with the American government on a regular basis, know what the reaction from the American government to the kidnapping would be? Or if you are a high-ranking government official who decides, for whatever reason, that your own best interest would be served by kidnapping and interrogating Camarena, would you trust the job to Rafael Caro Quintero and his men? I mean, one of the interrogators sounds like he might have been a police officer. But weren't there people in the Mexican military or government, trained in interrogation, who could have been called in to question Camarena, and presumably have done a more effective job?"

"Back up a sec." Erica looks back at James. "One of the interrogators?"

"Yes, it seems there are at least three interrogators on the tapes. None have been conclusively identified. I think someone in the DEA identified one of the voices as Caro himself, but I haven't been able to drill down on that identification yet. As I said, one of the interrogators seemed more professional, and that leads to a separate set of suspects.

Looking at these documents, I list something like ten people identified as interrogators, which we know is impossible."

Erica returns to the coffee table. "Are you finished?"

"I am. That was great."

"Keep talking while I take these to the kitchen." Erica piles the trash on the two plates.

"An interesting note on the interrogations," James says. "No one ever speaks English."

"So?" Erica yells from the kitchen. "I assume you'd like a Diet Coke?"

"Yes, please. And my point is: doesn't it seem to you that if you speak Spanish and English well, or more particularly, if English is your primary language and you're interrogating someone you know speaks English well, that you might slip into English at times during the interrogation, either inadvertently or for effect?"

"Okay, that does make sense to me," Erica says. "Can't you picture the interrogator getting close and saying in English, in essence, 'Cut the crap and tell me what I want to know?'"

"Precisely," James says. "And without getting too deep into the details, none of the interrogators appears to have anything other than a Mexican accent, either."

"That's significant how?"

"There is an allegation in *The Last Narc*—"

"Damn it." Erica sits on the sofa, facing James. "I'm only on episode two. I stopped watching to come feed you."

"Excellent choice," he says. "But the assertion in there is that a Cuban-American CIA officer was involved in the kidnapping and interrogation."

"No kidding?" Erica says. "A CIA agent?"

"Officer, not agent."

"You know what I mean, smart ass."

"For a while," James says, "there have been some allegations about the CIA's possible involvement with the cartel, and even the abduction. But they were made directly and substantially in *The Last Narc*, especially in episode four."

"Which reminds me," Erica says. "As I started to watch the documentary, it occurred to me that you submitted a FOIA request because you thought you might be able to slip it by people, totally disregarding that there had been the Netflix series, plus this documentary and its explosive and newsworthy allegations. Really?"

"Hey, it made sense at the time," James says. "In my head."

"And only there," Erica retorts.

"Something else that might be of interest," James continues. "The interrogators ask Camarena about several Mexican officials, important officials, like Mexico's Minister of Defense, the former premier comandante of the Mexican Federal Judicial Police, and chief of Interpol. And some witnesses, of varying credibility, have placed several of these Mexican VIPs at Lope de Vega during the interrogation itself."

"Not so fast," Erica says. "I'm still catching up. What's a Lope de Vega?"

"Sorry. After he was abducted from in front of the American consulate, Camarena apparently was taken to a home in Guadalajara, located at 881 Lope de Vega."

"Oh, right," Erica says. "Caro's estate."

"I guess you could call it that. In any event, the house had recently been purchased by Caro, but previously had been owned by a local businessman, Ruben Zuno Arce, who later also would be caught up in the net of Camarena investigations and prosecutions. The house came to be commonly referred to simply as Lope de Vega. If you can get past the idea of these officials involved in the kidnapping at all, why would they have all met, more than once, in relatively public places, such as a hotel, to plan the kidnapping, as the government alleged? And if there was a plan put into place by these officials—at least, some of whom were respected on both sides of the border—why would any of them be at the interrogation itself? Especially if the interrogation was to be audio taped. And as a side note, and going back to the congressional delegation theory, I'm not convinced that the timelines of the presence of the delegation's meetings in Mexico, and the alleged planning meetings, fit together."

"Maybe it's a mix of more than one logical path," Erica says.

"And thus, the puzzle this case presents. Even at a high level, the conundrums become readily apparent."

"Conundrums? What the hell? Who says conundrums?" Erica laughs.

James smiles and pauses for a moment.

"Before I forget," he says. "Back to the CIA argument. Isn't the flaw in this argument the same flaw I pointed out earlier, with respect to Caro kidnapping Camarena?"

"In what way?" Erica says. "You're giving me a lot of new stuff."

"The kidnapping would inevitably draw too much attention," James continues. "Let's assume, for the sake of argument, that the CIA was worried that Camarena either had found, or was about to uncover, the connection between the CIA, the cartel, and the CIA's support for the Contras, what is alleged in *The Last Narc*. How would kidnapping a DEA agent, and having that agent tortured and killed, help keep things quiet?"

Erica's eyes are wide, her voice carrying a lilt of excitement.

"It wouldn't. I don't think. Every law enforcement officer around would be looking for the reasons for the abduction and the killing. Instead of covering up the agency's forbidden activities, it would invite a whole new level of scrutiny. Everything Camarena had done, or was working on, would be put under a microscope."

"Absolutely," James says. "Unless the agents thought they could manage the fallout. But that's pretty ballsy, even for spies."

"It would seem," Erica says, " that the agency would want to minimize risk and maximize containment—two factors they lose control over if there is a massive investigation into the disappearance of a DEA agent. Of course, that ignores what I'd like to believe is that a federal agent is not likely to order the kidnapping and brutal interrogation of a fellow federal agent, under any circumstances, and certainly not these."

James mentally notes that Erica's summary was emphatic and spot-on, and he flashes a smile at her before picking up where she concluded.

"In short, it seems that a DEA agent more likely would be ordered picked up and interrogated as the result of an emotional impulse. But if it was an act of vengeance, there wouldn't have been planning meetings, and Mexican officials would not have been in attendance at the interrogation."

"Either you need to combine theories, or disregard facts," Erica says.

"Or find a new theory," James adds.

"Or new evidence," Erica says. "Basically, right now you have a lot of facts that don't add up to anything satisfying."

"Succinctly put. And unfortunately, I believe, accurate," James replies, with a trace of resignation in his voice.

"It's your hope that somewhere in this mass of paper is the answer?" Erica says.

"Oh heck no. My only hope is that somewhere in here is something that points me in a new direction."

"Points *us* in *some* direction," Erica says.

"That's what I meant to say."

Erica stands back up and moves to one of the paper piles.

"So Mister Butler, if you were a needle in this governmental haystack, where would you be hiding?"

CHAPTER EIGHT

THE FOLLOWING MORNING, Erica opens the office at 8:00 a.m., as usual. But unlike most every day, James has not yet arrived. Noting James's absence, Erica starts her day without much concern. By about 8:45, though, she begins to worry, but stops herself from overreacting.

Her anxiety is relieved when, shortly after 9:00, James struts into the office and pauses ever so briefly as he passes Erica's office, flashing a smirk masquerading as a smile. Erica leaps from her chair and follows him into his office.

"What's up?" she says, dismissing with the normal morning pleasantries.

"Good morning, sunshine. And whatever do you mean?"

"Cut the crap, Butler. You found something after I left last night, didn't you?"

"If you wanted to know, perhaps you shouldn't have been so lame as to go to a fancy dinner with your dad last."

"It was his birthday. Now spill your guts!"

James leans forward, sitting on the edge of his chair.

"I found a name."

"A name?"

"A name. There was a redacted name in a DEA-6 that I was able to make out with a bit of effort. I'm not sure how it slipped through, but it did. Based on the context, I think it's the name of someone outside of the DEA who was involved in, or sat in on, at least one DEA interview in Los Angeles in the early nineties. I hate to ask this, but—"

Erica says, "Jesus, don't be such a wimp. What do you need?"

"In your spare time, could you do your magic and find out everything you can about this guy? Here's the name. And thank you. I owe you. Again."

"Happy to help. And yes, you do. Again."

The glare of the computer screen illuminates James's face as he pounds furiously on the keyboard, his brow furrowed.

"Macho typing at its finest." Erica walks across the office and turns on the lamp on James's desk, then lays a file folder of documents in front of him. "Everything you'd ever want to know about your retired CIA agent, and now private eye to the beautiful people of Southern California, Timothy Speer."

"Holy crap. How'd you find all of this? And so fast?"

"I keep telling you—I'm good." She sits across from James. Flipping through the pages, James shakes his head.

"Is some of this even legal?" he says.

"I suggest we operate under the 'don't ask, don't tell' principle. His address is on top. Both his residence and office are in Palos Verdes. He has quite the house for a retired spook and a PI."

"Then he should be easy to find," James says.

"Find? What do you mean, *find*?"

"I'm going to make an appointment with him." James continues to flip through and scan the file documents.

"You're going to talk to him?"

"I have to. This may be the only new lead we'll ever get."

"James, I can see so many ways that could go badly, and fast."

"It'll be fine, and I'll be careful. Promise."

"James, my dear, my good friend, I'd never trust you to be *careful*. It's against your nature."

"That hurts." He turns his attention away from the file. "Even if it might be true. But this is a real opportunity. I told

Aguilar that I might be able to see things differently. I wasn't there. I don't know the main players. I'm trained to look at evidence from every angle, like when we investigate a crime for a defendant. Maybe I can talk to Speer in a way that gives me a unique perspective."

"I can't argue with that," Erica says. "But if I can't talk you out of it, will you at least promise to take Bobby with you?"

"I'm not sure that's such a good idea. I don't want to scare this guy off or give him reason to be overly suspicious."

"Just figure it out and have Booby there," Erica says. "Don't make me talk to Brian."

"Uncle. You win. I'll call Bobby."

Erica stands and winks.

"Thank you," she replies, as she leaves the office.

James spends a few minutes further perusing the materials Erica had compiled, before returning to the first page, a summary of key information. In addition to name, address, and phone number, Erica had left the email address for Speer's private investigation agency.

James quickly composes an email message: "My name is James Butler. I am in partner in the firm of Castle, Smyth & Palmer in Irvine. I'm working on a criminal defense matter that has an urgent need for some investigative work, and I was recently given your name as someone who could act quickly and discreetly. Because this is a bit of a high-profile matter, I'd prefer to explain it to you in person, and then you can decide if it's something you are interested in. This week would be preferred, if you have any openings. Please let me know. James."

He hits send and goes back to the file materials.

To his surprise, a reply email comes within minutes: "Mr. Butler. Tim happens to have some time available on Thursday, if that would work for you. Say 2:00 p.m.?"

James responds immediately: "2:00 p.m. Thursday works fine for me. I'll see him then."

With the meeting confirmed, James's mind returns to his promise to Erica, and quickly accesses up the contact information for Bobby Burgess.

Bobby was a star running back at UCLA, and Mission Viejo High School before that, and played a few years in the NFL—in Buffalo, of all places—before retiring and returning home to Orange County. James met him several years ago while defending one of Bobby's cousins on a relatively minor charge. During the case, they struck up a friendship.

After retiring from the NFL, Bobby started a small security business, both personal and electronic. What started out as a humble, after-the-playing-days side job, turned into a thriving career. Bobby has several employees and some high-tech capabilities. He has become James's go-to security/surveillance person, and has pulled James from trouble on more than one occasion.

James dials Bobby's number but gets his voicemail.

"Bobby, hi. James Butler. Hey, I need a bit of cover while I meet with someone in Palos Verdes on Thursday afternoon. On the real down low. I think everything will be fine, but I do worry a bit that if it goes bad, it could get ugly. And I'd feel much better if you were close by. I'll send you a text later, with the address and the exact schedule. Please send a text back if you can't make it. Thanks."

After hanging up the phone, James takes a slow deep breath. *Well, this just got real.*

CHAPTER NINE

RANCHO PALOS VERDES, together with a few other towns, sits in the Palos Verdes Hills. Colloquially, locals refer to the entire area as "Palos Verdes," and only make distinctions as needed.

The peninsula has a population of around seventy-five thousand residents, predominantly white, and overwhelmingly affluent, and is home to numerous parks, trails, and horse trials. Commerce in Palos Verdes is dominated by several high-end shopping centers.

Speer's office is located off Spur Road, a two-way major artery across from two shopping centers and just down the road from Palos Verdes Peninsula High School. James turns off Silver Spur onto Crossfield Drive and then into a parking area for several small office buildings, each in the ubiquitous and generic Southern California style. The sign in front of the tasteful office building in the middle of the row of buildings lists several professional offices, including, near the bottom, Speer & Associates, Private Investigators.

James takes a quick appraisal of the scene and drives off, across Silver Spur, and parks in front of the Starbucks in the Peninsula Shopping Center. Moments later, a black Mercedes sedan backs into the slot next to James, its driver's window slowly descending.

"Good to see you, Bobby. How's your mom? Trevor?"

"Everyone's good. Really good. My mom would love to see you."

"Soon. My appointment is in five minutes. You've got the details, right?"

"Yes. What did you tell him?"

"It really was pretty easy. I just said that it was a criminal matter of significance, with a short time fuse. Both of which are technically true."

"You're concerned about him?" Bobby says.

"Not really. But at some point, I'll likely tell him the real reason I'm here."

"It's Camarena related, I assume?"

"It is. And given the nature of that revelation, I'll just feel better with you close by, in case things go sideways. Though, I am hoping I present it in such a way that he doesn't feel blindsided."

"Not a problem," Bobby says. "I'll never be more than a minute or two away, and I'll have a visual on the office most of the time. Text or call, and I'm there."

"I really don't expect there to be any issues, but thanks. I'll text when I'm leaving."

James drives slowly back to the building and occupies an empty visitor's spot in front. The directory in the foyer shows that Speer's office is on the third floor. Foregoing the elevator, James climbs the central stairwell to the third floor. The Speer office directly faces the stairwell.

James walks in and is taken aback. The office is modern and well-lit, with potted trees in the reception and tasteful art on the walls. Not at all what he'd imagined.

You've watched too many late-night noir films.

The office is bright, tastefully decorated, and almost cheery. The receptionist at the desk smiles as she greets James, and offers him a seat in the small but professionally appointed lobby. James sits momentarily, looking to take it all in, when he is almost immediately greeted with an outstretched hand and a friendly smile.

"I'm Tim Speer. Nice to meet you, Mister Butler. Do you go by James or Jim?"

"James, please. And nice to meet you as well."

"Come on into the office. Can I get you anything? Coffee? Water?"

"I'm fine, but thank you."

James follows Speer into his office, and Speer shuts the door behind them. The office is large, well-decorated, and warm. Several pictures of Speer and his family adorn the credenza behind his desk. Pictures of Speer in what appear to be a variety of foreign locations, hang on several of the office walls.

James surveys the office and the former CIA officer sitting across from him. Speer, as with the office, is not as James had expected. With blond hair and blue eyes on a sturdy frame that stretches past six-foot-two, Speer is classically handsome and looks substantially younger than he must be.

"Go ahead and tell me about this criminal issue of yours."

"Well, to be frank, Mister Speers, it's somewhat of an older criminal matter."

"It's Speer, not Speers. There's only one of me, thank goodness. What is the older matter?"

"My apologies. I'm doing some re-examination of the Kiki Camarena case."

"For a client?"

"As far as you know." James runs a hand through his hair.

"Well, that's interesting, but I don't think I can help. I've never had anything to do with that case."

James pauses, silently calculating the amount of information to give away this soon before deciding to lead aggressively.

"I know you once were a CIA field officer, and I know you participated in some interviews of DEA confidential informants who testified during at least one of the Camarena criminal trials in the United States."

Speer pauses. Smiles. James speaks before Speer can.

"Look, I don't have an agenda." James mentally notes that he had used the same words to Aguilar. "I'm honestly just interested in background information. Some dialogue. Off the record. No notes. No recorder. Nothing."

Speer looks at him with the piercing eyes of someone who has judged people for a living, in much tougher situations than this. The pause lasts only a few seconds, which seem like hours to James.

Finally, Speer speaks, his voice earnest but not intimidating.

"Okay, off the record. Let's talk."

Speer rises and checks to confirm the office door is firmly shut. Upon returning to his office chair, he presents a half-smile to James.

"What do you want to know?"

A bit surprised by Speer's willingness to talk, James thinks carefully before speaking.

"All of my questions start with why a former SEAL and CIA operative would care about the DEA's interviews of two confidential informants in Los Angeles?"

"You've done your homework."

"Would you respect me if I hadn't?"

"Nope. And you start with a good question. But for me to answer it, I need to give you some background and context."

Speer leans back deep into his leather chair and stares into the distance as he speaks. James studies him, searching for any clue into Speer's mindset.

"I joined the Navy straight out of high school, disappointing my parents, my counselor, and my high school coaches. But I knew it was the right thing. For me. I had a high aptitude, and I was athletic, so I excelled. And I liked the discipline. Not the right thing for everyone, but a great fit for me. And it really was life-changing.

"It wasn't long before I was given an opportunity to join the SEALs. I thrived at the physical challenges, but it was the mental component to the training that I really loved. That, and the missions. See, we were doing things that had to be done. The sense of pride and achievement was palpable every single day.

"While in the SEALs, my high school Spanish bore fruit, and I was recruited to work with the CIA in South America, as part of the drug eradication projects in Colombia. Of course, the truth is more than that. We were working with the Colombia government to fight the Medellin and Calli cartels, with the most high-level objective being to find and capture, or kill, Pablo Escobar. I spent more days and weeks and months in the Colombian jungles than I care to remember.

"In the early 1980s, because of my knowledge of the Colombian cartels' operations, including their supply routes, I was assigned to operations in Central America, as part of the anti-Sandinista activities that ended up being part of the whole Iran–Contra affair."

James is impressed by Speer's willingness to admit involvement in the Iran–Contra affair without any apparent concern. The Iran–Contra affair involved senior officials in the second term of the Reagan administration secretly facilitating the sale of arms to Iran, which at the time was subject to an arms embargo. The administration hoped to use the proceeds of the arms sale to fund the Contras in Nicaragua who were conducting guerrilla warfare against the socialist Sandinistas in Nicaragua. Under the just-passed Boland Amendment, further funding of the Contras by the government had been prohibited by Congress. The plan was for Israel to ship weapons to Iran, for the United States to resupply Israel, and for Israel to pay the United States. Ostensibly, the arms sales were part of an operation to free seven American hostages held by Hezbollah in Lebanon.

However, the plan went astray in late 1985, when Lieutenant Colonel Oliver North, the deputy director for political-military affairs of the National Security Council, used some of the proceeds from the Iranian weapon sales to fund the Contras, a rebellion group that gained prominence in 1979, after the leftist Sandinistas overthrew Nicaragua's long-time dictator, Anastasio Somoza.

Speer continues his monologue. "In early 1980, I went to Nicaragua and worked with several groups opposing the Sandinistas. Most of them were former members of Somoza's National Guard. Around this time, I was discharged from the Navy, and officially joined the CIA. My operations and activities stayed the same. But let's say, I had significantly more operational freedom with the CIA than I did as a SEAL. Soon, Nicaragua became too active, and it was too dangerous for us to work with the opposition."

"You were training Contras?" James says.

"You know, as I said, a lot of the fighters, especially in the early days, were former National Guard, or even former military. So we didn't really train them, as much as we worked with them on mission planning and sharing intel and resources. In any event, we started scouting for different, more isolated places to train and equip the rebels."

"That's when you went to Mexico?" James says.

"Right. But doing that put us between the proverbial rock and hard place. We needed the airfields and supply routes, but this was also when the Reagan administration was really pushing its anti-drug policy. Frankly, I was far more concerned with the former, but we had to be cognizant of the latter. It really meant we had to be more secretive, more careful."

James listens carefully and watches intently. The more Speer speaks, the more James sees him as a true believer, a the-ends-justify-the-means type.

"How did your activities in Mexico involve the Guadalajara Cartel?" James says.

"First of all, at the time, we didn't know of anything called the Guadalajara Cartel. We knew who some of the primary drug traffickers in the area were, but we didn't really have a sense that there was an organization or a cartel. Regardless of how we characterize it, though, we learned that the narcos had facilities and supply routes we could utilize, and we made agreements to use their facilities and look the other way, at times, to allow them to continue their operations. That's really all there was to it."

"Did you train—I mean, work with—Contras on a cartel ranch?" James says.

"Contrary to persistent rumors, no, we did not. The ranch to which you refer had an airstrip on it that was primarily used by the traffickers to move cocaine from Colombia to Mexico before it was smuggled into the US. The airfield was perfect for us to move people and equipment into Nicaragua. We let the traffickers operate freely, and they let us use the airstrip. Occasionally, some money exchanged hands."

"Did you take and sell cartel drugs, and send the money to the Contras?" James says. "Did you supply the cartel with weapons in exchange for money to go to the Contras?"

"Look, James, I wasn't there for long, and I was not in charge, so it's possible things happened that I didn't know about. But to the best of my knowledge, the CIA never sold drugs for the cartel, and never provided the cartel with weapons. See, now you've got me saying cartel. Did things happen without my knowledge? Maybe, but I doubt it. Did they occur in other parts of Mexico, or after I left Mexico? Maybe, but I wouldn't know."

"How long were you in Mexico?"

"I was moved out of Mexico in January of '86. There was so much activity, so many investigations, our entire operation was imperiled. There were a lot of personnel changes around that time. Then, of course, the whole initiative blew up in Ollie North's face, and we all went scrambling. I was sentenced to Siberia, almost literally. I spent the next five years working in the Balkans, before going to Washington for the last few years of my career."

"Did you know Camarena, or ever meet him?" James says.

"I never interfaced with DEA agents in Mexico, and I can honestly tell you I never heard Camarena's name until after he was kidnapped."

"Then why would you get involved in the Camarena prosecutions, the interviews?"

"I can see you've never worked in an agency like the CIA," Speer says, "which is a behemoth monument to bureaucracy. Don't try to assign too much rationality to its activities and decisions. I was assigned to the DC office in the middle of 1991. I was there to quietly serve the next eighteen months so I could retire with full benefits. I hadn't been there long when I was told about a memo that came across someone's desk, discussing some interviews the DEA was doing in LA. We were told the DEA was asking a lot of questions about the activities about the traffickers in Mexico in '84 and '85. It was decided that the agency really should have some eyes and ears on the situation, and since I was the most knowledgeable and spoke Spanish, I was the logical choice. So I came to LA."

"For the interviews?"

"*An* interview. Only one. We just wanted to be sure that the guy...what was his name?"

"Jorge Godoy?" James says.

"That's right. Godoy. The memo I referred to, as well as some interagency rumors, suggested that he had been talking a lot, and might be saying things of interest to us at the agency. I went out and pried my way into an interview to see if he had any information on our activities."

"Did he?" James leans forward in his chair.

"Nope. As best I could tell, Godoy was one of those low-level guys that pretended he had been involved in, and knew, everything, but gave no indication he really knew anything unique. Most of what he said when I was there would best be categorized as either common knowledge or complete fabrication. I participated in part of one interview and gave up. During the interview, there was nothing said that even hinted at him having any knowledge about the CIA, and nothing was said that remotely touched on the Contras."

"No mention of Félix Rodríguez or a Cuban?" James says.

"Not a peep."

"Let me ask this." James rubs his chin as he thinks it through. "Didn't the DEA agents find it odd that a CIA person wanted to sit in on the interview?"

"Remember the time frame, James. The whole Iran-Contra affair really came to light around November 1986. North testified to Congress in the summer of 1987. If I remember correctly, he was convicted in 1989. So when I show up in late 1991 and say I wanted to confirm that their CIs weren't making allegations about things we were not aware of, I don't think it was a huge surprise."

"But he certainly didn't say, Thank God you're here. Now I can't get these guys to quit talking about the CIA. Right?"

"Nope," Speer says. "There was no mention at all about any CI at that time having said anything about the CIA."

"You're sure this was in fall of 1991?"

"Affirmative. October, I think. But don't hold me to that. But I know for certain it was still in 1991."

"How's that?" James says.

"My little girl was born on Thanksgiving night in 1991, and I distinctly remember getting back to DC from Los Angeles before she was born."

"Congratulations." James smiles, leaning back again. "Going back to your work with the Contras in '84 and '85, as far as you knew, was anyone in the DEA aware of your activities?"

"No. That's the point. There would have been no reason for them to have known anything. Our activities were discrete. The connections were minimal. Even within the CIA, we didn't know what other groups were doing. Discrete assignments. And think about it James, those guys were good at their jobs and knew their areas. If we had stepped out from our lane in any way, they would have known about it, which would have been contrary to our objectives."

"But even then, you wouldn't have killed one of them?" James says.

"Oh hell no. That's not how it works."

Speer's comment was so matter of fact, it particularly resonated with James.

A good questioner—and James is one—often will touch on a sensitive subject and then come back to it in a different context to judge the consistency and sincerity of the reaction.

James moves to a different subject.

"We touched on this a few minutes ago, but as you know, there have been some claims that Félix Rodríguez, or Max Gomez—or whatever his name is—was involved with the Contras and with the Camarena kidnapping and interrogation. Did you ever work with him?"

Félix Rodríguez, a Cuban American, is well-known in intelligence circles and has some general notoriety for having been directly involved in the capture and execution of Che Guevara in Bolivia. Rodríguez also was involved in the planning and preparation of the Bay of Pigs Invasion, may have met with Lee Harvey Oswald in Mexico City only months before the assassination of President Kennedy, and might even have been in Dallas on that fateful day. He is also a respected member of the Cuban-American community in Miami, and in September 2021, was awarded the Governor's Medal of Freedom by Florida governor Ron DeSantis.

Recently, *The Last Narc* aired allegations that Rodríguez was involved with the CIA's activities in support of the Sandinistas, and more significantly, that he had directly participated in Camarena's interrogation because Camarena had unearthed the connection between the CIA and the cartel leaders.

In a pensive mood, Speer pauses for a moment.

"Look, everyone in the agency knows about Félix," Speer replies. "He's a legend. There is no doubt about that. But his role in the missions for the Contras was limited, at best. And even then, he was in El Salvador. And to the best of my knowledge, never in Mexico. At least, not from an operational standpoint."

James leans forward again, now resting his hands on Speer's desk.

"So the million-dollar question is, do you think he was involved in the Camarena abduction?"

"No, I don't. It doesn't fit with what I know. But I'm not foolish enough to say it couldn't be true."

James's mind races. I know about the Iran–Contra affair, and even allegations that the CIA had worked with drug traffickers to fund the Contra efforts. But my information is general, at best, and obviously far inferior to Speer's.

James decides to move the conversation back to topics of which he has more familiarity.

"One of the things that has struck me in some of the allegations made recently is the comment that Camarena was *about to* uncover things regarding the CIA and the Contras, so he was picked up. Let that set in. He was interrogated, tortured, beaten in unconscionable ways, and killed because he was *about to* uncover things." James prepares for a leading question as he would to a witness on the stand. "Does that make any sense?"

"Of course not. You know that. And let me tell you something, James. I spent a lot of time with the SEALs and many of the covert CIA guys down there, and we got into some pretty messed up situations, most of which there is no record of. The guys operating down there included some real tough SOBs who took their missions and their duties uber seriously. They would defend this country to the death, and kill an enemy without hesitation or regret. But I can assure you, not one of them would have killed a fellow federal agent who was just doing his job. Not one. It simply did not happen."

Speer pauses for a moment. "Have you spoken to Hector?"

"Berrellez? No." James's response is both immediate and matter-of-fact.

Hector Berrellez is a former DEA agent and supervisor. And for a time, he was the head of Operation Leyenda, the DEA's code name for the investigation of the Camarena case. A highly decorated thirty-year DEA veteran, Berrellez retired from the DEA in 1996.

Since retiring, starting around 1998, Berrellez has appeared in various press and media outlets, commenting on the Camarena case, and is most notable for his assertion that Camarena was killed by the CIA when Camarena discovered—or was about to discover—that the CIA was training Contras on lands owned by Caro Quintero, and that drug money was helping fund the Contras in their insurgency against the Sandinista government in Nicaragua.

The 2020 four-part *The Last Narc* documentary aired on Amazon Prime, and was primarily a presentation of Berrellez's claims about the CIA's involvement in Camarena's murder, which were based on statements from three confidential informants.

The Last Narc also contained a previously unknown allegation: that Jaime Kuykendall, Camarena's supervisor and the resident agent in charge of the Guadalajara office, was being paid off by the narcotics traffickers, and that he identified Camarena for the kidnappers in the moments before Kiki's abduction.

Following the airing of the series, a book authored by Berrellez, of the same name, was published. The book contained the same allegations and added some additional details. In addition, Berrellez made many appearances on social media and in podcasts to reiterate the claims.

"After the documentary, the book, and his interviews," James says, "I kinda feel like I know what he would say. And frankly, I'm dubious."

"You don't believe Hector?" Speer replies sarcastically.

"Let's say I have my doubts about Hector's candor, his almost unchecked reliance on a few witnesses, and what some could characterize as a tendency to expand on the truth, usually to make himself look better."

"Good answer, James. If you had walked in here citing *The Last Narc,* chapter and verse, our conversation probably would not have lasted too long."

James continues to opine on Berrellez. "When I look carefully at what he has said, it seems to me that he talks about events with absolute certainty, when he wasn't there. He wasn't involved in Operation Leyenda for more than four years after Camarena's murder. But my real issue is that nearly everything he says, and the conclusions he reaches, come from three confidential informants—your buddy Godoy, Rene Lopez Romero, and to a lesser extent, I believe, Ramon Lira. They all were real bad guys in Mexico. Hell, Lopez Romero admits he participated in Camarena's abduction. They all fled to the US, were given protection and money, and said whatever the government wanted them to say, whenever the government wanted it said. I've seen investigations into them. They are proven liars."

"But that doesn't mean everything they say is a lie," Speer says in a definitive tone.

James pauses, pushes his hair back with his fingers, and emits a quiet sigh.

"True," he replies. "But that doesn't get anyone any closer to the truth."

"That, my friend, is the problem." Speer sits up in his chair and leans forward over his desk, looking at James to accentuate his point. "There is no truth. The truth depends on who you are, which side of the line you stand on, where your loyalties lie, who is paying you, who wants you dead."

"I get that. I really do. Maybe not the same way you do, but I can relate." James hesitates, avoiding any appearance of being either defensive or argumentative. "But that doesn't mean we should stop asking the questions, does it?"

"No, it does not," Speer says. "And I am not suggesting you should stop looking for answers to your questions. But what I am suggesting is that you don't try to find a golden truth that answers all the questions in a neat narrative that you can wrap up and put a bow on."

"That does make sense," James says. "After all this time, with so many people now dead, I'm starting to think there are only a handful of people who might really know what happened. And most of them are south of the border."

"Either safely tucked away in prison, or in hiding in the hills of Sinaloa."

Speer's not subtle reference to two of the leaders of the Guadalajara Cartel, Félix Gallardo and Caro Quintero, strikes James as curious. *Is he suggesting that the heads of the cartel were aware of the CIA's operations? Or only that they would have known why Camarena was picked up? Either way, I've probably gotten as much information from Speer as I am going to get.*

"Tim, this has been very illuminating and extremely helpful. I should let you get back to some real work now."

"James, if you really want to find some answers, I recommend you not spend too much time looking into the CIA. It will turn into a house of mirrors, and you'll be lost forever."

"Fair enough," James replies.

Both men stand, and Speer extends his hand.

"This has been a pleasure, James. If you have any other questions, here is my card. Give me a shout and save yourself the drive."

"I will. And thanks again." James puts the card in his shirt pocket.

As he starts to leave Speer's office, he notices a mid-sized rock on a stand sitting atop a marble mount in a corner of the office.

"That's an interesting rock. What is it?"

"That is a Eucrite meteorite I found it in Mexico. Very rare."

"Interesting. I'll have to Google it when I get home."

James walks through the reception and out of the office. As he reaches the stairs, Speer calls out to him.

"James. One more thought."

He turns to face Speer. "Oh, what's that?"

"Have you considered that, if the CIA was so intent on keeping its secrets secret that they had a fellow federal agent killed, what would they do to someone who starts digging too deep or gets too close?"

James shakes his head and starts down the stairs.

No, I really hadn't thought about it. But I am now.

CHAPTER TEN

STILL THROWN A BIT OFF by Speer's last comment, James texts Bobby as he walks out of the building. "All good. Thanks for being here."

The reply text is immediate: "Any time. But casually look due south in the parking lot."

James looks down the street, noting nothing out of the ordinary.

Bobby sends a follow-up text as James tries to scan the area. "The Black Suburban in the back corner of the lot, backed in to face the building about 5 minutes after you went in and has been there the entire time."

"So?" James replies.

"The driver has never gotten out."

James, both suspicious and curious, moves toward the Suburban, trying in vain to look causal. "Stay put for a minute, will you?"

Bobby replies immediately. "I ain't moving."

James nears the Suburban, when he recognizes the driver, who watches James's approach. The Suburban's window lowers as James reaches the door. "Did you and Tim have a nice chat?"

"Agent Aguilar. Quite interesting to see you here. Not a coincidence, I assume."

"Let's say I was interested in what you were up to." Aguilar flashes a friendly smile that was noticeably absent during their meeting in James's office.

Whether intended or not, James feels more at ease and significantly less guarded.

He returns the friendly expression. "Tell you what. I could use a beer before driving back home. How about I buy the first round?

"I could do that," Aguilar says. "I know a place not far from here. I'll wait here for you to get your car."

Once in his car, James texts Bobby back. "No worries here. I'll call you tomorrow."

Aguilar leads James to a small bar a few miles away. Tucked in the corner of a strip mall, it is quiet and dim—a perfect place to meet. James and Aguilar spot a table in the back, conveniently located adjacent to both the jukebox and the restrooms. The bartender/waitress, a middle-aged woman, is decidedly less than excited to have to follow the men to the back of the bar.

"My name is Jenna. What can I get you boys?"

Aguilar nods to James.

"I'll have a Corona." He glances at Aguilar. "Seems appropriate."

"Want a lime?"

"Please."

Barely turning her attention to Aguilar, Jenna says, "And you?"

"Same."

The men wait for Jenna to make her way toward the bar and out of earshot, before beginning their conversation, which Agular starts.

"I really didn't expect you to let things go. But I also didn't think you'd be talking to Speer. What's the connection?"

"You know Speer? How's that?"

"Not surprisingly, the number of former DEA agents and CIA officers with Mexican connections is not large. Let's say, we've met."

Jenna soon returns with two cold Corona bottles and sets

them on the table with an obligatory, "If you need anything else…"

James and Aguilar squeeze the limes into their bottles.

Aguilar is different than he was in James's office. The bravado is gone. Now, James sees a man worn and tired, but definitely not broken.

"Did Tim give you any new information, or have anything interesting to share?"

"I'm not sure I should answer that, given our conversation in my office. I don't really like being threatened."

"Trust me. You were not threatened." Aguilar chuckles.

James smiles. "Perhaps that was a bit of hyperbole, but your attitude was decidedly less than friendly."

"Look." Aguilar sighs. "This case has had far more than its fair share of whack jobs and naïve do-gooders. They make everything harder. If things start to open, and cracks appear, unfocused attention seals the cracks and drives the truth farther underground. After all this time, the number of leads and witnesses diminishes every day. I needed to see which one you were."

"Which am I?" James says.

"Frankly, neither. There's a chance that you just might be someone who can make some progress, and maybe even get something done."

James thinks for a moment. "You asked me, so I have to ask you. Why do you care? What's your connection?"

Aguilar takes a big drink, followed by another sigh, this one deep and guttural.

"In the early '80s, I was a young DEA agent in Texas. I was assigned to an office in Odessa, but as the new guy, I had assignments and traveled all over the state. In 1984, I had been moved to the San Antonio office and was tracking a relatively new flow of drugs apparently coming across the border from Nuevo Laredo. The surge was incredible, and we were doing little more than putting fingers in the dike. Morale among the agents was low, and I started looking for options. I applied for a few local police officer positions. But after a few months, our office, and others in Texas, started having some successes—making some significant busts and confiscating major drug shipments. We also made some good progress in trailing drugs from Mexico to some distribution points in the US. For the first time in a long time, the good guys were winning a little. I felt rejuvenated.

"In January 1985, I put in for a transfer to the Guadalajara office. I knew some agents had left that post, and they were operating shorthanded. There was a lot of activity, and I wanted to be part of the action. Make a difference. I even had a phone interview with Jaime Kuykendall, who, as you know—"

"Was the resident agent in charge in Guadalajara at that time," James says

"That's right. He was having a hard time keeping agents in Guadalajara. Keep in mind that during this time in the early '80s, DEA agents in Mexico could not carry weapons, could not make arrests, and were at the mercy of the local police and military, who often were in bed with the traffickers."

"It really was the Wild West," James says.

"It wasn't easy, that's for sure. But those who went and stayed, really believed in the cause they were fighting for."

"You were scheduled to replace Kiki?"

"I wouldn't put it that way. They needed people, and I was interested. I hoped to make the move sometime in the spring, but nothing was close to official. But then came the kidnapping. I went to Guadalajara to help with the investigation, like everyone else, but was there for less than a week. What I saw changed my mind. I had a family. I couldn't bring them into that world, and I knew I didn't want to live away from my children for the next five years. I withdrew my request and stayed in Texas for a few more years, before being moved out here. It's an odd feeling. I wasn't there, but his death hit me like I was. And part of me always felt like I let him down by not going to Guadalajara."

"I really can understand that sentiment," James says. "But it doesn't explain you coming to my office to try to dissuade me from looking into the case."

"Now that the criminal trials are over," Aguilar says, "the DEA and the DOJ have basically given up on the case, after new leads have all but completely dried up, even though it is classified as an open investigation. Rather than just let the case completely fade away, a few of us continued to monitor the case and track down leads on our own time. Over time, the number of legitimate leads became fewer and fewer. At the same time, frankly, there was no internal capital to be gained by continuing to investigate things, even if informally—a clear disincentive to questioning the official version of events. A friend in the DEA was notified about your FOIA and gave me the head's up."

"So you never worked with Camarena?" James says.

"No. I had intended to go to Guadalajara to meet with Kuykendall toward the end of February, and presumably, I would have met Kiki then."

"If he hadn't already left for San Diego by then," James says.

"That's right. You know your facts."

"As I said, this is more than a passing fad for me, and I'm good at putting information together. I am confused about one thing, though. In my office, you said you and Camarena were friends."

"Well, consider that my moment of hyperbole, as you put it."

Aguilar finishes his beer, and James quickly follows suit.

James stands. "I'll get us another round. I think I should go to Jenna this time."

"Smart man."

James slowly walks to the bar. "Two more please."

He surveys the bar: Jenna and four customers, none of whom seem to be anything other than mid-afternoon drinkers.

Damn, am I being paranoid all of a sudden? I wonder if this is how agents feel all the time? I don't like it.

James notices a patron at the far end of the bar to his left, wearing a black hoodie, the hood nearly covering his entire face, his head down, looking into the Coors Light bottle in front of him. In the dimly lit bar, he is virtually unnoticeable, until he turns to smile at James.

James walks to the end of the bar, noticing that the location is perfectly shielded from his table with Aguilar.

"Hi, Bobby," James whispers. "I'm both surprised and relieved to see you here."

"You didn't really think I would leave you alone, did you?"

Jenna calls out to James, "Your beers are here," placing them on the counter at the other end of the bar.

"I should get back to my table. Everything seems to be fine, but—"

"Don't worry. I'll be here, slowly milking my Rocky Mountain ale."

James returns to the other end of the bar to pick up the two Corona bottles, limes rising from the tops.

"On your tab?" Jenna says.

"Please. And I'm paying for both of us."

"Okay," Jenna replies.

James walks back to the table, a cold beer in each hand, and Aguilar resumes the conversation before James even sits.

"Now that you know my connection to the case, I'm still unclear as to yours. I did a bit of research on you. You've done a lot, and I was more impressed than I expected. But there is nothing connecting you to Camarena or the case. You're a white boy from the Midwest. I just don't get it."

James is assured by Aguilar's inquisitive, not accusatory, tone.

"All I can say is, it's personal." James strokes his hands back through his hair. "And it's very important to me. I've been curious for years, and only recently decided to be more assertive or proactive about it."

"Raising a few red flags in the process," Aguilar says.

"Yeah, that didn't go quite as planned."

James is not accustomed to misreading things, and is more than a bit sheepish owning up to it. Nevertheless, he presses forward.

"I'm curious, though, as to what you called the 'official story' earlier. Is that the narrative that Camarena was so successful that Caro picked him up, and the torture went too far and Camarena died?"

"Yes," Aguilar replies. "As well as the versions of the story about how the traffickers were aided by Mexican politicians, police, and the military who facilitated the abduction and interrogation."

"Neat and tidy," James says. "But leaves a few questions, does it not?"

"It does," Aguilar replies. "Starting, I think, with the tapes. If RCQ got pissed and kidnapped Camarena to find out how he was finding his fields, why tape the interrogations?"

James pauses for a moment. He knows newer DEA agents refer to Caro as "RCQ," but finds Aguilar's use of the reference interesting.

"At the same time," James replies, "if these high-powered Mexican officials were involved in the planning, and many of them allegedly were present during the interrogation, who were the tapes for?"

"Also a good question," Aguilar says.

"Not to be too circular here," James continues, "but my curiosity starts even further back. Why pick him up in the first place? No matter how upset or concerned the cartel was, didn't they know nothing good could would come from picking up an American agent? What did they really think could be learned that would be worth the risk? Or was there a different agenda? Different information to be gained?"

Aguilar contemplates for a moment. "One could answer that question by pointing to the tapes. The tapes show why he was picked up. Caro wanted to know more about the DEA."

"But doesn't that presuppose the answer?" James says. "The tapes show why he was picked up, but not why Caro, or whoever, thought it was a good idea in the first place. Look at everything bad that happened to the cartel and its heads as a result of the single decision to kidnap Agent Camarena."

"Are you trying to assign rational thought to an inherently irrational act by an irrational person?" Aguilar asks.

"You say that like it's a bad thing," James replies.

Aguilar laughs at his witticism, and James notes another crack in Aguilar's stoic exterior, before moving on.

"At the same time, though," James says, "Caro, to some extent, was responsible for the explosive growth of marijuana production, distribution, and sales. He might not have been well-educated, but he must have had some skills and talents. What could he have thought would be the result of picking up Camarena?"

"You know the response to that as well as I do," Aguilar says. "It's in in the documentary: the cartel killed the four Jehovah's Witness missionaries, whom someone might have suspected were DEA agents, without any repercussions. And then they killed Walker and Radelat, whom they thought were DEA agents, without any blowback. They thought they were immune and could act with impunity, even in kidnapping a DEA agent."

During the fall of 1984, there were large numbers of Jehovah's Witness missionaries, actively proselytizing in Guadalajara, many of whom had been threatened or harassed. Among the missionaries were Dennis and Rose Carlson, who arrived in late November or early December, from Redding, California. And Ben and Paula Mascarena, also Americans who had been in Guadalajara for about two years. On December 2, 1984, the four Americans returned to a neighborhood where the Mascarenas had visited the week prior. That morning, shortly after arriving in the neighborhood, the four were abducted by men in three cars, the missionary men separated from the women, and taken away. The Mexican government, not the DEA or any other American agency, investigated the case and came up with the story that the missionaries had inadvertently knocked on the door of a home owned by Ernesto Fonseca, and Fonseca had ordered them killed to keep them silent. The Mexican police advanced this theory, even though it was supported by neither the physical evidence or witness statements.

Shortly after the kidnapping of the missionaries, and only eight days before the Camarena abduction, two other Americans disappeared while in Guadalajara. John Walker was a Vietnam veteran who had moved to Guadalajara to pursue a career as a writer. His friend, Albert Radelat, had joined him in Guadalajara for a few days of fun and relaxation. On the evening of January 30, 1985, the two men apparently went out for dinner and were never heard from again.

As was the case with the missionary couples, the investigation into disappearance of Walker and Radelat, such as it was, was conducted by the Mexican police. In truth, most of the investigation was undertaken by Dr. Felipe Radelat, a Cuban refugee, medical doctor, and father to Albert Radelat, much to the annoyance and dismay of the Mexican officials.

The day after Dr. Radelat provided the Mexican police with information he'd learned about the whereabouts of his son and John Walker, newspapers in Guadalajara carried the story that the state judicial police identified two witnesses with details of the disappearances of Walker and Radelat.

The two witnesses were employees of La Longosta restaurant, who stated that the restaurant had closed at 7:00 p.m., and that Walker and Radelat had inadvertently walked into the restaurant after closing time, when a number of cartel members were meeting. Before the two men could correct their error, they were detained, tortured, and murdered.

James shakes his head before taking another drink of his beer.

"I've heard that explanation," he replies, "and I've heard smart people say it, but I'm just not convinced. The car the missionaries were driving was found in the middle of the street. They didn't park somewhere and then knock on Fonseca's door. There is nothing credible to suggest they were suspected of being DEA agents. With Walker and Radelat, within a day or two after they disappeared, it seems it was well-known who they were. While someone might have thought they were DEA when they were killed, they should have quickly learned they weren't DEA. So how could killing missionaries and two unlucky Americans given Caro the gravitas to think he could pick up Camarena—who they knew was DEA?"

"But wait," Aguilar says. "They apparently acted when they thought people were DEA. So why don't you think it makes sense for them to have acted the same way with respect to Camarena?"

"Two things," James replies, with increased energy and enthusiasm. "First, there was nothing about the actions of the missionaries that would indicate they were working for the DEA. Second, even if they thought Walker and Radelat were DEA—which, again, I question—they acted impulsively and killed them. Doesn't that seem more like how these butchers would act?"

Aguilar nods in silent agreement.

James continues. "But the fact that I don't believe that the missionary couples or the La Longosta incident were factors influencing the decision to abduct Camarena does *not* mean I don't think that the cartel members, and Rafa in particular, were so full of themselves, and so enamored with the DFS agents and police and politicians on their payrolls, that they implicitly thought they were above reproach."

"At the same time," Aguilar says, "they could have just killed Camarena, too. Shot him on the street. Easy."

"True. But instead, according to the government, they held planning meetings, kidnapped him, taped his interrogations, and had senior political and military people present at the interrogation. Really?"

"What, you think it is all going to get wrapped up in a neat explanation that ties up the loose ends, leaving no questions unanswered?" Aguilar says, continuing his obvious role as the devil's advocate in this conversation.

"No, that's not it at all," James says. "It's kinda like the OJ Simpson case. There may have been some open questions, but the evidence generally pointed to OJ, and virtually none of it pointed to not OJ. In that case, it was easy for me, analytically and emotionally, to say OJ did it. That's not the case here. There are things that point in many different directions, so I can't just accept the government's theory of the case."

"Instead, you do what?" Aguilar says.

"Apply the facts and evidence to alternative theories."

"Alternative theories, such as?" Aguilar says, with genuine curiosity.

"Well, there are many. But what about Sara Cosio, as but one example? You know the rumors, I'm sure. Sara Cosio was a debutante socialite from a prominent and well-connected family in the state of Jalisco, who was involved with Caro Quintero in the weeks leading up to the Camarena abduction. The details on their relationship are mostly speculative. Depending on the source, Sara was either a kidnapping victim or a young, sheltered girl who enjoyed the wild life she had with the handsome Caro Quintero. In Mexico, the affair between Cosio and Rafa made for headlines in the tabloids and was ample fodder for gossip, rumor, and innuendo. Cosio was in Costa Rica with Caro when he was arrested, and reports are that it was she who identified Caro for the military personnel and DEA agents looking to take Caro into custody.

"There had been some rumors that Camarena may have known Cosio, and that his friendship with her, however defined, may have enraged a jealous Caro and led to his kidnapping. During an appeal, one of the US defense teams presented an affidavit from a restaurateur who claimed to have seen Camarena and Cosio together the day before his abduction.

"Additionally, after the Camarena murder, an MFJP comandante investigated the case and apparently used *extreme* measures in his efforts to obtain information from witnesses. In September 1992, the comandante and a DEA agent said that Camarena was abducted because of his romantic relationship with Ms. Cosio, and that Caro Quintero initially intended only to slap Camarena around to teach him a lesson."

James knows many DEA agents have reacted strongly to any allegation that Camarena was involved with Cosio in any way, and worried he might have touched a nerve with his comment, so he quickly adds, "I never really bought that angle myself. Even if I thought there might have been something between Sara and Kiki, that motivation for the abduction would not explain the interrogation of Camarena, the recording of the interrogation, the absence of her name in the transcripts, the alleged presence of officials at Lope de Vega during interrogation, and the theory would render the alleged pre-abduction meetings wholly unnecessary."

Aguilar continues the conversation without any appearance of being offended by James's question.

"As far as I know, the DEA briefly looked into it, but no one had any reason to believe that Camarena was anything other than what he appeared to be. Cosio gave a statement or testimony in Washington, but I'm told she said nothing of note."

James says, "I know at least one of the American defense teams looked into the theory, and some other less favorable characterizations of Camarena, but elected to go with the don't-try-to-take-down-a-hero-unless-you-know-you-will-succeed strategy."

The conversation lulls for a moment as both men consider while drinking their beers. Soon, though, James breaks the silence.

"What about the idea that the congressional delegation spooked a government or military official enough to order the kidnapping?"

"Yeah, I watched *Narcos: Mexico,* too," Aguilar replies snidely.

"Any validity there, in your mind?"

Aguilar re-centers himself in his chair, leaning onto the table to look at James.

"Let's go back to one of your original points," he replies. "If we think RCQ was likely street smart or savvy enough to know better than to kidnap an American agent, and he was not a smart man, then surely high-ranking government officials would know the perils of such a course of action."

"Hard to argue with that," James says. "Which brings us back to the foundational questions of who picked him up and why tape the interrogation?"

Aguilar doesn't respond, but stares into the distance as he finishes his beer.

"One more before we leave?" he says.

"Sure, that sounds good," James replies.

Aguilar stands. "My turn."

He walks to the bar, and James remains seated. Nothing about this day has gone as I expected, and there is a lot to process. But I know one thing for sure: I'm on the right track, asking the right questions. But I have no idea where this will lead.

Aguilar returns with two cold Coronas and retakes his seat across from James, who picks up the conversation.

"Look, I know the cartel was heavily protected by the government and the military, and of course, the MFJP and DFS. And thanks."

"No, you're right," Aguilar says. "That's a given. But it is still hard to see what the endgame would have been."

"What about the CIA?" James floats the trial balloon as he takes a drink, watching for Aguilar's reaction.

Stone-faced, Aguilar replies, "Ah, the million-dollar question. Hence, Speer?"

"Hence, Speer." James nods his beer to Aguilar.

"I honestly don't know." Aguilar is deliberate in his word choice. "Over the last thirty-plus years, there has been little incentive for someone in my position to inquire too deep into the alleged CIA connection."

"But you know the allegations," James says.

"Of course I know the allegations and the stories," Aguilar replies, with a thread of irritation in his voice. "I also know the source for most of these allegations, and I don't have much faith in that source."

"You mean Berrellez and his allegation in *The Last Narc*?"

"Yeah, Berrellez. Together with the three informants he relies upon."

"But he has some support from other sources, doesn't he?" James says, now taking on the role as the provocateur, asking questions without believing the premise.

Aguilar shakes his head. "James, I'm betting you know this better than I. But from everything I know, if you boil down the allegations, they come from a couple of sources whose credibility is dubious, at best. All of the *facts* I've ever seen are either quite general and non-specific, or demonstrably false. And as far as support, if a CI tells a lie to three people, and all three say they heard the lie, they corroborate each other, but it's still a lie."

"My thoughts exactly," James says. "I'm also struck by the fact that in about twenty years, Berrellez has come up with almost nothing new in that regard, but completely relies on these three informants."

"Which brings us full circle to Speer," Aguilar says. "Did he give you anything?"

"Nothing we haven't seen and heard a million times. He

was helping the Contras, using cartel lands and supply routes. The CIA looked the other way on some drug trafficking operations. Yada, yada, yada."

"Mostly what I would have expected," Aguilar says. "At the end of the day, I still don't believe an American agent would be directly involved in something this sinister."

"Speer said the same thing, just in more graphic terms."

Aguilar glances at his watch and downs the last of his beer.

"I'm going to need to get going soon," he says.

"But Speer did seem to lend some credibility to Godoy and Lopez. And I assume Berrellez, by extension. Which I found curious."

"Why so?" Aguilar says. "They have helped convict some bad people."

"They are liars," James replies. "Proven liars. For every true nugget they put on the table, there are five more lies that embellish it."

James takes a drink and a deep breath before launching into an impassioned monologue.

"Let's think about this. Godoy and Lopez described meetings where the conspirators planned Camarena's kidnapping, and they assert that each of these meetings was attended by large groups of military officers, government prosecutors, state and federal police offices, and well-known politicians, as well as the drug lords and their henchmen.

"On their face, these don't ring true. For famous politicians and military officers to attend three or more meetings is implausible, at best. Even in 1985, without the paparazzi and social media of today, would a well-known politician risk his reputation to meet in person with cartel members, three times? And not just one-on-one meetings, but meetings with several other high-profile individuals, including Manuel Bartlett-Diaz, probably the second-most well-known politician in all of Mexico?

"If you read the transcript of the second Zuno trial, one thing stands out. The government's case had no corroboration. None. No witnesses, no receipts, no invoices, no photographs, no travel documents. That is, these two criminals, who came forward with testimony under questionable circumstances—the timing of which was dubious, at best—corroborated each other. Except, of course, when they didn't. And I know for a fact that some of these well-known men have solid, contemporaneous, third-party alibis for many of the meetings Godoy or Lopez allege they attended."

Aguilar smiles at James. "Ready to take a breath now?"

James laughs. "I do get a bit riled up. I'm just not prepared to indict the CIA and its agents, based on the word of these guys."

James and Aguilar pause. James knows the conversation is about to end, and makes the decision to close in a similar manner as he had with Speer earlier.

"One of the things I find interesting is that, at the end of the day, it seems there are only a few people still living who really know what happened. In Mexico, Félix Gallardo likely would know about the money trail, and I suspect, if and how the CIA was profiting from the cartel. And Caro would know how and why Camarena was picked up. But neither of them is talking."

"We can't ask them, so we may never know," Aguilar says. "I have to go. One last suggestion?"

"Of course."

"If you keep pursuing this, take everything you know or think you know, toss it to the side, and start only with the facts you deem credible, and avoid the mountains of misinformation and pure speculation. There. That's my kernel of wisdom for today, and now I really must be leaving. Drive safely back home."

"Thanks. You too."

James stands to shake Aguilar's hand, sits back down at the table, and watches Aguilar lumber out the decal-clad front door. James gives a nod of gratitude to Bobby, who follows Aguilar out the door, trailing a few seconds behind.

Jenna slowly walks back to the table. "Are you all done here?"

James shakes his head. "Nope. I'll have one more. At least."

CHAPTER ELEVEN

THE SUN HAS YET TO RISE VERY HIGH into the Southern California sky as James works furiously at his desk. His private investigation hobby has taken too much time from his real job, and this morning he is consumed by feelings of angst and worry.

"So????" Erica's voice echoes down the vacant halls as she walks toward James's office. "What the hell happened?" She plops down in the chair in front of James.

"Christ, you are a one-woman wrecking crew."

"Shut up. Did you talk to Speer?"

"Yes. And Aguilar, too."

"Shut the front door!"

"True. Shocked me, too."

"Tell me. Now!"

James recounts the prior day's events as Erica listens with rapt focus and attention. A pause follows James's recitation of the story before Erica finally speaks.

"Wow. I'm literally stunned. That's far more information than I ever expected you to get from Speer.

"Agreed."

"So what's next?"

"I don't know. It's been thirty-five years. If there was a big mystery behind it, wouldn't someone have found it by now? Maybe the story is exactly as it's been told, and that's all there is."

"Do you really believe that?"

"At this point, I honestly don't know. I really don't. Here is the issue I'm having. I don't believe the people making most of these allegations, most particularly Berrellez's informants—Godoy, Lopez Romero, and Lira. I don't trust them about anything. Literally, nothing at all. But they know enough that they cannot be completely discounted. At the same time, there are very few people in the US with firsthand knowledge that aren't either completely wrapped up with these liars or dead. The ones with real knowledge are the narcos themselves, and they haven't said much of significance in the last three decades."

"Do you know they won't say anything now?" Erica says. "Have you asked them? Has anyone?"

"That, my dear, is a good question."

"That's what I am here for. I'm going to get the coffee started before anyone else gets here. Let me know when you need some more of my brilliance."

James's phone rings, and he answers with the speaker phone, barely pausing from his typing.

"Do you need me to order you some lunch?" Erica says.

"Nah, I'm okay. I want to finish this brief."

"Okay, I'll be there in a sec."

Moments later, Erica is again in the chair in James's office.

"Which part of finishing a brief was confusing to you?"

"When is it due?"

"A week from tomorrow."

"See."

"I'm just uptight. I need to be certain everything here is being handled, and handled well."

"Everyone has your back, and you are too good to let the quality of your work slide."

"Why, thank you."

"So shut up and tell me more about Speer."

Saving his work, James moves his chair to be more directly in front of Erica.

"Smooth," he says. "Very smooth. He really wanted me to trust him. But I can't shake the feeling there is more."

"Then find it."

"I can't tell if you are being difficult or encouraging."

"Both." Erica displays a warm smile. "Let me put it this way, if you could do one thing now to advance the ball, if there were no restraints, what would you do?"

"I don't know. Maybe talk to Félix Gallardo..." James hits the speaker on his phone and dials a number, motioning for Erica to shut the office door. "Steve Williams." After a pause, "Hey, Steve, it's James. How are you?"

"I'm okay. What's up?"

"By the way, you are on speaker, and Erica is here."

"Hi, Erica. How are you?"

"I'm good, Steve. You need to come around more."

"I know. Just too damn busy."

James says, "So Erica and I were talking this morning, and...well, I want to go to Mexico and meet Félix Gallardo."

"And I want to go hot-tubbing with Kate Beckinsale tonight, but that ain't gonna happen either."

"Don't sell yourself short," James says, in a futile bid at whimsy. "But seriously, *in theory,* could you help smooth the path if I tried to get in to see him?"

"Honestly, James, I don't know. It's a crazy idea, and you are a freakin' madman."

"Is it possible, though?"

"Maybe?"

"Can you see?"

"I don't know. Let me make a few extremely quiet inquiries."

"Thank you. You know I appreciate it."

"I know. Erica, take care of my boy there."

"Always, Steve. Always."

James hangs up, and the office is silent for a moment.

Suddenly, Erica perks up, blurting out, "Damn it. I can't believe I didn't think about this until now. Did you know Brian knows the US Ambassador in Mexico?"

"That's an interesting bit of information I was not aware of," James snarks.

Erica stands and practically races out of the office.

"Come on," she yells to a trailing James.

Ignoring the closed door, Erica storms into Brian's office with unbridled enthusiasm.

"James needs your help to go meet with a narco in Mexico."

Trailing behind, James cringes upon hearing Erica's words.

"It's not quite as unsavory as that sounded," he says.

Brian looks at the two in front of him, both breathing heavily, their mutual excitement tangible.

"Why don't you two take a seat and a few deep breaths, and tell me what you are talking about."

James and Erica look at each other for a moment, before James starts.

"You know my off-hours hobby is looking into the Camarena case, and it has recently produced some interesting information. One of the big issues are the allegations that the CIA was connected to both the kidnapping and the interrogation. But as you can imagine, getting information on that is difficult. But if we really wanted to pursue the allegations and understand what role the CIA had with the cartel, including possible involvement with Camarena, a logical step forward—something I don't think anyone has really pursued—is to talk to Miguel Angel Félix Gallardo, who is now in a penitentiary in Guadalajara."

Erica chimes in to draw the connection to a close. "And James and I were discussing it, and I remembered that you and Juan Abun are friends, and...well, here we are."

Brian looks at James with an expression of exasperation and a hint of fatherly worry.

James tries to talk, but Erica steps on his words. "We've just been talking when he needs an ear or my superhuman research skills."

Brian smiles and looks at James. "Okay, why don't you give me some more details. But shut the door first."

James recounts the meetings with Speer and Aguilar, and his current theories on the investigation.

"That's why I think getting information from Félix Gallardo or Caro is a unique opportunity. Since we know where Gallardo is, he seems to be the logical choice. He is in bad health, but he gave his one and only television interview not too long ago. So maybe he is more willing to talk than he would have been previously."

"That's when I thought of your connection, and here we are," Erica says.

"You are now caught up." James flashes a wry half-smile that comes off more like a grimace.

Brain pauses and looks out the window at the Pacific Ocean.

"Let me see if I understand this correctly. You want to go to Mexico and meet with a notorious drug dealer and killer in order to satisfy your curiosity about the case, even though you have no idea if he will talk to you, or what he might say if he does."

"Correct," James replies, before reluctantly adding, "But it's a bit worse than that."

"Of course it is."

"I don't speak Spanish," James says. "But Erica is fluent."

Brian looks to Erica. "Is this where I should give the outraged, overprotective father speech? Angrily forbid you from going?

"You could." Erica laughs. "If you thought it would make any difference."

"You know I hate the idea of either one of you going down there."

Brian looks at James, who leans forward to meet Brian's gaze.

"You know me, Brian. Probably as well as anyone ever has. You know I hate the idea as much as you. But we will be safe and smart. If your friend can help set it up, that is."

Brian shakes his head. "I'll tell you what...send me the details on where he is incarcerated, what you would like to do, and I'll give Juan Abun a call. But no promises. He'll think this even crazier than I do."

"No expectations whatsoever. Thanks, Brian."

Later that night, James rests on his couch, barely watching the basketball game on the television, when the buzzing of his phone on the coffee table alerts him to a text from Steve Williams. "Interview scheduled. Next Thursday. 1 pm local. 15 minutes only. Ask for Comandante Perez at the prison gate. That's ALL I know."

James stares at the phone before forwarding the message to Erica with a simple message: "Holy crap. Get your passport ready."

CHAPTER TWELVE

THE FOLLOWING FEW DAYS ARE A BLUR for both James and Erica. Erica handles travel details and coordinates with the American consulate in Guadalajara, while James addresses his cases and clients.

The following Monday, just three days before their trip, a few moments before 5:00 p.m., James approaches Erica at her normal position at the front desk. Erica willingly covers the desk starting at 4:30 p.m. so the full-time receptionist can catch an earlier bus home and be able to pick up her son at his grade school on time.

James leans on the reception desk in front of Erica.

"Any plans tonight?" he says.

"Not really."

"Great. Let's go."

"Okay. Where are we going?"

"San Diego, of course." James walks to the elevator.

"San Diego, of course," Erica mockingly repeats, as she follows James.

Once in the car, heading south on the 405, James says, "We are going to see Doctor Javier Mirada. He is a professor at UCSD in the history department, with a specialty in modern Mexican history, and a focus on the development of the Mexican cartel structure and the influence of the cartels on Mexican society, politically, socially, and economically. I thought if we were going to go to talk to one of the founders of the cartel, we should understand it better."

The drive down the San Diego Freeway is quick, peaceful, and relaxed. Soon, James's Audi enters into north San Diego County and approaches the town of La Jolla, home to University of California, San Diego. Founded in 1960, UCSD is one of ten campuses in the University of California system, and home to some forty thousand undergraduate and graduate students. The school sits on almost twenty-two hundred acres of prime real estate near the Pacific Ocean.

James exits off the 5 Freeway, onto La Jolla Village Drive, heading west. In about a mile, the road curves to the north, past the Scripps Institute of Oceanography, one of the first research and education facilities in the area.

Heading north, James drives past Revelle College, one of seven residential colleges on the campus. Immediately past Revelle College are John Muir College's athletic field and tennis courts, and James turns right immediately after the tennis courts, onto Scholar's Lane. The road quickly bends to the right, with the Humanities & Social Sciences building on the left at the bend. In another block, the lane dead ends at a small parking lot in front of the gymnasium. James glides into one of the two open visitors' parking spots.

"Just like it was waiting for us," he says.

James and Erica walk back the short distance to the H&SS building, and enter through the front door. The elevator is directly in front of them, and they ride it down one floor to the main level.

"Doctor Mirada has a seven p.m. class, and he agreed to meet us in the large classroom on the first floor, prior to his class," James says, before he and Erica exit the elevator.

Looking around, they soon spot the classroom at the end of the hall to the right.

Upon entering the classroom, James walks toward the stage, where a man awaits.

"Javi!" he says, and Dr. Mirada reciprocates, "Mi amigo!" as the two men warmly embrace.

Dr. Mirada appears to be in his late forties or early fifties.

He is shorter than James and has a bit of a paunch, but looks to have been fit in his earlier years. He wears a dark beard, neatly trimmed, and the suit of a banker, not a college professor. His baritone voice echoes off the acoustic tiles in the auditorium.

Trailing slightly behind, Erica says, "You two know each other?"

"Yes, we are *old* friends," James replies.

"And you know each other how?" Erica says.

"It's a long story," James replies.

"That means James could tell you, but then one of us would have to kill you," Dr. Mirada says.

Erica laughs, assuming—or hoping—it was a joke.

"Doctor Javier Mirada, this inquisitive lady is Erica Walsh, the best paralegal in California, and a very good friend."

Dr. Mirada faces Erica. "It is a pleasure to meet you. That is high praise from James."

Erica shakes Dr. Mirada's hand. "James is being too kind."

Dr. Mirada points to the seats in the front row. "Here. Have a seat and tell me what brings you all the way to La Jolla on a weeknight?"

"We need your brilliance and expertise," James replies.

"Hah. I'm happy to share what little I have."

"Erica and I are working on a case that relates to the early days of the cartel system in Mexico. The early 1980s, and more specifically, the Guadalajara Cartel. I was hoping you could give us a down-and-dirty primer on that period."

"Sure, but you know most of this as well as I do." Dr. Mirada says. "What's up?"

"For reasons that don't really matter right now, I'd like you to give us the stripped-down version. Strip away the hype and the movies, the publicity, and the stories. Treat us like freshmen with no prior knowledge."

"Well, that I know how to do. Stop me if I'm not giving you the information you need."

Dr. Mirada turns on his computer, which projects a large

map of the United States, Central America, and northern South America onto the large screen behind the stage.

"In the 1970s, until the early 1980s," he says, "most of the drugs shipped into the United States came from South America, mostly Colombia, but also countries such a Bolivia. During that period, a central point of entry was in or near Florida, for the obvious logistical reasons. However, in the mid-1970s, the US government made a concerted effort to stem the drug flow into Florida, so the traffickers needed another route. This time, by land."

"Through Mexico," Erica says.

"Give the lady a gold star. Mexico has a long history of smuggling contraband into the United States, including during Prohibition. So when the South Americans needed a new way to the US market, it made sense for them to look to Mexico. Mexican traffickers started to establish routes to bring the drugs, mostly cocaine, into Mexico from South America, and then utilize its already-established trade routes to move the drugs into the US. At the same time, Mexico's production of marijuana was growing at an astounding rate, and Mexican traffickers were shipping it, as well as heroin, into the United States.

"By the early 1980s, the Mexican drug trade was largely controlled by what became known or referred to as the Guadalajara Narcotics Cartel. Over time, there came to be three individuals who were generally viewed as the heads of the cartel—Rafael Caro Quintero, Ernesto Fonseca, and Miguel Angel Félix Gallardo. It would be a mistake to minimize the number of narcos that were involved in the drug trade around this time, or to overstate the organizational structure of the cartel. In many ways, even to this day, little is known about the ways in which they shared power and ran the cartel. It is unlikely that reality matches the popular cultural version of events. For example, we know that a Honduran national, Juan Ramon Matta Ballesteros, was heavily involved in the cocaine side of the business, and his influence likely has been understated for years. In Guadalajara, Javier Barba Hernandez was a fast-rising leader in the cartel who appears to have had significant influence in the latter days of the cartel's operations.

"The key, though, is that, however defined or comprised, the group known as the Guadalajara Cartel had an enormous impact on the drug trade in Mexico and the US, and its influences and affects are felt to this day. Through the political and business mastery of Félix Gallardo, Félix's successful transportation of Colombian cocaine into the United States, and Caro Quintero's ability to grow large volumes of high-quality marijuana in the Mexican deserts, the Guadalajara Cartel was, at the time, by far the largest player in the drug trade in Mexico. The cartel and its associates oversaw the explosive rise in the production and distribution of marijuana and cocaine into the United States.

"In order to grow and maintain its operations, the Guadalajara Cartel unquestionably had close relations with many of Mexico's police, military, and political leaders, though whom and to which extent remain subject to differing interpretations. Or better said, differing speculation.

"Though the general outlines of the development of the cartel have been documented, the specifics are fuzzy, at best. The same is true of the backstories of the cartel leaders, many of the facts having been lost to time and replaced with folklore, conjecture, and an insubstantial amount of pure fabrication.

"It is known that all three of the reputed cartel heads came from the Mexican state of Sinaloa, and each had some involvement with Pedro Aviles Perez, who ran the drug trade in Sinaloa during the 1960s and '70s, until his death in 1978. Each of them probably moved to Guadalajara in the late '70s, possibly as a result of the successful raids by the US and Mexican governments on a number of Sinaloan poppy fields used to produce and distribute heroin into the United States, as well as the death of Aviles Perez. Plus, Guadalajara was a vibrant city and has great weather year-round.

"Born in Sinaloa in 1952, Rafael Caro Quintero was the youngest of the three. Rafa, as he was called, apparently started growing marijuana as a teenager, a task for which he seemed to have an aptitude. It has been widely reported that he was successful enough to acquire several farms and a small fortune while still in his teens. Caro is generally given credit as being one of, if not the most influential developers of the marijuana trade in Mexico.

"Ernesto Fonseca, also known as Don Neto, was the oldest of the three narcos, and his experience in the drug trade dated back many years. Though generally regarded as one of the cartel heads, Fonseca's particular role in, or function for, the Cartel during the '80s has remained somewhat of a mystery. Often portrayed in popular culture as an old man with minimal education, Fonseca, in fact, was very savvy and astute, and usually well-dressed. One DEA agent who visited him in prison in the early days of his incarceration said Fonseca was wearing silk pajamas. It is widely assumed that Fonseca's contacts and his knowledge of supply and transportation routes fueled a large part of the rise of the cartel. Fonseca was related to Caro by marriage. But again, the real relationship between the three men, and others, has never been definitively presented.

"Miguel Angel Félix Gallardo was known in the drug world as 'El Padrino'—literally, 'The Godfather.' Born on a ranch in Sinaloa, Félix Gallardo graduated from high school and took at least some college classes before becoming an agent with the Mexican Federal Judicial Police. While working for the MFJP, Félix Gallardo served as a bodyguard for, and apparently became friends with, Leopoldo Sanchez Celis, the governor of the state of Sinaloa, and his family. It is widely believed that this relationship, and the political connections it brought, were the foundation for the political power wielded by Félix Gallardo not only to control the various drug factions in Mexico, but also to arrange protection from the Mexican police and military. The cartel was the primary driving force in the Mexican drug trade until it was broken up following the Camarena killing in 1985."

James says, "All of this has been very helpful. Could you touch upon the Camarena case briefly?"

"Of course. Enrique "Kiki" Camarena was a DEA special agent assigned to the Guadalajara Field Office. Whether or not it was all him, Camarena has been credited with having a great deal of success in finding marijuana fields operated by the Guadalajara Cartel, most of which were located far into the deserts, where it previously had been assumed that there would not be sufficient water supplies to grow marijuana in any material quantities.

"On February 7, 1985, Camarena was abducted from in front of the American consulate in Guadalajara. He then was taken to a house in a residential neighborhood not far away, and for the next thirty-six hours or so, was tortured and interrogated, eventually succumbing to the injuries inflicted on him during the interrogations.

"The United States government responded to the Camarena kidnapping and murder with the full force of its power, and the DEA launched the largest DEA homicide investigation ever undertaken, known as Operation Leyenda. Eventually, the US virtually closed the border with Mexico, putting overwhelming pressure on the Mexican government and economy.

"On March 5, 1985, Camarena's body, and that of a Mexican agricultural pilot who had worked with him, Captain Alfredo Zavala Avelar, were discovered outside the town of La Angostura, in the state of Michoacán, under circumstances properly characterized as dubious, at best. There is significant speculation and evidence that they were buried somewhere else originally, perhaps in La Primavera Forest outside of Guadalajara, and later moved. There were three autopsies that were somewhat inconsistent and inconclusive.

"Eventually, the three cartel leaders we've talked about were arrested and imprisoned, and there were three trials in the United States, resulting in several convictions.

"Camarena's murder led directly to the destruction of the Guadalajara Cartel. When Félix Gallardo first was jailed, there was a period of time where he seemed to be able to run things from his confinement. Soon, though, the terms of his confinement became far more austere, and he could no longer wield power or influence in the outside word. When this happened, the drug trade in Mexico splintered and became fractionalized and localized. A very direct and real, though unintended, consequence of the dismantling of the Guadalajara Cartel was the rise of the violent cartel system now running the drug trade in Mexico and Central America. It is no stretch to say that the demise of the Guadalajara Cartel directly led to the rise of the Sinaloa Cartel—El Chapo apparently started out working as a henchman for Gallardo—the Juarez Cartel, the Tijuana Cartel, the Gulf Cartel, and by extension, Los Zetas, and others, as well as the intercartel violence that has plagued Mexico for years and accounted for tens of thousands of lost lives."

"The law of unintended consequences," Erica says.

"What do you know about the DFS?" Mirada asks.

"It was the Mexican CIA," James replies, "and had a reputation for being heavily involved with the cartel. Other than that, not much."

"If you want to understand Mexico at the time of the Camarena case," Dr. Mirada says, "you'll need to understand the DFS. The Direccion Federal de Seguridad was a Mexican intelligence agency formed in 1947, as the Cold War was in its infancy, with the assistance of the CIA. The United States, at the time, was acting pursuant to the Truman Doctrine, which focused on the containment of Soviet and communist influence in the Western Hemisphere. Soviet Containment. Ostensibly, the DFS was charged with the duty of 'preserving the internal stability of Mexico against all forms of subversion and terrorist threats.'"

"In practice, the DFS operated much like the secret police of many dictatorships. From 1968 to the late 1970s, the DFS was accused of illegal detentions, torture, assassinations, and forced disappearances, and many, many complaints alleging state crimes were submitted to the United Nations. It is no wonder this period is commonly called the Mexican Dirty War.

"The DFS was widely known to have collaborated with the Guadalajara Cartel in the Cartel's drug trafficking activities, including providing protection for the cartel's marijuana fields. There are several stories of the DFS running interference to assure that DEA-precipitated raids by Mexican military units did not result in the capture of key traffickers.

"The agency was also suspected of having a hand in the CIA's assistance to the Nicaraguan Contras. Several infamous criminals in Mexico, including the founders of the Juarez and Sinaloa Cartels, started as DFS agents.

"If you investigate the Camarena case, the DFS is prominent. Its agents appeared to have been assigned to serve some of the cartel leaders. Most notably, Fonseca and Caro. There also are many allegations that one or more DFS agents were involved, directly or indirectly, in Camarena's kidnapping, interrogation, and/or murder.

"In 1985, during the presidency of Miguel de la Madrid, at the direction of the secretary of the interior, Manual Bartlett Diaz, the DFS was disbanded and merged into the Centro de Investigacion y Seguridad Nacional, or CISEN."

As Dr. Mirada paused, the door to the auditorium opens and college students start streaming in.

"My seven p.m. class is starting soon. Did that help?"

"Immensely," James says. "As always."

"Someday, you'll have to explain this to me." Mirada looks up to see more students entering the classroom.

"Someday, my friend." James smiles.

"Thank you for brightening my evening, Erica. Next time, we will have to talk more."

"I look forward to it." Erica gives Dr. Mirada a hug.

He and James embrace.

"I love you, man," James whispers.

"Stay safe, mi amigo," Mirada replies.

James and Erica leave the auditorium to find the dark of night descending upon the north San Diego campus. James drives back down Scholar's Drive, to Revelle College Drive, and stops at the traffic light at North Torrey Pines Road. He turns right, but rather than staying on the road, James makes another right onto Torrey Pines Road.

"You're the driver," Erica says, "and I don't want to give directions, but I think you missed the turn to the freeway."

"I know." James smiles. "I thought maybe a bite to eat and a drink before we head back would be nice."

"No objections, Counselor."

James continues his route down Torrey Pines Road, toward the Village of La Jolla and the coast. As he enters La Jolla, James turns onto Prospect Place, and then onto Prospect Street, driving in front of several restaurants with amazing coastal views. Crawling past Eddie V's and George's at the Cove, and just before the famous Duke's La Jolla, James pulls into the valet line at Antonio's Casa al Mare, a smaller but well-received restaurant specializing in Italian seafood.

As they enter the crowded restaurant, James waives to the bartender across the room. The hostess starts to speak to James, when she is interrupted by a man in a tuxedo.

"Sophia, I'll seat Mister Butler and his guest at table nine. How are you, James?" The man extends his hand.

"I'm well, Tony." James embraces him. "Tony, this is Erica Walsh. Erica, this beautiful place is Tony's. The best scenery and food in the county."

Tony shakes Erica's hand and leads her and James to a table on the railing overlooking the ocean.

As they are seated, Erica smiles at James.

"You, Mister Butler, are a man of many secrets."

CHAPTER THIRTEEN

THURSDAY MORNING ARRIVES, and Erica and James take an early morning flight to Guadalajara from LAX, scheduled to land in plenty of time for them to make their scheduled visit to the Puente Grande Penitentiary. After taking their first-class seats, they lean close and whisper.

"Do you have a plan yet?" Erica says.

"I'm still not sure. I have ideas, but it would be a stretch at this point to call it a plan."

Erica shoots him a look of incredulity and disgust.

"I really never expected this to happen," James says. "Hell, a week ago, I'd never even considered the possibility. We have fifteen minutes to get him to talk to us, and to ask him something useful. I figure we will only be able to ask, what, five or six good questions. So the objective for us is to determine what we most want to know, and what we think he is most likely to answer, and answer truthfully...to two Americans he has never met before, after being mostly silent in jail for three decades..." James goes into deep thought.

"I love your use of the word *us* when it is something difficult!" Erica says. "I was thinking about this earlier and wanted to ask. Presumably, he has lots of dirt on a number of important people. Why hasn't he used that to help his situation, or even just out of spite? In that one television interview, he didn't come close to pointing a finger at anyone else, other than saying, those guilty are in prison."

"La Familia," James replies. "That's the only thing I can think of. As bad as the government has been to the leaders, at least in their minds, they have taken a somewhat hands-off approach to their families. Fonseca is under house arrest in a mansion. Félix's family lives well in Guadalajara. Rafa has two families that, at a minimum, are not in jail. Hell, one of his sons represented Mexico in the Olympics, as an equestrian athlete, of all things."

"Makes sense." Erica nods. "Family first."

"By the way," James says, "Javi helped me on a civil forfeiture case years ago, and we found out we had a lot in common. We became good friends, and have done a few favors for each other over the years. Later, he helped me out on a big drug case before I joined the firm. Nothing too crazy, but we got ourselves into a bit of a predicament, and we bonded. I trust him like a brother."

"I didn't think it was anything too nefarious," Erica says. "Plus, you didn't owe me an explanation."

"You're about to walk into a Mexican prison and talk to one of the most notorious drug dealers in history, all because I have nightmares. Secrets, even benign, seem unnecessary."

Erica smiles and looks out the window. James's description of what they were about to do scares her for the first time since she started helping him. But she knows she has to quell the fear and not show it.

In the seat next to her, James also realizes the depth of danger they both were in. *What am I doing? Why am I risking Erica's life? Is this really worth it?"*

To distract him from his fears, James reaches into his pack to pull out some materials he had compiled.

Following the Camarena murder, Caro Quintero, Fonseca, and several other of the primary members of the Guadalajara Cartel were arrested and jailed, on both sides of the border. Félix Gallardo, however, stayed out of prison for years. But his fortunes turned, and he apparently was betrayed by the politicians who had protected him. Mexican officials finally arrested Félix on April 8, 1989, more than four years after Camarena's murder.

Upon his arrest, Félix faced criminal charges both in Mexico and in the United States, in connection with the Camarena kidnapping and murder, as well as many other crimes befitting the head of a major narcotics organization.

Mexico refused to extradite Félix to the United States. Instead, he was tried and convicted in Mexico, and received a thirty-seven-year sentence. Initially, Félix was jailed in a minimum-security prison with many amenities, from which it is believed he was able to continue his involvement in the drug trade in Mexico, even if he was no longer the sole power broker in the country.

In 1993, though, the Mexican government, as part of a renewed "get tough on the cartels" effort, changed the terms of Félix's confinement. Félix was transferred to a maximum-security federal prison, Altiplano, located in Almoloya de Juarez, in the state of Mexico, where he faced much worse conditions than he previously had experienced.

After years of complaining about his failing health and the allegedly deplorable conditions of his incarceration, in December 2014, he was transferred to a medium-security prison in Guadalajara. In February 2019, his request to complete the remainder of his sentence at his home was denied by a Mexican court, though the same release had been granted previously to Ernesto Fonseca. Now, the infamous Félix Gallardo, El Padrino himself, is almost blind and deaf.

The three-hour flight from Los Angeles passes quickly, and James and Erica soon see the suburbs of Guadalajara below. The landing into the Miguel Hidalgo y Costilla Guadalajara International Airport is smooth, and both James and Erica silently hope it is an omen for the trip.

Deplaning with only backpack-styled briefcases, the two

breeze through customs and proceed down the concourse, following the signs to the taxi line. Shortly before reaching the doorway to the cabs, Erica spots and points to a man in a navy-blue suit, carrying a sign with James's name on it.

Before either James or Erica can speak, the man, shouts out in English, "Mister Butler, your car is waiting for you."

James approaches the man, strategically keeping himself between the man and Erica.

"How do you know me?"

"Relax, sir. I work at the American consulate. My name is Jesús, and I have been instructed to drive you to the prison."

"Okay," James replies. "Can I see some identification, just to be safe?"

"No problem." From inside his jacket pocket, Jesús produces a consulate identification card with a picture matching his appearance. "Don't worry. Everything will be just fine."

"Okay, and this is—"

"Miss Walsh, a pleasure to meet you." Jesús displays a warm smile. "Please, let me take your bags."

He grabs Erica's bag off her shoulder, then reaches for James's bag, but he politely refuses.

"The car is this way." Jesús leads the way out the glass doors, across a street and into the bottom level of the parking garage, and toward a late-model black Suburban.

"Inconspicuous," James mutters.

Once in the car, Jesús slowly drives out of the airport.

"The airport is about fifteen miles from downtown Guadalajara," he says, "but only ten miles from the prison. We should be there in about twenty minutes."

James and Erica sit silently, taking in their first on-the-ground view of the Guadalajara metropolis. With more than 5.2 million people in the metropolitan area, the city covers 151 square kilometers, making it the second most population dense city in Mexico. The drive to the prison is through an urban area. Store fronts and shops are intermixed with graffiti-filled walls and vacant lots.

Erica leans over to James. "This is not what I was expecting."

"Nor I. Definitely more urban."

Soon, Jesús turns onto a long road leading to the prison. The car approaches a checkpoint and is waived through, and the same happens at the second and third checkpoints.

"That's just a bit disconcerting," James says to no one in particular.

Soon, the Suburban approaches the penitentiary—a huge structure of metal, wire, and concrete—and pulls to a stop in front of the entrance to the commissary and cafeteria.

Jesús points as he gives directions. "If you go straight, past that vending machine, you will go to the commissary. Go to the left, just past that entryway, and there should be a guard to direct you."

"Should?" Erica whispers as she reaches for James's hand. "Are you sure you can't accompany us."

"No, señorita. I have my instructions, and you have yours, right?"

"Yes, we do." James steps out, holding the door for Erica, who slides across the seat to use James's door to get out.

Jesús tuns to look directly at James. "I'll be back here in about thirty minutes. I'm supposed to tell you that once you step inside the prison, there is no one in there or out here to help you. Understand?"

"Got it," James says. "We are on our own." *For better or worse.*

CHAPTER FOURTEEN

JAMES AND ERICA STEP AWAY from the protection of the Suburban and walk toward the front gate with trepidation. The anxiety building in each grows heavier as they watch Jesús drive away, down the driveway toward the main road.

You've done some stupid things before, James, but nothing like this.

Upon reaching the gate, the guard stationed in the booth just inside looks at James and Erica with an obvious air of disdain.

"What are your names?

Erica responds in perfect Spanish, developed over many years of high school and college Spanish, a summer in Barcelona, and of course, numerous trips to Mexico.

"We are James Butler and Erica Walsh. We have an appointment with Comandante Perez."

The guard frowns but pulls a clipboard from a hook on the wall, flipping through some papers with annoyance, and nods approval. The front gate opens, and Erica and James step inside, and are noticeably startled when the gate crashes closed behind them. The guard motions to the building at the end of a long wire-fence-lined corridor.

"The administration building is straight ahead. Someone there will be waiting to direct you to Comandante Perez."

Erica and James start the walk, and Erica starts to translate for James, but he interrupts.

"My gringo Spanish could handle that one. But probably not much more."

Upon reaching the administration building, the pair is buzzed inside. A guard at the front desk awaits. James speaks before Erica is able.

"Comandante Perez, por favor." He grins and gives a wink to Erica.

Almost immediately, the two are greeted by Comandante Perez. Short and stout, meticulously groomed, in a well-pressed uniform adorned by a chest of ribbons and polished boots, Perez presents an imposing figure. As he walks from behind the desk, Perez speaks in Spanish directly to James.

"Mister Butler, welcome to Puente Grande Penitentiary. You speak Spanish?"

Erica does not wait for James to respond. "He speaks very little Spanish, Comandante. But I am fluent."

Perez smiles at Erica and continues in Spanish. "Very well, Miss Walsh. And may I say, you are much more delightful to talk to, anyway?"

"What did he say?" James whispers.

"He likes me more than he likes you."

"Wise man."

The guard behind the desk stands and asks James and Erica for their bags.

"But my notes and materials are in here," James blurts out in English.

Perez barks in English, "You can bring nothing in with you, and take nothing when you leave. Fifteen minutes. No more. Those are the rules, or you can leave."

"No, that will be fine." James hands his bag to the guard and empties his pockets into a tray on the counter as Erica follows suit.

"We'll get these back, right?" Erica reluctantly hands her Chanel bag to the guard. *This bag costs more than she probably makes in six months.*

"Trust me, Miss Walsh. Everything will be very secure. Follow me."

Perez leads them to another door located below a windowed security control room on the second floor. He looks up and nods to a man sitting behind smoked glass, and the door opens, accompanied by a startling horn sound. Perez points to the end of a hallway about thirty feet away. "Go there," he says in Spanish, to Erica. "Once inside, the guard will take you to a room with Señor Félix waiting."

As they enter the hallway, the large metal door slams behind them. Their footsteps echo off the pale white walls as they walk with trepidation to the other end.

Once they approach the interior doorway, James and Erica's walk slows to a near crawl before they finally stop just in front of the massive metal door.

"They've got us trapped," James jokes.

Erica flashes a nervous smile but does not respond.

Finally, a buzzer sounds, the large metal door opens, and they walk through to find a guard waiting for them.

"Come with me." The guard hurries down a corridor to the right.

James and Erica follow, hearing the door slam shut behind them, until they reach a row of several small rooms, each with a window in the door. The guard leads them to the room on the far left with the door open. As they get close, James can see a man sitting at a table in the room.

"Is that him?" James says.

"Sí. That's Señor Félix."

Oh my god. He looks dead.

CHAPTER FIFTEEN

JAMES AND ERICA WALK IN and stand in front of the table. Félix Gallardo sits across from them. In the pictures from his trafficking days, Félix was lean, almost skinny, but someone with an imposing presence. The man in front of them now is old and frail, dressed in prison clothes—gray sweatpants and a white t-shirt covered by a blue knit vest. Félix clearly has a hearing aid in his right ear, and his right eye is droopy.

He looks at the Americans in front of him and motions for them to sit in the two chairs across the table from him. A plastic jug of water and three paper cups sit on the table's edge.

In Spanish, and a soft voice, Félix says, "Who are you?"

Erica responds in Félix's language. "My name is Erica Walsh, and this is Licenciado James Butler. We are from Los Angeles. America."

"Why are you here, disturbing my day?"

"We would like to ask you a few questions."

"Why would I care what you want, or about any of your questions?"

Erica looks at James. "He wants to know why he should answer our questions."

James talks directly to Félix while Erica translates.

"Maybe we can help you?"

"I've been in prison for more than thirty years. I've endured the harshest conditions. My eyesight is virtually gone. I'm sick and tired. The friends I had are either dead or have abandoned me. You tell me, how could you possibly help me?"

"What is the one thing you would like most in this world?" James says, and then answers his own question before Gallardo can respond. "To serve the rest of your sentence on house arrest. With your family."

"Sí, my lawyers have asked for that many times. We have another petition with the court. You aren't from here. You don't know anything. You have no influence on where I spend the last years of my life."

"Would you have ever thought there was a chance that the two of us, two Americans you've never met or even heard of, would be let into this prison and escorted to this room to talk to you? Of course not. But we had enough influence with someone to make that happen. Do you really want to bet that we have no influence on the terms or circumstances, including location of your confinement?"

Erica's translation is shorter and more direct, but conveys the forcefulness behind James's words.

Félix looks at both James and Erica, but he focuses most intently on James. Pensive. Doubtful. But intrigued.

James finally breaks the silence. "What have you got to lose? A few questions and answers. We can't record anything. We can't even take notes. It's just us. We are particularly interested in three things all around the time of, or regarding, the Camarena kidnapping: the activities of the CIA in connection with the drug trade in Mexico, your interactions with the DEA, and the decision to kidnap and interrogate Camarena. That's it. More importantly, this goes nowhere. We do not tell the police, the media, my mother. No one. It is information for us only. You have my word. Our oaths."

Félix deliberates in silence. James feels each second of their fifteen minutes slipping away, but he refuses to move or say anything more.

At least five minutes, which seem like fifty, pass before Félix speaks.

"So ask."

James promptly says, "As I'm sure you are aware, there are stories that your organization worked closely with the CIA, including the sale of drugs and weapons. Is that true?"

"I have heard these stories as well, for many years," Félix replies. "Did we know about the CIA's involvement with the DFS? Of course we did. I'm also told that the CIA used the airstrip on Caro's ranch."

"Did the CIA sell drugs for you?"

"Never."

"Did you ship weapons to the CIA or act as a middleman for weapons to be provided to the CIA?"

"Never."

"Did the CIA train people on that ranch?"

"I don't know. That was Rafa's ranch, not mine."

"Do you have any thoughts on how it was being used?"

Félix takes a long pause, wiping his brow. His focus wanes, and his eyes glaze slightly.

Finally, he says, "It was a small ranch. I assume they liked the airfield and it fit their purposes. Rafa might have flown planes out of there. I'd imagine, if they used it, too, we just let each other be. That was it. Mutual convenience."

Félix's answer sapped even more energy from his nearly limp body. Erica picks up the jug of water and pours a glass for him. After she slides it close to him, Félix drinks without acknowledgement.

"In your interview with Univision," James continues, "you said you did not know Caro or Fonseca."

"I said I did not know them, as in, I did not do business with them. We were not partners. Of course I had known them. I knew who they were."

"I'd like to ask you about some people, and ask if, around the time of the Camarena kidnapping, you knew, or had heard about, any of the following people? Again, not whether you've heard of them since then, but whether you did at the time?"

"Okay."

"Félix Rodríguez?"

"No."

"Max Gomez?"

"No."

"Lawrence Victor Harrison?"

"I think he was the American who helped set up our security and electronic surveillance systems."

"Did he work for the CIA."

"I have no idea, and I'd have no way of knowing that."

"Did he ever tell you he worked for the CIA?"

"I never spoke to the man. I remember his name as someone who worked security because he had such an American name, and he was a very tall gringo."

"Fair enough. A few more names, please. Jorge Godoy?"

"No."

"Rene Lopez?

"Not then, but later."

"Tim Speer?"

"No."

"Tomas Morlet?"

"He was a DFS comandante."

"Did he work for the CIA?"

"As I've told you, I wouldn't know."

"Did he work for you?"

"Never."

"James Kuykendall?"

Erica gives James a look of surprise and urgency.

"I believe that, at a time, I knew he was the leader of the DEA agents in Guadalajara."

"What was your relationship with the DEA around that time?"

"There was no 'relationship.'"

"Did the cartel payoff any of the DEA agents prior to the kidnapping?"

"You refer to a cartel. That's your word, not mine."

"Okay. Did you pay off any of the DEA agents?"

"No."

"Did Caro Quintero?"

"I don't know."

"If he had, would he have told you?"

"Maybe. It might have been he'd let me know, but he wouldn't have gone out of his way to tell me."

"When was the last time you spoke to Caro Quintero?"

"Rafa left the country in one of my planes, a few days after the agent died. We spoke before he left."

"Not since then."

"No."

"Who gave the order for Agent Camarena to be picked up?"

"Rafa, I think."

"You think?"

"I wasn't there, so I don't know."

"Did you order him to be picked up?"

"I did not."

"To your knowledge, did someone in the Mexican government give the order for Camarena to be abducted?"

"I have no knowledge of that."

"So as far as you know, the decision was all on Rafa?"

"Yes. That pendejo." Félix's voice grows increasingly agitated.

James's gringo Spanish was peppered with Mexican curse words, and he was quite familiar with the word "pendejo," which loosely translates to "asshole." Sensing Félix's irritation, James sees an opportunity. He looks at Erica, whose gaze meets his as she gives him a subtle nod of approval.

"Did you give your approval to Rafa to abduct Agent Camarena?"

Félix explodes into a fit of anger. "Of course not! Why would I do that? Why would I want the Americans looking more into my business? Let them keep looking for marijuana fields. I could not have cared less. Rafa was making more money than he expected to see in twenty lifetimes. What did I care if some of his fields were found?"

"Is that why Rafa was going to get out of the marijuana business and focus on cocaine?"

"Why do you say that?"

"It was clear from items found with him in Costa Rica. Was he going to be a competitor?"

"Not a competitor. We cooperated with one another."

"Are you sure? Did you know Rafa was working with the CIA to establish new locations for cocaine shipments to land in Mexico before being shipped to the US?"

"I told him I would kill him if he betrayed me. That illiterate son of a bitch would have been farming dirt in Sinaloa without me."

"Was Camarena taken to the house at 881 Lope de Vega after he was picked up?"

"That's what I was told, yes."

"That house was owned by Rafa?"

"I was told he lived there. I never went to the house. I'm an old man. I'm tired. I'm sick. Why do you keep asking me these questions?"

"Were you there when Camarena was being interrogated?"

Félix becomes consumed with rage as he musters the energy to respond as El Padrino.

"No. No No. Why would I go there? It wasn't safe. For any of us."

"Was the CIA present during the interrogation?"

"I just said I wasn't there."

"Did anyone ever tell you someone from the CIA was present and participated in the interrogation of Agent Camarena?"

"We didn't sit around with a bottle of tequila and discuss the events after the agent died. Once I got word that the agent was dead, I knew hell was going to reign down on us."

"Did you know the interrogations were being taped?"

"I found out about that, yes."

"Who requested or ordered that the interrogations be taped. Or, said differently, who were the tapes for?"

"You have to understand that, at the time, there were a number of interested parties. Some of them knew of each other. Others did not. My role, in part, was to keep all of those interests pacified."

"And the tapes?"

"As I came to understand it, the tapes were..."

The guard opens the door without warning, interrupting Félix in mid-sentence.

"Time is up."

James protests. "Can he just finish his sentence? We are almost done."

Looking at both the guard and Félix, he quickly realizes the futility of his request.

Félix stands slowly as the guard moves a wheelchair in front of him. Félix contorts himself into the chair and begins to roll out the door, where yet another guard waits.

"Gracias, Señor Félix," James says, as Félix wheels himself through the doorway.

Félix pauses for a moment, turns his head ever so slightly, but neither speaks nor looks back.

After Félix has exited the room, the guard who originally brought them to the room appears.

"You have to wait here."

He starts to shut the door, but James puts his hand out to catch it.

"What do you mean, wait? We have someone meeting us. We have a plane to catch."

Annoyed, the guard forcefully reiterates, "You *must* wait here," then shuts the door and leaves.

A quiet overtakes the room. Erica feels the hair on the back of her neck stand on end, while the pit in James's stomach grows exponentially.

"What do you think is going on?" she whispers.

"I have no idea. None."

"I'm assuming we are well-advised to not talk about anything important here," Erica says.

"Nothing more substantial than the weather, I'd think."

They both sit back in the chairs at the table, waiting.

"What do we do?" Erica says.

"The only thing we can do. Wait."

"Great."

After nearly thirty minutes, the room's door finally opens. A new guard enters the room with a friendly demeanor. James and Erica stand as he approaches.

"Señor Butler and Señorita Walsh, my apologies for the delay. My name is Sergeant Ramirez. I will take you to get your belongings, and then I'll show you out."

Ramirez speaks perfect English, and James and Erica find their nervous tension slowly abating.

Ramirez extends an arm toward the door. "This way, please."

James and Erica leave the room at Ramirez's direction, before Ramirez shuts and locks the door behind them. He takes the lead, walking the Americans down the long corridor to return to the front desk.

Ramirez speaks in Spanish to the guard at the administration desk, clearly a subordinate to Ramirez.

"Please give Mister Butler and Miss Walsh their belongings, and I'll escort them to the gate."

The guard responds affirmatively and walks to a cabinet just behind the desk. A key turns the lock on the top drawer, and the guard retrieves James and Erica's packs. Taking hold of their bags, they look to Ramirez, who starts to lead them toward the series of gates that lead to the front prison entrance. As the three walk, the voice of Comandante Perez, speaking English, stops them.

"Señor Butler. A word please." Perez stands rigidly on the other side of the room, expecting James to walk to him.

James darts his gaze at Erica and then at Ramirez, who has stopped and is standing at near attention. Ramirez gives

James a subtly nod, which he mentally notes to be both odd and reassuring.

James sets his bag at Erica's feet.

"Here goes nothing," he says to her, with a fake smile.

"Be careful," she replies, though she knows James has no control over the situation.

James inches to Perez, who extends his hand as James nears. "Be safe and well on your travels home."

James shakes Perez's hand and feels something slipped into his palm. Concealing it, James ends the handshake.

"Thank you," he says. "And thank you for your hospitality today."

James turns to walk back to Erica, when Perez says, "I might recommend you proceed directly to the airport."

James looks back at him. "That is our plan."

Perez nods. "I'm happy to hear that. Stick to the plan."

James reaches Erica, and together they follow Ramirez to the gate leading to the main entrance.

"You will exit through here, just as you came in earlier."

"We know the way from here," Erica replies in matching Spanish.

The door opens, and James and Erica walk through.

"Be safe," Ramirez says in English, as the door closes.

James and Erica navigate the labyrinth of doors to the main gate. As they approach, the guard calls for the gate to open without word or acknowledgement to either James or Erica. Walking through the main gate, they both spot Jesús in the Suburban.

"Thank God," whispers Erica.

CHAPTER SIXTEEN

"YOU HAVE NO IDEA how good it is to see you, Jesús," Erica breathlessly says.

"I was starting to get worried about you."

"That makes three of us," James replies.

"Before we head back to the airport, would you like to drive by the US Consulate?

"How did you know?" asks a surprised James.

"Don't worry, Mister Butler. I was briefed on your visit and your interest in more than just the prison."

Clearly distracted, James replies, "If we have the time before our flight, I would love to see them. Thanks."

Erica whisper to James, "What did Perez slip you?"

"You noticed?"

"Yes, but only because I was watching you closely. No one else would have seen."

"Good. He totally caught me off guard. Pun decidedly not intended."

James opens his palm to reveal a rolled-up piece of white paper that he carefully unfolds to reveal a handwritten note.

Lo siento no pude ser de mas ayuda.
420 South Grand Avenue
Los Angeles, CA

"What does it say?" James asks.

"It says, I'm sorry I could not be of more help."

"It's from Félix?"

"Seems that way. What's the address about?"

"I have no idea," James says. "But I have a pretty good idea what we'll be looking at when we get home."

"We? Do you have a mouse in your pocket or something? After the last hour that took ten of my best years off of my life?"

"If you want, of course," James replies.

"What do you think? I just like messing with you occasionally." Erica smiles, and the two relax back into their seats, allowing themselves to be tourists for a few moments as Jesús navigates the Guadalajara traffic.

"I'm going to take you on the scenic route to the consulate, which is a bit longer but not bad. Locals would not take this route."

The drive from the prison to the consulate takes about thirty minutes without traffic. But there is always traffic in Guadalajara. A few minutes from the prison, Jesús turns from Highway 131, onto the Guadalajara Zapotlanejo, a major artery into the heart of Guadalajara. Several minutes later, the highway turns into Calz. Lazro Cardenas and the beauty and history of Guadalajara become even more apparent. On the left, James and Erica notice the Parque de La Liberacion, a large, beautiful park at the edge of the city's historic district.

Soon, the black Suburban reaches the Arcos del Milenio, a unique art installation in Guadalajara's central district. At a height of fifty-two feet, the project is comprised of six huge yellow metal arches, each slightly larger than the previous, with a twisting and turning design intended to give the impression that each is growing from one another in a natural, organic way. The sculpture weighs more than fifteen hundred tons, and was the unfortunate backdrop to news of drug cartel violence when the bodies of twenty-six murder victims were once discovered under the arches.

At the arches, Jesús turns onto Ave Mariano Oero, and

they soon reach the roundabout at Glorieta de Los Niños Heroes, Jesús exits onto the second road off the roundabout, Ave Chapultepec Sur, to take them into the neighborhood of the consulate.

"Mister Butler, we are getting close to the consulate."

James and Erica sit up and look outside.

"Onto which street will we be turning?" he says.

"I was going to take us to Calle Manuel Lopez Cotilla, and then turn in front of the consulate on Progresso."

"Can you turn onto Libertad instead," James says, "and park near its intersection with Progresso?"

"Sure. That is no problem."

The Suburban slowly drives toward the Libertad intersection. This part of Guadalajara is an interesting blend between old world and modern Mexico. Long-standing authentic Mexican family restaurants occupy the same city block as a Starbucks and a ramen noodle house.

At Libertad, Jesús turns right and proceeds down the one block to the intersection at Progresso. James points to a parking spot on the right near the corner.

"There. Can you get that spot?"

"With ease." Jesús guides the Suburban into a spot just a few yards from the intersection.

As he puts the vehicle in park, James starts to open his door, inciting screams from both Jesús and Erica.

"Mister Butler, please."

"What do you think you are doing?" Erica yells, as she grabs his arm.

"Whoa, I just want to get out and get a perspective."

"Not a chance," Erica roars.

"Mister Butler, I cannot allow that. We have no security, no notice."

"Come on. You're both overreacting. Do you really think there is a hitman hanging out in front of the consulate, on the off chance I might show up?"

"We're being reasonable," Erica says. "You, on the other hand, have lost your mind."

James stops and looks at her. The worry on her face hits him hard. Damn, she is really scared. Maybe she's right. I can't put her in such an uncomfortable situation.

"Think about it, James. You just left a prison where you met with Miguel Angel Félix Gallardo, for Christ's sake. Isn't it possible we might have raised a few eyebrows, a few red flags? Maybe, just maybe, someone would like to know if he told you anything important? You are not going to go and stand on the street for just anyone to see."

"She's right, Mister Butler. Please try to see whatever you need from the car. We are safe in here, if you get my meaning."

"I'm not sure if he does, but I do, and I feel a lot better." Erica's heavy breathing nearly muffles her words.

Jesús looks ahead a block, in front of the Café Libertad, and spots three members of the Jalisco State Police eating lunch out of the back of their SUV.

"You two wait here. I'm going to go speak to the police up there."

"Sounds good, and thanks," James replies, as Jesús exits the car.

"I don't like this, James," Erica says.

"Now that I think about it, and not to further fuel your worry, but both Ramirez and Perez made it a point to tell us to be careful. In fact..."

"In fact, what?" asks an annoyed Erica.

"As we were leaving, Perez asked if we were going straight to the airport. He seemed relieved when I said we were."

"Why didn't we?"

"I got so caught up thinking about the note, and then opportunity to see the consulate was so exciting. I just really wasn't thinking about anything else."

Jesús opens the driver's door, looking back at James and Erica.

"The officers ahead have assured me you will be fine. I told them you were attorneys from the United States, working on a case for the consulate, and that you wanted to take a walk around and take some pictures. They just asked that you not take pictures directly of the consulate."

"Perfect," James says. "Thank you, Jesús."

He digs through his pack and retrieves two documents: a spreadsheet on legal paper, and a printout from Google maps of the area around the consulate."

"I'll wait here for you, but we should leave in about fifteen minutes."

"No problem," Erica replies, as she and James exit the Suburban.

Once they have stepped away from the vehicle, she turns her attention back to James.

"Now that we are here," she says, "and know we are safe, and you can look around, it must be so powerful for you. To be here."

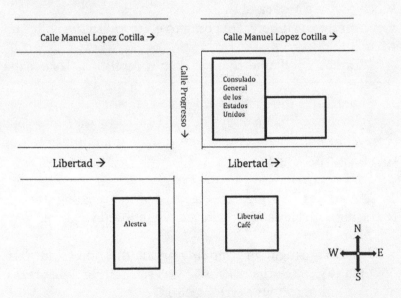

"It is. I'm in awe." Standing on the southwest corner of Libertad and Progresso, James looks around, slowly taking it all in. "There, across the street is the consulate. Of course, it didn't have the green fencing around it in 1985, and those planters are post-9/11 security structures. The main public entrance is up there on the Progresso-facing side of the Consulate."

He turns to look behind him, facing the white Alestra building and the white steps leading to the building entrance.

"In 1985, this was the Camelot, a bar/restaurant where the agents often drank after work, and they frequently met with informants here. There was a balcony and a patio, which would have been right about in front of us. In front of the patio, the agents would often park their vehicles, having received permission from the Camelot's owner. They apparently preferred this location to the main lot on Lopez Cotilla, another block up on Progresso. We are standing right about where Agent Camarena's truck was parked that fateful day."

"I don't even know what to say," Erica replies. "It's emotional for me. I can't imagine how you feel."

"It's an unusual feeling," James says. "Seeing this, being here, it's almost like a weight has been lifted. It's a cliché, but it's the only feeling I can articulate."

James and Erica stand in silence for a moment, taking in the scene.

"Do you know what is particularly interesting to me, as we stand at the site of the kidnapping?" James surveys the surroundings.

"What's that?" Erica replies.

"How little we really know. We know that Camarena left a little after two p.m., and was running late to meet his wife for lunch. We also know he was headed to his truck, and we know that Kuykendall had parked behind him, blocking Camarena in. And that's about it. We don't know precisely which street he crossed to get to his truck. We don't know if an employee pointed him out, and, if someone did, when it occurred. We don't know when he was approached. Where the car that took him came from is not known, and we have only limited information on where the car went."

James pauses and looks around again before showing the spreadsheet to Erica.

"I've been identifying and then breaking down the various versions of the abduction. And right now, I think there are at least six, including two from Lopez Romero and one from Berrellez's book. None of them match up, and they all differ in significant ways. I've started to put the analysis on this spreadsheet, but it's a work in progress."

"How are the two versions from Lopez different?" Erica says.

"His two versions vary materially. I'm also pretty sure that none of them can be completely correct. And I say that, even while accepting that Lopez Romero was likely one of the kidnappers."

"Okay, so let's look at this like a crime scene and investigate," Erica says. "Where did Camarena exit the Consulate?"

"You'd think that would be an easy question to answer, but surprisingly, it is not. Several statements seem to allege that he left through the door over there on Libertad, across from the café, which was not a café at the time."

"Where were the kidnappers?" Erica says.

James looks at his map and the notes he had made on it.

"They likely were in a car here on Libertad somewhere. Likely that way, down the street and on the other side." He points to the left, down Libertad, away from the consulate.

"Let's walk it, then." Erica starts to walk across Libertad.

James quickly follows. "You're awfully froggish for someone who was afraid to get out of the car a few minutes ago."

"Jesús relieved my concerns. And now I want to help." Once across the street, Erica stops. "I have an idea. Why don't I stand halfway down the block where the car might have been, and you can walk from the consulate exit, and we can see when you would have been visible?"

"I like how you think," James says. "I'll call you when I am in position."

With that, the two split off in separate directions. James walks up Progresso, across from the consulate, crossing the street at the main entrance/exit. Erica retreats down Libertad, to a spot a bit more than halfway to Ave Chapultepec Sur.

Erica answers James's call.

"Start walking," she says, "and I'll let you know when I can see you."

James elects to take what seems to be the more expeditious route for someone in a hurry, like Camarena was. Eschewing both straight lines and crosswalks, James cuts a diagonal path across Progresso, to the Libertad corner, before starting across Libertad, veering slightly to his right to take a direct angle to the parking spot that would have been in front of the Camelot.

As James reaches the edge of the sidewalk, just before stepping onto, Erica calls out.

"Stop. Stay right there."

James stops and waits for an approaching Erica.

"That was the first spot where I really could see you from back there," she says. "The trees might be a bit bigger now, and the streets a little busier, but I bet, even then, it's a pretty accurate location."

"If it is, then he would have been, what, ten seconds, at most, from his truck?" James says.

"Sounds about right."

"Interesting. What about the other exit? Should we try that one, too?"

"Definitely," Erica replies. "I'll call you when I'm there."

She returns to her location on Libertad, while James crosses Libertad to stand near the other entrance to the consulate. He stands up against the fence to mimic someone exiting the consulate.

"Heading your way now." James steps out from the fence, edging toward the Progresso/Libertad corner.

As he nears the corner, Erica tells him to stop.

"Make a note of where I am," he says. "I want to try something else out."

"Standing by," Erica replies.

James walks back to his initial location against the fence, then crosses directly across Libertad, toward the Café Libertad patio, across Progresso from the Camelot.

"Now I see you," Erica says.

"Perfect. Meet you back where we started."

James walks the one block and meets Erica in front of the Alestra building, getting more than a few curious looks from passersby and people entering and exiting the building.

"What did we just learn?" Erica says.

"Let's walk through it," James replies, "assuming the pickup car was across the street and down the block a bit. If Camarena left from the main exit on Progresso, he would not have been seen until he was pretty much crossing Libertad, at which point he would have been only a few seconds from his truck."

"He could have reached his truck," Erica says, "saw Kuykendall's truck behind him, and started to radio for him to move it, and then have been approached by the abductors."

"Entirely plausible," James replies. "But none of the alleged percipient witnesses mentions the truck. Scenario two has him leaving from the Libertad exit, walking down Libertad, and crossing to his truck at or just after Progresso— again, assuming he wasn't using crosswalks."

"In that situation," Erica says, "he likely would have been seen a little earlier, but not a lot."

"Right. So he either would have gotten to his truck, or he would have been approached by the abductors as he crossed Libertad, as some of the statements suggest."

"Okay, and the last scenario?" Erica says.

"If he crossed Libertad way before Progresso, he would likely have been seen long before he got to his truck, and could have been approached."

"Maybe I'm overthinking this," Erica says, "but Camarena was a trained agent, in a hostile environment, where tensions were high. Could a couple of guys really have just walked up to him and abducted him?"

James looks down Libertad Street, trying to imagine the scene in his head.

"That's bothered me, too," he replies. "Two possible explanations come to mind. First, if one of the abductors flashed DFS credentials soon enough, maybe Camarena let down his guard. Second, there is always the possibility he knew one of the abductors, and that let them get close."

"I suppose we should also remember that he likely was not armed," Erica says, "narrowing his options."

"Another good point," says James. "Which brings us back to the idea that there was a consulate employee in the car with the abductors, which I find implausible, at best."

"And if some of the abductors were on foot," Erica says, "and others in the car, they couldn't sit there all day. They'd need to know when Camarena would be leaving."

"Agreed," James says, while deep in thought. "It would be extremely hard to believe the kidnappers sat there for any significant time without being notice."

"They likely would have had to have arrived here closer to the time of the abduction," Erica says, "witness timelines be damned, and fell into the perfect scenario."

James flashes a confused grin. "I'm not sure I follow."

"Look at it this way," Erica says. "If the plan were to abduct Camarena, they picked a great day to do it. He walked out of the consulate alone, to go to lunch with his wife. He could have left with one of his fellow agents. Or an agent could have been close by, coincidentally. He could have been meeting a fellow agent for lunch, and that agent might have been more suspicious, and might not have waited as long to sound an alarm as Missus Camarena did. If there were abductors waiting on foot, how did they know where to wait? Did they know he was going to his truck? If they didn't know him, did they know which one was his truck? What if he had decided to walk the other direction to go to lunch? Were they going to wait there every day until he fortuitously walked in the right direction? Did they know he was going to meet his wife for lunch. And if so, how?"

"None of that makes sense," James says. "Unless..." He looks into the sky shaking his head. "Unless the kidnapping did not happen the way it's been told!"

CHAPTER SEVENTEEN

JESÚS, WHO HAS BEEN WAITING in the Suburban with the air conditioning on, rolls down his window.

"Mister Butler, if you are almost ready, I have another place to show you before we head to the airport."

"On our way now," James replies.

He and Erica return to the back of the Suburban.

"Thanks, Jesús. That was extremely helpful."

"That is good to hear, Mister Butler. If you would like, we have enough time to see the house at Lope de Vega and still get you to the airport in plenty of time for your flight."

"Oh man, I'd love that. I'd love to see it."

"We will be there in about seven minutes."

As Jesús drives toward Lope de Vega, James and Erica take mental notes of the path and the timing, picturing the drive with the abducted Camarena crammed into a small car, being carried from the consulate to the venue of his demise.

"Have you lived in Guadalajara long, Jesús?"

"All of my life, Mister Butler."

"How long is that, if you don't mind my asking?"

"I don't mind at all. I'll be thirty-one next month. I was born about four years after the Camarena murder."

"What is the public's knowledge of the case? Was it a big event?

"Everyone in Jalisco who was alive then remembers it. Some say it is like your Kennedy assassination."

"Do people know the facts of the case?"

"I don't think they do in the way you are talking about it."

"What do you mean by that? I find this fascinating," Erica says, losing track of the route to Lope de Vega.

"I don't think most people know much more than the basic facts, as they've been told to them. Caro got mad. Picked up Camarena and killed him. Fonseca went to jail, along with Caro after he was found in Costa Rica with that girl."

"What about Félix?" James says.

"Who?"

James and Erica share a confused glance before James responds.

"Miguel Angel Félix Gallardo."

"I've heard of him, but I don't know much."

"That's who we met in the penitentiary," James says.

"I wasn't given that information. I guess it was a need-to-know thing."

"Does the average person care about any of the nuances of the Camarena case?" James says.

"I'm not sure I know what you mean."

"Things like the interrogation tapes, or the alleged presence of high-ranking officials at the interrogation."

"I can only generalize," Jesús replies. "Whenever the case comes up, I almost never hear anything about the tapes or any specific officials. I think there is a wide-spread presumption that the cartel paid off politicians, police, and military figures, but I don't think there is much focus on who they were specifically. As I said, I think the relationship between those events and the increased drug violence are the thing people think about the most now. I suppose many of the older people in Jalisco view it as something of black eye on Guadalajara. The city is beautiful, with a long and rich history, and significant contributions in art and science. But when I talk to American tourists or Americans at the consulate, it seems beautiful Guadalajara is most known for being home to the Guadalajara Cartel, and for the killing of Camarena."

"What about Bartlett Diaz?" James says. "There were many stories that he was involved in planning meetings, and was even present when Camarena was interrogated."

"As I said, the idea that Mexican politicians, even someone as powerful as Bartlett Diaz, were involved with the traffickers is generally accepted. Some level of corruption is part of the Mexican culture."

"There are stories that Bartlett met with cartel leaders at the Las Americas Hotel."

Jesús laughs out loud. "That place was not in the best area of town, and was not even close to fancy. Bartlett Diaz would not have been caught dead there. It was not the sort of place his 'type' went to."

"What about the CIA?" James asks.

Jesús does not answer, but instead informs his passengers that, "Lope de Vega is coming up."

He drives up Calle El Sol and halts at a stop sign directly across from the house, before turning right onto Calle Lope de Vega and parking a few feet down the street. The house sits on the intersection of Lope de Vega and the continuation of Calle El Sol.

"The house is now a Montessori school for kids ages three to twelve, as I am sure you know. It is called Casa Yinú Montessori."

"There's something just wrong with that," Erica says.

"What does Casa Yinú mean?"

"Frankly, Mister Butler, I have no idea."

"You don't mind if we get out and walk around, do you Jesús?"

"No, sir. I'll be here waiting for you."

"We won't be long," James replies, as he and Erica climb out of the Suburban.

James walks across the street and stands on the sidewalk looking at the house. The present-day home has a large white-painted brick fence around it that might not have been there in 1985. Even though he is only able to see the top of the house, but from a variety of vantage points, James is taken aback looking at the wooden block with white 881 numbering near the official Calle Lope de Vega sign.

"I've seen pictures of this for years. It's beyond surreal to actually be here."

"My mind is officially blown today," replies Erica, who had been hanging back a bit behind James, but now moves closer to talk.

"I don't really know what to say," James mutters, his voice filled with emotion. "At the end of the day, it's just a building. Somehow, it should be more. A man lost his life here. He was tortured in the most brutal ways. And yet, here it stands."

Erica starts to speak, but stops as a gate opens and a young man in his early twenties emerges. Without saying anything to James, Erica takes a few steps to meet the man, and they engage in a brief conversation. Soon, the man walks off and Erica returns to James.

"I asked if we could see inside, but he said he would lose his job if he let anyone in. I even offered him money. Sorry, James."

"It's okay. I wouldn't want to cause him any trouble."

James and Erica walk around the two sides of the house before returning to the area near the gate and the 881 numbering.

"I'm trying to get my bearings," he says. "I think we actually need to go back over to Calle El Sol. Sorry."

"Don't apologize. I'm with you wherever you go."

James and Erica stand in front of a gate on Calle de Sol.

"The Atlantic," he says, "with as many as five people in it, makes its way from the consulate and probably enters through the gate here, as opposed to the one on the other side of the house."

"Okay, I can picture that," Erica replies.

"There are two buildings or portions to the house. There is the main house, which is the large one in front of us, with two stories. Then there is a smaller building to the rear of the main house, or just to our right, commonly referred to as the guest house. But I think it was really more of a servant's quarters. The two buildings are connected now, but they were a few feet apart 1985. It's sometimes been referred to as a guest house, but I think it the better name would be 'servant's quarters.' Whatever we call it, there was a small room, again, generally referred to as a guest room, with an adjoining bathroom, and then a maid's room. Forensic evidence and testimony make it pretty clear, I think, that Camarena was interrogated and tortured in the guest room."

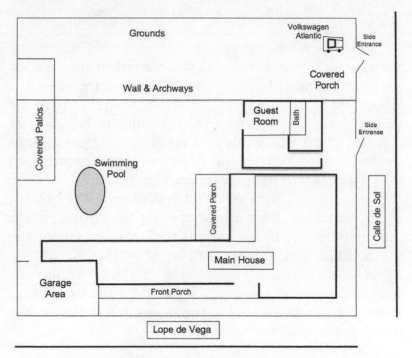

"I find that interesting," Erica says. "It's not connected to the main house?"

"No, I don't think it is or was. But it's not far."

Erica continues. "But someone wanting *to look in* on the interrogation would have to go from the main house to this little guest house, and then to this small bedroom?"

"I think that is right," James says. "Not really conducive to lots of oversight by all of the dignitaries supposedly at the house during some or all of the interrogation."

"Not even a little bit."

James walks closer to the gate and peaks through the crack to see a bit of the yard while continuing to talk.

"There was a swimming pool on the grounds. But if I remember correctly, the pool was mostly drained, and/or was a mess. I don't think the house was a model of good housekeeping."

"This is where most of the forensic evidence came from, right?" Erica asks.

"It is. There was some from Bravo Ranch, where the bodies were found, but this is where most of the forensic work was conducted. Keep in mind, too, that the place had been swept by DFS agents before anyone from the FBI or the DEA got in. This is also where the FBI found the hair samples that tied Matta Ballesteros and Verdugo, among others, to the house, and ultimately, in the eyes of the prosecution, to the Camarena interrogation and murder."

"Just curious," Erica says, "but if Caro owned the house, and if there had been any socializing there, how would the presence of hair be indicative of involvement in the Camarena abduction, as opposed to just another party?"

"A good question," James says. "I think the answer, according to the government, is that the hairs were found in the guest room, where Camarena was, rather than in the main house itself."

"Okay, I can follow that logic."

Jesús, who has walked to the corner of Lope de Vega and Calle El Sol, calls out, "Mister Butler, we should be heading to the airport soon."

"Sure. Just a few moments longer," James replies.

He pulls out pictures from the interior of the building and tries to picture the scene: Where did Camarena arrive? Who was there? Who interrogated him first? When did the interrogation turn irretrievably violent? When did Camarena know he was going to die?

James is overwhelmed as he tries to imagine what those moments must have been like for Camarena.

"What are you thinking?" Erica says.

"Something Camarena apparently said to Kuykendall after the congressional investigators had come to Mexico, and left without taking any action."

"What did he say?" Erica asks.

James clears his throat for composure. "He said, 'Does somebody have to die before anything is done? Is someone going to have to get killed?'"

CHAPTER EIGHTEEN

JAMES AND ERICA JOIN JESÚS in the Suburban, and Jesús quickly puts the Suburban into drive and pulls into traffic, leaving Lope de Vega behind. The three have traveled only a few blocks away from Lope de Vega when Erica detects a change in Jesús's demeanor.

"What's wrong, Jesús?"

Cool and calm, he replies, "We have company behind us."

Instinctively, James turns to see two black Mercedes sedans following them closely.

"Those two cars have been close to us since we left the consulate," Jesús says, his expression stoic.

"Are you sure they're following us?" James says, not realizing that Jesús had not taken the most direct route to Lope de Vega from the consulate.

"Let's find out." Jesús speeds up a little and makes an abrupt left turn across traffic, onto Calle El Sol, followed by a quick right into Tormenta.

The two cars continue behind the Suburban, maintaining a consistent trailing distance, erasing any doubt as to their intentions.

One block later, Jesús approaches intersection with Ave Mariano Otero in the first of two left turn lanes, taking advantage of the fact that both traffic directions on Mariano Otero can be used to get to the airport. As the lights turn, Jesús cuts across traffic to take a right turn to head west on Mariano Otero, eliciting a chorus of honking horns from the other drivers. One of the trailing cars gets stuck in the intersection traffic, while the other manages to follow onto Mariano Otero, but further back now.

Jesús reaches a roundabout and weaves through cars to efficiently take the second exit onto Calz. Lazaro Cardenas Pte. for a few blocks, before a U-turn places the Suburban on Ave Paseo de la Arboleda, putting further distance between them and the trailing car. A few moments later and they are on Highway 23, which merges with Highway 44, leading directly to the airport.

James, who has been watching the car behind them, looks back toward the front.

"Nice job, Jesús. Think you lost them?"

"Not a chance. And that was the easy part."

"Easy part?" Erica says.

"We have about twenty kilometers on this highway, and they will catch up. This car is designed for security, not speed."

"Should we get off and take another route?" James says.

"No. Our best bet is to take the most direct route and stay as public as possible. But I won't worry about speeding."

"Okay, we trust you," James says, offering more reassurance to himself and Erica than to Jesús.

Jesús hurls the Suburban through traffic, toward the airport. In a few kilometers, the white Mercedes reappears.

"I knew they would catch up."

James and Erica look back to see the Mercedes closing ground at a rapid pace. Soon, the Mercedes is directly behind, inching closer and closer.

"Should you hit your brakes?" Erica says.

"No!" James replies. "They haven't done anything to us. Maybe they just want us to know they are there."

"I bloody well know they are there!" says Erica.

Soon, the traffic sign indicates that the exit for the aeropuerto is only one kilometer away. Jesús takes the exit, and the Mercedes follows. At the roundabout, Jesús follows the route to the terminal, and upon exiting the roundabout, sees the Mercedes pull alongside the Suburban on the left.

"Remember, this car is safe," Jesús says, in a fleeting effort to be comforting.

James looks out the window and sees the rear passenger window on the Mercedes roll down. A passenger in the back seat sticks an AK-47 out the window.

"Get down!" James yells to Erica.

Both duck, but James is still able to look out the window to see the terminal approaching. The man in the Mercedes pulls the gun back inside, waives and smiles, before the Mercedes speeds off toward the airport exit.

"It's okay," Jesús says. "They are gone. You will be safe once inside the terminal. Besides, if they wanted you dead, I think you would be dead."

"That point was made clear," James says.

He and Erica each grab their bags.

"I know they're gone, but I'd prefer to run like hell into the terminal," he tells Erica.

"Right behind you," she says.

"Thanks for everything, Jesús. Be safe."

James opens his door and hurries to exit, with Erica sliding across the seat to follow closely. He slams the door shut, takes Erica's hand, and they run the fifty feet to the terminal doors, which automatically open, providing sanctuary.

James briefly looks back to see Jesús pulling away, before turning to Erica.

"So how was your trip to Guadalajara, Miss Walsh?"

CHAPTER NINETEEN

ONCE THROUGH SECURITY, James and Erica feel slightly more at ease. While walking to their gate in silence, James sees a bar not far ahead.

He looks at his watch. "A drink before we board?"

"That better have been rhetorical," a still shaken Erica replies.

The airport is quiet on this weekday afternoon, and they quickly find two seats at the bar. The bartender greets them, and James asks for a house margarita and a float of Patron Silver.

The bartender nods and looks at Erica. "Dos, por favor."

The drinks arrive, and each pour the float into their margarita. James holds his drink aloft and toasts to Erica.

"Here's to our first trip to Guadalajara. May it also be our last."

"I'll drink to that!"

The two each sip from their drinks as some of the anxiety slips from their bodies.

"Who do you think was behind that?" Erica says.

"I don't know." James shakes his head. "There are lots of possibilities. What I do know is that they were sending a clear message."

"I, for one, received a message loud and clear," Erica says. "I'm just not sure if the message is stop the investigation, don't talk to Félix, or get out of Mexico."

"Or all three," James says.

After a moment of silence to drink from the large margarita classes, he continues.

"Do you want to know what worries me, though?"

"Sure, why not," Erica says.

"Not many people knew we were coming to Mexico in the first place. Then, on the way out, Perez asked if we were going straight to the airport, and I said we were. I had no idea we were going to the consulate until Jesús suggested it when we were in the car, and at that point, I hadn't even entertained a thought about going to Lope de Vega."

"So how did they know to find us at the consulate?" Erica says.

"That is the question. Or did they follow us from the prison without Jesús knowing?" James pauses and drinks more of his margarita. "Is it possible that Jesús tipped them off?

"Not a chance," Erica replies. "I was watching him when he first realized we were being tailed. He was surprised and concerned. I am convinced of that."

"Then, yet again," James says, "we know nothing that helps."

"Don't be such a glass half-empty guy. Almost being killed aside, it was a productive trip. We talked to Félix Gallardo, and he gave you an address."

"Do we know that?"

"Which part?" Erica replies.

"Do we know he gave us an address? I got it from Perez. We really don't know if it came from Félix or Perez, or someone else, for that matter."

"No disagreement," Erica says. "But that only means we know even less than I thought we did thirty seconds ago. Thanks a lot."

James flags the bartender. "Dos tequilas y el cheque, por favor."

"Look at you go with your gringo Spanish," Erica says.

The bartender pours the shots and leaves the check in

front of James. Erica raises her glass and James touches shot glasses before they each down the tequila.

Erica grimaces as the she swallows the silver liquid. "Smooth."

James looks at the bill in front of him and lays down cash to cover the drinks and a hefty tip.

"Let's get on the plane," he says. "We can talk about this more on the flight home."

The two walk the short distance to the gate, and arrive right as the boarding has begun. After walking over the blue lane reserved for first class passengers, they display the boarding passes on their phones, scan their passports, and walk down the jetway to the plane. They take their places in seats 3A and 3B, and buckle in.

"Do you want to talk more about today?" Erica asks.

"I do. But maybe we can just rest our eyes for a few minutes first?"

"I like that idea better," Erica says.

James closes his eyes and falls into semi-consciousness almost immediately. Erica looks at him and smiles. After resting her head on his shoulder, she quickly joins him in sleep.

James and Erica rest peacefully until awakened by a flight attendant to complete the required customs forms. Shortly after the forms are presented, the plane touches down safely at LAX and begins the long taxi trip to the gate.

James looks to Erica as she pulls her carry-on bag from the seat in front of her.

"I don't know about you," he says, "but I'm even happier to be home than usual."

"I completely agree. What's your plan now? We've gained two hours coming back, so it's, what, 6:30?"

"Before I do anything," James says, "I want to check out this address. We can run by the office to see what we can figure out. Or we can just swing by my place. Or I can take you home. Depending on how tired you are."

"I'm freakin' exhausted," Erica says. "But there is no chance I'm going to sleep until we get some answers. Let's just go to your place. I'm not really in the mood to see the office." She pauses for a moment. "What do you think the meaning of address is?"

"Honestly, I have no idea. Maybe we're supposed to find something, or we're being led to something."

"I'll follow your lead, James. Please just don't lead us into a trap!"

CHAPTER TWENTY

UPON ENTERING JAMES'S CONDO, James and Erica leave their packs by the door.

"Come on." James heads up the stairs to his office, with Erica following close.

He sits down at his computer as Erica looks around.

"Interesting," she says.

"It's not that interesting."

"No, I just realized, I've been here dozens of times, and yet this is the first time I've been in your office."

"Is it everything you expected?"

"And more." Erica is drawn across the room to the corkboard with the pictures, focusing on the picture with the two tuxedo-clad men, and the woman.

"Me, you, and my dad at the bar association dinner, three—or was it four—years ago. I'm surprised you have the photo, and so prominently displayed."

"It's important to me," James says. "That was the day I knew I finally had a family. I look at that picture often, and think about what it signifies."

Erica walks over to sit in an oversized guest chair near James's desk.

"You never talk about your family," she says.

James works on his computer as he talks, not looking at Erica.

"There isn't much to talk about," he replies. "My birth

certificate says I was born in Indianapolis, on September 21, 1984, to Mary Alice Johnson. Though, I never met her. There is no father's name on the birth certificate. I was raised in foster homes in Terre Haute. I left the foster home and moved to Bloomington the day I turned sixteen. Once there, I was able to become legally emancipated, and I changed my name to James Butler, no middle name, which seriously confounded college registration computers. James Butler was the ninth Earl of Ormand in mid-1500s England, who nearly married Anne Boleyn to resolve a family dispute. He died from a poisoning, which remains an unsolved mystery to this day. Yes, I was a history nerd back then, too. Anyhow, I finished high school, and then, as you know, went to IU for both undergrad and law school, before moving to LA to go to work at Gibson Dunn in Century City. There were some nice people in the foster families, but no one I keep in touch with after all these years."

Erica pauses, unsure what to say, until she is saved by James.

"Come look at this," he says. "As we knew, it's downtown, and it's close to the federal courthouse. I wonder if there is a way to see who is in the building..."

"Shut up and get out of the way." Erica takes James's seat in front of the computer, and he retreats to a position looking over her shoulder as she works. "Using Google Earth, street view, we might be able to get a view of the front of the building and see if there are any names."

Both are transfixed on the computer as the image focuses into view, revealing it to be the home of at least one large Los Angeles law firm.

"I can see the name of the management company," Erica says. "Let's look at their website. Sometimes they have a list of tenants. And presto!"

As she slowly scrolls through the list of tenants, in alphabetical order, she and James look for any name that appears interesting, significant, or out of place.

Suddenly, James startles to attention, almost yelling to Erica.

"Wait! Go back." He watches carefully as the cursor moves back up the alphabet. "Much, much higher. More. Around G or F, I think. There!" He points to the screen. "Suite twenty-seven hundred. Eucrite Import and Export Partners."

"So?" Erica intones.

"In Speer's office, he has a meteorite on a stand. It's a eucrite. He told me about it."

"A coincidence?" Erica says.

"Let me ask you this, Miss Walsh. Have you ever heard of a eucrite before?"

"I can't say I have."

"I rarely believe in coincidences, as it is," James says. "But in this case, never. Can we try to see who else is on the floor?"

Erica slowly scrolls up and down the list of tenants.

"I don't see any other tenants listed for that floor," she says. "Which, of course, only means we can't find any, not that there aren't other tenants on the floor. But we'd know for sure if we went and looked tomorrow."

"Hold up just a second," James says. "We have to be careful. If there is a connection to Tim Speer, he's seen me. I can't just go waltzing onto the floor, looking around."

"I can go," Erica says.

"Not by yourself, you can't. Let's get Bobby in on this."

James pulls his cell phone from his front pocket and makes a call. Puts it on speaker when it starts to ring.

"This is Bobby."

"Hey, Bobby, it's James."

"Mister Butler. What is up?"

"Erica and I need a little more help on something that may be connected to our recent Palos Verdes trip."

"Interesting."

"We have some information about a company with an office in downtown LA. Erica and I would like to go and gather some information, but for reasons I can explain later, I can't show my face on the floor, and I don't want Erica to go alone. Is there any chance you could meet us there and help us figure out how to get some intelligence on the company and the people that work there?"

"Of course. When?"

"I know it's last minute, and you can say no, but could you do it tomorrow morning, maybe around ten?"

"For you, I can juggle."

"Great. I'll text you the address. We can meet up somewhere close and make a plan. Thanks, man. You know I always appreciate it."

"And I appreciate the work. I'll see you in the morning, my friend."

James hangs up the phone. "We are set."

"And now I am back to being very tired!" Erica says. "I requested an Uber."

"I can take you."

"No, you need to sleep, too. Just come get me in the morning. Eight-thirty?"

"I'll be there. Text me when you get home."

"You'll be crashed out."

"I said, text me. I didn't say I'd read it."

Erica and James walk down to the main floor, where Erica retrieves her bag.

James opens the door. "What a day."

"So true." Erica walks out the door, toward the elevator.

As she waits for the elevator, James calls out to her, "You know, I couldn't do all of this without you."

"Sure, you could. But I love that you don't have to."

James watches her leave, before grabbing a water from the refrigerator. He lumbers up the stairs and sits on the end of his bed.

Nothing today went as planned, but what a day. I have to be careful, though. I have to make sure Erica is careful, too. There is still much going on that I don't understand.

James undresses and crawls into bed, placing his phone on the pillow next to him. He turns out the lights and sinks into the pillow, laying on his back, staring at the ceiling. A few minutes pass before he is stirred by the ringing notification of a text message on his phone.

As expected, it is from Erica: "Made it home. Not dead. Eucrite? WTF? See you in the morning."

James smiles, turns off the phone, sets it on the nightstand, and rolls over into a sound slumber.

CHAPTER TWENTY-ONE

JAMES PULLS UP TO ERICA'S COTTAGE to find her waiting in the wicker chair on her front stoop. She walks quickly and smoothly in her Valentino heels to meet James. As Erica opens the car door, she spies a Starbuck's cup in the cup holder of the center console. Knowing James doesn't drink coffee, she smiles at him.

"You are the sweetest."

"Good morning. Sleep well?"

"Like a rock." She shuts the car door.

"Me, too. Bobby is going to get there before us and check things out. He said he'd text where to meet."

Traffic north toward LA moves particularly well today, and using the HOV lane, James and Erica make good time. The two are silent as James navigates the spaghetti network of freeways covering LA and Orange Counties. Shortly after the 405 Freeway seamlessly blends into the 110, soon to turn into the 5, the silence is disrupted by a call to James's phone, which is picked up by the Bluetooth in his car.

James looks at the display. "It's Javi," he says to Erica, before answering through the car's speaker phone. "Good morning, Professor. Erica and I are in the car."

"Was it you?" Dr. Mirada says.

"Well, good morning to you, too."

"Forgive my bad manners. Good morning, James. And especially, a lovely good morning to Erica. Now, was it you?"

"Was what me?" James says.

"The gringo that met with Félix in prison."

"You heard about that?"

"Did you really think it would go unnoticed?"

"If I did, that idea was dispelled pretty quickly."

"And you drug Erica along with you?"

"No, I went willingly," Erica says.

"If I'd had any idea what you two were planning when we talked, I likely would have altered my discussion."

"How's that?" James says. "I thought you gave us a pretty detailed analysis."

"I gave you the standard interpretation. The most widely accepted historical analysis."

"I'm sensing it's a narrative you don't fully buy into," Erica says.

"That's right, Erica. I have a somewhat different hypothesis. But frankly, there hasn't been much of an incentive to publicize it, or to even investigate further."

"You have our attention," James says.

"Let's start with the most basic premise. You asked me to discuss the Guadalajara Cartel and the lead-up to Agent Camarena's murder, right?"

"That is correct," James says.

"Well, I think the question itself starts with a false premise. That is, there was no real cartel, in Guadalajara or anywhere else in Mexico, at the time of Camarena's unfortunate murder. Remember, prior to Félix Gallardo, Mexico operated on the plaza system, whereby the geographic territories were divided up, and largely, they each left one another alone to operate. That system worked well for marijuana and heroin trafficking, and for what essentially were smaller, more localized, operations. The genius of Félix was that he realized the plaza system was not good for the multi-continent shipping of other drugs, most notably vast quantities of cocaine going from Columbia into the United States, through Mexico. Félix was able to convince the plaza bosses to play nice with one another so shipments could be moved, stored, and transported without running afoul of the various plazas. Félix's operation also required a level of organization theretofore unseen, because it had never been necessary. But the idea that there was a *cartel* with Félix, Fonseca, and Caro at the head is really off base. The term was used later, as investigators and prosecutors tried to explain the drug trade in Mexico. Pre-kidnapping, the DEA never used the term 'Guadalajara Cartel.'"

James gives Erica a puzzled, but curious, look.

"Okay," he says. "If there was no cartel, how did Caro, Fonseca, and Félix work together?"

"You are missing my point, James. The answer is, they didn't, really. Contrary to media representations, Caro was far from the only marijuana cultivator in Mexico. And in some material respects, he was really just starting to rise to prominence in 1984, with his operations in Zacatecas, and of course, Búfalo. The DEA has reports with informants from the early spring of 1984, where the informants suggest that going into that growing season, Caro would become the largest grower. There is a March 1984 DEA-6, where an informant explains that there are eighteen to twenty loosely related groups with fields in Zacatecas. That report specifically mentions the fields of Fonseca and an Abelardo Fernandez, and even notes that Samuel Medina from Culiacan is expected to have some two thousand hectares alone. You know who is not mentioned in that DEA-6?"

"Caro, I assume," Erica replies.

"Another gold star for the beautiful lady. And there is more. There is no evidence that Caro had anything to do with the cocaine side of the business, which likely was run by Félix and Matta Ballesteros. And there is little to no evidence of any significant interaction between Caro and Félix, other than Félix perhaps being a financier from some of the larger farms established by Caro."

James speaks quickly to interject. "That fits with some of what Félix said to us."

"What was he like?"

"He is old and frail, as you know. But he got feisty when we mentioned Caro and Camarena."

"That makes sense. Did you know that there is almost no mention of Félix being involved in the kidnapping, until well after-the-fact? When Sergio Espino Verdin, a comandante with the MFJP who worked extensively with Fonseca and Caro, was arrested and interrogated in Mexico City, he initially told the investigators, including DEA agents, that Félix was not at Lope de Vega. It was only after further *interrogation* by Mexican officials, without DEA agents present, that Espino *remembered* that Félix was there. Otherwise, Félix really isn't implicated again until the early 1990s, by Mexican witnesses in the criminal trials."

James says, "Okay, assuming we accept your analysis—"

"Which we do," Erica interjects.

"...then how did the narrative get its start."

"I'm not sure," Dr. Mirada replies. "But I have two theories, which are not mutually exclusive. First, it was easier for investigators, journalists, and prosecutors to get their arms around the Camarena events by creating a cartel-type structure. Second, if the focus quickly was on Caro, does anyone really want to say a DEA agent's life was lost because of the actions of one mid-level marijuana grower? Or were people immediately looking for more? A cartel. Mexican officials. Later, the CIA. Sometimes the myths outrun the facts. As an example, there are many who challenge the concept that El Chapo was the head of the Sinaloa Cartel, and insist he was, at best, number two or three, under El Mayo. But El Chapo escaped from prisons. He gave an interview to a Hollywood celebrity. It was a better story."

"Damn, Javi," James says. "That makes a lot of sense. But what about the times when it appears Caro, Fonseca, and Félix got together?"

"Of course they did. Fonseca and Caro were related by marriage. They all came from the same areas of Sonora.

They all were *outsiders* in Guadalajara. If there were parties and celebrations, it's perfectly logical that they would be together."

"I understand that idea," Erica says. "One of my old sorority sisters is Greek. If they have any event like a wedding or a baptism, every Greek in a five-hundred-mile radius attends."

"Precisely," Dr. Mirada says. "Taking it one step further, if they are at social events together, what are they going to talk about?"

James replies, "Drugs and trafficking. Everyone talks about what they know and have in common, whether they are cops, or lawyers, or doctors."

"Which does not mean they were the heads of a cartel," Erica says.

"That's right, Erica, it doesn't. I am terribly sorry we didn't get into this the other night, and I hope it didn't negatively impact your meeting with Félix."

"We had fifteen minutes to talk to a frail old man with a faded memory," James says, "who had no real reason to trust or cooperate with us. Nothing you didn't say changed any of that, but this information does make sense of a few things he said and how he reacted. We appreciate it."

"Of course. If I hear anything that I think might be helpful, I'll pass it along. Drinks are on me next time, as long as Erica comes."

"Wouldn't miss it, Javi," says James.

"Excellent. Be safe, mi amigo."

"Thanks, Javi. Nos vemos."

James disconnects the call and silence returns for a moment, before being interrupted by Erica.

"Well, that was interesting," she says, and then mimics Dr. Mirada's voice. "Hi, James and Erica. Everything you thought you knew about the cartel and Caro is wrong. Have a nice day."

CHAPTER TWENTY-TWO

JAMES CONTINUES TO DRIVE on near autopilot as the high-rises of central Los Angeles start to appear on the horizon. James's daze is broken by the appearance of a text message from Bobby on the car's navigation screen. "There is a coffee vendor about two blocks away, with lots of places to sit and talk."

James enters the address affixed to the text, into his navigation system. He finds a metered spot on the street a block away from the coffee shops, and effortlessly parallel parks. He and Erica bounce along the sidewalk until they see the coffee cart, and then Bobby at a table a few feet away in a small park.

"Good morning, Bobby. Good to see you."

"Good to see you, too, Mister Butler. But it is especially good to see this pretty lady."

"You are too sweet."

"Do you want some coffee?" Bobby says.

"Nah, we had some on the way up," Erica replies.

"What do you think?" James says.

"Well, I went to the floor and looked around quickly. Super high-end security, including stuff you'd never know was there if you didn't know to look for it. I also tried to trace the company name, and it is a shell with absolutely nothing tangible behind it. I mean, nothing at all. Last, I was able to access the electrical meter for the building. One floor is using way more energy than the rest of the building."

"Which means?" James says.

"Computers," Erica replies. "Lots and lots of computers."

"She's so smart and pretty. Why is she hanging around with you?"

"It's a mystery," Erica says.

Ignoring the others, James says, "So we have a shell company housing lots of computers on a whole floor. And the answer is?"

"Spook central," Bobby replies, with vigor.

"Really?" replies a genuinely surprised James.

"It has all the hallmarks of some intelligence operation, and the connection to the only spook we know—Speer."

"Okay, then what's the plan?" James asks.

Erica says, "I'm going to go up to the office and see what I can figure out."

"There's no way that can be good idea," James says.

"Look, if there is a connection to Speer, you can't go up there. The cops will be called if they see Bobby wandering around on the floor again. It only makes sense."

"Okay, but we are going to be close," James says.

"Of course," Erica replies, her tone casual. "That's why I'm not worried."

"Follow me to the building," Bobby says.

The three slowly walk the three blocks to the building, and as they near, Bobby stops them.

"James and I should wait here. I don't want us showing up on security cameras."

"That makes sense," Erica says.

"Are you sure about this?" James asks.

"Of course I am. Seriously, what could go wrong?"

"Never, ever, ask that question!" James says.

"I'll be fine, silly."

Bobby says, "Get as much information as you think you can, then get out of there. If there is an issue, or you feel insecure in any way, text anything to me and I'll be right there."

"Got it," Erica replies.

"I'm texting you right now, "Bobby says. "So I'll be the first one on your list."

"I'll be careful," Erica replies, with self-assurance.

She strolls into the building lobby and looks around, but sees nothing out of the ordinary for a business tower in Los Angeles. She looks to the elevators and sees that the middle elevator bank includes the twenty-fourth floor. Erica heads to that bank, pushes 24, and is directed to Elevator C, which she enters as the doors open. She breathes deeply as the doors close.

As the doors open on the twenty-fourth floor, Erica steps out and surveys the area. Tasteful but not overdone, the hallway to the right leads to a closed door with what appears to be a retinal scan access system. The hall to the left leads to two glass doors. Behind the doors is a reception desk made from granite, and large black onyx letters spelling out EUCRITE IMPORT AND EXPORT PARTNERS adorn the wall behind the desk.

Erica walks to the glass doors and is noticed by the receptionist, who presses a button to permit her entry. She walks to the front desk. The receptionist greets her with a warm smile. Erica walks slowly, taking in as much of her surroundings as possible. As she approaches the desk, she shares a friendly smile.

"Tim Speer, please."

The receptionist gives her a puzzled look. "I'm sorry, but no one by that name works here."

"Really? I thought this was Tim Speer's business. I must have been misinformed. My apologies."

"It's no problem," the receptionist says in a friendly, only slightly condescending, manner.

"If you don't mind my asking, what do you deal in?"

"Not at all. Most of our business is with Mexico—everything from major construction equipment to food products."

Erica starts to walk toward the doors leading back to the elevators. Her mind races, thinking of what else she can do to get some useful information.

She stops and turns her head. "You don't happen to have any facilities actually in Mexico, do you?"

"As a matter of fact, we do. We have a major facility in Los Mochis, regional facilities in Acapulco and Guadalajara, and an office and warehouse outside of Mexico City."

"Sounds like business is good."

"It certainly seems that way."

"Thank you again."

"My pleasure. Have a wonderful day."

The door unlocks as Erica approaches, allowing her to press the doors open and walk to the elevators. She presses L on the panel by the elevators, and car C opens. Erica enters, texting James: "On my way down."

Another direct trip and Erica's elevator car opens in the lobby. Her phone pings with a response from James: "Meet us in the same place."

Erica nearly jogs to the park, where she finds James and Bobby sitting at the same table.

"The receptionist said 'there is no Tim Speer.' that the company imports from and exports to Mexico. She also said they have Mexican facilities in Los Mochis, Acapulco, and wait for it...Guadalajara, as well as Mexico City."

"Did you believe her?" James says.

"She's not telling the truth, but she thinks she is. That's my read."

"Good enough for me. So what's the next step, Bobby?"

"I think I should observe for a bit. Check who comes and goes, and see if anyone *special* appears. Maybe the illustrious Mister Speer himself."

"Do you know what he looks like?" James says.

"Of course I do," Bobby replies. "Do you really think I let you go to the meeting in Palisades without doing some due diligence? I have pictures of everyone in the office and on that floor. Especially Speer."

"You are a sneaky son of a bitch." James smiles. "Thank you."

CHAPTER TWENTY-THREE

JAMES AND ERICA LEAVE BOBBY to conduct his surveillance, and return to James's car and head toward their Orange County office. They sit in silence for a few minutes, taking stock of the day's revelations.

"What's our next move, Captain?" Erica finally says.

"I was just thinking through that."

"I know. That's why I asked." Erica smirks.

"I think we let Bobby take his time with our friend Mister Speer, and we go back and try to fill in some gaps."

"Gaps?"

"Something we discussed in Guadalajara has stuck with me."

"Which would be?"

"The abduction was never really investigated like a traditional crime, nor the area around the consulate like a crime scene."

"Okay, but thirty-five years later, we change that how?" Erica says.

"It seems to me that there are two periods of time that are of special significance. First, there is the time immediately preceding the abduction, through the immediate aftermath and investigation. The second is once the investigators really started to talk and listen to some of the Mexican nationals who worked with the narcos, and their version of events became the focus of the investigations."

"Okay, that seems to make sense." Erica says.

"What if, for at least a bit, we look at this as we would any other criminal case, and we look into the crime scene and the facts

"You know I'm game," Erica says. "But what, specifically, are you thinking?"

"I'm just making this up as I go. But what if I try to find all of the statements and evidence I can, that are within the first couple months following the abduction?"

"Okay. And for me?" Erica says.

"Can you do a crime scene reconstruction and analysis of the abduction?"

"Easy."

"At the same time, and as always," James says, "be on the lookout for any other percipient witnesses—preferably living—and any other paths we should follow. We know enough now to be able to spot new issues or areas of inquiry."

"I'm good with this approach," Erica says. "It does seem like so much of the focus has been on information provided by witnesses—namely, Godoy and Lopez—given more than four years after the fact. Even if they were present at some things, and even if—and it's a big *if*—they were trying to be truthful and helpful, memories fade. Add to that the fact that they likely were being pressured by Berrellez, and probably Medrano."

Manuel "Manny" Medrano was the Assistant United States Attorney in charge of several of the Camarena-related criminal prosecutions in the United States. He has been outspoken in recent months about the guilt of several defendants, including those not convicted in court. Medrano lent support to the conspiracy theories of Hector Berrellez by appearing on camera in *The Last Narc*.

Erica continues. "Hell, they may well have been coached before they even left Mexico. There is this morass of information with seemingly little way to siphon the facts from the fraud. Maybe starting at the beginning will provide some guidance."

She pauses to reflect on the breadth of the task in front of them.

"One other thing," James says. "We still have work to do. I don't want Brian firing either of us. What if we try to get our information together and compare notes in the conference room tomorrow evening?"

"It's a date," Erica says. "In the meantime, I'll make sure you have the support you need at the office, and I'll pay special attention to Brian. On a different note, it meant a lot that you shared some about your past last night."

"I thought it was important," James replies. "I wanted you to know. I'd like for you to know me. Not many people really do, which I am good with."

"Well, I appreciate it."

"It is a little odd," James says. "We know so much about each other, and yet there is so much we don't know."

"True."

"What about your childhood? How was it growing up as Brian's daughter?"

"I don't want to disappoint you, but it was pretty normal. My mom was a writer, so she worked from home and was always there. And my dad was there for most things. There were some things he missed, but again, I never felt left out because my mom never missed anything."

"His work was never an issue?" James says.

"Not really. I suppose if I were to really scrutinize my memories, I'd find a time or two when I wished he had been there more. But I soon realized how good he was at what he did, and how many people he helped, and that made up for everything. He really tried to be present, and I don't think he ever missed anything important. Frankly, there was never a serious issue until I was at college."

"At Stanford?" James says.

"Right." Erica watches the scenery speed by outside the car window. "My mom was diagnosed in the middle of my junior year. As a family, we made the decision that I would stay where I was, and not transfer to be closer to her. It was always intended that I would be a lawyer. Dad wanted me to be a partner with him. By the end of that year, though, as my mom got worse, I decided being a lawyer didn't really fit into the things that were most important in my life: family, friends, helping people.

"I remember when I informed my parents of my decision to be a paralegal so I could still work with the law, but that I was going to study nutrition and volunteer and do other things. My mom was so sick and frail, but she listened patiently as I explained my reasons. I knew my dad was disappointed and didn't really understand. My mom, though, when I was done, she looked at me, took my hand in hers, and simply said 'I believe in you, and I trust that you will do what is best for you. I want you to be happy more than anything else.'"

Erica pauses for a moment. James starts to interject, but stops himself, his silent support saying more.

"That was all my dad needed to hear. After mom finished, dad went to the wine cellar and returned with two bottles of stupidly expensive wine. And though my mom shouldn't have had alcohol, we got hammered on both bottles. We talked and laughed into the wee hours of the morning. Two weeks later, she was gone. My dad and I never discussed my career choice again. And since then, no one could have been more supportive of my path than he has been."

"I'm sorry I never had the opportunity to meet your mom," James says.

"She was a good woman. She was ridiculously talented, super smart, and the most selfless person I've ever known."

James glanced at Erica while driving. "I feel as though I know what she was like, though, through you, because that's how I'd describe you. You must be a lot alike."

"We are. But I am my own person, too." Erica turns back to look at James.

"I would never doubt that for a second," he says. "Is that

why the last name of Walsh?"

"It's part a tribute to my mother, and part a way to be distinct from my father and his well-deserved and hard-earned but omni-present shadow."

"Makes sense," James says. "How you live now says a lot about your relationship with both of your parents, and I see all the things you do for people without fanfare or notice."

"You are sweet. Right now, I am immensely proud of and thankful for the relationship I have with my dad. To me, that is the best way to honor my mother and her legacy."

"Think Brian will ever remarry?" James says.

"I don't think so. I really don't. He misses her, and I know he is lonely. But I just don't see him really opening up to someone else. I'd be completely supportive, but he seems happy. If it's possible to be lonely and missing the love of your life while also being happy, he has found that space, and I intend to let him enjoy it."

"Well, I know Brian doesn't lack for friends and activities. I am fortunate to know both of you."

"It's more than that, and you know it. You have a special place with both of us."

"I hope you both know it means a lot to me."

"Never a question."

The conversation has carried them to Erica's house.

James pulls up front. "Are you going to the office?"

"Yes, I'll go in and juggle work and my assignment so I'm prepared for tomorrow night," Erica says.

"Sounds good. I think I am going to go home, go for a run, and then work from my deck."

"We are making progress, James. I feel it." Erica leans over and gives him a quick kiss on the lips that is neither romantic nor platonic. "Call me if anything new develops."

"Be well," he replies. "And thank you."

Erica shuts the door and walks off. James stays in place and watches as she unlocks her front door and steps inside. He leaves only after she is completely out of sight.

CHAPTER TWENTY-FOUR

THE FOLLOWING DAY, shortly before 5:00 p.m., Erica calls James's office.

"See you in a few minutes, in the conference room?"

"Yep. I'm prepared," he replies.

"See you then." Erica hangs up the phone.

Seconds later, she rings James again.

"Didn't we just talk?" James says wryly.

"We did. But that was before Agent Aguilar showed up in our lobby."

"Wow. Okay, do you want to bring him with you to the conference room?"

"Sure, I can do that," Erica says.

"Give me a couple of minutes to get there and get settled."

"Okay."

James sits at the head of the massive conference room table, waiting for Erica and Aguilar. He stands to greet them as they enter the room, and shakes hands with Aguilar before motioning him to sit in the chair to James's left. Aguilar takes that seat, and Erica sits in the chair across from Aguilar, to James's right.

"I must admit, I am surprised to see you," James says with a cool but friendly tone.

"I wanted to check in and see if you were making any progress, and to see if I could be of any help."

"We are plugging away," James says. "Learning things, but making progress or not would be a subjective determination, at best."

I wish I had a better sense of what Aguilar knows about our investigation and the Guadalajara trip. I don't distrust him really, but he has an agenda. Is it compatible with mine and Erica's? Maybe the only way to find out it is to let him participate. Tonight's topics are pretty straightforward. There might not be any harm in letting him sit in. Besides, there's a chance Aguilar will contribute something to the discussion.

"We have taken your advice and tried to deconstruct everything and review things with fresh eyes and open minds. Tonight, Erica and I plan to go back over some of the foundational elements of the case."

Like a fine-tuned machine, Erica picks up from James.

"We have gone back to square one—the abduction and its immediate aftermath. Perhaps there is evidence from those early days that is more significant than originally realized because it is not tainted with the knowledge of Camarena's fate or the identities of those charged in connection with the crime. I've been looking at the scene of the abduction and comparing the scene itself to the statements about how the abduction occurred."

"As for me," James says, "I've been looking at the evidence and statements contemporaneous to the events, before either Lopez or Godoy, before Berrellez became involved in Operation Leyenda, and comparing those with the statements of Berrellez's witnesses."

"Sounds interesting," Aguilar replies.

"Our hope is that, by starting from the beginning," Erica says, "we can formulate some material hypotheses to inform our investigations going forward."

She looks at Aguilar, who has been paying rapt attention, and takes the leap.

"You are welcome to stay and hear what we've found and are thinking."

Aguilar smiled. "I'd like that. Since I think I'm the only one here who has been to Guadalajara, or was involved in the initial investigation, perhaps I can add to the conversation."

James nods subtly at Erica, and they both implicitly accept Aguilar's statement. If Aguilar could be of help, there seemed to be no sense in compromising his forthrightness by revealing their Guadalajara adventures. If, on the other hand, he already knew, they might as well play along."

"Before Erica gets into the substantive," James says, "I'd like to point out something that we both find intriguing, if not confounding, which is the incredible lack of attention to the details of the abduction itself. In *The Last Narc*, the abduction discussion itself lasts a total of four minutes and forty-five seconds. Berrellez's book devotes maybe three pages to those events. *Desperados* spends little time on the kidnapping itself, because it just didn't seem to warrant much discussion, other than a description of the basic events. Even at trial, Lopez Romero testifies on the subject for maybe five minutes. We want to change that."

"With that lead in, I'll start," Erica says. "From our research, we have identified six descriptions of the abduction, and that includes the documentary and the book. We have broken down each of the descriptions and tried to analyze them, both collectively and individually." She puts two large maps of Guadalajara on the screen. "As you can see, the map on the left, which is the most important of the two for our purposes, is the area around the American consulate, and the other is a broader view of Guadalajara."

"Again," James says, "the idea is to use our experience and training, and Erica's skillset, and treat this like a crime scene in a more investigative sense."

"I'm with you," Aguilar replies.

Erica puts a map of the area immediately surrounding the consulate on the screen.

"Hopefully, this map will help for orientation," she says. "We know that Camarena's truck was parked in a lot outside the Camelot restaurant on Libertad. The Camelot was the building now labeled as Alestra. The parking area was in front of the Camelot, or to the north, and just west of the intersection of Progresso and Libertad. Close to here." She places an electronic T on the approximate location of Camarena's parked truck.

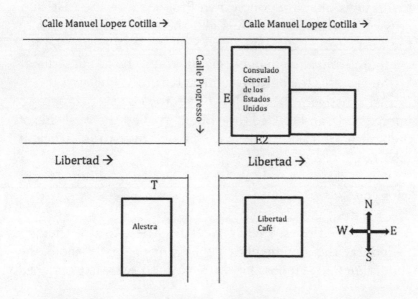

"T for truck," James wisecracks. "I get it."

"You're such a smart boy. Now shut up," Erica says. "The main entrance to the consulate was on Progresso, facing west. At that time, anytime a visitor came to the consulate, a consulate employee would greet the visitor and check them in. The employee would then check with the employee or department the employee wanted to visit, and only send them to the appropriate office after receiving permission and confirmation. There are two other entrances. One goes to the library, and the other to the visa office. Every statement we can find from former DEA agents, or anyone who worked at the DEA office, says the agents always used that Progresso exit." She has an E affixed to the map. "Skipping ahead a moment, there may be statements asserting that Camarena left from the exit onto Libertad, so I'll note that with an E2." Which then appears on the screen.

"We know he was running late to meet his wife for lunch," Erica continues. "So it's safe to assume that Camarena headed straight toward his truck upon leaving the consulate. To get there, he could have gone down Progresso on the east side, crossed over Libertad at the light, then crossed Progresso to the west, at the light. Like this." She presses a button on her computer, and a red line reflects the route she has described.

She presses the button again, and a green line appears.

"Alternatively, he could have crossed over Progresso immediately, and walked toward Libertad on the west side of the street. He then would have crossed over to his truck at Libertad."

James stares intently at the screen in front of him. "Okay, with you."

"Me, too," Aguilar says.

Erica continues. "What we have tried to do, then, is to look at the statements that have been made about the abduction and the possible witnesses. To see what matched up."

"And?" Aguilar says.

"You are going to have to be patient," Erica replies. "*Both* of you. A key to understanding the abduction witness statements is to recognize certain things we know that the witnesses simply could not have known."

"What didn't they know that helps us?" James says, though he knows the answer.

"Start with the assumption that, for all practical purposes, the only detailed description of the abduction itself comes from Rene Lopez, and he provides this statement to Berrellez when he is in Los Angeles in April 1992. At that point, Elaine Shannon had written *Desperados*, but I doubt that Rene read it. Or Hector, for that matter. It would be years until

Kuykendall wrote his book. As a result, three key facts likely were not known to Rene or his handlers.

"First, Camarena left the consulate a little after two p.m., and was running late for lunch with his wife, which was to be at two p.m. Second, at one p.m. on the day of the abduction, Kuykendall and Alan Bachelier met with an informant at the Camelot. Camarena joined them from the consulate at one-thirty. Camarena and Kuykendall left around one-thirty-five and walked back to the consulate, and Bachelier remained at the Camelot. Third, there was little, if anything, in the public record to indicate that Camarena's truck was found unlocked the following day."

Erica pauses.

Aguilar says, "Does that mean we know a timeline that Rene didn't know, from which we can assess the veracity of his account?"

"Very good, Agent Aguilar," she replies. "Notwithstanding the fact that you sounded a bit too much like Vincent Gambini. Have you done this before?"

"Once or twice, ma'am. Once or twice."

James says, "Unless I am mistaken, and I don't think I am, aren't there other witness statements that don't give a record of the abduction, but do talk about the timing that people left from and returned to Lope de Vega?"

"Also correct, of course," Erica says. "With that in mind, as a preview of coming attractions, I can state with confidence that Lopez's version of the abduction gets the timeline significantly wrong."

"Those lying bastards," Aguilar mutters under his breath.

"Can you give us a bit more detail?" James says.

"My dear James, I would *love* to explain more," Erica says, doing her *My Cousin Vinny* impersonation, the turns back to the map on the screen. "Lopez says he was in a cream-colored Atlantic with four passengers: Lopez Romero, El Sammy, Guadalupe Torres-Lepe, and the unidentified, alleged consulate employee—and we will get back to him—who was going to point out Camarena. He then alleges that they took up a surveillance position at the intersection of Libertad and Progresso Streets, covering the west entrance to the consulate."

"Which means that the abductors were across the street from Camarena's truck and from the Camelot, right?" Aguilar stares intently at the area map projected behind Erica.

"Maybe," she replies. "But it gets more curious. Rene does not specifically state where on that intersection the car was waiting. Only that they were covering the exit from the consulate onto Libertad. He says that the consulate employee was almost positive that was the door he would exit from."

James sits upright in his chair. "Stop right there. The idea that Camarena was going to exit through the Libertad door just does *not* make sense. Every DEA agent, or other employee in the DEA office at the time, that I've talked to, or heard from or about, says the agents always exited through the main entry point on Progresso. More significantly, how in the hell would this consulate employee have any idea which door Camarena would be leaving from, particularly if it was not the normal door of departure, and if he was running late?"

"There is no explanation," Erica says. "All Lopez said was that this consulate employee arrived at Lope de Vega that day, at around twelve-thirty p.m. In his book, Kuykendall says that none of the other agents knew Camarena had a lunch date with his wife until he announced it and left the consulate."

"After *The Last Narc*," James says, "there was some random Internet speculation that this consulate employee was Kuykendall. But of course, the timeline is all wrong for that, because we know Kuykendall had a phone call with the CI at noon, and was at the Camelot at one p.m., with Bachelier. More importantly, I have it on good authority that the DEA knows exactly who that person was, and he was another narco that Lopez apparently did not know, not a consulate employee."

"One thing we know for certain," Erica says, "is that it was not Rene Verdugo, as alleged some thirty years after-the-fact, in *The Last Narc*."

"No, it was not," James says. "Another obvious false statement from *The Last Narc*."

Aguilar stands to get a better view of the map.

"Nothing is adding up," he says.

"Nothing does, Agent Aguilar," replies Erica. "But let's look at the timeline more. Lopez's story would have to put them in the consulate area around one-fifteen p.m."

"Right," James says. "But Kuykendall and Bachelier were at the Camelot at one p.m. Camarena walked across from the consulate *alone* at one-thirty. And he and Kuykendall returned to the consulate together about five minutes later. Not one witness statement mentions seeing Camarena walking across the street while they were waiting, even those that, by their own timelines, would have already been in position."

"They couldn't have been there when they said," Aguilar replies.

"Correct," Erica says. "Moreover, despite almost all versions placing the abduction car across from the Camelot well before two p.m., neither Kuykendall, Bachelier, nor Camarena noticed anything suspicious, despite the well-accepted fact that these streets were not overly busy in 1985."

"And the unbelievable luck of the abductors on that day continued," James says.

"Excellent word choice James," says Erica. "Unbelievable. Now let's talk about the alleged sequence of events that Rene says led to the abduction. First, Rene says Camarena left from the exit to Libertad. Though, as discussed, the common and standard practice was to use the main exit on Progresso."

"The one marked with an E2. See, I'm paying attention." James snickers.

Erica casts a disapproving look toward him, but does not respond.

"Looking at Rene's version for a moment," she continues. "If Camarena leaves from the south exit and is running late, to get to his truck, do we imagine he walked to the intersection and waited for the crosswalk lights. Or..."

"Or does he walk directly across Libertad and head to his truck?" Aguilar says. "If I was late for lunch with my wife, I know I would take the most direct route to my car."

"Especially since that apparently was not a busy street in those days," James says.

"Let's go with that assumption and put that route in red," Erica says. "Like this. Now, Camarena is walking directly toward the car. Note also that Rene doesn't mention anything at all about Camarena's truck."

James perks up. "Wait, I thought that Camarena was getting into his truck when he was approached and abducted?"

"That's always been the conventional story, all the way back to *Desperados*," Erica says. "But Rene says nothing about it."

"But his truck was found unlocked the following day, right?" James asks.

"It was," Erica replies. "Kuykendall says they would always lock their vehicles, especially on that day when Camarena parked there early in the day and was going to leave it for several hours."

"As a former agent," Aguilar says, "I can assure you that is standard practice."

"Instead, Lopez says the three abductors got out of the Atlantic," Erica continues, "left the consulate employee in the car by himself, and then approached Camarena as he 'walked west across Libertad Street.'" Erica reads directly from a DEA-6 report of the DEA's interview with Lopez Romero to precisely restate Lopez Romero's words. El Sammy flashes a DFS badge and says to Camarena, 'The Comandante wants to see you.' When Camarena protests, El Sammy flashes a gun at Camarena, and he orders and guides Camarena into the Atlantic, with El Sammy and Lopez Romero flanking Camarena in the back seat. Torres-Lepe got in the front passenger's seat, while the consulate employee stayed in the driver's seat."

"The consulate employee was left alone in the driver's seat, with the keys, while Camarena was accosted on the street?" James says, incredulous.

"Standard kidnapping practice, I'm sure," Erica says.

Aguilar returns to a standing position. "Hold on. Three people walk up to him, basically on the street, from half a block away?"

"That's how it sounds," Erica replies.

"Bullshit," Aguilar says. "With all that was going on down there, he would have been on alert. I find it hard to believe they could have just walked up to him."

"Lopez says that they put Camarena in the back seat," James says, "told him to bend over and keep his head down, and then they all drove off to Lope de Vega."

"I will also note two things, gentlemen. First, Lopez can't keep his story straight. As a tiny example, in an *LA Weekly* article, Rene says he was the one who pulled the gun on Camarena, when in every other version where it is mentioned, El Samy is the one with the gun. The second thing of importance is that all of the descriptions of the abduction from government informants vary in material respects from the others, and each deflates under any scrutiny, just as easily as the Lopez scenario we just looked at."

"None of the scenarios are accurate?" Aguilar says, incredulous.

"Not one," James replies. "They had seven tries, and botched each one."

Erica says, "Before we leave the topic of the abduction itself, I would just like to lay out on other part of the timeline."

"No objections here," James says.

Erica puts a slide on the screen and reads it to James and Aguilar.

- One p.m. —Alan Bachelier and Kuykendall go from the Consulate to Camelot.
- One-thirty p.m.—Camarena goes from the Consulate to Camelot.
- One-thirty-five p.m.—Kuykendall and Camarena return to the Consulate, Bachelier remains at Camelot.
- Noon to two p.m.—abduction car arrives at Libertad and parks.
- Two-ten p.m.—Camarena abducted.
- Two-thirty p.m.—Kuykendall's first recollection of Bachelier being back in the office.
- Two-forty-five p.m.—Bachelier and Shaggy Wallace meet contact at the Camelot.

"What does Alan say about this timeline?" Aguilar asks.

"As best we can tell," Erica replies, "he says he really doesn't remember the meeting at the, Camelot or his activities around the meeting."

James says, "We know the agents in the office were asked on the eight—the day after the kidnapping—to write down their activities of the prior day, and we have seen Kuykendall's recollection. But to this point, we are not aware of anyone having a copy of Bachelier's recap of the events of that fateful day. It obviously would be nice to be able to plug in when Bachelier went back to the consulate, and the route he took."

"So what we know," Erica moves the screen back to the map of the consulate area, "is that none of the abduction scenarios fits with the timeline. And the window between there not being any other agents around, and Camarena being abducted, is narrower than anyone seems to have understood previously."

Aguilar takes a deep breath while looking over the map again. After a few minutes, he breaks the silence, looking at

Erica and James sitting at the head of the conference room table.

"So to summarize, are you saying it is possible that the narrative that someone identified Camarena to waiting cartel members who nabbed him in the street is not true?"

Erica looks directly at Aguilar. "No, sir. It's more than that. We are saying that many of the details of Camarena's abduction were likely part of one or more after-the-fact, manufactured stories."

CHAPTER TWENTY-FIVE

"I HAVE MORE," James says.

Erica stands up from her chair. "I'm certain you do, but I am going to order some dinner. Does Italian food work for you, Agent Aguilar. It's kind of our standard delivery?"

"First of all, at this point, you probably should call me Joe. And second, Italian is great. Thank you."

"I'll step out and order while you get ready," Erica says to James.

"Since it's Italian, we should have a little wine." James presses on the panel next to the credenza, unveiling a hidden wine refrigerator.

Aguilar whistles. "Nice."

"What's the saying? Membership has its privileges." James pulls out a bottle, opens it and pours three glasses as Erica returns.

She says, "Just in time, I see. Andre will have dinner here in about thirty minutes."

"Sounds good. In the meantime," James raises his glass, followed by Aguilar and Erica, "here's to following the facts and seeking the truth, wherever they may lead us."

"Salúd," says Aguilar.

"Salúd," James and Erica say in unison.

James excuses himself for a few minutes, before coming back. He returns to his seat, drinks a bit more wine, and resumes where the conversation had left off.

"While Erica was dissecting the abduction scene, I went back to find whatever I could that was contemporaneous to the events. As we mentioned, for all the obvious reasons, and not to cast aspersions on anyone, this was treated as a rescue mission from the beginning. The goal was to find Agent Camarena. It was not to process evidence and witnesses as part of a criminal investigation. For that reason, there are substantially more DEA-6 reports talking about the case that originated in 1991 and 1992, than all the preceding years combined."

"At the risk of repeating myself, have you found anything of significance?" Aguilar says.

"Significance is a tricky word," James replies, "and may very much be in the eye of the beholder. But I promise you, there are some interesting things. What I'd like to do is to avoid looking for conclusions at this point, and to just examine these statements and documents. Later, we can see if there are conclusions that should be drawn, which will tell us where to look next."

"That seems to me to be the right approach, James." Erica smiles.

"I'm in," Aguilar says.

"Let's start with a person," James continues. "Tomas Morlet Borquez."

"The name sounds familiar, but that's it," Aguilar says.

Erica ponders for a moment. "I'm pretty sure I remember that name being mentioned in Kuykendall's book. But at the moment, I can't remember why."

"Morlet, indeed, was mentioned," James says. "Kuykendall says that on February 13th—so six days after the abduction—a federal law enforcement agency in the US passed a message that an agent had received a phone call from a William Wayne Collins, who said he was less than a hundred feet away when Camarena was abducted. Quoting directly from the book: 'According to Collins, he had recognized two of the men as being members of the Tomas Morlet drug trafficking organization.'"

"What!" Aguilar says.

"It gets better," James continues. "Morlet purportedly oversaw the security detail for the Shah of Iran when the Shah was living in exile in Acapulco. Who recommended him for that position?"

"What is the CIA, Alex?" Erica says.

"Correct, for two hundred dollars. Apparently, Morlet was a comandante with the DFS, and we all know the presumed connections between the DFS and the CIA. Kuykendall's book goes on to say that the person identified as Collins claimed Morlet was heavily involved in drug trafficking, and that, as a DFS comandante, had provided protection for drug traffickers and large marijuana growers. But here is the wild part. According to Kuykendall, the 'DEA had no record of Tomas Morlet.'"

"How is that even possible?" Erica asks Aguilar.

"I have no idea," says an agape Aguilar.

James continues. "Moving forward, I note that Kuykendall identifies two particularly interesting items from the interrogation tapes. He said that the interrogators regularly said they needed directions to places being talked about because 'we are not from here.' Moreover, he says that at least one of the interrogators had an accent not unlike that of someone raised on the border. So much so, that an MFJP comandante who listened to the tapes, described one interrogator's voice as sounding like that of DEA Agent Art Rodríguez, who Kuykendall notes is a native Texan who grew up on the border."

"I assume Morlet grew up on the border?" Erica says.

"He is from Mexicali," James replies. "But it gets even more curious. I've found a news report from UPI on the 27th of February 1985, where Francis Mullen, the departing head of the DEA at the time, discusses the investigation. In the report, Mullen says four people had been arrested in connection with the kidnapping. Here's where it gets good. The report says, and I quote: 'the arrested suspects include the purported mastermind, Tomas Morlet Borquez, and three former Mexican federal agents.'"

"The purported mastermind? What the hell?" Erica blurts out.

"That makes no sense to me," Aguilar replies.

"The statement is not a direct quote from Mullen," James says. "But where else would the reporter have gotten that information? And why would Mullen label Morlet the mastermind, when Kuykendall says the DEA had no record of him?"

Aguilar thinks for a moment. "Here is what I find odd. As I have said several times, the DEA agents in Guadalajara and the rest of Mexico were damn good at their jobs. Just look at the vast amounts of information the agents in Guadalajara uncovered. It seems incomprehensible that there could be a DFS comandante who was deeply embedded with the traffickers, and the DEA would have no record of that person."

"I completely agree," James says. "And yet we have the Mullen statement. It's also important to note that in Kuykendall's book, he maintains that an informant in a US prison confirmed most of the information the Collins person had said about Morlet."

"Where is Morlet now? Aguilar says.

"Dead," James replies. "The most widely circulated story is that he got into a disagreement with a narco and was shot twice in the head in the doorway to his restaurant. Some sources say the Mexican police who killed him since they could not arrest a DFS agent. Either way, he's a dead end. Literally."

Erica stands up from the table. "Perfect timing. Dinner is

here, and this is a good point to take a break."

She leaves the conference room and lets the delivery person up the elevator. Aguilar and James sit in silence as Erica shows the delivery person into the conference room. Soon, conference the table is assembled with an assortment of Italian salads and pastas.

Erica hands the bill to James. "I believe this is yours."

James smiles, adds a generous tip, and slides it back to Erica, who then walks the delivery person back to the elevator while James and Aguilar politely wait for her to return before eating, and James opens another bottle of wine and refills their glasses.

Erica enters the room. "Let's eat."

The three load their plates and begin to eat.

"This is fantastic," Aguilar says.

"We tend to order out a fair amount, with the hours some of the attorneys here keep," James says, "and we've found a few really good places close by. We love Il Piacere, which translates to The Pleasure. Andre, the owner/chef, knows us well and always does a bit more for us."

"Let me know the next time you order, and I'll come back."

CHAPTER TWENTY-SIX

JAMES RESUMES THE CONVERSATION while still eating.

"The link between these more contemporaneous reports and the prolific reporting in '91 and '92, is one Antonio Garate Bustamante."

"Ah, yes. Garate," Aguilar says. "I've had my own dealings with Garate."

Prior to the Camarena abduction, many officials in the United States suspected that elements of the Mexican government, be they political, military, or police, were actively aiding the cartel in its operations. However, despite these suspicions, there was little evidence of a broad conspiracy. In fact, in the first criminal trial in the United States, brought against three defendants, the government did not present a broad conspiracy case. Instead, the case focused on evidence that allegedly showed the defendants' direct involvement in the murders of Camarena, as well as those of Walker and Radelat.

The scope of the government's case changed, though, when Antonio Garate Bustamante began working with some of the Operation Leyenda agents. Garate, a former Mexican police commander with ties to drug cartel members, said he knew people who were privy to what had happened to Camarena. Soon, witnesses were telling DEA agents about the involvement of several prominent Mexicans.

"What I've never understood is why the DEA would start dealing with someone as shady as Garate," Erica says.

"Simple," James replies. "They were desperate. The US government wanted to expose the Mexican corruption it believed precipitated Camarena's abduction, and they wanted convictions. In the Verdugo trial, they pretty much tried and convicted everyone they had any solid physical evidence against. They needed something else, something more. Garate had to be desperate after his protector, Fonseca, was arrested, and Garate was later ostracized from the MFJP. His way out was to go to the DFS and offer to provide information to the DEA."

"Talk about sleeping with the devil," Erica says.

"True. But investigators and prosecutors use informants all the time," James says. "I know you've both heard a million times that it takes a criminal to catch and convict a criminal. The key, though, is to have controls on it. The evidence seems to indicate there were few, if any, controls with Garate."

"So Garate tells the DEA he knows of people who have direct knowledge of the Camarena abduction and torture," Erica replies, "and the DEA says, 'Great. Bring them to us?'"

James stands. "That seems to be about it, but I suspect there was more. If Garate was desperate, if he needed the protection of the DFS and wanted to be certain he got the attention of the DEA and the American prosecutors, it seems likely it was about more than just witnesses. I think there had to be a representation from Garate that he also could implicate prominent Mexicans from Mexico's government and military. That had to have been part of the enticement. Otherwise, you are right. Why use someone like Garate to get low-level narcos, who you might not be able to convict without being able to show a larger conspiracy?"

James starts to pace, and his voice takes on the tone of a trial lawyer casting a spell on the jury.

"We know Garate *interviewed* a large number of potential witnesses and sent many to the states. Most notable among those were Godoy and Lopez. But to understand the role of Godoy and Lopez, up to and including their involvement in

The Last Narc, we must go back to the early 1990s."

"Does he always pace like that when he talks?" Aguilar whispers to Erica.

"He does. He says it sends oxygen to his brain. Around here, we refer to it as 'kinetic intelligence.'"

CHAPTER TWENTY-SEVEN

"THERE HAVE BEEN THREE Camarena-related trials in the United States," James says. "All of which took place in the Central District of California, before Judge Edward Rafeedie. The first of the three, most well-known for the *abduction* of Rene Verdugo, has been discussed. The other two each involved, as a defendant, a Mexican businessman named Ruben Zuno Arce, who happened to be the brother-in-law of a former president of Mexico. This is going to seem to be a little deep into the weeds, but I think it will be worthwhile."

"We will follow along and stop you if we get lost," Erica says.

"In August 1986, Zuno was on a trip to the United States when he was detained by the DEA and arrested as a material witness for a grand jury proceeding in Los Angeles, relating to the Camarena murder investigation. During his testimony before the grand jury, Zuno apparently was asked if he knew Rafael Caro Quintero. 'I don't think that I ever met him,' was his response.

"Another witness, a character by the name of Lawrence Victor Harrison—who we could spend an evening talking about—testified to the grand jury that he'd been working for the CIA, and also for the traffickers installing communications equipment, and that he had attended a party where Caro was riding a dancing horse, and he dismounted the horse, then greeted and hugged Zuno. Notwithstanding Harrison's dubious nature, and his past work as a communications specialist for the cartel, based on Harrison's testimony, perjury charges were filed against Zuno."

"Really?" Aguilar says. "Based on Harrison. That dude was smart, but he was about three beers short of a six pack, if you know what I mean. I'm not sure if he ever really worked for or with the CIA. And from what I heard, his tales got wilder the more he talked, and he'd tell almost anyone almost anything they wanted to hear."

"No argument here," James says. "But nevertheless, perjury charges were filed. Zuno was granted bail and permitted to return to his home in Mexico. Three months later, Zuno openly returned to the US for trial on the perjury charge. But upon arrival, Zuno was re-arrested and charged with Camarena's murder. What happened in the interim, you might ask."

"Yes, you've got us both wondering," Erica says.

"The DEA *found* a new informant named Hector Cervantes Santos, who had been a bit of a gopher/security guard for some of the cartel leadership."

"Convenient," Erica says.

"In fact," James continues, "Cervantes was anointed the star witness in the government's case against Ruben Zuno and two other defendants. Suddenly, Ruben Zuno had become a major figure in the cartel who had conspired with drug lords to kill Camarena. Despite the defense's presentation of evidence to question Cervantes's testimony, Zuno and two co-defendants were convicted of conspiracy.

"In addition to implicating Ruben Zuno and his co-defendants, Cervantes's testimony sated the DEA's thirst for evidence of involvement by Mexican officials with the cartel and in Camarena's abduction. Cervantes, though, went beyond their wildest expectations and implicated the heads of the Mexico City Police Department, Interpol, and the country's anti-drug agency, as well as the police commander initially responsible for solving Camarena's murder. Cervantes also was the first to directly implicate Manuel

Bartlett Diaz, Mexico's Interior Minister, in the Camarena abduction.

"Following the jury verdict, Zuno was granted a new trial by the district court because Medrano mischaracterized evidence against Zuno during closing arguments. I once thought Medrano just made an error without a malevolent intent. Now, I'm not so sure. In any event, the government appealed the new trial order to the Ninth Circuit.

"During the pendency of the appeal, while Zuno remained in jail, Cervantes's background and testimony were analyzed, and it became obvious that Cervantes had fabricated large portions of his testimony. Years later, Cervantes told multiple sources that his testimony against Zuno was a lie devised by the prosecution. That he had never seen Zuno in person in his life, and that Berrellez and Medrano wrote a script for him to follow at trial.

"I hate to interrupt," Erica says, "but is there a point at the end of this very long Cervantes tunnel?"

"Indeed, there is," James replies. "Godoy and Lopez. Listen to this very carefully. Godoy was first interviewed by the DEA in Los Angeles, on August 30, 1991, and his initial meetings with the DEA continued through October 1991. For reference, the first Zuno trial and the District Court's new trial order was early in 1991. The Ninth Circuit affirmed the new trial order came in an unpublished opinion on March 27, 1992.

"In Goody's first set of meetings with the DEA, Godoy does not implicate Zuno in the Camarena conspiracy, though he identifies Zuno in a picture, noting that Zuno is well-known in Jalisco. Godoy was interviewed by the DEA in October 1991, and then apparently not again until April 7, 1992, less than two weeks after the Ninth Circuit's affirmance of the new trial order. Not until these April 1992 meetings did Godoy say anything that implicated Zuno in any way. Berrellez signed off on, and/or conducted, each of these Godoy interviews.

"Lopez did not start speaking to the DEA until even later than Godoy. His first interview apparently was in March 1992, after the Ninth Circuit arguments, and a mere weeks before the appeals court's affirmance of the new trial order. Like Godoy, however, Lopez's initial interviews with the DEA did not implicate Zuno, and it was not until *after* the Ninth Circuit ruled that Lopez began speaking of Zuno's alleged involvement in the conspiracy."

"They really didn't implicate Zuno until after the new trial order," Aguilar says. "Seriously?"

"Seriously," James replies. "And there is more. In a stunning change of strategy, the government did not call Cervantes to provide any testimony whatsoever. Instead, Godoy and Lopez were the new star witnesses. Though Berrellez once assured a Camarena grand jury that he would not present witnesses who had been personally involved in the Camarena case, Lopez figured prominently in the second Zuno trial despite that he admitted to personally participating in Camarena's kidnapping, and that he was present during and had witnessed much of Camarena's torture and interrogation."

"Son of a bitch," Aguilar mutters.

"On top of all of this," Erica says, "we've read and analyzed the trial transcripts, and one thing is glaringly absent."

"What's that?" Aguilar asks."

"There is a stunning absence of any corroboration of Godoy and Lopez," James replies. "The government introduced no witness testimony, no receipts, no invoices, no photographs, no travel documents. That is, these two criminals, who came forward with testimony under questionable circumstances—the timing of which was dubious, at best—corroborated each other. Except, of course, when they didn't."

"I honestly had no idea about this," Aguilar says.

"Most people—even those close to the case—don't," James replies.

Erica says, "I contrast Zuno's fate with that of Doctor Machain, Zuno's co-defendant at the second trial."

Dr. Humberto Alvarez Machain, commonly referred to in the US as Dr. Machain, was a gynecologist in Guadalajara who was known to *hang around* the city's drug traffickers.

In 1990, a federal grand jury in Los Angeles indicted Machain for complicity in Camarena's kidnapping, torture, and murder. On April 3,1990, Dr. Machain was picked up on the streets of Guadalajara and flown to El Paso, Texas, where he was arrested

Along with Ruben Zuno, Dr. Machain was tried for Camarena's kidnapping, torture and murder in 1992. After the conclusion of the government's case, Judge Rafeedie granted Dr. Machain's motion for judgment of acquittal, on the grounds of insufficient evidence to support a guilty verdict. Judge Rafeedie expressly stated that the government's case was based on "suspicion and hunches, but no proof," and that the theory of the prosecution's case was "whole cloth, the wildest speculation." Dr. Machain was thus released from federal custody and immediately repatriated to Mexico.

Erica continues her presentation on Dr. Machain. "The charges against Doctor Machain were dismissed by Judge Rafeedie after the prosecution's presentation of its case upon a finding that the case against him was too speculative. There should be no doubt in anyone's mind, that if Rafeedie had let the case go to the jury, Machain would have been convicted, too."

"Wait," Aguilar says. "In *The Last Narc*, don't Berrellez and Medrano make some definitive statements about Doctor Machain and the things he did to Camarena?"

Erica responds with excitement and agitation. "They absolutely do. Berrellez talks about Machain injecting Camarena in the heart with lidocaine. Medrano, an alleged officer of the court, talks about Machain's actions and guilt with absolute certainty, as if he is stating facts—facts he did not, and apparently could not, present in the trial. He even dramatically shows how Machain plunged a syringe into Camarena's heart, despite no evidence of this being presented at Machain's trial. I cannot tell you how infuriated I became watching him."

"In the end, then," Aguilar says, "we are left with the feeling that the US government convicted several people, and did so based on inherently flawed and suspect testimony derived from an unchecked investigative apparatus."

"Well said," James replies.

"I know we need to wrap up and go home since tomorrow is a workday," Erica says, "but I personally think this has been very helpful. I truly believe that exposing these flaws in the conventional narrative, and the government's case, will lead us down the path to a better understanding of what really happened. Ruben Zuno died in prison, and Doctor Machain was kidnapped—basically dumped out of a plane, jailed, and tried, and given no compensation, because the US justice system betrayed them. And there are many more who have been harmed."

Erica pauses for a second, drawing in a deep breath to control her emotions.

"The people who committed these acts dishonored Agent Camarena and his legacy, and they further that malfeasance every time they repeat the lies."

CHAPTER TWENTY-EIGHT

THE FOLLOWING MONDAY, James rises early to appear on the motions docket at LA Superior Court in downtown Los Angeles. In this court, motions are heard at 8:30 a.m. every day. Typically, the motions are handled quickly, and judges are incentivized to move things along expeditiously to get to their trial docket.

The court emailed James and his opposing counsel a tentative ruling last night that was in James's favor. Often, the party losing on the tentative ruling will submit on the tentative and forego the need for a hearing. Other times, though, the losing party wants another chance in front of the judge. Such is the case today, and James is bit annoyed to be dealing with the traffic on I-5, for what likely will be a waste of time.

James parks in a lot a block down from the courthouse and enjoys the cool fall air as he walks to the courthouse. Past the security line, he takes the stairs to the third floor, finds his courtroom, and checks the docket posted outside the door. Happily, James finds that he is number two on the docket. The judge has fourteen motions to hear this morning, so the process should be quick and efficient.

James starts to enter the courtroom when he receives a text. Reversing course, he waits until he is in the hallway to see a text from Bobby. "James. I need to talk to you ASAP!"

James reluctantly replies. "Heading into a courtroom. I'll text as soon as I'm out."

He turns off his phone and puts it in his suit jacket pocket before taking a seat in the second row. As the first case is called, he nervously contemplates what Bobby could have been calling about. Unlike most motions, the court allows the parties to argue for several minutes, with James's agitation and irritation expanding as each word is spoken.

Finally, the case is resolved, and James's case is called. The hearing lasts less than two minutes, as opposing counsel's efforts to persuade the judge to change from the tentative ruling are unsuccessful. The case is dismissed, and James hurries out of the courtroom. Opposing counsel—a nice, but inexperienced, attorney from a large downtown firm—runs after James, asking if they can discuss the case and settlement options. James, exhibiting far less patience than is his norm, asks to be called at the office. As the chagrined associate walks away, James mentally notes he will do something to make it up to him.

Once outside, James calls Bobby. "What was so urgent?"

"Where are you? You need to see something?"

"I'm just leaving LA Superior. Where are you?"

"Well, that's convenient. I'm at the Speer building. Can you come over?"

"I'll be there in ten minutes."

"Park away from the building. I'm across the street. By the bus stop."

"On my way."

"Be invisible, James."

He hops in his car and drives to a parking lot with an open spot not too close to the building. Walks the two blocks to Bobby, trying to look as inconspicuous as possible, but likely failing miserably.

Bobby smiles as James approaches. "Nice threads for a stakeout."

"I was in court. What can I say? What's up?"

"We had a visitor this morning." Bobby raises his camera, showing James a picture of Tim Speer entering the building.

"Gotcha, you son of a bitch," James says. "How long has he been in there?"

"Since I called you. What do you want to do?"

"Wouldn't it be good to see if he leaves with anyone or anything, and where he goes?"

"Okay, I'm on it."

"Can I come along?" James says.

"Of course, but it might be pretty boring. Who knows how long we will have to wait."

Bobby starts to walk toward the building, and James follows suit.

"I think I can handle it. Let me text Erica and let her know not to expect me at the office right away."

"Text quickly," Bobby says.

James looks up to see Speer walking out of the building, carrying a large envelope. He is alone. Well-dressed, Speer has the appearance of a man in total control as he heads down the street.

"You follow him, but not closely, and I'll get my car." Bobby runs in the opposite direction from Speer.

James watches Speer while keeping a safe distance behind so Speer cannot see him in the periphery.

A block down the road, James sees Bobby's black Mercedes pull up next to him, and he hops in. Skillfully following Speer three-quarters of a block ahead, Bobby focuses on the surroundings. Looking ahead, he and James watch Speer make a right turn into the parking garage below a building. Bobby makes an immediate U-turn against traffic.

"What are you doing," James says.

"We are getting out of here."

"Why?"

"I know that building."

"So?"

"The CIA field office is inside."

"Leaving is good!" James concurs.

Bobby quickly returns to the lot where James had parked

his car. He puts his car in park and looks at James.

"Need more proof?"

"Something's not right," James mutters, under his breath.

"What's not right is that we are following a CIA officer, and we have no idea what his intentions are."

"No. It's too easy. All of it. The note, the directory, Speer showing up and leading us to the field office." James's mind races, combining variables.

"Félix must have wanted you to know that Speer was still connected with the CIA," Bobby says.

"Why do you say that?"

"Well, let's start with, he gave you the damn note."

"Did he?" James says, as his thoughts begin to crystalize.

"Come again."

"I've never been certain it really came from Félix. Nothing about it, or how I got it, indicates that it had to be from him."

"But irrespective of who wrote it," Bobby says, "wasn't the point the same—to show that Speer is still working for, or with, the CIA?"

"Maybe. But it might be simpler than that, and I don't like being played."

CHAPTER TWENTY-NINE

JAMES RETURNS TO HIS OFFICE, becoming more agitated and more determined with each passing moment.

Walking by Erica's office on the way to his own, he leans his head inside.

"You're going to want to hear what just happened in LA."

Intrigued and concerned, Erica locks her computer and follows close on his heels. Once in his office, James hangs up his suit jacket while Erica shuts the door, gets a Diet Coke from the mini-fridge and opens it before handing it to James, then sits in the chair across from his desk. James sits and takes a deep breath. Meticulously, he recounts the events of the morning, leading to Speer's entry into the CIA field office.

"No way!" Erica says. "I can hardly wrap my head around it. You really think Speer is actively working for the CIA, and he arranged for the prison note? I'm certainly not shocked that there was something else going on with him, but I would not have guessed this."

"The breadcrumbs line up so well, a blind man could follow them."

"I think you are supposed to say, visually impaired," Erica cracks, taking a slight edge of the intense discussion. "Where do we go from here?"

"I'm not sure, but I have some ideas," James says.

"If you tell me you are going to go confront Speer, I will go get Brian right now."

"No. At least, not yet. Right now, I'm thinking that the

more we learn about the CIA's possible involvement with the cartel, the more opportunities we will have to learn things from Speer. I think we can find ways to use our friend Tim to our advantage."

James's chain of thought is disrupted by the ping notification of an incoming text.

He shows Erica the phone. "It's from Javi, and the timing is almost spooky. Dr. Mirada's message said: "I had a call today with Doctor Anna Garcia-Dias from the University of Guadalajara, to discuss recent cartel developments in Mexico, which has seen a resurgence of cartel-related violence and open wars between rival cartels. While on the call, I thought about our recent discussion, so I asked her who she thought was responsible for Camarena's murder. Her response surprised me and should interest you. She said, 'Everyone knows it was the CIA who killed him.'"

James knows full well that others have asserted that the CIA was, at a minimum, involved in, and at most, responsible for, Agent Camarena's abduction and interrogation. The theory, as advanced by Hector Berrellez in *The Last Narc*, is that Camarena learned of a connection between the cartel and the CIA's Central American activities, including its covert, and largely illegal, activities to support the Contras in their fight to overthrow the government of Nicaragua. Because he got too close to such sensitive information, the argument goes, he was picked up and interrogated.

James and Erica already had spent considerable time combing through the publicly available records to see what corroboration, if any, they could find to these theories. Dr. Mirada's text increased the urgency of their task, and they spent the next few days re-doubling their efforts to somehow connect Camarena—or at least, the DEA in Mexico—the Contras, and the CIA.

A few days into their efforts, James sits at his desk, pouring over Iran–Contra government reports and tracking down notations and attributions in obscure books and articles. He has called virtually every contact he had who might be able to steer him and Erica in the right direction.

James answers his ringing office phone by pressing the speaker phone with nary a glance.

"James Butler."

"Mister Butler, you don't know me, but I'd like to talk to you about your CIA inquiries."

James startles to attention. "May I put you on hold for a moment to close my door?"

"Sure. That's fine."

James places the call on hold and races to his door.

He yells down the hall, "Erica. Come here. Fast!"

James returns to his chair as Erica flashes through the doorway, slightly out of breath. He points to the speakerphone and then to the chair across from him before turning the call from mute to the speaker.

"Okay, I'm back. Thank you. Now, you were saying Mister...?

"Who I am is not important. I know you have been asking questions about the CIA and Camarena. You are looking in the right directions, but there is more."

"I have no trouble believing there is more," James says. "Where else should we be looking?"

"I'm not at liberty to give you that information, but you should know it all starts with and flows from one Juan Ramon Matta Ballesteros. You know of him, I'm sure."

"Of course I do."

James was familiar with Matta, who was widely known as a significant player in trafficking cocaine from South and Central America into the United States in the 1980s. In 1984, he was indicted for his role in a smuggling ring in Van Nuys, California. When that operation was discovered in 1981, some 114 pounds of cocaine and $1.9 million in cash were seized.

Matta also was indicted in 1985 for his alleged activities in connection with a significant cocaine-smuggling operation in Southern California and Arizona.

More important, James has begun to surmise that Matta played an important, and very under-recognized, role in Mexican drug trafficking. As early as 1975, Matta was working with Félix Gallardo, providing the critical link between Colombian cocaine suppliers and Mexican traffickers, leading to the establishment of new transportation routes for moving South American cocaine into the US.

Most reports say that Matta was in Mexico at the time of the Camarena murder, and that after the murder, he somehow was able to elude Mexican and American authorities and flee Mexico. Matta later was tracked to Cartagena, Columbia, and in April 1985, the DEA convinced the Columbian authorities to arrest Matta. Matta was able to escape—or bribe his way out of—the Columbian prison a year later, before the judicial process had cleared the way for his extradition to the US.

Matta fled Colombia for his home nation of Honduras. The Honduran Constitution prohibited the extradition of Honduran citizens, and for two years, Honduran authorities rejected US requests to extradite Matta. Finally, in April 1988, Honduran police arrested Matta and put him on a plane to the Dominican Republic. The Dominican government then put him on a flight to Puerto Rico with US marshals, who arrested Matta when they reached the United States territory. At the time of his arrest, Matta had amassed a large fortune.

In the first Zuno trial, Matta was convicted of being part of the conspiracy behind the Camarena kidnapping, torture, and murder. Later, in a separate trial, Matta was convicted for his role in the Van Nuys and Arizona distribution rings. Matta continues to be incarcerated in a federal prison in the United States.

"Then you know his connection to Félix Gallardo and that their alliance could be seen as forming the foundation for the Guadalajara Cartel."

"We do know some of that," James replies. "But of course, there aren't records of those activities, and the reports are limited and somewhat contradictory."

"If it was obvious, everyone would already know the answers, and no one would need you, Mister Butler."

"What can you tell me about SETCO," James says.

SETCO was a Honduran airline formed by American *businessmen* aligned with Matta, that was found by a congressional committee to be the principal company used by the Contras in Honduras to transport supplies and personnel for the Honduras-based FDN—one of the earliest Contra groups. SETCO was also found to have been an important player in the transportation of narcotics from Central and South America to the United States.

"Don't believe everything you read or think you know. Look at it fresh. If the connections are there, you will find them. That is all I have for you right now, Mister Butler. The rest is up to you."

The call ends.

"Well, that was helpful," Erica says with biting sarcasm.

"I'm getting tired of everyone telling me to look at things new," James says. "What do they think we have been doing?"

"So do we trust him? Whoever he is? Someone with a Deep Throat fetish?"

"I think we have to, don't you? He sounded knowledgeable."

"All right, but before we go too far," Erica says, "can we step back and evaluate whether the CIA angle is worth exploring in the first place?"

"Of course," James replies. "Apparently, we are meant to look at everything anew."

"Okay, then," Erica says. "I keep going back to one central question: What could Camarena possibly have discovered that would be sufficient to cause the CIA to essentially order him to be killed?"

"Berrellez himself says that Camarena was about to discover the CIA's narcotics trafficking operations and its work with the Contras," James replies.

About to discover? Come on. I'm not naïve, James. Not by a long shot. But I cannot accept that the CIA would torture and kill a fellow federal agent on something he might be about to find. Especially if he was being transferred back to the States, which I would assume they would know. I mean, you'd assume they would thoroughly vet him before they had him killed, right?"

"Absolutely," James says. "That has to be right."

"What about the lack of any documentation? Aren't you bothered by the fact that there doesn't appear to be any contemporaneous documentation that Camarena found out anything about the CIA, or even mentioned the CIA?"

"I'm beyond bothered," James says. "In the mounds of documents we have gone through, the only semi-direct reference I can find is an allegation of a late 1984 meeting in Phoenix, with attendees including Camarena and Plumlee, where Plumlee claims Camarena talked about the CIA-Contra connection. But as we know, there is nothing to show Camarena was in Phoenix in late 1984. No travel requests or documents. No reports. No one from the office, including his partner the last few months of '84, remembers such a trip. And Kuykendall has said it absolutely did not happen."

Erica frantically ruffles through a stack of documents, talking as she searches.

"Wait, wait, wait. There is more than that. There is Plumlee's article from the *San Diego Weekly Reader,* and then are two stories by a reporter—Conroy, I think—that I just came across the other day."

She pulls two documents from the stack on her lap.

"Here. Right here. October 27th and December 7, 2013, the first from Bill Conroy, and the other, my mistake, seems to be from the *Salem News*. But in both, Plumlee references the 1984 Phoenix meeting and says it was attended by members of the Phoenix Organized Crime Task Force and the Arizona Tri-State Task Force."

"Pretty specific," James says.

"That was my thought, too. And both of those organizations apparently exist. Plumlee says that Camarena was at this meeting and was disturbed by the discussion of the links between the CIA and the traffickers, which may have included both drugs and guns."

"Wow." James whistles. "That could provide a CIA link."

"It could," Erica says. "And there is more. Plumlee says he told his CIA handler about Camarena's reaction, and was told Camarena would be handled."

"Which does not mean he would be kidnapped and killed by the CIA a few months later," James says.

"No, it does not. But are you ready for the most interesting part?"

"Hit me with it," James says. "I can take it."

"There is hearsay, or probably hearsay on top of hearsay, that Plumlee has said there were several more meetings of this type at the Oaxaca Café, that the DEA regularly participated, that Camarena was regularly there, and that another DEA agent often accompanied him. Care to guess who?"

"Berrellez?" James replies half-heartedly.

"That would be good, but this one is better. Kuykendall."

"No way!" James says. "Is there any evidence to support that assertion?"

"At this moment, I have found absolutely none. In all the research I've done, I've seen nothing else at all."

"So other than unverified hearsay," James says, "and Plumlee's statements—"

"Let me interject for a moment. One of these articles specifically mentions that Plumlee met with and provided information to Senator Hart and his security advisor Bill Holden, and Holden later said he had no reason not to believe Plumlee."

"I am certainly not suggesting Plumlee is lying," James

says. "But as we sit here now, we have no hard evidence that Camarena was aware of the CIA activities with the cartel, assuming they even existed. On top of that, as you know, no one from the Guadalajara office we know of recalls any mention of the CIA at all. None. Susie Lozano, the DEA office secretary, says she heard nearly all of the *talk* in the office, and never heard any of the agents talk about the CIA, or even mention the CIA, and none ever expressed any concern about the CIA. It's not just the Guadalajara office, either. None of the agents I've talked to who were working on Operation Padrino from the Mexico City office say that, at the time, they were not aware of any alleged CIA connection to the cartel. Not one DEA-6 report that anyone has seen from the time period says says anything at all about the CIA."

"On that cheery note," Erica says, "can I add one more related item that also makes me shake my head in bewilderment?"

"Why not," James replies.

"In addition to Berrellez saying Camarena was about to discover the CIA connection, in *The Last Narc,* he also says that Camarena was the *first one* to start tracing the money. That cannot possibly be correct, can it?"

"Of course it's not," James says. "It's well-documented that Operation Padrino had been working on the money angle with Félix for at least the two prior years, and probably longer than that. David Herrera has stated that he coordinated with Camarena in his efforts on Operation Padrino, which primarily dealt with the cocaine traffic between South America, Mexico, and the western United States. So Camarena knew of the efforts to trace the money, but no, he was not the first."

"That's what I thought," Erica says, "and I'm not a criminal investigator, but follow the money doesn't seem like a novel investigative theory that no one in the DEA would have thought of until Kiki got the idea. Hell, anyone who watched *All the President's Men* knew to follow the money."

James pauses for a moment. "If I recall correctly, doesn't Berrellez also say that Camarena had been able to freeze some of Caro's assets?"

"He does," Erica replies.

"That's another obviously false statement that apparently is believed by many, without questioning."

A dejected Erica looks away for a moment. "That's my point. The narrative has been told and accepted, willingly."

"The public can be gullible, I guess. Especially on issues such as the CIA."

"But then why do we keep going down this road?" Erica says. "Why put so much at risk? Does anyone care? Wouldn't it be easier to accept the CIA narrative and move forward on the kidnapping itself and what happened in Lope de Vega?"

"We know people care." James pauses with emotion. "Why do we keep going? Because the allegations are still out there being accepted as if they are the gospel brought from Mount Sinai. The truth needs to come out, whatever it is. The public deserves to know. Camarena's legacy deserves to be clear."

CHAPTER THIRTY

THE FOLLOWING EVENING, James sits on his sofa, a wine glass in front of him. The Lakers game plays on the television, but the sound is low, and James pays minimal attention.

He picks up his cell to answer a call from Erica.

"Hey, what's up."

"I have it," she says.

"You have what?"

"I might understand the Matta connection. Are you home?"

"I am."

"Good, because I'm out front. Pour me some wine, and I'll be right up."

Erica disconnects, and James does as instructed and texts the security desk to let her up, before he pours a second glass of wine while also filling his.

James turns off the television as he hears a knock on his door. He opens the door to find Erica bouncing with excitement.

"Damn, I'm happy you were home. I was driving home after a date—which was terrible, by the way—and it came to me."

"Sit down. Have a drink and then explain. Slowly." James leads her to the sofa and hands her a wine glass as they sit. "Here."

"I could use it. Thanks." Erica takes a drink and lets out a loud sigh. "Okay, I'm better. Now, let me explain."

"The floor is yours. Literally," James says, as Erica approaches the whiteboard.

"Okay. When looking at the question of whether the CIA had some involvement in Camarena's abduction, there are two schools of thought. What I'll call the 'No CIA Involvement,' and the 'Of Course CIA' contingent."

"No objections to that characterization," James says.

"In the No CIA camp, we have Kuykendall, the DEA agents in Mexico who never heard anything about the CIA being involved with the traffickers, people persuaded by an absence of contemporaneous documents, and those, like me, who are hung up on the lack of a concrete motivation. This group maybe summed up with the Kuykendall statement that, if the CIA had been involved, the DEA would have known about it because they had good informants and were good at their jobs.

"On the other side, we have those that talk matter-of-factly about the CIA's profound involvement, including Berrellez, Jordan, Tosh Plumlee, Harrison, and Berrellez's witnesses."

"I'm still with you," James says, as Erica takes a drink of wine.

"Now, what we have been doing is what everyone seems to have done, and asked which of these two camps was correct. Which of these two groups had the factually correct position? Who tells the true story?"

"You're telling me you know which story is right?" James says.

"No. Better than that. I'm telling you, they both are right."

"Both yes and no are correct," James replies. "Let's say I'm intrigued."

"One name, James. Matta. Matta can make both sides correct."

"I'm curious, but I need more wine." James starts to walk to the kitchen, and yells back to Erica still standing at the board, "Don't let me stop you."

"No, I'll wait. I want your full attention."

James returns with a bottle of wine and a corkscrew. He opens the bottle, fills both glasses, takes his and reclines into the sofa.

"You once again have my full and undivided attention," he says.

"Thank you. Let's go back to the No CIA group and start with the premise that, to the extent that the CIA was actively involved with the Contras in mid- to late 1984, most of that activity would have been centered on cocaine trafficking, mostly in Central America, largely as part of its alliance with Matta and SETCO. In addition, we know that Camarena had been focused more on the money end of things in his last few months, and working on Operation Padrino. It's entirely conceivable that Camarena stumbled onto some money that ran from the Matta–Félix connection to the CIA, with or without him knowing that he had found it."

Erica pauses to look at James, who has been playing careful attention.

"That scenario appears plausible," he says. "Except for the lack of evidence."

"Hold on. Work with me here."

"I'm here to help."

"Now, the flip side could also be true," Erica says. "If the CIA was involved in some with traffickers who had connections to the Guadalajara traffickers—"

"Such as, their involvement with Matta..."

"It's possible that Harrison heard something about it and told Berrellez," Erica continues. "It also is possible, if not likely, that some of the CIA personnel in Mexico knew some of the DEA agents there. Now this is the important part. It is eminently reasonable to accept both without accepting everything the trio of witnesses alleges."

"Like the presence of Félix Rodríguez at the interrogation?" James asks.

"Like the presence of Félix Rodríguez at the interrogations. But it seems to me, he is a huge red flag, either way.

"Okay, I think I need some clarification," James says.

"I haven't even started to really dig into Matta's connections with the CIA, but we know that SETCO was used by the US government to supply the anti-government Contra rebels in Nicaragua."

"Does the timing fit?" James says. "I've never really investigated, but I'd somehow come to assume the timelines don't match."

"You tell me," Erica replies. "According to the Kerry Committee report, SETCO was the principal company used by the Contras in Honduras to transport supplies and personnel for one of the earliest Contra groups, carrying food, uniforms, other military supplies, and at least a million rounds of ammunition for the Contras, from 1983 to 1985."

James sits in quietly for a moment, his gaze flitting over the material on the board. After another large drink of wine, he sits more upright.

"You are as brilliant as you are beautiful. I love it. The CIA and the DEA operated in the same areas, sometimes with the same people. That doesn't mean they were connected, and it certainly doesn't mean the CIA was willing to kill Camarena, irrespective of what he had found or was investigating."

CHAPTER THIRTY-ONE

JAMES SPENDS THE NEXT SEVERAL DAYS researching the Contras and their alleged connections to the CIA and Mexican drug traffickers.

The term "Contras" is the name commonly given to a variety of US-backed and funded right-wing rebel groups that, during the period from around 1979 to the early 1990s, opposed to the Marxist Sandinista government in Nicaragua. In 1987, virtually all contra organizations were united, at least nominally, into the Nicaraguan Resistance.

From the first days of the Sandinista government, the rebels received financial and military support from the United States. The US government, especially the Reagan administration, viewed the leftist Sandinistas as a threat to economic interests of American corporations in Nicaragua, and to national security because of its leftist ties to Cuba and the Soviet Union. In 1983, President Reagan proclaimed that "the defense of [the country's] southern frontier" was at stake. The United States continued to oppose the Sandinista government, even after the Sandinistas remained in power after elections in 1984.

In January 1982, Reagan signed the secret National Security Decision Directive 17 (NSDD-17), giving the CIA the authority to recruit and support the contras with $19 million in military aid.

In 1985, Congress cut off all funds for the Contras through passage of the Boland Amendment, which originally outlawed

US assistance to the Contras for the purpose of overthrowing the Nicaraguan government, but later was amended to forbid action by not only the Defense Department and the Central Intelligence Agency, but all US government agencies.

Over the years, there have been a number of allegations that the CIA was involved in Contra-related cocaine trafficking operations. Such allegations have been the subject of several hearings and investigations, including hearings and reports by both the US House of Representatives and the Senate, the Department of Justice, and the CIA's Office of the Inspector General.

It has been reported that as early as 1984, US officials began receiving reports of Contra cocaine trafficking. On March 16, 1986, the *San Francisco Examiner* published a report on the 1983 seizure of 430 pounds of cocaine from a Colombian freighter in San Francisco, and alleged that a cocaine ring in the San Francisco Bay Area helped finance the Contras.

An investigation by the US Senate Foreign Relations Committee's Subcommittee on Terrorism, Narcotics, and International Operations, chaired at the time by Senator John Kerry, held a series of hearings in 1987 and 1988, on drug cartels and drug money laundering in South and Central America and the Caribbean. The subcommittee's final report, issued in 1989, said that Contra drug links included involvement in narcotics trafficking by individuals associated with the Contra movement; participation of narcotics traffickers in Contra supply operations through business relationships with Contra organizations; provision of assistance to the Contras by narcotics traffickers, including cash, weapons, planes, pilots, air supply services and other materials, on a voluntary basis by the traffickers; payments to drug traffickers by the US State Department, of funds authorized by the Congress for humanitarian assistance to the Contras, in some cases, after the traffickers had been indicted by federal law enforcement agencies on drug charges, in others, while traffickers were under active investigation by these same agencies.

According to the report, the US State Department paid over $806,000 to four companies owned and operated by narcotics traffickers, to carry humanitarian assistance to the Contras.

James walks into Erica's office without either knocking or speaking, and sits in the chair across from her.

"No, please, by all means, come on in and be comfortable."

James says, "You know I monitor some sub-groups on Reddit, right?"

"Yes, you have mentioned it, and I think I told you to get a life."

"Well," James says, with trepidation, "I think someone there might by sending me information."

"Really. Like your secret caller and the message from the prison? Are you seeing smoke signals or messages in the clouds, too?"

James replies, "Or it's possible that someone is just posting a lot of information on the case, some of which is actually interesting."

"Call me crazy," Erica says, "but that sounds like more of a plausible explanation. Have you tried to communicate with him or her?"

"By the name, I'm pretty sure it's a him. I almost reached out, but then I thought that if I did, it might stop the flow of information. I think I'd rather keep looking at the information than know who is sending the info and why. At least for now."

"Makes sense," Erica replies.

"Want to see what was on the site last night?"

"Nah, I'm good." Erica giggles. "What the hell? Of course I do."

"For a smart, beautiful woman, sometimes you have the mouth of a crusty old sailor."

"Ignoring the offensive patriarchal nature of that comment, when you are smart and beautiful in a male-dominated industry, with an alpha male for a dad, it can be a bit of an equalizer. And now, it's just me. What about you Mister Boy Scout?"

"The first time you almost drop an F-bomb in court is enough to curb you of the habit," James says. "Mine was in front of the Ninth Circuit in Pasadena. It didn't slip, but it was close."

Erica laughs. "That would have been hysterical to watch."

"Anyway, look at this chain. It's easier to see on my phone." James hands over his iPhone.

Erica reads through the fifteen or so posts, each one presenting an article or report connecting the CIA to drug trafficking in the United States in the 1970s and 80s. After finishing scrolling through the documents, she hands the phone back to James with a look of incredulity.

"Okay, so the CIA had some bad actors," she says. "And they sold drugs in the US to make money to send to the Contras. None of that has ties to Camarena."

"Agreed," James says. "But the guy posting the information sure thinks it does."

"Who cares. He's a nut job with too much time on his hands."

"A nut job who has uncovered a lot of information."

"That either of us, with a bit and effort, could have found," Erica says. "Hell, I'm pretty sure we have found most of it, even if we haven't dug deep into it."

"Isn't that the point. He spent the time to look. We haven't. Maybe he has found the link, but just doesn't want to share it?"

"I don't buy it." Erica shakes her head. "Plus, he's a belligerent little punk, and I don't like him."

"I don't like him either, but maybe we can use him."

CHAPTER THIRTY-TWO

FOR MANY YEARS, James has been well-aware of the allegations of a connection between the CIA, drug trafficking in the United States, and the Contras. In 1996, James had read, with great interest, a series of reports titled the "Dark Alliance" in *The Mercury News* of San Jose, California, by Gary Webb, which explored the origins of the crack-cocaine epidemic in America. In the series, Webb alleged that the Contra rebels played a key role in creating the crack trade, using the profits to fund their rebel activities in Nicaragua. Most explosively, Webb's series claimed that the CIA knew of, and protected, these Contra activities, and may even have directly facilitated and participated in the trafficking of crack-cocaine in America's inner cities.

Though there were reasons to question the journalistic rigor of Webb's series, it cast the public eye on the Contras and drug trafficking, and precipitated several governmental investigations. One such investigation, from the CIA's Inspector-General's Office, did not find support for the specific allegations in Webb's reports, but in late 1998, acknowledged that the agency had covered up Contra drug trafficking for more than a decade.

At the same time, it has been widely acknowledged that, in the early '80s, leading up to Camarena's murder, the Guadalajara Cartel operated with, or as if it had virtual impunity, both because of its deep connections within the DFS, and because it believed many of its activities secretly had been sanctioned by the CIA. It was reported that when Fonseca and his men were arrested in Puerto Vallarta, Fonseca told his men not to run because they all would be released when the CIA intervened on their behalf.

As best James has determined, the allegations of a CIA connection to Camarena originated in a series of events, or alleged events, involving Berrellez, Lawrence Harrison, and Dale Stinson, a DEA agent assigned to Mexico City, who worked on both Operation Padrino and Operation Leyenda. In his book, Berrellez alleges that, when he was getting ready to first interview Harrison, Stinson traveled from Mexico City to Los Angeles to observe the interview, and even more suspiciously, according to Berrellez, requested to speak with Harrison alone, prior to the interview. Finally, Berrellez asserts that when he was finally able to speak with Harrison, Harrison stated with certainty that Stinson was a CIA operative working within the DEA. Stinson, of course, categorically denies working with or for the CIA.

After looking into the Stinson connection more, James unearths a few more curiosities, none of which lead to any conclusions, but perplex and bother James, nevertheless.

First, Stinson was one of two witnesses at the Zuno I trial to identify one of the voices on the interrogation tapes as being Caro Quintero.

If, as a completely wild hypothetical, without any factual basis or credibility, James thought the CIA wanted to point the blame at the cartel, it would be helpful to have one of your own identify Caro as being one of the interrogators. This would even fit into some conjecture that Caro was *manipulated* into kidnapping Agent Camarena.

The bigger anomaly, though, related to Stinson's possible time in Guadalajara, is that Stinson has recounted that he went to Guadalajara in the fall of 1984 to fill in as a temporary agent while the office was short staffed. Stinson also said he was partnered with Kiki for a couple months, rode in the truck Kiki was going to the day he was abducted, and even had Thanksgiving dinner at Kiki's house in 1984, before returning to Mexico City in December. Stinson even describes a stakeout at the Guadalajara airport, where he was almost discovered by Caro himself. Stinson's description of his time in Guadalajara is detailed, vivid, natural, and bears the hallmarks of accuracy.

The problem confounding James is that Jaime Kuykendall, the resident agent in charge of the Guadalajara office at the time, has been adamant that Stinson was never assigned to the Guadalajara office, on a temporary basis or otherwise. It would have been easy for James to chalk the discrepancy up to faded memories of events occurred almost forty years ago, until Susan Lozano, the office secretary, also said she was certain that Agent Stinson was never a part of the Guadalajara office. James has walked through these facts over and over, trying to find a way to make them fit, but reluctantly concludes each time that they are the proverbial round peg and square hole.

Could one of them be wrong? Possibly, but Stinson can't be mistaken about a temporary assignment with Camarena, and it is hard to imagine Kuykendall not knowing who was assigned to his office for a few months.

James reaches out to a contact with a wealth of detailed information about the DEA in Mexico before and after the Camarena case, to see if he has any information that might reconcile this discrepancy. The source is well-known for loquaciousness, often answering a seemingly simple inquiry with several paragraphs of information. In response to this inquiry, however, the connection simply wrote, "I'm not sure. Let me think and get back to you."

Curiouser and curiouser, James muses, upon reading the email.

CHAPTER THIRTY-THREE

BOBBY'S SURVEILLANCE of the Los Angeles building has revealed an unusual pattern— Speer parks in the surface lot one block down the street, and enters the building on Tuesday and Thursday mornings at 9:00 a.m., leaves again at 11:00 a.m., and travels directly to the CIA office building. Having confirmed this pattern for four weeks, James, Erica, and Bobby intend to use that routine to their benefit.

On a Tuesday morning, the three arrive in downtown Los Angeles at 8:30 a.m., having devised and confirmed their plan several times over the preceding weekend. Erica takes a position inside the lobby of the office building. Dressed in business attire, she blends in with the small army of office workers entering the building this morning.

As Erica was ensconced in the lobby, Bobby sets up surveillance near the parking lot used by Speer. Sitting in his Mercedes with tinted glass windows, he is obscure to those outside, but has a clear view of the lot.

At five minutes to 9:00, Bobby comes to attention as Speer's silver Range Rover pulls into the parking lot and occupies one of the few open spots. Speer climbs out, brief case in hand, pays at the central kiosk, and starts toward the building.

Bobby texts Erica that Speer is on his way. As Erica sees Speer approach, she times her entry into the revolving door to be slightly ahead of Speer from the other side. Exiting the revolving door, she bumps directly into Speer.

"Oh my god. I am so sorry," she says to a slightly stunned Speer.

"It was totally my fault," he replies. "I should pay more attention. Are you okay?"

"I'm fine. Thank you, and have a wonderful day."

Erica keeps walking as Speer exits the revolving door into the building. She glances over her shoulder to confirm Speer is getting on the elevator. Moments later, she sits in the passenger seat of Bobby's car.

"Any problems?"

"None. I stuck it on his suit jacket, just like we practiced."

"Perfect. If everything is working correctly, we should be able to see his location on my iPad."

Bobby shows Erica the tablet, and both watch as a small blip illuminates on the screen.

"And there he is," Bobby says.

Moments later, the icon goes dark.

A startled Erica says, "Oh no! Did it fall off?"

A cool and calm Bobby provides assurance. "I was expecting this. Somewhere within that office, there had to be security to block the signal."

"But not enough to locate the tracker?"

"I don't know, but we will find out in about two hours. Let's get some coffee."

Bobby and Erica take a short walk to a coffee shop, where they wait and talk and do other business until 10:45 a.m., when they head back to Bobby's car.

Shortly after returning to their surveillance positions, Bobby says, "There he is!" while showing Erica the iPad screen, with the revived icon reflecting Speer descending in the elevator. "Let's go."

Bobby drives to a location about a mile away. Shortly before a traffic light, he pulls to the side and parks, placing the tablet in front of both he and Erica. Soon, the screen shows the Speer icon moving rapidly.

"He is in his car and heading our way." Bobby watches the

screen and the traffic light, knowing optimal timing is key.

Revving the engine, he waits patiently.

"Now." Bobby pulls black Mercedes into traffic at the perfect moment—in front of Speer's Range Rover and stuck at a red light.

Soon, the light turns green, but Bobby does not move. Speer honks from behind, and Bobby opens his window and gestures to reflect car issues. Waiting a bit longer, and relying on the midday LA traffic to keep Speer behind him, Bobby remains in place until the light turns red again. This time, though, Bobby hops out of his car and jogs back to talk to Speer, who rolls down his car window as Bobby approaches.

"Car troubles?"

"Not exactly." Bobby pulls an envelope from his sport coat pocket and hands it to Speer. "This is for you."

Bobby turns and runs back to his car. He guns the engine and makes a turn into traffic, leaving Speer stranded at the light.

"Okay, so now..." Erica says, thankful that Bobby's maneuver didn't result in a traffic calamity.

"Now we go to the park and wait. The note in the envelope instructs Speer to be at the park at 11:15—enough time for him to make his drop at the CIA, but not enough time to get reinforcements. Hopefully."

"Hopefully?" Erica says. "I'll be the sitting duck!"

"Would I do that to you? I have people at the park. We will know if anything is amiss."

"You know I trust you, Bobby."

"Besides," he says, "from what little we know about Speer, I doubt he is quivering in fear right now. But he must be perplexed."

After pulling into the park, Bobby drives to a somewhat secluded spot with a view of the central fountain.

"As soon as we see him move in this direction," he says, "you'll take your spot by the fountain, with your earbuds in, facing away from the parking lot. We don't want him to see you until you turn around in front of him."

The two sit in silence for a few minutes, until the monitor indicates Speer is proceeding toward the park. Bobby makes a call on the car's speakers.

"Yes, sir?"

"Any unusual activity? Bobby says.

"None. Nothing at all. Quiet as can be."

"Are you sure?"

"Positive."

"Good. Stay in position until it goes down." Bobby hangs up and turns his attention back to Erica. "You're up."

Erica steps out of the car with shaking legs. Before shutting the door, she leans back in and emits a nervous laugh.

"Please don't leave."

Erica shuts the door and walks the twenty yards to the fountain at the park's center. As instructed, she keeps her back turned to the parking lot. Soon, Bobby speaks into her earbud.

"He's here."

Erica tenses and takes a deep breath, reminding herself that Bobby is a pro, and she is well-protected.

"He is walking toward you now. Don't turn around until I say."

The seconds drag interminably as Erica waits, unable to observe anything happening behind her.

Suddenly, Bobby's voice says, "Turn."

Speaking as she turns, with a warm smile forced upon her face, Erica sees Speer a few feet away.

"Nice to see you again, Mister Speer."

Speer looks into Erica's eyes. "You? What the hell?"

"Relax, Tim. It's all good. I have one more instruction for you. Café Mazatlán. Fifteen minutes. The booth in the far back right corner. There will be a man in a blue plaid sports coat."

"Do you think I'm stupid?" Speer says. "I'm not going to walk into a setup."

"Setup? Who said anything about a setup, Tim? He just wants to talk."

"I'm not going." Speer turns to walk away.

"Your choice, Tim. And your loss. I assume, then, you won't object to having your picture on the front page of the *Times* in the morning? CIA domestic activities and all. Which is your better side? Left or right?"

As the last words leave her lips, Erica strolls back to Bobby's car, hoping Speer doesn't grab her.

"He's not moving," Bobby whispers into her ear.

Erica reaches the car, and before she opens the door, she looks back and shouts to Speer.

"Mister Speer. You really should go. It will be informative. Besides, the food is exceptional. I recommend the sopes."

Erica hops into the car, shuts the door, and smiles at Bobby.

"Damn, girl, you are good!" Bobby races away from the park.

A few miles away, James sits in the Café Mazatlán booth, wearing his lucky blue sports coat, waiting patiently. Soon, he sees a text from Bobby. "He'll be walking into the Café in 30 seconds."

James sits up and waits, more anxious than nervous.

Suddenly, Speer's voice comes from behind as he walks toward the booth.

"I don't know who you are or who you think you are messing with?"

He reaches the booth, and James turns to look at a taken aback Speer.

"Butler?"

"It sucks when things aren't as they appear. Doesn't it, Tim?"

CHAPTER THIRTY-FOUR

"ND NOW THE TRUTH COMES OUT." Speer sits in the booth across from James.

"Some of the truth, at least," James retorts. "I have lots of questions."

Before Speer can answer, the conversation is interrupted by the waitress handing them menus and asking for drink orders.

"I think a house margarita is in order," Speer says.

"Two, please," James says to the waitress.

"A pitcher would be cheaper," she tells him.

"What the hell," James replies, before she leaves.

"Why all of the Thomas Crown subterfuge, James?"

"Frankly, I wanted to have an honest conversation with you, and I didn't think marching into your office and saying, 'I know you still work with the CIA,' was going to change your position. I needed to get your attention in a way that let you know what we know."

"Mission accomplished there," Speer says. "But before we get too far, I have to tell you, as I have before, if you are looking for the puzzle key that makes all the parts fit together and paints a clear picture, you are going to be disappointed. I don't think it exists. I certainly don't have it."

"In your office," James says, "you told me there was not a truth, which I believe is correct. But I think there are untruths out there that need to be exposed. I also note the irony of you saying anything about the truth when you lied to me about almost everything."

"I didn't lie about everything," Speer says.

"Please!"

"Okay," a chagrined Speer replies. "I admittedly was less than forthcoming, but most of what I told you was accurate."

The semantic debate is mercifully interrupted by the waitress returning with the pitcher of margaritas and two glasses, both of which she fills about two-thirds full. After ash asks for their orders, Speer nods for James to go first.

"You have the best sopes north of Tijuana. I'll have two. One carne asada, and one carnitas. And a side of guacamole and chips."

"And you, sir?"

"Since this is my first tim,e and my friend here seems to be experienced, I'll have the sopes, too. But make mine both chicken, please. And thank you."

As the waitress walks away, Speer says, "A lovely young lady recommended the sopes as well this morning, as she and her friend were jerking my chain across downtown Los Angeles."

"Yeah, sorry about that," James says.

"Truth be told, for a lawyer, it was pretty damn good."

"Let's go back to the cartel and the CIA."

"Let me stop you right there, James. I think we sort of alluded to this when you were in my office. At this time, there was no such thing as a cartel. Frankly, there wasn't even a real organization. At best, I think there was an alliance of sorts between the marijuana dealers—Caro and Fonseca—and the cocaine network of Gallardo and Matta."

"I agree with that," James says. "Though, it drives me crazy that so many people seem to acknowledge that, and still the perception of the big bad cartel, run like a corporation by Félix Gallardo, persists. I also know that the DEA compiled two reports proximate to the case—one about the Rafael Caro Quintero organization, and the other about the Félix Gallardo organization. The most striking part? The RCQ memo barely mentions Félix, and the Gallardo report goes into extensive detail about the web of connections and influence wielded by Félix. Though it identifies Caro, it hardly places Caro and Félix on the same level, nor does the report evidence Caro having a significant influence on Félix's network. That report also lists dozens and dozens of people with whom Félix was involved. The report says Félix Gallardo was responsible for an estimated hundred million dollars in income and expenses in 1984 and 1985. One more thing."

"What's that?" Speer says.

"Neither report mentions Fonseca in any material way. Now the two reports were written at different times, by different people, with differing agendas and audiences, but I think the point still stands— these guys weren't partners in any sense of the word. It also makes sense, since we know Félix got word to the DEA through a DFS agent, that the DEA should be looking into Caro and not him. It's also likely that Félix *arranged* for the confrontation at the airport with the DEA, DFS, and Caro."

James had read numerous reports indicating that the DEA had long been monitoring some of the communications of Félix and his associates in and around Guadalajara, and it is reasonable to assume that Félix either knew, or strongly suspected, the monitoring was taking place. One such report stated that, on the morning of February 9th, the DEA intercepted a communication from Félix to an associate, instructing the associate to bring a large quantity of money to the airport because Félix was preparing to leave the country. But when the DEA agents arrived at the airport, Félix was nowhere to be found. Instead, Caro had a jet at the airport and was preparing to flee to Costa Rica.

Despite the protest of the DEA, the MFJP comandante, after speaking with Caro on the plane, told the DEA agents that Caro had DFS credentials and would be allowed to leave. The agents present that day reported that Caro stood at the door of the plane with a champagne bottle, and told the agents, "If you want to play, next time bring bigger toys."

Contrary to common portrayals, the DEA agents at the airport likely assumed the person on the plane was Caro, but did not know for sure, because no one in the DEA knew for certain what Caro looked like at the time. All the DEA had was a very old and blurry photo of Caro.

James assumed Speer was generally aware of these events.

"Though that latter incident might well have had more to do with getting the heat off of him," James says, "and even if Caro was a friend or business partner, Félix was willing to sacrifice him to save himself."

Speer nods in agreement. "The point being, tying the three together, or analyzing events based on a perception of coordinated activities and interests, presents a false narrative."

"Or at a minimum, a subject to distortion," James says.

"Perception bias in its simplest form."

"Right," James says. "Ascribing intent to Félix from an act by Caro is an illusory correlation. The conspiracy theorists who want to find meaning to support their conspiracy, find meaning because they are looking for it. This case sets up as a textbook example of confirmation bias. You find what you are looking for, whether it's there or not. And frankly, some of this is so bizarre, it sounds like a conspiracy."

James thinks for a moment while finishing off the margarita in front of him.

He continues. "I am also intrigued by the statements from the pilot who flew Caro to Costa Rica, saying that Caro was intent on getting into the cocaine side of the business because it was easier and more lucrative."

"Let me ask you this, Mister Butler. If we assume, for purposes of this discussion only, that the CIA was interested in using drug traffickers to sell drugs and funnel money to the Contras, or similar elements, which side of the industry do you expect that would look to."

"The cocaine side, of course," James replies. "Especially

since they had a relationship with Matta and SETCO."

"Fair enough," Speer says. "To start with, it's probably common knowledge that the CIA used the airstrip at the Veracruz ranch to move arms and people into Nicaragua and Honduras as part of the effort with the Contras."

"Pardon the interruption," James says. "But was there really a Rancho Veracruz? I know many people have mentioned or referred to it and accepted it as fact, but I also know there are former DEA agents who are convinced it never existed."

"As someone who was there," Speer smiles, "I can assure you it existed. Perhaps some of the confusion stems from its location near the town of Nautla, in the Mexican state of Veracruz, about a hundred fifty clicks north of the city of Veracruz."

"And it had an airfield big enough to land a C-130?" James says.

"As well as other large aircraft," Speer replies.

"Then why is it so hard to track down exactly where this field was?"

"I can't solve all of the complexities of life for you, James. But as I told you when we first met, there was no training of militants there. There was no cooperation with drug smuggling. I have no doubt the CIA used Matta and SETCO to help move things around in Central America, but all of that was really focused on the anti-Russia and anti-Cuban efforts. To the best of my knowledge, the CIA—at least, in the period prior to Camarena's murder—had no affiliation with, and provided no support to, the traffickers. At least, not on a systematic basis."

"I can buy that," James says. "And I can accept the focus of the CIA around that time. But why, then, when Fonseca and his men were being arrested in Puerto Vallarta, did Fonseca tell his men not to run because they would be released soon since the American government approved of their actions? Why did defense attorneys in Zuno I try to admit evidence that the US—that is, the CIA—had supported or endorsed their activities."

"I don't know, James. I really don't. Perhaps they took small actions by CIA officers in the field to imply larger authorization. But if there was greater support, where's the evidence?"

"That's where I end up, too," James says. "Somewhere, there would have to be at least one piece of paper, one memo, one note, saying the CIA backed Caro or Fonseca, or someone, in 1984 and early 1985."

"I agree with that. I can also say that you and Erica were right about one other thing."

"What's that?"

"These sopes are really good."

CHAPTER THIRTY-FIVE

WHILE JAMES AND SPEER ARE ENGROSSED in their conversation, Erica enters the restaurant and spots them in the back booth.

"I thought I should stop by and make sure you boys are playing nice together."

Upon hearing her voice, James stands and turns to greet Erica. Speer stands as well.

"Tim Speer, this beautiful lady is Erica Walsh."

Speer extends a hand. "Very nice to meet you, Miss Walsh. Again."

Erica slides into the booth, on the inside of James.

"So what have I missed?"

"Tim and I have had a lively discussion about the cartel and the CIA, and even delved into some basic psychology."

"Fascinating, I'm sure," Erica says. "Sorry I missed it."

"In fact," Speer says, "I think our conversation was starting to wind to a close."

"Well, then, before you go," Erica says, "can we talk about one issue that, though not directly CIA-related, has bothered me?"

"Why not," Speer replies.

"I continue to be fascinated by the so-called planning meetings. Ten meetings with all those notable attendees? Really?"

"I'm just the CIA guy here," Speer says. "So I'm probably not the right person to ask. Nor do I really have a good reason to opine. But since you asked, I'll tell you what I think. Didn't happen."

"Ooooh, interesting," Erica says. "All of them? Some of them?"

"All of them," Speer replies. "There were no meetings. Except, maybe one directly proximate to the abduction. First of all, planning what? The kidnappers picked him up on the street. All the traffickers knew where the consulate was. You and I could plan that in, I don't know, five minutes?"

James says, "I've always thought the depiction of them as *planning* meetings, rather than just *conspiracy* meetings, was problematic."

"Agreed," Speer says. "But even then, do you need—what did you say, Erica—ten meetings?"

"Someone once said to me that what the government describes as planning meetings, we would call happy hour," James says. "Traffickers get together. That's who they hang out with. When they are partying, isn't it inevitable that they talk about their drug businesses and things going right and wrong. The DEA was doing a good job of finding Caro's marijuana fields. If they were together and talking, of course they were also bitching about the damn DEA causing them problems. It's also likely they said something about finding out what agent or agents were causing them the most losses."

Erica says, "But would well-known public figures from Mexico City be in several of these meetings?"

"The question answers itself," Speer replies. "No way."

"Without going into too much detail," James says, "it is easy to poke substantial holes in the stories around several of these alleged meetings."

"Okay, I'll admit that since I'm convinced no one has all of the answers," Speer says, "can you give me an example or two of your *holes*?"

"Of course he can." Erica snickers.

"Let's start with the last one," James says. "Near the beginning of episode four of *The Last Narc*, Ramon Lira describes a meeting of what he called cartel leaders, the night before Camarena's kidnapping. There are several notable things about his description of the meeting that call its veracity into question.

"First, Lira makes it very clear that the meeting was the night before the kidnapping, and was held at a house on Hidalgo Avenue, owned by Caro Quintero. At the Zuno II trial, Lopez Romero testified to a meeting that occurred *just prior* to the kidnapping, but he does not say it was the night before, and he says the house was owned by Fonseca."

"So he got a small detail wrong," Speer says.

"But it's a small detail someone who was there would know," James says. "If you are a bodyguard for Fonseca, you'd know if Fonseca or Caro owned the house. It's a small detail someone trying to remember a lie would err on."

"Okay," Speer replies.

"Think of it this way," James continues. "Early in my career, I worked on a case where two partners were dissolving their partnership which owned and operated a very large, very famous Southern resort. One of the partners, our client, had been a silent partner for many years, while the other partner operated and really was the face of the resort. One of the allegations was that the managing partner had been running personal expenses through the resort for years. One of my favorite pieces of evidence was a set of timecards showing that the managing partner would send resort maintenance people to his mansion about twenty-five miles away, twice a year, to change all the clocks in the house when the time changed. Was it a huge item? Of course not. But it showed just how the partner had completely intertwined personal and business. It was a very powerful piece in the arbitration. Sometimes it's not the biggest or the flashiest item that makes the point the best."

"I can see that," Speer says. "I like that analogy."

"I think it is also interesting that Lopez identified twenty-five people present at the house, including traffickers and their security, but never mentions Lira."

"A curious omission," Erica says.

"In addition to omitting Lira, who says he was there, Lopez also did not identify Félix Rodríguez as being present. Nor did he mention any unidentified Cuban, or anyone working with the CIA. Both Lira and Lopez place Bartlett Diaz and General Gardoqui at this meeting, and then Camarena's interrogation the following day. Bartlett and Gardoqui were both widely known and recognizable. Is it reasonable to believe they could hang out in Guadalajara for two days, at least, without being identified? Where did they stay on the night of the sixth? Did they just camp out on a hide-a-bed in the guest room, waiting for the kidnapped DEA agent to arrive?"

"You certainly would think someone would have seen them," Erica says. "Could Bartlett have flown back and forth?"

"Doubtful," James replies. "His activities were regularly and routinely reported. It's not just this one meeting, either. Some Mexican press report public events with Bartlett Diaz in other cities in Mexico other than Guadalajara, conducting government business and having publicized meetings when he is alleged to have attended conspiracy meetings. On a similar note, an investigator explored the Las Americas Hotel when it was still standing, and he looked at the rooms and interviewed then-current and former employees. He submitted sworn statements that directly refute the claims of Godoy and Lopez in particular.

"As another example, Godoy describes a meeting at the hotel in a suite on the ground floor, consisting of a living room area and two bedrooms, with each room having a door to an outside patio. It is alleged that the suite was large enough for a meeting with at least twenty-nine different identified individuals, not to mention around twenty named bodyguards.

"Notably, the hotel was on a main thoroughfare, and a huge meeting, attended by well-known politicians, driven to the meeting in expensive cars, would have stuck out like the proverbial sore thumb. One more thing, the allegations of a large conspiracy meeting at the Las Americas Hotel must be false as well. Pictures and descriptions of the hotel, supported by sworn statements from hotel employees, reveal, to any reasonable person's satisfaction, that the descriptions of a large meeting simply could not have taken place there.

"Bartlett Diaz also was alleged to have been present at Lope de Vega on the date of the kidnapping—February 7th—and Lopez testified that he was definitely there from seven p.m. to eleven p.m. Putting aside for the moment that there are no reports of him coming in or out of the airport, and the concern about where he would stay, Bartlett's official calendar for that day included at least *nine significant meetings* in Mexico City, the last of which started at nine p.m. Investigators have verified that these meetings took place, and have obtained statements, letters, and other verification from figures such as the governor of Nuevo Leon, and a senator from Michoacan. Most significantly, Jose Maria Morfin Patraca, the official in the Secretariat of Government responsible for elections, whose meeting with Secretary Bartlett started at nine p.m., has verified that the meeting occurred as scheduled, and lasted between one and a half and two hours. There are many more glaring inconsistencies in the assertions against Bartlett, which directly call into question the veracity of the allegations made by, in particular, Godoy and Lopez Romero, as well as the motivation behind the allegations. Not to mention the due diligence of the prosecution." James sighs.

After he finishes, the table is silent for a moment, before Erica says, "One additional comment. If you chart out all of the alleged meetings—and I have—there is no internal consistency, on several key issues, such as whether or not the participants had identified Camarena as the DEA agent *causing them problems*. It's almost as if their stories were prepared in isolation."

"Doesn't the fact that they are different show that they weren't schooled," Speer says. "Not reading from a script?"

"That is a good question, Agent Speer. But I don't see how it helps the government's assertions when it is easy to show that their main witnesses are either liars, or too stupid to keep a story straight. The fact of the matter is that Lopez and Godoy don't tell the truth, and I think it is clear that they tell different stories at different times, based upon what their benefactor, the US government, in the persons of Berrellez and Medrano, told them to say at the time."

"I must say, James and Erica, it seems you have given me more information than I've given you."

"Maybe," James says. "But the important part is that the information essentially fits together and supports our narrative."

Erica flashes him a brief smile.

"That, my friend, is for you to decide," Speer says. "If you need me again, give me a call. It's easier that way." He looks at Erica, smiling. "Though, I wouldn't mind chasing you around town again."

"Thank you for being a good sport," Erica says, with a twinkle.

She and James wait in silence until Speer has left the restaurant.

"So?" Erica says.

"He has some interesting thoughts."

"Do they fit with the narrative?"

"I think so. But maybe not the exact narrative I had in mind."

CHAPTER THIRTY-SIX

AFTER *THE LAST NARC* WAS RELEASED and the allegations against Félix Rodríguez and Jaime Kuykendall aired, Kuykendall filed a federal court defamation action against Amazon Studios, Berrellez, the director, Tiller Russell, and others.

Rodríguez, on the other hand, aside from a few statements of protest, has remained mostly silent, and he has not joined Kuykendall in pursuing litigation against those behind the production. James concludes that Rodríguez's history holds a key to his motivations, and does not support the allegations of Rodríguez's involvement in the Camarena abduction.

Félix Ismael Rodríguez Mendigutia was born on May 31, 1941, in Cuba, the son of a wealthy family of landowners, whose uncle was the minister of Public Works in the administration of dictator Fulgencio Batista. Rodríguez and his family fled to the United States after the overthrow of the Batista regime by Fidel Castro in 1959.

Rodríguez attended the Perkiomen School in Pennsylvania, but dropped out to join the Anti-Communist League of the Caribbean, which had been created by Dominican leader Rafael Trujillo, with the intention of ending communism in Cuba. That planned invasion of Cuba was a failure, and Rodríguez went back to Perkiomen. He graduated in June 1960, and moved to Miami with his grandparents. Miami—then, as now—was home to a large community of Cuban exiles.

In September 1960, Rodríguez joined a group of Cuban exiles in Guatemala called Brigade 2506, that received military training from the CIA.

Rodríguez participated in the Bay of Pigs invasion as a paramilitary operations officer with the CIA's Special Activities Division, and with CIA-backed Brigade 2506. A few weeks before the invasion, Rodríguez clandestinely entered Cuba, and he was able to gather critical intelligence for use in the planning and preparation of the ultimately doomed invasion.

In 1967, the CIA again recruited Rodríguez to train and head a team to hunt down Che Guevara, who was attempting to overthrow the US-backed government in Bolivia and replace it with a communist government. Upon tracking down and capturing Guevara, Rodríguez alleges he was given orders from the president of Bolivia, that Guevara should be summarily executed. Rodríguez, whose cover was that of a Bolivian Army major, repeated those orders, and later stated it was a Bolivian decision for Guevara to be killed. Rumor, however apocryphal, is that Rodríguez has Guevara's hands in mason jars in his home.

Rodríguez became a US citizen in 1969. During the Vietnam War, Rodríguez flew over three hundred helicopter missions and was shot down five times. In 1971, Rodríguez trained Provincial Reconnaissance Units, CIA-sponsored units working for the Phoenix Program.

There is extensive documentation of Rodríguez's ties to then-vice-president George H.W. Bush during the Iran–Contra affair from 1983 to 1988. In fact, it has been reported that, in 1985, Rodríguez was reporting personally to Vice President Bush's office about his logistical support for the Contras, from a base in El Salvador.

In 2005, Rodríguez oversaw the opening of the Bay of Pigs Museum and Library in Little Havana, Florida, and became the chairman of the board of directors.

According to *The Last Narc*, and the witnesses presented

therein, Rodríguez participated in the planning of the kidnapping of Camarena, and was personally involved in the agent's interrogation and torture, and perhaps even his murder. The alleged motive for the crime was that Camarena had supposedly discovered that the US government had collaborated with the Guadalajara Cartel in the importation and the transfer of drugs from Colombia through Mexico and into the United States to use the proceeds to sponsor the Contras in Nicaragua in its war against the Sandinista government. The witnesses describe specific alleged planning meetings, where they assert Rodríguez was present.

Rodríguez apparently denies having been in Mexico in 1984 or 1985, but in his 1996 memoir, former CIA pilot Terry Reed recalls meeting with Rodríguez in the Mexican state of Veracruz in August 1985.

Finally, of note is the assertion by the Mexican news magazine *Proceso,* that Rodríguez introduced Matta Ballesteros to the Guadalajara Cartel. The veracity of this alleged connection is dubious, though, because there are reports of a connection between Félix Gallardo and Matta well before Rodríguez went to Central America in support of the Contras.

James is working at his desk when his concertation is broken by a loud voice from just outside his office.

"I found it!"

"I'd be very excited about that, Billy, if I knew what *it* was."

Billy is William Garza, a law clerk at Castle, Smyth & Palmer. Billy grew up in the Irvine area, the only child of a successful neonatal neurosurgeon and a middle school teacher. Billy attended Pacific Academy, a prominent private school in Irvine, through high school. As both a scholar and a letterman in both baseball and cross country, Billy had many options for college, but chose to stay close to home and ursue degrees in economics and history at UCI. Surprising no one, he stayed at home to attend UCI's highly ranked and well-regarded law school. Billy was a summer associate at the firm last year and worked closely with James on several matters. Billy is in his third year of law school, and he works as a law clerk at the firm, part time, helping James and several other attorneys in the firm mostly with legal research. It is expected he will join the firm after he graduates and passes the bar.

He replies, "I found proof—or at least, near proof—that Félix Rodríguez was not in Mexico in early February 1985."

James sits up in his chair and smiles. "That is interesting. Sit down and let's talk about it."

"The curious part is that may be the least interesting thing I've unearthed about Rodríguez."

"Okay, Billy, I'm intrigued."

"For example, did you know Rodríguez was an original member of Operation 40?"

"You say that like I'm expected to know what Operation 40 is or was," James says.

"Operation 40 was a CIA-backed deep black ops group formed in 1960, after the Cuban Revolution. Ostensibly, it was comprised of Cuban exiles, with the intent of fermenting a regime change in Cuba. But there is a lot of evidence that it was much more than that, and had some well-known members."

"Do tell," James says.

"Among the members are our friend Rodríguez; Frank Sturgis, one of the Watergate burglars; Porter Goss, later head of the CIA under President George W. Bush; and Barry Seal."

"*American Made* Barry Seal?" James says.

"The very same Barry Seal," Billy replies.

American Made is a 2017 movie starring Tom Cruise, telling the story, or a story, about Barry Seal, who is depicted in the movie as a pilot for TWA who gets recruited by the CIA to do reconnaissance missions of Sandinista bases, and soon was a bag man for Panamanian dictator Manuel Noriega and the Medellin Cartel. Identifying Seal as a member of Operation 40 would be contrary to the narrative that Seal was a happy-go-lucky family man who made extra money smuggling Cuban cigars before he was recruited by the CIA.

"Fascinating," James says.

"It is. But it gets even better." Billy continues. "Allegedly, Operation 40 operated a training camp in the Florida Everglades in the early 1960s. Care to take a wild guess who else was seen there at that time?"

"I have no idea," James replies.

"One Lee Harvey Oswald."

"Really?"

"I can show you pictures." Billy hands James three pages with photographs that Billy has copied off Internet pages revealing these connections.

"Just when I thought his case couldn't get much weirder," James says.

"Do you want more?"

"Of course," James replies.

"A former CIA officer has claimed that she drove from Miami to Dallas a few days before the Kennedy assassination, with members of Operation 40, including Frank Sturgis and—"

"Oswald?" James says.

"Correct."

"Holy crap. Does any of this tie into Camarena?" James asks.

"Not directly. But it ties into the Iran–Contra affair, which is how Rodríguez ended up in Central America."

"Okay," James says, "let's not go too far into the weeds on the Kennedy assassination stuff unless it directly ties to the Contras, the cartel, or Camarena. Or unless it's really, really interesting."

"Got it," Billy replies.

"For now, I want to understand what exactly 'not directly' means. But first, let's back up to what you said when you came in. That you had *found it*."

"Which again ties into Iran–Contra," Billy says. "During the hearings, the connections between Bush Senior and his aides and Rodríguez were examined, and revealed two main things. First, an offshoot of Operation 40 was the Brigade 2506, which was a group of Cuban exiles that fought in the Bay of Pigs. Rodríguez was involved in Brigade 2506, and many of the first anti-Sandinista operatives in Central America were members of the long-since disbanded Brigade 2506. Second, in the mounds of papers surrounding the Iran–Contra investigations were various reports of meetings and travel, and other references to the locations of various people during the critical periods."

"You're burying the lead, kid," says James.

"Rodríguez wasn't in Guadalajara during the first week in February," Billy replies. "He was in Miami."

"If you'd like to keep your job," James says, "you'll tell me more without my asking."

"Let me give you the full picture first," Billy continues. "Félix was preparing to direct operations in support of the Contras from an air base in El Salvador, at the direction of the staff of the former head of the CIA, or the man himself— then-vice-president George H.W. Bush."

"Really?" James says.

"Bush's National Security Advisor, Donald Gregg, was a superior of Rodríguez in Vietnam, and clearly the person who brought Félix into the burgeoning Contra movement. There are several references to Rodríguez attending meetings in the White House, and with both Gregg and Bush."

"That's quite an alibi," James says, "and would explain why he hasn't shouted it to all of those accusers and their believers."

"I have a lot more on the Iran–Contra affair and Mister Rodríguez, if you'd like to hear it."

"I would, and I know someone else who would like to hear it as well." James picks up his phone and dials Erica's extension. "I'm here with Billy, who is about to tell us everything we want to know about the Iran–Contra affair, Félix Rodríguez, and their relation to the Camarena case. Come on down if you'd like to participate." He hangs up. "She'll be right down."

Moments later, Erica walks in and takes the guest chair next to Billy and across from James.

"Thanks for waiting for me."

"Of course. You did miss Billy here telling me he knows that Félix Rodríguez could not have been in Guadalajara on February 7, 1985. But he's about to give us the details."

"Interesting. Good work, Billy." Erica takes the chair next to him.

"Okay," Billy says. "But first I want to note that between the Kerry Committee report and the CIA inspector general's report, and a few miscellaneous committee hearings, there are literally tens of thousands of pages of reports, exhibits, documents, and the like, on the entirety of the efforts to fund and support the Contras and Félix Rodríguez figures prominently. Félix testified to the Kerry Committee, and though it might be most remembered by some for the contentious back-and-forth between Rodríguez and Kerry, Rodríguez really was pretty candid and talked a lot. Given the magic of modern data retrieval and analysis tools, I have been able to dig into these documents, which would have been nearly impossible if someone tried to just read it all."

"That's why you were the man for the task," James says. "What did you find?"

"For all intents and purposes, I found nothing. Nothing at all." Billy sits with a Cheshire cat grin, while James looks dumbfoundedly at Erica.

"I'll be honest, Billy," he says. "'Nothing' was not what I was hoping for."

"Unless 'nothing' really is something!" Billy replies.

"Damn. You two talk like each other," says an irritated Erica. "Billy, I'm going to give you about three seconds to tell us what you've found before I kick your ass."

"Since you put it that way, in all the testimony, all the reports, all the documents and exhibits, the amount of nothing is staggering. There is no mention of Mexico in any operational sense. No mention of Félix Rodríguez ever having gone to Mexico. No mention of any of the major traffickers. No mention of Camarena. Nothing about Mexican politicians.

"In his testimony, Félix comes across as a true believer—anti-Communist to the core. He proudly talks about his efforts in Central America, and many of his action in the years prior. But he never talks about Mexico. At all. There is nothing—and I mean nothing—at all."

"Wow." James whistles. "That is very intriguing. As I've said several times, in order to accept the idea that the CIA had Camarena killed because of what he knew, there first had to be something to know that was important enough to have a fellow agent tortured and killed."

"Something that significant would have fingerprints, wouldn't it? Erica says.

"One would think so." James looks back at Billy. "Is there anything else?"

"There is. Let's look at a few key dates on a timeline."

"Let's do that." Erica smiles.

Billy continues. "The record indicates that the first time Rodríguez is really brought into the fold, with respect to the issue of the Contras, is in late December 1984, and specifically, December 21st, when he meets with Oliver North at the White House. He had several meetings on the matter in late January 1985. He met with Vice President Bush on January 22nd, visited CIA headquarters in Langley on January 23rd. Then he had other CIA-arranged meetings on January 27th and January 30, 1985. The trail next finds Félix at an El

Salvador meeting with General Paul Gorman, the chief of the US Southern Command, on February 14, 1985."

"So there is a gap between January 30th and February 14th, and the Camarena kidnapping fits right in that window?" Erica's says, with dejection dripping from each word.

"That I can prove right now, yes," Billy replies. "But it's also consistent with things written by former DEA Agent Celerino Castillo. Agent Castillo provided a written statement for the House Permanent Select Committee on Intelligence that sharply criticizes the war on drugs, and the roles of the CIA and the DEA in Central and South America. In support of his stinging criticism, he details some of the actions of Rodríguez, and the timing matches up on when Félix was introduced to North and then to Bush. In addition, Castillo alleges the Félix went to the Ilopango airbase in El Salvador on January 24, 1985, 'to set up his base of operations.' Castillo makes no mention of any relationship between Rodríguez or any of the Mexican traffickers, and never places Rodríquez in Mexico. So I can't prove Félix wasn't there, but there is nothing I've found that even hints at it."

"This is excellent, Billy!" James stands from his desk chair and walks to the other side of the office to gaze out at the ocean. "You're right. In all the work Erica and I have done, we've found nothing to support the allegation that he was in Mexico, let alone at Lope de Vega, other than the word of Godoy, Lopez, and Lira. Of course, as we have discussed repeatedly, when initially debriefed in Los Angeles, Godoy and Lopez provided many new and dubious claims, duly noted in multi-page DEA-6 reports. Not one of those reports, though, even mentions Félix Rodríguez, a Cuban, or the CIA. Maybe we need to take the excellent information Billy has compiled and look at it differently."

"Go on," Erica says.

"Based on this timeline, in order to have Félix involved in the Camarena interrogation—and for the moment, I'm just looking at the interrogation—one would have to believe that someone who had been involved in the Contras mess in any way for only a month, with no operational history in Mexico, who was planning a major operation out of the base in El Salvador, was tasked with taking a diversion and going to Mexico to interrogate Camarena on something? And if he did, how would he have known when to be there, when it seems the decision to pick up Camarena was made that morning? And if he did get there, why would Caro, or whoever else was there, let him in? Did he just show up flashing CIA credentials? It makes no sense."

"Further to your point," Erica says, "if the CIA was allegedly involved in encouraging the abduction, as has been suggested, it would have been virtually impossible for Rodríguez to have been involved in those efforts. But he whisks in, interrogates Camarena, and then goes back to his real passion of ridding the world of communists? Please."

Billy says, "But I decided to look in other directions, and it turns out, there was a humanitarian aid project to take refugees, including wounded Nicaraguan rebels, to Miami for aid and medical treatment, headed by our friend Félix Rodríguez."

"Really?" Erica says.

"Really," Billy replies. "It was a big deal. The mayor of Miami was there. So was the press, including photographers, and I have found references to pictures of Félix at the hospital. The date of the photograph, you might ask. February 8, 1985."

"You could have started with that information!" James says.

"That would have spoiled all the fun," Billy replies.

"Do you have a copy of the picture?" James asks.

"I was expecting that question. I have searched everywhere, and I've come up empty. But the rumor on the web is that Félix has a copy of the newspaper article and photograph, and that it has been deemed legitimate by those that have seen it."

"So Félix really couldn't have been at the interrogation," James says.

"Not unless he had the ability to be in two places at once," Billy says. "The news articles say the event lasted from February 7th through the 9th."

"Not to be the naysayer," Erica says, "but if Félix has an alibi, and in *The Last Narc* he is accused of being at the interrogation, then why the hell wouldn't he have shown it to the world and told Berrellez and the Berrellez witnesses to kiss his ass."

"I thought of that, too, Erica," Billy replies, "and I have no reasonable explanation."

"Unless it opened the door to more questions about his Contra involvement," James says.

"That must be it," Erica replies. "Or it ought to be the theory we run with until we come up with a better one."

James thinks for a moment. "Billy, this is a great find, and it fits in nicely with what Erica and I have begun concluding about the CIA's alleged involvement. We know Plumlee says CIA operations were taking drugs from Rancho Búfalo or Rancho Veracruz to the United States, but those could have been wholly unrelated to the Contras. And if so...there would have been nothing for the CIA to be significantly concerned about. Iran–Contra conceivably could have taken down the Reagan administration, and certainly Bush, if it came out, so I get the logic of the argument. But not this." He pauses for a moment. "Do you know what else is a significant nothing?"

"Ignoring the tortured grammar, I'd love to know," Erica replies.

"If Camarena had found something out about a CIA link to the cartel, or something else CIA-related significant enough to get him killed, wouldn't he have written it down somewhere? A DEA-6, a memo, a letter, a notepad, his diary? But you know what the investigation revealed?"

"Nothing," Billy says. "But what about the telephone call with the Mexican reporter?"

Manuel Buendia was a Mexican reporter who was murdered in Mexico City on May 30, 1984," says James. "At the time of his murder, it is thought that he was investigating CIA activities in Mexico, including its relationship with the DFS. But it's also well-known that he was working on other high-profile and controversial stories.

"For goodness sake, not that," Erica says. "Buendia died almost a year before Camarena, and there is no record of what he and Camarena talked about. He could have been asking Kiki if he knew anything about a CIA connection, and Camarena could have said no."

"Even without speculation, though," James says, "Berrellez would like us to believe that a phone call a year earlier provides a definitive causal link between Buendia's investigation and the Camarena murder, which is ridiculous on its face. In fact, in a documentary on the Buendia case, Berrellez says with absolute certainty and conviction that the CIA was responsible for both murders, because both Buendia and Camarena had discovered the CIA's activities with the cartel in aid of the Contras. But I repeat for emphasis, while it is said in that same documentary that Berrellez acquired all Camarena's office papers and found Buendia's number in Camarena's folio, there is nothing else. Putting aside that there is no evidence Buendia found such a connection, not to mention the complete incredulity of the story that years after the fact, Berrellez found something in Camarena's folio that no other investigator had found, even if accepted that is the only thing Berrellez found. If Camarena had gotten into something sufficiently deep that it caused the CIA to arrange his abduction, there absolutely would have been more. I am convinced of it."

Erica says, "Which means we can dismiss the alleged CIA role in the abduction and murder?"

"I wouldn't say dismiss it," James replies. "But let's not spend much more time or effort on it unless we get some real, hard evidence."

"Works for me," Erica says. "And now I need to get back to work, while I still have my real job."

As Erica stands to leave, she thanks Billy for his good work, and tells James, as she walks out the door, "I'll check back in with you later today."

Billy starts to leave James's office right behind Erica, but he pauses, then turns to face James.

"Do you mind if I ask one other question?"

"Of course not," James replies, even as his attention returns to the computer screen in front of him. "What's on your mind?"

"I assume you've read *Eclipse of the Assassins*?" Billy says. "*Eclipse of the Assassins* is a book written the husband-and-wife team of Russell H. Bartley and Sylvia Erickson Bartley, which purports to be centered on the CIA's role in the Buendia assassination, but also deals with the Camarena case, and ends with a full-throated endorsement of Berrellez and his claims of CIA involvement.

"Yes, I've read it a couple times," James says. "Why?"

"I'm just curious. The authors raise some interesting questions about the lawyers in the Camarena case, most notably the lawyers for Bartlett Diaz and Zuno."

James turns his focus directly to Billy. "Let's be candid here, shall we. The authors excoriate both."

"What do you think?" Billy says. "Could they have done a better job, recognizing that only Zuno was tried, and that the Bartlett Diaz representation came later?"

"Interesting question," James replies. "First, let me say that it is always easy to look back and question the strategy and tactics of attorneys. Brian could come in here right now, pick up almost any case file, look through it, and wonder what the hell I'm doing or thinking in places. The same would be true if I looked at his cases. Everyone has different styles, methodologies, and thought processes. And as I've often said to you, there rarely is only one right way to do things. One of my mentors was fond of saying that painters use different brush strokes, but many make art.

"Second, keep in mind that Zuno's counsel was in the heat of a trial where documents were being produced, and witnesses disclosed, by the prosecution on a daily basis. Everything Zuno's team did or did not do during that time has to be viewed in that light, and unless someone has been in a case like that, their opinion matters little to me. Last, I have my own issues with the conclusions the authors draw."

"Such as?" Billy says.

James stands up and walks over to his bookshelf, where he pulls off a three-ring binder and tosses it to Billy.

"This is one of three binders compiled by Bartlett Diaz's counsel. Put together, any reasonable person would conclude there's substantial evidence that Bartlett simply could not have been involved in most, or all, of the meetings, as alleged by the Zuno II prosecution."

"I had no idea," Billy says.

"Of course you didn't. You'd have no reason to know. Nor would the people watching *The Last Narc*, because the filmmakers did not have the integrity to present alternatives or contrary facts. In the *Eclipse of the Assassins*, the authors come to a grand conclusion that the evidence of US complicity in the Camarena murder is persuasive, through what they called a 'judicious application of Occam's Razor.' With genuine respect for their efforts, I think William of Occam rolled over in his grave when those words were published. The leaps in logic are profound, and the Bartleys rely almost entirely on the unchecked allegations and assertions of Hector Berrellez, which discredits their conclusions in my mind.

"You also would have no reason to know that I've worked with Michael Lightfoot, who represented Bartlett, and I knew Zuno's lead counsel, Ed Medvene. I'd trust either of them over the opinions of almost any two journalists. What's more, I doubt that I am alone in that opinion."

James hits the speaker phone and dials three numbers. After one ring, the phone is answered.

"What's up?"

"Brian, I'm here with Billy, and I have a quick question. On a scale of one to ten, how would you rate the legal acumen and judgment of Michael Lightfoot."

"Somewhere around a ten," Brian says.

"What about Ed Medvene?"

"A twelve or so."

"That's what I thought. Thanks."

"Any time."

James hangs up and looks at Billy. "I have a lot of respect for many of the journalists who worked on this case and have unearthed amazing amounts of information, but I am going to trust the people I know—or knew—the facts we find, and our analysis. And frankly, I don't care even a little who disagrees with our facts, or who takes the hit if the allegations that have been spread wide and far turn out to be false."

CHAPTER THIRTY-SEVEN

JAMES HAD BEEN TRYING FOR WEEKS to contact Ernesto Payan, as former DEA agent who had worked under Berrellez on Operation Leyenda in Los Angeles. Finally, a returned text leads to a meeting with the long-since retired Payan at his home in Temecula, California.

Temecula is a town of around 125,000, in southwestern Riverside County, known for its wineries, hot air balloon festivals, golf courses, and world-class spas and resorts.

Payan said he lived in a retirement village trailer park on the north side of town, which James was relieved to see was only a few miles off the freeway. *Easy in, easy out,* he thought while driving to meet Payan.

As he turns into Yucca Estates, it become clear that the term "trailer park" did not apply. A beautifully landscaped area housing a collection of some of the finest mobile homes James has ever seen. Each home has its own yard, each impeccably maintained.

James parks in Payan's driveway and is met at the door as he starts up the steps.

After introductions, Payan points to his left. "Let's sit on the patio. It's cooler here."

To the left of the trailer is a beautiful stonework patio with a fire pit, chairs, and an awning with a ceiling fan. Large lilac bushes provide seclusion, add shade, and the scent from their flowers wafts through the air.

As the two men sit down, Payan leans to look directly at James.

"I want to repeat what I said in my text. I don't have a dog in this fight. I'm not out to get anyone. I like my quiet retirement. And frankly, I liked Hector most of the time. But I'll tell you what I know."

"I understand and appreciate that," James says. "Frankly, I have no agenda. I'm really just trying to understand. Hector has made some pretty amazing claims. Some of which, frankly, I think are false. And I'm trying to understand the motivation."

"Let me start with this," Payan says. "Hector was a pretty good investigator, but Hector wanted to be a famous investigator. In my mind, Hector became a paid mercenary who would say anything if it had the chance of making him rich and famous."

"Okay," James says. "That's certainly not inconsistent with anecdotes I've heard before. Does that pre-date *Drug Wars: The Camarena Story*?"

Drug Wars was an NBC mini-series directed by Michael Mann, based on Elaine Shannon's book *Desperados,* starring Steven Bauer, Treat Williams, and Craig T. Nelson, as a thinly fictionalized Jaime Kuykendall.

Payna replies, "I think Hector's desire to be more than just a DEA agent started well before that, but certainly was fueled by that filming and the events that followed. I once spoke with Elaine Shannon, and she said that, when she met Hector on the set of the mini-series, he told her, 'The next movie Michael Mann makes, it's going to be about me.'"

Payan's wife interrupts the conversation, bringing both men a tall glass of lemonade, before returning to the trailer.

James takes a long drink. "In his IMDB bio, Hector says he was the inspiration for the Ray Carson character, played by Treat Williams."

"Yes, I've seen that, too," Payan says. "We both know that is not accurate. The series involves events that occurred long before Hector had any involvement with Operation Leyenda. Everyone in the DEA knew that character was basically a composite of Bill Coonce, Matty Mahar, and maybe another person."

"Yes," James says. "I've also read where Treat Williams said he got the role, in part, because he was *not* a Hispanic actor."

"As I understand it," Payan says, "the DEA liaison on the show had invited Berrellez to come to the set to coach Steve Bauer how a buy-bust would be conducted. Hector told the story that he had concocted a fake undercover buy-bust, in which he played the undercover role, and had recruited other people to play the bad guys. Hector said that Bauer thought it was real. Apparently, Bauer was legitimately terrified, and Hector thought it was hysterical that Bauer bought it. He relished the whole process."

"He must have hated that the main DEA figure in the show was based on Kuykendall," James says.

"I know he recounted more than once," Payan replies, "how it was disgusting to see Jaime there at the Hollywood premier, getting all of the attention."

"I wonder if that has anything to do with his later claims against Jaime."

"Look, James." Payan motions to his surroundings. "I'm an old, retired agent. I'm not a psychologist. I don't want to try to guess why anyone has done anything. I told you I would tell you what I know. But that's it."

"Fair enough. I respect that." James takes a drink of the lemonade and ponders for a moment. "You know, Agent Payan, I think you have answered what I needed to know." He stands and finishes the glass of lemonade. "Please thank your wife for the hospitality."

"Are you sure there is nothing else?" Payan says. "Seems like you drove a long way for such a short discussion."

"No, sir, you were more helpful than you know, and I

really appreciate it." James extends his hand, and the men shake.

"There is one other thing I might mention," Payan says.

"What is that?"

"The allegations against Jaime Kuykendall are complete fiction."

"I've always thought that, too."

"No, Mister Butler. I know they are fiction, because the DEA had good information—I mean, *very* good information—that Caro was being scammed by a DFS agent into thinking he was paying off the DEA, when in fact, the DFS officer—I wish I could remember his name—was pocketing the money."

"That makes so much sense," James says. "Did Hector know that the DEA had that information?"

"He certainly should have known," Payan replies.

"Well, that is a fascinating piece of information to end on. Thank you again."

"Any time at all. And you have my email if you have any other questions."

James leaves the trailer park and is racing down the on ramp to I-15, toward his Irvine office. Once on the freeway, he presses the voice activation button on the steering wheel.

"Call Billy Work."

The phone dials the number, as instructed.

"Hi, James. How was the meeting?"

"It was fine. Nothing earth-shattering, but confirmation and some nuance."

"You love your nuance."

"Did you find anything on that issue I left for you?" James says.

"In that case," Billy says, "you may be interested in some news reports I found. In an article from October 16, 2013, in Progreso Weekly, former DEA agent and Berrellez supporter Phil Jordan is quoted as saying, 'The CIA ordered the kidnapping a torture of Kiki Camarena. And when they killed him, they made us believe it was Caro Quintero in order to cover up all the illegal things they were doing in Mexico.'"

"So?" James replies. "That's consistent with what he has been saying other places and on *The Last Narc*."

"Agreed," Billy says. "But here's what's interesting. Less than two months later, in an article in the *Costa Rica Tico Times*, Jordan takes a different posture. Reading directly from the article: 'We're not saying the CIA murdered Kiki Camarena, Jordan said. But the consensual relationship between the Godfathers of Mexico and the CIA that included drug trafficking contributed to Camarena's death,'" he said.

"That is interesting, and a good find," James says. "Thank you."

"What do you think it means?" Billy asks.

"At this point, I'm not sure. But as we've discussed many times before, knowing what someone did is only part of the story. Knowing why they did it gives the complete picture."

"Then I have one last thing to share," Billy says. "You know the whole story about Caro getting away after a confrontation at the Guadalajara airport, right?"

"I am familiar with the incident, yes."

"Well, I have a *FoxNews.com* report from October 10, 2013," Billy continues, "and there is one very similar in *USA Today* around the same time, where Hector describes the confrontation at the airport. Can I just read it to you?"

"Read away, Billy."

"Here is exactly what it says:

> Upon arrival, we were confronted by over fifty DFS agents pointing machine guns and shotguns at us—the DEA. They told us we were not going to take Caro Quintero," says Berrellez, recalling the standoff. "Well, Caro Quintero came to the plane door, waved a bottle of champagne at the DEA agents, and said, 'My children, next time, bring more guns. And laughed at us.'"

"Wow," James laughs aloud. "I don't even know where to start."

"Maybe with the fact that Sal Leyva testified at trial that there were eight gunmen," Billy says, "and admitted that when he first described the incident, there were five. But whether it was five or eight, it sure wasn't anywhere close to fifty."

"Good point," James replies. "Plus, since Leyva was once his partner, Hector had to know that fifty was an overstatement of exponential proportions. Since we are talking about Agent Leyva, it also is interesting that he testified, on direct examination by Medrano, that he had heard of Caro Quintero before the incident, but didn't know what he looked like, and that he didn't confirm that the man on the plane was Caro until the next day, when he saw a grainy old photo of Caro. No one at the airport knew for sure it was Caro, though the DEA agents suspected it was."

"How about the phrase, says Berrellez, recalling the standoff?"

"That's crazy, too," James replies. "Berrellez wasn't there. He was nowhere close at the time. Remember he took over Leyenda in January 1989, almost four years after the kidnapping. He is a percipient witness to virtually nothing."

"Do you remember the *LA Weekly* article with him on the cover?" Billy says.

"Sure. It's been a while since I read it, but I do remember it. Why?"

"Well, in the article," Billy says, "among other crazy things, it says Camarena led the raid on Rancho Búfalo, which they spell 'B-u-f-f-a-l-o,' like the animal."

"It was a common misperception," James replies.

"Yes, it was," Billy says. "But Hector *knew* it wasn't true. On page one-seventy-nine of his book, he says that Camarena was not part of either the discovery of, or raid on, Búfalo."

"Okay, meaning what? James says.

"If the article is about Berrellez, and he is on the cover,

and there are interviews with his three witnesses, wouldn't you assume he had an opportunity to review the article."

"I think that would be a safe assumption," James says.

"Then why would he allow such a factual assertion to be publicized and allow the false narrative to be further disseminated?"

"That is another excellent question," James replies, "for which I do not have an answer. Good work, Billy."

"Thanks. That means a lot. Anything else you need from me?"

"Nope," James says. "Go back to working for clients that pay us, and I'll do the same on my drive back. See you in a bit. And thanks."

James hangs up and turns on the car radio for background noise as he thinks. *Great job, James. You've spent weeks to get absolutely nowhere.*

CHAPTER THIRTY-EIGHT

JAMES HAD A LONG-STANDING THOUGHT that the common axiom that you can't prove a negative is both misleading and poorly constructed. In fact, James often said he could prove with reasonable exactitude that there was not a purple kangaroo sitting on the coffee table on Erica's porch, where he sits pondering his next move.

In mathematics, Euclid's theorem proves there is no largest prime number, for example. Nevertheless, James wonders how he can prove that the CIA had no role in the tragic events that befell Agent Camarena?

"Maybe that is the point," James says, out of the blue, as Erica sits across from him, sipping a homemade margarita.

"I'd love to comment, but for the fact that I have no idea what you are talking about," she says.

"I've been sitting here thinking that it will be impossible to prove that the CIA was not involved in Camarena's abduction," James says. "I mean, we will never be able to say with absolute certainty that it did not happen."

"But we know it didn't," Erica replies, "because the vast balance of the information indicates it did not."

"Which is the point precisely," James says. "It cannot be proven with absolute certainty that magic unicorns don't exist. But we can prove they did not, beyond any plausible doubt, and that is all this, or any, investigation should require."

"Meaning that if we combine all the evidence we have compiled," Erica says, "with respect to the CIA, Matta, and Félix Rodríguez, we can disprove the claims of CIA involvement to such an academically significant degree that it cannot be questioned reasonably?"

"Right," James replies. "And you said it perfectly. We will never be able to convince everyone. Some people still believe the world is flat, or that dinosaurs didn't exist. But that's never been my goal, to convince everyone."

"You wanted to know the truth, for you. That's why I wanted to help you. So the question for you, my dear James, is are you there? Do you have enough information to make a conclusion?"

James ponders for a moment in silence. Erica fills their glasses from the margarita pitcher, emptying it.

"You contemplate while I refill."

Erica moves to the kitchen while James peers out into the ocean in front of him. Suddenly, he leaps to his feet, yelling to Erica as he walks in from the porch.

"Can I use your laptop?" James repeats himself, trying to be heard over the blender crushing tequila-soaked ice.

On his third effort, Erica finally hears him as she switches off the blender.

"Sure," she replies. "It's on my nightstand. It's plugged in, so just unplug it and go. It's connected to Wi-Fi."

James rushes to Erica's bedroom. He unplugs the laptop and returns to his seat on the patio, joining Erica, who had returned with a fresh pitcher of drinks.

"What's the urgency?" she says.

"The clown on Voat. Let's see if he really has anything."

James types away on the laptop as Erica slides her chair next to him. Once on the website, he opens a chat that he had engaged in with user WiseGuy420.

I'm still at a loss to understand how you think the CIA was involved in the Camarena murder, other than blindly accepting the word of the three amigos in The Last Narc.

"This won't take long," James tells Erica.

As predicted, the response is received in less than ten minutes. Rather than a direct response, WiseGuy420 sends a list of ten or so links to various articles and reports linking the CIA to drug trafficking in the United States, and the funds from those activities going to finance the Contras in Nicaragua.

James replies immediately. "I will agree, for these purposes, that the CIA was engaged in drug dealing, and that it worked with drug traffickers. I'll also agree that the CIA skirted federal law by working with and providing illicit financing to the Contras. But that doesn't say anything about its alleged role in the Camarena murder.

"He is going to get petulant very soon," James predicts to Erica.

The snarky reply is almost immediate. "Can't you read? The CIA worked with SETCO for years. SETCO was owned by Matta. The cartel leaders had DFS credentials, and there were DFS officers involved in the kidnapping and interrogation of Camarena. Everyone knows the CIA started and controlled the DFS."

James smiles at Erica. "Told you."

He drafts a quick response. "Surely you are not conflating every action of the DFS and everyone in the DFS as being a CIA action? Other than the three bozos, who directly provided evidence of the CIA being involved in Camarena's murder?"

WiseGuy420 replies, "Lawrence Victor Harrison and Phil Jordan."

"That's funny," James writes. "Harrison says the CIA was involved with the cartel, but even Berrellez's book doesn't say that Harrison provided any real evidence of a connection to Camarena. Jordan has no firsthand knowledge of anything CIA-related, and the claim that Camarena said the CIA was following him is BS. At most, Camarena said that the DFS followed him. Contrary to perception, the DFS and the CIA were not joined at the hip, and the average DFS officer was not working for, or even with, the CIA."

WiseGuy420 replies, "Félix told people his operation was protected because it was endorsed by the US government. Fonseca said the same thing when he was arrested."

James smiles while responding, having confirmed for his own satisfaction that WiseGuy420 has nothing new to offer. "They believed their drug trafficking was protected. No one has ever alleged that they said that killing Camarena was protected by the US government. In fact, Fonseca's alleged response when finding out Camarena was dead indicates just the opposite. Do you really not have anything new or original?"

WiseGuy420 replies in a rage. "You either are a DEA-lover or a complete moron. It's all there? Why would the judge in the federal criminal trials prohibit the defense from discussing the CIA connection? Because he got the case specifically to hide the government's secrets. He was a co-conspirator."

"Well, that's a new one," James says aloud, reading the allegations against Judge Rafeedie.

Edward Rafeedie was a United States District Court Judge in the Central District of California, commissioned after confirmation by the United States Senate on September 24, 1982. He went on Senior status on January 6, 1996 and served in that role until his death on March 25, 2008. Prior to becoming a federal judge, Rafeedie was a California Superior Court Judge for eleven years, where he had a reputation for the efficient management of trials and his reticence to grant continuances, earning him the nickname "Speedie Rafeedie."

Judge Rafeedie presided over the three Camarena criminal trials in the US. His judicial temperament, before and during these trials, was often difficult and irascible, but fair and impartial. One attorney who had practiced before him, said of Rafeedie: "He could be a mean son of a bitch, but he was a mean son of a bitch to everyone."

In the years since the last Camarena trial in 1992, there has been no evidence of any kind that Rafeedie was involved in any type of coverup of the CIA's activities, or otherwise. Even attorneys who argued for the admission of evidence regarding the CIA scoffed at the occasional suggestion that Rafeedie's decisions were less than forthright, or that he somehow had ulterior motivations.

James considers his move for a moment. "I've had about enough of this," he says, and writes, "The judge's rulings were legally correct. Notice that none were ever overturned on appeal. Hell, even the attorneys that tried to introduce the CIA evidence don't think he was a bad judge, and certainly not a corrupt judge. Can you point to one document, any document, anywhere at all, that directly connects the CIA to Camarena's abduction or interrogation?"

The reply from WiseGuy420 is as James expects. "If you can't see it, you are blind and stupid, and part of the coverup."

"Question answered. Thank you. Enjoy your delusions." James shuts the laptop.

"It's getting chilly. Can we move this inside?" Erica says, alerting the oblivious James to the setting sun.

"Of course," he replies. "Let me help you."

The two grab the pitcher, glasses, and laptop, and move inside. James shuts the French doors behind them and watches Erica walk to the kitchen.

"I always forget how short you are when you don't have your heels on."

"I'm not short. I'm five-six, and don't you forget it."

"You're right. You're not short. It's just that in heels, you are—"

"If you say huge," Erica replies, "I swear I'll punch you."

"No. I was going to say, even prettier."

"Nice try, Butler, but I ain't buying what you're selling. What did that the discourse with your friend prove to you?"

"You've seen some of the things he has sent before," James replies. "He, or someone he works with, has spent a lot of time going through the Contra investigations, the Webb articles, and various other sources. If there was something out there that connected the CIA and Camarena, I honestly believe he, or one of his compatriots, would have found it."

"Would he share it with you?" Erica asks.

"You saw his tone," James says. "If he has something where he could show it and say, 'Here, I told you, you dumb bastard,' he would have done it. Hell, I'd love to see some real, solid evidence that would give us answers to some of the questions we've been asking. I don't even care what the evidence said, or where it led. Just something solid and real. Is that really too much to ask for?"

Erica lays her head on the pillow, leaning against the arm of her sofa.

"Are you tired?" James says.

"A little. But keep talking." Erica pulls the pillow from the arm cuddling it as she extends her legs onto the length of the sofa.

"I'll clean up as I talk," James calls from the kitchen.

"Leave it. I can get it in the morning." Erica moves into a fully relaxed, fetal position on the sofa.

"Nonsense," James replies.

He takes the pitcher and the glasses into the kitchen, where he finds the remnants of the fruit, cheese and crackers from lunch, and the blender. He opens the dishwasher and rinses the dishes as he talks.

"Would I be completely astounded if we found out something that provided that CIA–Camarena link? Not really. But we've found nothing. And I think the three witnesses screwed themselves by providing dates for Félix Rodríguez that simply don't match up. Plus, remember in the interrogation tapes, Camarena mentions Veracruz, and the interrogators don't bite at all, but instead they turn the focus back to Búfalo. If the CIA was involved in the interrogation, wouldn't it stand to reason that they would be interested in what Camarena knew about Veracruz?"

Erica yawns and talks. "They would jump all over it, I would expect. So what do you think?"

"I think the CIA was in Central America and Mexico," James says. "But they were, as Kuykendall says in his book, focused on the Cubans and the Russians, or the Contras. They funded the Contras any way they could once the Boland Amendment went into effect. They used the traffickers when it benefitted them. But there is nothing that even hints that Camarena was *on to* them, or that the CIA would be at all worried about him. And maybe I'm still a bit naïve, but there had to have been a lot more for them to have him brutalized."

James searches the kitchen for a sponge to wipe down the counter.

"Here's the best way I can put it," he continues. "Gary Webb wrote a whole series on the links between the CIA and drug trafficking, and traced nothing back to Camarena. From the Iran–Contra affair, there are tens of thousands of pages of reports, and testimony, with nothing linking any of it to Camarena. We should not forget that Kerry was leading the charge, and he would have loved to lay Camarena's fate at the feet of Reagan and Bush. Even though, the Kerry Committee and its report have been critiqued for focusing on the questioning of high officials rather than the foot soldiers who worked for Oliver North in efforts to supply the Contras, and who would know better the lengths to which North and his network went to aid the Contras. I suppose we also should not avoid the reality that any real investigation and review of the CIA would reveal too many bad things done under the watch of, or at the direction of, both parties, and so maybe both had an incentive not to go in certain directions. If, as we've learned, some of the same figures trace all the way back to the days right after the Cuban Revolution, it wouldn't be too much of a logical leap to assume they have enough damning information to keep the lid on the cookie jar tight from the prying eyes of anyone of either party.

"But however I look at it, I cannot discount that, for four years after the murder, not one DEA agent or report mentions the CIA, a connection between Camarena and the CIA, or a mysterious Cuban—not Mexican, but Cuban— operative being involved. It's not until the great Hector Berrellez becomes involved that all the cards fall into place and the CIA connection is revealed. Please. Not even to mention that there is no evidence the CIA did anything to try to determine what Camarena knew prior to his abduction. If, just for the sake of argument, the CIA was involved, and if they were concerned about what Camarena knew, would their first step to have a fellow agent kidnapped, tortured, and killed, bringing dozens of DEA and FBI agents into Mexico to investigate? To ask the question is to answer it."

James finishes wiping down the counter, places the towel on the door handle of the refrigerator, and walks back to the living room to find Erica sound asleep on the sofa.

James shakes his head. Damn, that was a great recap. You would have liked it.

He looks around before retrieving a light blanket from the foot of Erica's bed. Gently removes Erica's white deck shoes and places the blanket over her. He turns out the living room lights, leaving a kitchen light on for some illumination, before kissing Erica tenderly on the cheek.

"Good night, beautiful lady. Sleep well."

James shuts the door quietly and uses the spare key kept in a hidden compartment in the large ceramic vase on the porch to lock the door. He strolls down the sidewalk, to his car parked two blocks down the street. Looking out into the night sky, he has a sense of satisfaction. Definitely not closure, but satisfaction.

Before he gets too comfortable, though, a gust of the breeze off the ocean reminds James of the work still to be done. *Don't get cocky. There still are many questions to be answered.*

CHAPTER THIRTY-NINE

THE NEXT MORNING, James rises early and dresses in his running gear. He frequently uses a long run along the Newport Beach coastline to clear his head.

Once back home, he calls Erica.

"I went for a long run this morning, and was going back over everything we had looked at and analyzed. I'm thinking there's one thing in particular we might have given short shrift to."

"The interrogation tapes?" Erica yawns.

"Yeah. How did you know?"

"Last night, I remembered that in my first telephone call with Kuykendall, he told me he thought the answers to many of the questions around the case can be found in the interrogation tapes."

"That's interesting," James says. "I was thinking we probably can extract some relevant information through a study of the tapes. I think some statements from *The Last Narc* also can be disproven through the tapes themselves."

"Do you want to get together and dissect them?" Erica says.

"I really do," James replies. "I know it's the weekend, but the big screen in the office would be really useful."

"I'll be there, but I need some time to pull myself together," replies a perkier Erica. "Can we say, one or one-thirty?"

"Let's say one-thirty. I'll meet you there. And thanks."

⊕

One of the most intriguing, and even baffling, aspects of the Camarena case is the existence of recordings of the interrogation of Agent Camarena. At an undetermined time after Camarena's body was recovered, the CIA learned that the Mexican government was in possession of audio tapes that apparently were recordings of some, or all, of Camarena's interrogation. In or around April 1985, the CIA informed some in the DEA's administration about the existence of these tapes. Jaime Kuykendall says he became aware of their existence on April 16, 1985, in a phone call from Walter White, then the assistant agent in charge of the DEA's office in Mexico City.

According to Kuykendall, a note from the CIA indicated that the person being interrogated had referred to a Jesús Ramirez, which Kuykendall knew was an alias for a confidential informant who had worked with both Kuykendall and Camarena, and it was an alias known to no one else. The voice on the recording had to have been Agent Camarena's. As described by Kuykendall, the interrogators had Mexican accents, and the interrogation was conducted entirely in Spanish.

The CIA received a forty-three-page transcript of the interrogation a few months later, but it was not until the end of August 1985, that the DEA received copies of the tapes from the Mexican government.

The tapes were plain audio cassettes, numbered five in total, and were identified as "copias," or copies. Copia One was a short recording of radio traffic recorded from the DEA radio in Guadalajara. Copias Two and Four were recordings of Agent Camarena's interrogation. Copia Three was the interrogation of a different person. Copia Five, which was nearly unintelligible, was later determined to be another copy of Copia Four. Most curiously, though, the interrogation transcript originally provided to the CIA did *not* correspond to any of these five tapes.

James gets to the office well before 1:30, to be prepared before Erica arrives. The computer is on the big screen, and he pulls up the transcripts of the tapes up for easy viewing. He places the rolling white board to the side of the screen and lists out categories:

- RCQ
- Félix Rodríguez
- Zavala
- Comandante
- Why?

"I should have guessed you'd already be here." Erica enters the conference room.

"Holy crap, you scared me to death!" James says.

"Deep in thought again?"

"I don't think I'd go that far, but I do have things ready for us."

"Great, let's get to work," Erica says.

"I have the transcripts—or one of them—loaded on the computer, but I'm not really sure how much help they'll be."

The interrogation tapes are known to have been transcribed a few times, and there are differences in the transcriptions. It is apparent the recordings were stopped and started, likely omitting portions of the interrogations when the torture of Agent Camarena was most severe.

The translations are bit stilted at times, as a result of the change Spanish to English. Plus, the interrogators often speak over each other, in choppy, partial sentences. Add to those factors, the morbid fact that Camarena's life is literally draining away from him as he tries to respond to the interrogators, and the interrogation is difficult to follow and understand, even when reading a transcript.

"But," James continues, "I have identified a few areas where I think we can make progress."

"Let's do it," Erica replies.

"Okay, one of the items I find interesting is the assertion that Caro was on the tapes," James says, "and one of the main interrogators. In testimony at the Zuno I trial, DEA Agent Dale Stinson identified two of the voices on the interrogation tapes as being those of Caro Quintero and Sergio Espino Verdin. Agent Stinson had met Caro in a Mexican prison not long after the arrests of Caro and Fonseca. Stinson has said he was sitting in the prison when Caro approached him from behind him, yelling and screaming at him. Stinson was later escorted out of the prison by some of Caro's men, and he says it was one of the few times in his career when he truly was afraid for his life, and also why he remembers Caro's voice so distinctly."

"Makes sense to me," Erica says. "I'd sure remember someone who threatened me like that."

"Stinson was not the only one to testify about the voices," James says. "DEA Agent Robert Castillo was present when Caro was taken from Costa Rica to Mexico City and was interrogated. Castillo testified that he sat in on three interrogations of Caro, recorded two of them, and that he used his memory and the tapes he had made to identify Caro's voice on the Camarena interrogation tapes. Castillo testified about Caro's accent, his speaking style, and his grammar."

"It sounds persuasive," Erica says.

"I think it was," James replies. "There was not a lot the defense contested in their cross-examinations. But at the time, defense counsel seemed to be more concerned with the tactics used by the Mexican officials in interviewing Caro and others, and in keeping the interrogation tapes out of evidence. There was little incentive for any of the defense teams to question the accuracy of the voice identifications. There was testimony of the defense expert who tried to separate out the voices of the interrogators, but that didn't impact the identification aspects of the testimony of Agents Castillo and Stinson."

"Do you think that Caro wouldn't be there during the interrogation, and participating in it?" Erica asks.

"I'm not sure I can even guess what Caro might have done," James says. "I do know there are places in the transcripts where, based on the Castillo testimony, it appears that Caro is asking questions about Caro, and he doesn't strike me as someone who referred to himself in the third person often. I just don't think anyone at the time had a reason to question it."

"Okay, James, let's say I agree with you—which I do—and that there is a legitimate question as to whether Caro is one of the interrogators, or how long he participated in some of the interrogations. So what? How does this get us closer to knowing who had Camarena kidnapped, and who gave the orders that killed him?"

"I have a couple of responses," James says. "First, stop being so mean. Second, the more we know about the events in Lope de Vega on the seventh and eighth, the closer we will be to finding those answers. And I must admit, at this point in the process, a large motivation is the simple desire to understand it all. I don't care what the answer is. Only that there is an answer."

"Agreed, and moving on." Erica looks to the next item on James's list. "The next point is Félix Rodríguez. Forgive the ill-timed metaphor, but haven't we beaten that dead horse enough already?"

"True," James says, but perhaps a recap here could put the tapes as a whole in perspective."

"Then buy all means, recap away," Erica intones, successfully avoiding a tone of condescension.

"Remember," James says, "the allegation is that Rodríguez interrogated Camarena. But no one—and I mean no one—reported hearing anyone with a Cuban accent on the tapes. Dale Stinson does not recall any such voice on the tapes. David Herrera, who transcribed the tapes upon their arrival to Washington, DC, does not believe any of the Camarena interrogators had a Cuban accent. No one listening to the tapes at any of the criminal trials recalls a Cuban-sounding voice. I'll also note that in all the reports of the various people at Lope de Vega during Camarena's interrogation none, not even one names Rodríguez, or his alias, Max Gomez, or even says, 'a guy with a Cuban accent that I don't know.'"

Erica says, "Isn't the response that the tapes have been altered, and are clearly incomplete. At some point, they were given to the CIA. Who better to alter them to hide the identity of its agent interrogating Agent Camarena? Its's the same argument used to counter the revelation that the CIA is not mentioned on the tapes at all, which seems to belie the assertion that the CIA was looking for information about what Camarena knew about their activities."

James becomes more animated. "I reject that argument, categorically. I have to. Initially, it defies credulity to believe that the CIA was conducting some of the interrogations, but somehow managed to get every reference to the CIA or CIA-related questions deleted from the tapes. But more importantly, one simply cannot make allegations—wild allegations—and claim the support would have been on the tapes if they were unaltered and complete. Or if one wants to make that argument, they must have some other evidence, even inferential, to support it."

"But they do," Erica replies. "They have Lira, Godoy, and Lopez."

"And there it is again," James says. "The circular argument that Lira supports Godoy, who supports Lopez, who supports Lira. See all the support. It must be true. And the complete tapes would prove it. The same is true, in some respect, with Berrellez and Phil Jordan. That is not support. If someone—"

"Like Berrellez," Erica says.

"If someone," James continues, "like Berrellez, is going to make wild claims and allegations, then there has to be some support in the record for the claims. It cannot be sufficient to say, 'our paid and protected criminal informants say so.'"

"But many people do believe it," Erica says. "Many people say the witnesses would never lie, because they would lose their immunity."

"They will not lose their immunity if they say what Berrellez wants them to say," James replies, "irrespective of the truth. Who has the motivation to prosecute these guys, even if someone proved they fabricated things? The DOJ? Does anyone in their right mind really think the DOJ wants to come out and say, 'So sorry. We convicted Ruben Zuno, and others, based on the testimony of witnesses, including one of Camarena's kidnappers, who we now know were providing false testimony. We are sorry. We will make it up to Ruben Zuno. Oh, wait, he's dead.'"

"That all makes sense, James, but it really doesn't tell us anything more about who killed Camarena."

"No, it doesn't. But the tapes can be used to help refute a number of false claims."

"Now we are getting somewhere," Erica says. "Do tell."

"In his book," James continues, "Berrellez makes a stunning assertion regarding Camarena and Captain Zavala. He asserts, with no evidentiary support, that on the second day of his interrogation and torture, February 8th, reading directly from the book, 'Kiki gave up the one and only name interrogators would ever get from him. It was the name of the pilot who'd supposedly flown him and other DEA agents over the marijuana fields the cartel owned at Rancho Búfalo. The pilot's name was Alfredo Zavala.'"

"I call BS," Erica says.

"That would be a good call," James replies. "We know it's not on any of the interrogation tapes anyone has listened to or transcribed, unless Berrellez has heard one no one else has. We also have heard from Hector's own mouth that Camarena had nothing to do with the Búfalo investigation and raid. More importantly, it is contrary to all of the evidence that Zavala was grabbed the same day as Camarena."

A DEA report detailing agents' interviews with Captain Zavala's sons affirms, without qualification, that Captain Zavala was kidnapped on the afternoon of February 7th, when the car he was riding in was pulled over on the highway from the airport. That report also states that Zavala and Camarena had a lengthy telephone conversation on Sunday, February 3rd. Following that conversation, Agent Camarena apparently told his wife, "We're getting on to another big one."

The sons also stated that they had been interviewed by the MFJP, told the same story to the MFJP, and had been told by the MFJP not to share the information with the DEA.

In addition to the DEA report, Susie Lozano, a secretary for the DEA in Guadalajara, confirms the timing of Captain Zavala's abduction. According to Ms. Lozano, she had an appointment first thing on the morning of February 8th, the day after Camarena's kidnapping, and was a little late, getting to the office around 9:30 a.m. When she arrived, Kuykendall called her into this office, informed her that Camarena was missing, and asked her to help in the efforts to locate Kiki. Ms. Lozano says that she then went to her desk, and a short time later, likely around 10:00 a.m., she received a call from one of Captain Zavala's sons, who told her his dad had been abducted off the highway from the Guadalajara airport, and Captain Zavala had told his son that if anything ever happened to him for his son to "call Susie" at the Consulate.

"So Berrellez is just wrong?" Erica asks.

"About such a crucial fact? Such an easily checked assertion?" James ponders his own question.

"I see your point," Erica says. ""Your last bullet is *why?* That one needs no explanation."

"But I'll provide one, nevertheless," James replies. "Every theory seemingly falls apart at the tapes. If Caro got mad and acted on his own to find out how the DEA was finding his fields, why would he tape the interrogation? If major Mexican politicians, and other officials, were involved with the cartel and wanted to know what the DEA knew, why would they tape the interrogations and still be present at Lope de Vega, as alleged by the government and Berrellez's boys? If the CIA ordered the abduction to find out what Camarena knew, and if he was close to finding out about their narcotics trade, why would they need, let alone want, a tape out there that could provide further evidence of their activities?"

"Okay, James, you know I'll sit here and discuss this with you all night, if you want. But where does this painfully circular analysis of the tapes get us?"

"Maybe the only conclusion is that this the rare instance where Kuykendall is mistaken," James says. "The answers are not to be found on the tapes. At least, not the ones we have."

CHAPTER FORTY

WORRIED ABOUT HIS LACK OF OFFICE TIME the prior week, James forces himself to wake early to go into the office, where he knows he will be more productive than if he tried to work from home. Once at his desk, James quickly becomes immersed in the work at hand, momentarily forgetting about Speer, Aguilar, and even Camarena.

Mid-morning, though, his focus is interrupted by the distinctive sound of an incoming text. As expected, it was from Erica. "I assume you are at the office."

"Am I that transparent?"

"Only to me. How long do you expect to be there?"

"Most of the day, I assume."

"An early dinner, then?"

"Sounds great."

"What about 6 pm? Same place?"

"See you there."

James sets the phone down, looking out toward the ocean. The day was crystal clear, the water deep blue. James reflected on the parallels.

We've learned so much and developed such clarity on so many issues. I just need to draw it all together somehow.

By the time 6:00 p.m. came, and James arrives at Duke's Huntington Beach, just off the Huntington Beach Pier, the weather has taken an ominous turn. Dark clouds roll onto the coast, and there is a cool mist in the air.

James arrives first—his disdain for being late, and penchant for arriving early, being well-known. Normally, he and Erica would sit under the heat lamps on the patio above the water, but not tonight. Instead, James secures a table by the window, orders a Buffalo Trace Old-Fashioned, and stares at the tumultuous waves as he waits.

"Started without me, I see." Erica approaches the table.

"Noting your love-hate relationship with promptness, I thought it prudent." James stands.

They embrace for a moment, before James pulls out Erica's chair and holds it for her to sit.

"Brian is not far behind me," she says. "I hope you don't mind that I invited him."

"Not in the least. It'll be nice. We don't get a chance to talk nearly as much as we used to."

James waives for the waitress and explains that there will be another person, and she adds a chair and a place setting. Erica orders a club soda and lime, and James eschews another drink, instead ordering a bottle of a 2012 Caymas cabernet sauvignon, without looking at the wine list.

Erica admires the sight of the iconic eighteen-hundred-plus-foot pier, and out at the ocean beyond.

"It sure is beautiful here," she says. "But you know, there are a lot of nice places closer to all of our homes, with almost as great of views. Why do we come here so often?"

"When I first moved to California after law school," Brian replies, "I didn't know anyone. There were many nights when, after working late at the office, I would drive down here, sit on the pier, and just watch the ocean for hours. It was relaxing and somehow comforting. I guess coming back here brings back those feelings."

Before Erica can respond, the waitress returns with Erica's club soda and the bottle of wine, which she promptly opens.

"Would you like a taste?" Erica asks James.

"Nah. I'm sure it's good."

The waitress pours James's glass and looks to Erica, who moves her wine glass to the center of the table.

"What the hell," Erica says. "Might as well start now."

The waitress pours her glass and promises a return when the third member of the party arrives. As she leaves, James and Erica clink glasses while continuing to soak in the view.

"So my dear, where do we go from here?" Erica asks.

"About the Camarena case?"

"No, right now I'm really totally stressing about my fantasy football team," Erica says. "Yes, the Camarena case."

Before he can answer, James stands to greet an approaching Brian.

"I almost didn't want to interrupt you two." Brian extends his hand to shake James's.

"Don't be silly. We're glad you can join us," Erica says, as Brian leans over to kiss her on the cheek.

The waitress returns to pour Brian's glass, and James asks her to decant another bottle as she leaves. Once she is gone, Brian raises his glass for a toast.

"To good friends."

"I like that," James says.

"James and I were about ready to discuss the next steps in the Camarena case," Erica says.

"I don't know, Erica. Maybe Brian would prefer to have a relaxing evening, and not hear us prattle on about the case. Hell, sometimes I even bore myself talking about it."

Erica smiles. "Well, truth be told, part of the reason I asked Brian to join us was so we could get his thoughts. A neutral party, so to speak."

"It's okay, James," Brian says. "I'm interested, and I'd like to help if I can."

"Only if you're sure," James replies.

"I am," Brian says. "If I get bored, I'll drink more."

Sensing the issue resolved, Erica returns to her talking points.

"As I said, we were just getting ready to talk about next steps."

James's expression turns somber. "I'm not sure. Maybe we've gone far enough. Found what is going to be found."

"If I thought for a second that really is how you feel," Erica says, "I'd reach across the table and smack you. But what I know is that you started this with two main questions—who ordered the Camarena kidnapping, and who killed him? We know a lot more today than we did a month ago, but we don't have answers to those two questions. I have no doubt that you won't stop until you either answer them, or you know, definitively, that no one can."

"Maybe you're right," James says. "Sometimes it's hard not to get discouraged. While I was having a drink before you arrived, I was trying to reconsider where we are and how we got here. After Speer, and the compilation of information we have from a variety of sources, I think we really do have a decent idea about the CIA's actions with the cartel, and how that relates, or doesn't relate, to Camarena's abduction. But as Erica aptly notes, unfortunately for us, that doesn't resolve all the key issues. Any way you view the facts as we know them, there is a hole. Something missing. We need to learn more."

"More with the CIA? Brian asks.

The waitress approaches, and the three halt their conversation. She refills the wine glasses and takes dinner orders.

"I'll get some bread for you," she says, "but leave you to your clandestine discussions."

James, Erica, and Brian laugh as she walks away.

"Not necessarily with the CIA," James continues, "but as a whole. We have many more facts, and some better hypotheses, but we don't have conclusions."

Brian reflects for a moment, hesitating before speaking.

"At Erica's insistence," he says, "I watched *The Last Narc* the last two nights."

"It was a request," Erica replies.

"A strongly worded request," Brian says. "Be that as it may, I tried to watch it as an objective third party, and I have to say, it was well-done. It's well-produced, and it advances its position well."

"But it's not a true documentary," Erica says.

"No, it's not," Brian replies. "But do you really think that most of the people finding it on Amazon and watching four episodes were really looking for a well-balanced, objective presentation of the case?

"Brian's right," James says. "It was even advertised as providing a shocking revelation about Camarena's death and the CIA."

Erica replies, "The filmmakers still had an obligation to present both sides."

"Even if they did," Brian says, "that's not how it was presented. And again, my point is they made the case reasonably well. Godoy was a crazy man, and the scenes in the cemetery were over the top, but it makes a compelling case for the involvement of the CIA, if—and this is the important part—if you know nothing other than what has been presented."

"We have volumes of material that cut directly against its claims," Erica says.

"I know," Brian replies. "But before we get there, I have one other question. As you said, the advertising seemed to focus on the CIA aspect, and that was the general focus for much of the four episodes. And then, almost out of nowhere, comes the allegations against Kuykendall."

"Do you think it is clear that's who they are referring to?" Erica asks.

"It is crystal clear," Brian says. "So why him?"

Erica looks at James, who sweeps back his hair and furrows his brow.

"Brian, I honestly have no idea," he replies. "I have thought about it a lot. I don't know what is gained by throwing him under the proverbial bus."

Brian says, "Should you at least keep an open mind to the possibility that Kuykendall was involved with the cartel? That he set Camarena up?"

"No!" James blurts out.

"Hold on," Brian says. "I'm not suggesting it's true. Just asking if you do a disservice to the inquiry if we exclude the possibility."

"I get it Brian, I do," James replies. "But I just can't give it any real credibility. The DEA investigated and found nothing. The stories just don't make sense. There is no evidence presented, other than the statements of those witnesses, and we have solid evidence to cast doubt on virtually everything they say."

Erica says, "But James—and I know you'll hate me saying this—but what about Tosh Plumlee's assertions of more than one meeting in Phoenix where the CIA connection was discussed, and where both Camarena and Kuykendall were present?"

"If there was any way to provide any corroboration to those claims, I might agree with you and Brian. But as of now, we have none. I'm not saying Plumlee's accounts are false. I'm just not convinced to pull hard on that thread without some type of corroboration."

"And if we find such corroboration?" Erica asks.

"I'll be the first one to yank on the thread," James replies.

"Fair enough," Erica says, with a smile and a twinkle.

Brian continues. "But what about the allegations that Kuykendall was paid millions of dollars in bribes. Bribes that were paid directly to him at the consulate?"

"I have a number of responses," James says, "but will give you the primary ones. First, no one from the DEA who was in Guadalajara before or after the abduction, had any indication or belief that anyone in the DEA was on the take. Alan Bachelier, who was stationed there with Camarena and Kuykendall, said he was offended just by the question, and every one of the former agents said they would have reported it if they had even a suspicion.

"Second, even though security was laxer in '84 and '85, there still was security. Someone could not just waltz into the consulate with a briefcase filled with millions of dollars and give it to Kuykendall or anyone else. Susie Lozano also says she doesn't remember anyone, other than the agents, ever having a briefcase while in the consulate.

"Finally, Agent Payan, a former Leyenda member, says that the DEA discovered that the bribe money Caro thought was going to the DEA, was instead kept by a DFS agent who Caro had intended to use as an intermediary. Caro was being scammed. The bribe money never made it to any DEA agent."

"Okay, you've sold me," Brian says. "We can put the allegations against Kuykendall to the side."

The waitress approaches with a large tray carrying dinner.

"Excellent timing," Brian says.

The conversation pauses while the meal is served and wine glasses refilled.

"While we eat," Brian says, "can you give me the CliffsNotes version of the case against the story presented in *The Last Narc*?"

James again springs to life. "I'd be happy to."

For the next twenty-five minutes, with Erica's timely supplementations, James lays out the arguments. He details the character of Godoy and Lopez, the factual inconsistencies in their stories, the dubious timing of their claims against Ruben Zuno, Bartlett Diaz, and others. He recounts discussions with DEA agents who worked in Mexico during the time surrounding Camarena's abduction, who never heard anything about CIA entanglement with the cartel. The discussion flows freely and naturally, accented by the passion of James and Erica.

Dinner ends, the table is cleared, and each glass is filled one last time.

Brian pauses, reflecting. "I've listened carefully to everything you have said, and I know how smart and skilled you both are, so I have no doubt the evidence is as you represent it. With all of that, playing my role of the detached observer, and feeling like an overused trope, it strikes me that maybe you are trying too hard."

"What do you mean by 'too hard?'" Erica says. "Trying to find too much meaning?"

"Just a thought," Brian replies. "But when in doubt, I like to fall back on the principle of parsimony."

"What is the simplest explanation that fits all the evidence?" Erica says.

"Correct. I know you both have heard me talk about that concept in connection with litigation strategy and trial presentations."

"How do you think it applies here?" James asks.

"Frankly, I'm not sure it does," Brian says. "But if we were to try to apply the concept, we could look for the more reasonable explanation, or explanations, consistent with the evidence as presently known. As an example, is the simplest explanation that the CIA participated in the kidnapping and brutal murder of a fellow government agent? Or is the most basic explanation that many government and military officials would meet over and over to plot a rudimentary kidnapping, and then be present for the interrogation? Is it that Kuykendall would set up his friend?"

"Or is it that Caro Quintero was a hot head and acted emotionally, irrationally, and on his own?" Erica says.

"Precisely," Brian replies.

"Which raises another point we've glossed over with respect to the CIA," James says. "Even if it was involved somehow, that doesn't mean it ordered that Camarena be brutally tortured and murdered. It could have been more... shall we say, subtle than that, and would that have been their first step? Wouldn't they have taken other steps to either guide Camarena in a different direction, or try to find out what he knew through different sources, before having him kidnapped?"

"Again, I agree," Brian says. "In fact, Caro acting irrationally, without regard for the consequences, seems far more plausible on the face of it, doesn't it?

James asks, "But what about the tapes? Why tape the interrogations? Who benefits from the tapes?"

"I don't know," Brian replies. "You say there's no doubt that some political and military figures were working with the drug dealers. Maybe one or more of them really did want to know what the DEA knew. But in any event, there is nothing that says a theory is correct only if it resolves all issues. Sometimes life is messy. Sometimes people are not perfectly rational actors. Not everything always gets wrapped up like in a Richard Castle novel."

Erica says, "Especially when talking about the actions of an uneducated, anger-prone, hormonal, drug-using young man."

"That's right," Brian says. "At the same time, though, that is not to suggest that you don't follow the evidence and revise your hypotheses to fit the new evidence—if, and as, needed. Regardless of where that evidence leads you."

Erica sits straight up. "Back this train up. I think there is a simple explanation for the tapes. One I'd never even considered until a few seconds ago."

"The floor is yours," James says, with anticipation."

"Okay, if we start with the assumption that Rafa kidnapped Camarena, and it had nothing directly to do with the CIA, then the question is why would Rafa tape the interrogations, right?"

"Right," James replies. "And..."

"Was Rafa going to sit in on all of the interrogations?" Erica continues. "Would he rather get secondhand information on what Camarena said, or be able to hear it for himself? Wouldn't he want a record of what was said for future reference? What if Camarena said something that could be useful in other ways, such as against Mexican government officials?"

James says, "Suddenly, I can think of many reasons why someone might want to take the interrogations that have nothing to do with the CIA or Mexican officials. Would Caro have been present enough to think of that?"

"If he wasn't," Erica replies, "think of the people around him who might have been. Fonseca, Javier Barba Hernandez, Espino Verdin, El Samy. It's not like someone had to be Stephen Hawking. They just needed a little foresight!"

"That wouldn't necessarily address the *missing* tapes," James says.

"No, but back to my point," Brian says. "It doesn't have to. In order to be the best theory, it just needs to provide the best explanation based on the available evidence and the supportable information you have. It just needs to be malleable enough to adapt to and incorporate new evidence and new facts, should they be found."

"That, of course, is good advice, Brian," James replies.

"My work here is done, and now I am going home." Brian stands from the table. "Let me know if you need anything else, or if you have any further epiphanies."

"Thanks, Brian," James says. "You know I appreciate it."

"Yes, I do. Which is why I'll leave the check for you." Brian shakes hands with James and gives Erica a kiss as he leaves. "Get some rest. Both of you."

CHAPTER FORTY-ONE

JAMES SITS BACK DOWN NEXT TO ERICA as Brian leaves. Erica leans close to him as she resumes the conversation.

"To follow up on Brian's last thought, and following the evidence—or in this case, the logic—though I was dubious about the documentary when I first watched it, and am more so now that I know more about the case, there was one thing that did stick out. In it, someone said that after the killing of the missionaries and then Walker and Radelat, when there was no real blowback to the cartel, Caro felt empowered, and that he could go after a DEA agent with impunity. That resonated with me, and could support the idea that Caro acted impetuously."

"That argument struck me the first time I heard it as well," James says. "And Aguilar advanced that idea when we spoke after the Speer meeting." He moves his glass out of the line of his hands as he talks. "But I don't think the logic withstands scrutiny, and here's why. In the documentary, the people making that argument are the same people who endorse and rely upon the statements from Godoy and Lopez. But Godoy and Lopez, and Cervantes before them, detail planning meetings that were said to have taken place well before the missionaries were kidnapped."

"If they were having planning meetings to kidnap the DEA agent causing trouble," Erica says, "then they had to have disregarded or minimized the risks associated with picking up a DEA agent long before the kidnapping of the missionaries, or the Walker-Radelat murders."

"That's my thought, too," James says. "But more than that, we know the missionaries' story is not as alleged because their car was left in the middle of the road. They were not walking door-to-door and happened to knock on the wrong door. Also, there is nothing about the description of the missionaries to suggest that anyone at the time really thought they were DEA agents, especially since we know the cartel regularly surveilled DEA agents. The idea that they were killed because Fonseca or his sicarios thought they were DEA is suspect, at best."

"Okay, but Walker and Radelat were closer to the time of the kidnapping," Erica says, "and clearly involved Caro. What about the response to their executions?"

"The answer," James leans back and looks out over the ocean, "is the same. I am certain that if Caro, or anyone around him, had listened to the news at all in the day or two after the La Longosta incident, he either would have known for sure that they were not DEA agents, or at a minimum, had a strong sense that they were not. Hell, he probably figured that out as they were tortured in La Longosta, even though one of the two men apparently agreed that he was a cop after being tortured."

"Frankly, James, I find the whole story hard to believe. From what we are told, La Longosta was a known place. DEA agents and staff had eaten there, though, admittedly, during the day. Caro is going to have an important meeting, leave the doors open, and apparently not guarded from the outside, and then assume the two men walking in the door are DEA and kill them? It just doesn't seem likely."

"I agree with you, as usual," James says. "Another thought just for conversation. If one runs with the theory that Caro got mad and acted impulsively, then why pick up Zavala, too."

"James, my dear, you are, as Brian said, thinking too hard. Kuykendall has said that if the cartel knew about Kiki, it would not be hard for them to find out about Zavala, too. If Caro wanted to know about the investigations and the riads, too, and made the decision to pick up Camarena, wouldn't it make sense for him to also want to find out what Zavala knew?"

"That does make sense," James says, "unless you buy into the idea that someone had to point Camarena out to the kidnappers—ignoring for the moment, that no one can seem to keep a consistent story on who it was or how the identification was made. If they had to point out Camarena, did they also need someone to point out Zavala? Or did they simply know who the pilot for the DEA was, irrespective of the agent's identity?"

Both catch their breath for a moment and let the last question lay unanswered. James starts to pour some more wine into Erica's glass, but she waives him off. James reflects for a moment, and then deflects to an adjacent topic.

"This may sound a bit grandiose, even for me, but what if everyone, including us, has been looking at this the wrong way since day one?"

"Not too grandiose, for you," Erica says. "What do you mean by the 'wrong way?'"

James sits up and adjusts his chair to be closer to Erica.

He replies, "Start with the narrative that Camarena was abducted by the big bad Guadalajara Narcotics Cartel. Remember, no one had ever used that term before the kidnapping. The idea that it was a coordinated *cartel* now seems far-fetched. Then you get the apparent desire from US officials to find that Mexican officials had been involved. Those two concepts lead to a vast conspiracy, with planning meetings and discussions held over several months, including some of Mexico's most well-known politicians and military leaders. This, of course, fuels people like Berrellez and Medrano to find witnesses to spin even more elaborate stories and implicate the CIA directly into the kidnapping and interrogation."

"What's the alternative story?" Erica says.

James reflects momentarily. "The story is, there is no story. Caro was losing money from raids he blamed on the DEA in Guadalajara. He may have even owed Félix Gallardo money in connection with the production at Búfalo. He got mad, he had Camarena picked up, Zavala too, and reckless thugs took it too far. End of story."

"But it's not a story that sells books," Erica says, "pressures the Mexican government, or makes former agents famous."

"No, it's not," James says. "Think about it. Could it also fit in with the Reagan administration's war on drugs—just say no. Did the story of the cartel getting to Camarena support the narrative? If drugs were going to be sold to support the Contras, wouldn't the government's response provide an element of cover?"

"When all the time it was one man who was deranged, powerful, and rich—a dangerous combination." Erica hesitates for a moment. "It does make sense. But doesn't Berrellez make a big deal about the fact that Búfalo could not have been the reason for Camarena's abduction because he was not involved in the Búfalo investigation?"

"He does," James replies, "and I think it's a monumentally stupid argument. The issue is not whether Camarena was actually involved in the raids on Búfalo. The issue is whether Caro thought he was. If he thought so, the abduction makes sense, irrespective of the validity of that belief."

"Agreed," Erica says. "So every rendition of the cartel and Camarena's abduction has been false?"

"Not completely false," James says. "But like so many other examples in this case, the truth gets lost in the midst of dramatic license, self-serving commentary, exaggerations, and flat-out lies."

James pauses again, looking out over the ocean and finishing his wine.

He continues. "You know, Rafa has given a couple of interviews over the years. Totally self-serving, but nevertheless.

One was after his release in 2013."

"Anything of note? Erica asks.

"As I said, most of it was self-serving. I didn't kill Camarena, etc. But the interviewer, at least from the article, didn't really try to follow up or ask probing questions."

"'Where is he now?" Erica says.

"He's been at large for several years now, with a huge bounty on his head—and nothing. What does that tell you?"

"James, if this case has taught me anything, it's that nothing *tells* me anything."

"I know there have been some press reports that he is running the Sinaloa Cartel," James says, "and that he is involved in a *war* with El Chapo's kids and successors. But I don't know how much of that is real."

"Maybe we should find out," Erica says.

"Maybe we should. Tomorrow. For now, it is time to go home and get some sleep."

James stands and pulls the chair out for Erica. They walk slowly to the front of the restaurant, their faces refreshed by the crisp night air carried by the ocean breeze.

"Are you okay to drive?" James asks.

"I'm fine. Not sure I want to go, but I know I should."

James and Erica walk to the valet stand, where James pays for both cars. Erica's Tesla arrives first. Upon seeing it pull up, she hugs and thanks James. He barely reciprocates the hug, instead staring ahead, lost in thought.

Erica slides into the driver's seat and clips in her seat belt. Before driving off, she looks up at James, who is still deep in thought.

"What is it?" she asks.

"I feel like Nic Cage in *National Treasure*."

"You're going to steal the Declaration of Independence?"

"No, but we are going to find Rafael Caro Quintero," James says, as he shuts Erica's door.

CHAPTER FORTY-TWO

THE CELL PHONE ON JAMES'S NIGHTSTAND plays music denoting an incoming phone call, but he ignores it, silently hoping he can go back to sleep. When the music plays a second time, he again ignores it, this time giving a fleeting thought that it might be an emergency. Seconds later, the now exceedingly annoying music plays again, and James rustles to a semi-alert state and picks up the phone.

"Hi, Erica," he says, slightly annoyed.

"Good morning, sunshine. When will you be here?"

"Which here is here?"

"I'm at the office, silly. Come join me. And will you bring a breakfast burrito from Nate's, and some OJ?"

"Sure. Give me thirty minutes or so."

"Okay, but hurry. I've found some good stuff."

James hangs up the phone and looks at the clock on the nightstand next to him. *8:15? What the hell? It is Sunday, right?*

"I have food," James says.

"Yummy!!!"

"What exactly are you doing here? I thought we were planning to get some rest today."

James lays the breakfast burritos and juices on the conference table in front of Erica.

"If you want us to find Rafa," she replies, "shouldn't we know a lot more about him?"

"Sure," says a hesitant James, sitting at the end of the table adjacent to Erica's chair.

"Look, if we look at this whole investigation," she says, "what is the one thing we clearly did wrong?"

Trying not to sound annoyed, James replies, "You tell me."

"We went to talk to Félix too soon. We should have prepared better. Known more. I woke up thinking about that this morning—early this morning—and wanted to help assure that we don't make the same mistake twice. If we are going to track Caro, let's get to know him."

"I'm game. Tired, but game." James unwraps one of the burritos and slides it in front of Erica before open the second for himself.

"Even better, my time has not been a waste," she says. "I think there's some interesting information. As an example, what if I suggested Rafa has been running—or at least, helped to run—a cartel both inside and outside of prison, and that he has power in a cartel to this day?" Erica takes a bite of her burrito.

"I'd say I'm not surprised," James replies. "Intrigued, but not surprised. Eat more of your burrito and explain."

"Consistent with our approach on this case," Erica continues, "I tried to start from the beginning. The background is, as Professor Mirada described it, murky, at best. Frankly, lack of information known about his early time in Sinaloa is astonishing. I mean, I know it was rural Mexico. But it was still the twentieth century."

"It seems we know more about Europe in the Middle Ages than Mexico in the 1980s," James says.

"Here is some of what we do know," Erica says. "Or believe to be true. He was born on October 3, 1952, in La Noria, Sinaloa, the oldest son of twelve children. His father, a farmer and rancher, died when Caro was fourteen years old. The details of his father's death are not completely clear, but a version has Rafa witnessing his father being killed.

"Sometime around the age of sixteen, Rafa moved to Caborca, Sonora. By most accounts, for a time, he worked in livestock grazing, and later as a truck driver in Sinaloa, and maybe even at a bean and corn plantation. At some point, though, he made the decision to become a full-time drug trafficker—initially, in the state of Chihuahua.

"We know most of the story from there and how he ended up in Guadalajara with other traffickers from Sinaloa. What is most interesting, I think, is what he has done since he was released from prison in 2013."

In the early hours of August 9, 2013, Caro was ordered released after twenty-eight years in prison. After a motion by Rosalía Isabel Moreno Ruiz, a state judge and magistrate, the Jalisco State Court ruled that Caro had been tried improperly in federal court because he was sentenced for his conviction on the charge of murder, a state crime, and not the federal crime of drug trafficking. Caro was given an immediate release after credit for time served.

Caro's release was not well-received on either side of the border. On August 14, 2013, a Mexican federal court, upon request of the Office of the General Prosecutor, issued an arrest warrant against Caro. For a while, there was a question if Caro would be extradited to the United States if he was arrested. A recent court ruling ended that speculation, and thus, if arrested, Caro could join his fellow trafficker El Chapo in an American prison.

"Since Rafa's release," Erica continues, "there are no confirmed reports of him being seen in public. Though, there are rumors he has visited his hometown of Badiraguato, Sinaloa, traveled to Caborca, Sonora, and even visited his wife in Mazatlán. In March 2018, it was reported that Mexican Marines used Black Hawk helicopters to search for Caro in the mountain villages of the Badiraguato Municipality. And as you know, the US government has a well-publicized twenty-million-dollar bounty out for his capture."

Erica stops and scarfs down the remainder of her burrito.

James stands and cleans the table, talking as he walks to the trash and back to his chair.

"You mentioned his business earlier. Since his release, has he been put back in power?"

"The answer to that question seems to depend on to whom it is asked and when," Erica replies. "After his release, initial intelligence indicated that Caro was retired from drug trafficking and living in recluse. Those initial reports were disputed late,r though, as it became clear to many that Caro had forged an alliance with El Mayo, Ismael Zambada Niebla, El Chapo's partner atop the Sinaloa Cartel before Chapo's arrest. It is believed that El Mayo wanted to give leadership roles in the Sinaloa Cartel to Rafa and his brother Miguel, but that was doomed when El Chapo's sons objected. It is suspected, though, that Rafa and Miguel continue to be aligned, formally or otherwise, with the factions of the Sinaloa Cartel more loyal to El Mayo than Los Chapitos."

"Los Chapitos. I love that term," James wisecracks.

Erica continues. "As you mentioned previously, Rafa has given at least two interviews since he was released from prison."

On July 24, 2016, Caro Quintero granted an interview to *Proceso* magazine, where he claims he did not kill Camarena. Rafa also alleged that once released from prison, he had been visited, on separate occasions, by both El Chapo and El Mayo, and that he rebuffed both their offers for him to get back into the drug trafficking business.

In April 2018, journalist Anabel Hernandez visited Caro at a shabby mountain home Rafa claimed was his. Ms. Hernandez described Caro as appearing aged and frail. During the interview, he said he wanted to be left in peace, and that he also spends his days looking for drones. Caro also claimed, in this interview, that he was not speaking with his wife or any of his children, and of course, that he was not in business with any cartel.

"Neither of these interviews tills any new ground," Erica says. "And frankly, I found both somewhat ridiculous. Miss Hernandez has stated that she believed Caro when he said he was not back in business, and there are some who support that position. For example, I read where former DEA agent Mike Vigil described Caro Quintero as a 'shell' of his former self, and asserted that the allegations that Caro might have a leadership role in the Sinaloa Cartel were *ludicrous*. There was even speculation that Caro's cousin Sajid—who was arrested by US authorities in October 2017, and pled guilty to charges of drug trafficking and money laundering in 2018— may have started these allegations in order to make a deal with prosecutors."

"Where does that leave things now?" James says.

"Most of the intelligence reports I've read suggest that Sonora is a battleground state where La Linea, Cartel De Jalisco, Los Salazar, Los Chapitos, and the Caro Quintero organizations—whatever they may be—are at in conflict. At least one report, that is here somewhere, asserted that Caro maintains strategic points of collaboration with Cartel De Jalisco.

"Recently, violence also has erupted in Quintana Roo, and many have suggested that this plaza is subject to a battle for control between Caro, the Gulf Cartel, CDN, and the Guerrero Unidos, all of which have an established presence in Quintana Roo.

"I think it is safe to conclude that it is highly unlikely that Rafa is truly retired and has no role in any cartel or trafficking operations, and I seriously doubt that Caro lives in a hovel in the hills, in abject poverty."

Erica is interrupted by the sound of a text on James's phone sitting on the conference room table. James picks it up to see a text from Aguilar. "Can you meet me tomorrow around 4? I have some RCQ information for you."

James shows the message to Erica.
"Coincidence?" she asks.
"I don't know."
"But you are going to meet with him, right?
"Damn straight I am."

CHAPTER FORTY-THREE

JAMES ARRANGED TO MEET AGUILAR at a bar chosen by Aguilar, near Aguilar's home in Tustin, not far from the old El Toro Marine Corps Air Station, which was largely decommissioned in 1999, and now houses a huge recreational center, as well as numerous residential and commercial developments.

As James approaches the address, he sees what could only be described as a cowboy bar in the middle of California suburbia. He parks in the lot next to the bar, his Audi notable amid the pickup trucks of every brand and description.

James steps out of his car and surveys his surroundings. He removes the tie from around his neck, loosens the top two buttons on his tailor-made shirt, and puts his jacket in the car. *Won't be needing this here.*

As James walks into the bar, he feels the eyes of the local patrons on him. After scanning the room, he is relieved to finally spot Aguilar at a table in the back of the room, again near the ubiquitous tavern jukebox.

"Why am I singing that Sesame Street song in my head?" James says while shaking Aguilar's hand. "Which one is not like the other? Which one doesn't belong?" He takes a seat at the table.

Aguilar chuckles. "You'll be fine. They don't do Corona here, so I ordered you a Bud Light."

"Works for me. Thanks."

"Erica's not with you?" Aguilar asks.

"No, she had some other commitments. But she sends her regards."

As James speaks, the bartender—a tall, thin man in western boots and a NASCAR hat—sets two beers on the table, and with a nod from Aguilar, leaves without a word.

"Too bad. What have you and Erica been working on recently, Mister Butler?"

"Such formality." James chuckles. "Recently, we've been doing a deep dive into Caro Quintero, his life, and his actions after his release. You don't happen to know where he is, do you?"

"There's a twenty-million-dollar bounty on his head. If I knew—and I don't—I wouldn't tell you!"

As the two men talk, another man approaches. He is non-descript. James guesses he's about forty, six-feet tall and 180 pounds, dressed in tennis shoes, jeans, a blue flannel shirt, and a light jacket. His expression is stoic as he approaches the table.

As Aguilar sees him approach, he nods and motions to the empty chair at the table, between James and Aguilar. The man sits, still silent.

"James Butler, this is my friend Tom."

"Hi, Tom. Nice to meet you. How do you two know each other?"

"James, you are not listening. His name is Tom. He is a friend. He might contribute to our conversation."

"Got it."

Aguilar returns to the conversation, while Tom sits in silence.

"We were talking about Caro Quintero?"

"We were. And now I am wondering..." James adjusts in his seat and brushes his hair back, "if someone wanted to find him, how would they go about it?"

Aguilar's replies, "Short answer is, they shouldn't."

"That, I know," James says. "But hypothetically. Or stated differently, how is it he has not been found after all this time?"

"How was Osama bin Laden able to hide for all those years?" Aguilar says. "It's a big world."

Tom leans onto the table. "Much of Sinaloa is still very rugged and unsettled. The mountains between Sinaloa and Durango, in particular, are fertile ground for laying low. Add to that the idea that if RCQ has taken refuge in Sonora, he has family connections throughout the state who will shelter and protect him."

"Can someone both hide and run a drug operation from there?" James asks.

"Are you asking if RCQ is still in the drug trafficking business?" Aguilar replies.

"Yes, that is a better question than what I asked."

"As far as we know," Tom says, "he never stopped being a significant part of the trafficking operations."

"How is that even possible?"

"It's Mexico, Mister Butler," Tom replies.

Aguilar says, "Let me try to help. As you know, the notion that the various cartels are run by a single person, or otherwise are a unified, seamless operation, is a fiction created mostly to make reporting on the cartels easier. For instance, as we've talked about before, in what commonly is referred to as the Guadalajara Cartel, was involved in both marijuana and cocaine, and it appears, at least until near the end, that RCQ took care of the marijuana business, and Félix ran the cocaine side, and the two rarely mixed businesses. But even on the marijuana side, it wasn't RCQ alone. There were others, including El Azul, who had substantial roles in the operations."

"I can understand that," James replies.

Tom says, "Even in prison, Caro had a knowledge base that was impressive and valuable. Add to that his familial and business connections, and it would be naïve at best to think he just went away, even if he took refuge for periods of time in the hills of Sinaloa."

"That's where the *Progreso* interviews took place, right?" James asks.

"It appears that way," Tom replies. "If I had to surmise, when Caro was let out of prison, though he was immediately on the run and in hiding, he took advantage of his connections and knowledge to begin working with the Sinaloa Cartel. At that time, though, the Sinaloa Cartel had a divided leadership with both El Chapo and El Mayo."

"Notwithstanding the public perception that El Chapo was the one and only leader," James says.

"Correct," Aguilar replies. "Which may explain why one is in jail in the US, and the other is not. Though, El Mayo's days of freedom may be numbered, too."

"The reports we have," Tom says, "are that El Mayo was willing to share power and leadership with RCQ. But in recent years, it is said that El Mayo's diabetes has severely limited his abilities, and there have even been reports that he has died. Whichever is the case, El Chapo's sons have exerted greater leadership roles in the cartel. It is believed that they have been willing to *work with* RCQ, but have no willingness to put him in a leadership role, or otherwise to share power with him."

"That wouldn't seem to be a fight a man on the run would want to be involved in," James says.

"Apparently not." Tom continues. "It seems that RCQ has moved back to his family's home state of Sonora, and taken control in or around the town of Caborca, which has seen the dual phenomena of a meteoric rise in both luxury car sales and drug-related violence. In May 2020, an icebox with human remains was abandoned and accompanied by a message: 'We are informing the people of the Coast that we are the people of Caro Quintero. This square belonged to us, and now all those producers, traders, miners of the region, will have to pay the square. Here we are to clean. We are the

Sweeper twenty-four-sevn, the R Rodrigo Paez and Cara de Coch, and together we are the Caborca Cartel.'"

"So Caro is in Caborca." James sits taller in his seat. "That narrows it down."

"No, he likely is somewhere in the big state of Sonora," Aguilar says. "And he has supporters and soldiers throughout Sonora, particularly in Caborca. He also could be somewhere in Sinaloa."

"Are you familiar with the Spanish term 'zozobra,' Mister Butler?" Tom asks.

"No, sir, I am not."

"It is a term that conveys a sense of gloom, anxiety, and despair," Tom continues. "Santa Fe, New Mexico, has an annual festival where a fifty-foot-high marionette effigy is burned to destroy the worries and ills of the prior year. The people of Caborca live in a sense of 'zozobra.' Those that are not associated with drug trafficking have seen the violence and ills of the traffickers' lives come to their doorstep. RCQ is an omni-present figure, but not one to be spoken of."

"Doesn't this lead back to my initial question of how has he not been found?" James asks.

Aguilar replies. "The answer is the same. Sonora and Sinaloa are large states, with lots of places to hide. He has a large network of family, friends, employees, and paid-for officials to keep him hidden and allow him to be able to move before he can be found."

"There are also the practicalities of dealing with the Mexican government," Tom says. "Generally speaking, the DEA has to find him, tell Mexico, and then the Mexican Marines will go get him. That's how it worked to get El Chapo, but he was in Las Mochis, and it was easier to get to him once Mexico decided to take action. So far, RCQ apparently has not made the same mistake. Wherever he is."

"I guess going to Caborca and asking to meet with Rafa is not a good idea."

Aguilar scowls at James. "A deadly one for a gringo."

The three men pause their conversation for a moment, before Tom stands.

"If there is nothing more I can help with, I should be going."

James stands and extends his hand to shake Tom's, but the gesture is ignored.

"Thank you, Tom. It has been very informative. If I have any further questions, how might I reach you?"

"You can't."

"Fair enough." James sits back in his chair and takes a large drink from his still chilled beer.

Tom nods to Aguilar and leaves the bar. James and Aguilar watch him leave, before Aguilar sits back down."

"That was helpful," James says.

"It wasn't designed to be helpful. I was concerned about you. You are smart and headstrong—a bad combination. I wanted to show you how foolish it would be to investigate Caro in Mexico."

"That point came through loud and clear," James says.

"I'll drink to that."

As James drives home, he gets a call from an unidentified number. Despite his normal reluctance to answer unknown calls, he picks up this one.

"James Butler."

"Mister Butler, do you remember me?"

James immediately recognizes the voice as that of the anonymous caller who had provided information about Matta, SETCO, and the CIA.

"I do remember you. Are you working with Tom?" James asks, thinking the call might be related to his meeting with Aguilar's friend.

"I don't know a Tom. I just wanted to see if my information was of help to you."

"Frankly, it was interesting in connection with some of

our research," James says. "But I think Matta is a dead end for us. At least, on this part of the investigation."

"Where are you now?" the man asks.

"In my car, driving home."

"No, in your investigation."

"You wouldn't believe me if I told you," James says.

"Try me."

"We are looking for Caro Quintero himself."

"Interesting," the man replies. "How is it going so far?"

"Frankly, we have only started the investigation, and we have little to go on at this point."

"Might I make an observation?"" the man asks.

"Sure. Why not."

"Many of those around Caro are much younger than he," the man says, "and they have made great use of certain social media elements to conduct their business, recruit sicarios, and even monitor their rivals."

"Fascinating," James says. "But I don't see how that applies to what I am doing." His growing annoyance is more evident with each word.

"The governments on both sides of the borders have tried to use this more modern communication methodology to gain information on the actions of the traffickers, and to identify Caro's movements, but with limited success."

"Maybe the traffickers are smarter than the government agents trying to find them?" James says.

"Or alternatively, they have a different perspective on the scope and breadth of the Internet. If you could find some with a similar mindset, maybe they could find breadcrumbs others have missed. You might even be able to get to Caro through them."

"Interesting," James says. "I'll keep that in mind. I have to go now. I'm about to pull into my garage."

"Very well. Best of luck to you, Mister Butler."

The call disconnects, and James descends into his garage. He summons the elevator and leans back against a wall, pondering the significance of the meeting with Aguilar, and his mystery call.

Suddenly, he stands up straight, eyes wide. *The dark web. That's a great idea.*

CHAPTER FORTY-FOUR

"IT SHOULD BE EASY. We just need to get Caro to come into the open to talk to us," James says to Erica, who is sitting on the patio at The Dock in Newport Beach.

Two iced teas, with lemon and chips and salsa, adorn the table, shielded from the afternoon sun by a well-angled umbrella.

"James, I love you. So when I say you've lost your mind, I mean it in the best way possible."

"Hah. That's probably fair, but hear me out before you have me committed."

"Very well. The floor is yours." Erica puts chips and salsa on a small plate in front of her.

"Thank you," James says. "I draw your attention to the various interviews given by Caro since his capture. Both the television interviews right after he was brought back from Costa Rica, and his two interviews. What is his consistent theme and story?"

"That he was not involved in the kidnapping or murder of Camarena?" Erica says.

"Ding, ding. Correct answer, Miss Walsh."

"But no one in their right mind believes it," Erica says, in between bites of crunchy chips.

"That contention—true as it may be—is not relevant to this discussion. For these purposes, focus on the fact that he continues to say it."

"Okay," Erica says. "I'm hoping to get a meal out of this, so I'll play along."

James continues. "We know there is some press indication that Caro has an elevated status among the Mexican traffickers because of the Camarena murder—which I'm not prepared to give much credence to—but he never publicly takes credit for it."

"Are you saying he has an interest in having the public believe his protests that he was not involved?" Erica asks.

"Exactly! The public perception seems to be important to him. Nevertheless, he has only pled his case in the most perfunctory way, to a Mexican reporter with a limited audience."

"But what if he had the opportunity to explain how he was not involved," Erica says, "and to implicate those who he believes were, to someone with a broader audience, but also in a safe manner?"

"I could kiss you right now," James says. "That's precisely what I've been thinking. Why can't we give him the opportunity to state his case while also answering the questions important to us and our investigation!"

"Do you know a willing reporter?" Erica says.

"No." James rubs his face and adjusts his hair. "We are going to do it ourselves."

"You are going to journalism school?" Erica says. "Won't that take too long?"

"Funny. We are going to get him to willingly talk to us."

"Hello, Mister Caro, the Narco of Narcos," Erica says. "My name is James. Can I buy you a cup of coffee?"

"You are hysterical. But your underlying point is well-taken." James eats some chips and salsa directly from the serving plates. "Irrespective of how we approach this, we have to be very careful and very subtle. So after the call last night—which, admittedly, was too weird and coincidental for me—it seems that the way we can reach out to him, or those around him, is through the dark web."

"Right," Erica says dubiously. "Do you know anything—anything at all—about the dark web?"

"Not a single thing. But Bobby knows someone, and we are meeting with her tomorrow afternoon."

Despite the mysticism surrounding it, the dark web simply refers to those websites that exist behind multiple layers of encryption, and cannot be found by using traditional search engines, or visited through traditional web browsers.

While there are many nefarious, illegal, and infamous uses, there are also legitimate purposes for the dark web. One simple example is that people operating within closed, totalitarian societies can use the dark web to communicate with the outside world.

In addition to the dark web, there is a part of the Internet known as the deep web. Though often confusingly used interchangeably, there are nuanced differences between the two. The deep web refers to all web pages that search engines cannot find. That is, not everything stored electronically is indexed and made accessible by search engines like Google. Thus, the deep web includes the dark web, but it also includes all user databases, webmail pages, registration-required web forums, and pages behind paywalls, most of which exist for perfectly mundane and benign reasons.

Added to the mix is the utterly confusing term "dark internet," which sometimes is used to refer to networks, databases, or even websites that cannot be reached over the Internet. Often, this is niche information that few people will want. Or in some cases, is private data.

A noted UK technical site provides a useful summary: "A basic rule of thumb is that while the phrases 'dark web' or 'deep web' are typically used by tabloid newspapers to refer to dangerous secret online worlds, the 'dark internet' is a boring place where scientists store raw data for research."

James and Erica turn off of Harbor Boulevard into a strip mall a few blocks from the office, and James glides into a front row parking spot."

"A Starbucks, really?" Erica says. "Couldn't come up with anything more stereotypical?"

"Hey, it has outdoor seating and Wi-Fi. I thought it was perfect." James gets out of the car and walks to the Starbucks doors.

"Who are we meeting?" Erica asks.

"Her name is Julia. She is a friend of Bobby's, and he says we can trust her completely. That, literally, is everything I know."

"Enough for me." Erica says.

As they open the door to the coffee shop, and the overwhelming smell of freshly ground coffee beans wafts through the air, James grimaces.

"Damn, I hate the smell of coffee."

"Why don't you get us a table outside," Erica says, "and I'll get my coffee? Do you want anything."

"How about a hot chocolate." James replies.

"Hot chocolate? It's eighty-seven degrees outside!"

"Good point," James says. "I'll have a large vente grande iced chai tea."

"Shut up, dork. Here's my computer."

James takes Erica's laptop and walks through the store, to the outside seating area. The sun is hot, but the mid-afternoon crowd is minimal, so he's able to find a table in the corner with a sliver of shade. He sits in the sunny part of the table, opens Erica's laptop, and places it in front of a seat in the shade. Erica arrives a few moments later with two drinks.

"I got you an iced tea. Do we know what Julia looks like?"

"No idea," James says. "She's supposed to be able to recognize us."

He pulls his cell phone from his pocket and scrolls through emails while Erica connects to the free Wi-Fi.

A few moments pass, then a voice says, "Excuse me. Are you James Butler?"

James looks up. "Yes, I am."

"Hi, I'm Julia. Bobby sent me." She extends her hand.

James stands to shake her hand. "This is Erica Walsh."

Erica and Julia also shake.

"Please have a seat," James says. "I think we saved some shade for you."

Julia sits next to Erica, directly across from James.

Far from what James visualized, Julia looks to be in her mid-forties, professionally dressed—a bit out of place for a Saturday afternoon—with a distinct Midwestern accent.

"Bobby says you could use some tutoring on the dark web," Julia says quietly.

"That's right," James replies. "We are doing some research on an important case, and we think we might need to access some information or people in less than conventional ways."

"At least for us," Erica says.

"Exactly," James replies.

"That should be no problem," Julia says. "What do you know about the dark web?"

"Only what we've read from some Google searches," James says.

"And only those parts we understood." Erica winks to James.

"Fair enough," Julia says. "I'll start with the basics, and you can stop me if you find it too elementary."

"Which we won't," James tells her.

"Almost all sites on the dark web use an encryption tool called Tor to hide their identity," Julia says. "Tor acts like a normal VPN to allow you to hide your identity and activity. You know what a VPN is, right?"

"I know I have one on my phone and my laptop," James says. "Does that count?"

"Close enough." Julia continues. "In simple terms, a VPN, or Virtual Private Network, allows you to create a secure connection to another network over the Internet. When you browse the web while connected to a VPN, your computer contacts the website through the encrypted VPN connection. The VPN forwards the request for you, and forwards the response from the website back through the secure connection. A VPN can allow you to access region-restricted websites, or to keep your activities private when using an unsecured Wi-Fi."

"Or search the dark web?" James asks.

"Or search the dark web," Julia confirms. "With Tor, the effect of a VPN is accelerated so that an accessed website is bounced through several layers of encryption to appear to be at another website address on the Tor network, just as it does with an IP address. Now, not all dark web sites use Tor. Some use similar services such as I2P, but the principle is the same. You use the same encryption tool as the site, and you must know where to find the site in order to type in the URL and view it."

"We are with you so far," James says.

"Technically, this is not a difficult process. You simply need to install and use Tor." Julia turns her attention to Erica. "Do you want to do that now?"

"Now?" Erica looks around. "Here?"

"Sure. Why not?" Julia says. "You're connected to the Wi-Fi through a VPN."

"Yes, I am." Erica points to the VPN icon on her screen.

"Then we're set. Go to www.torproject.org and download the Tor Browser bundle. This will have all the tools you'll need."

Erica works diligently as Julia speaks.

Julia points to the laptop. "There. Go ahead and run the downloaded file. When an extraction location comes up, just extract to your C drive. Now open the folder." She pauses while Erica catches up. "Good. Now click on 'Start Tor Browser.' Presto. That's all there is to it. As soon as Tor is ready, the browser will open, and you can use it much like any other web browser. Then you can just close it to disconnect from the network."

"Wow. There we are!" Erica shows her laptop screen to

James, who has craned his neck to see what they're doing.

"You could have found the directions for what we just did on a thousand different sites," Julia says. "My guess is, you really need help to know where to look on the deep web."

"That would be highly accurate," James replies.

"So are you going to tell me what you're looking for?"

"Who," James says.

"Excuse me?" Julia replies.

"We aren't looking for something," James says. "We are trying to communicate with someone."

Julia turns to Erica. "Does he always talk like this?"

"Unfortunately, yes. But after a while, it becomes part of his charm."

Julia returns to looking at James. "I can't help you if I don't know what you want to find."

Despite knowing Julia is correct, James remains hesitant to say too much.

He replies, "We want to contact a criminal who, of course, does not have a Facebook or LinkedIn profile. We are hoping that there might be resources on the deep web to allow us to reach out."

"Bobby said this was a bit outside the box," Julia says.

Erica leans closer to her. "If this worries you in any way, we can stop right here."

"Oh, no." Julia waves her off. "Sounds like a fun challenge."

"Good," Erica replies. "We want to try to contact Rafael Caro Quintero, or someone in close to him in his current organization."

Julia sits up, hands on her hips. "I seriously have no idea who or what you are talking about."

"Sorry." Erica puts her hands up in a placating gesture. "Sometimes we forget. Rafael Caro Quintero is a narcotics trafficker in Mexico that is wanted by both the American and Mexican governments. He is a very bad guy."

"But you want to talk to him!" Julia asks.

"We do," James says.

"So you want me to troll some key sites on the dark web to see if I can get someone associated with this Caro guy to bite and engage in a conversation with you, without them knowing it's you? Kinda like dark web catfishing?" Julia says, with a twinkle.

"You lost me a bit on the last part," James replies. "But yes."

"You all are crazy," Julia says. "But let me see what I can do."

She goes to work on her computer and for the next twenty minutes or so, as James and Erica watch, without having any real idea what she is doing.

As Julia types, James whispers to Erica, "Look at her go. I couldn't type that fast if I wasn't trying to make words."

Julia flashes an annoyed look. "This is going to take a few minutes, you know."

"It happens much faster on TV," James says.

"Well, this ain't TV. You might want to do something other than stare at me until I'm done."

James and Erica bide their time with several trips to the Starbucks bathroom, an additional drink for all, and several minutes of work on their phones.

Finally, Julia stops. "There."

James perks up. "There? What there? What does 'there' mean?"

"I've put feelers out on several social networks that focus on the seedier side of life."

"Those things really exist?" Erica says.

"There are many of them," Julia replies. "More than you'd expect, I'd guess."

"What do we do now?" James gazes at the computer screen.

"We all go home." Julia clutches her purse and stands up. "And you wait."

CHAPTER FORTY-FIVE

FOUR DAYS LATER, James returns home from a long run, retrieves a bottle of water from the refrigerator, opens the balcony doors and admires the view while he cools down. Upon returning to the air-conditioned condo a few minutes later, he eyes his cell phone on the kitchen counter. Turns it over and sees he has missed a text.

Damn it. The one time I go for a run without my Apple watch.

The text is from Julia. "I've been monitoring the sites I accessed for you. There is a message on one. Open the files on your laptop, as I showed you, and you should be able to have a chat. Be certain you have your VPN working. Text me if you have any technical issues."

James thanks Julia and immediately texts Erica to come over to his place. "Julia's magic worked. Come over and we can find out together. I won't do a thing until you get here—except shower, which you will appreciate."

Erica's response is quick. "On my way!"

A few minutes later, a freshly showered James descends the steps to the living room, his running gear replaced by a navy polo shirt and Tommy Bahama shorts. He opens his laptop on the coffee table and checks to be certain the VPN is working, when Erica buzzes from downstairs. James lets her in without speaking, and opens his door, leaving it ajar. He is back on the sofa in front of the laptop when Erica enters.

"I have it set up, but haven't started anything."

"Smart man." Erica sits next to him.

"As you know," James says, "Julia said she left messages on several dark web social media sites, with the information we gave her. Enough to pique an interest perhaps, but nothing more."

"We got a hit?" Erica replies.

"A response, for sure. Are you ready?"

"Open it!"

With a crisp press of a button, James opens the message: "I know who you are looking for, but why should he care about you?"

With a slight nod of approval from Erica, James replies, "We have something to offer. We can help."

"Now what?" Erica asks.

"I guess we wait."

To the amazement of both, the wait was short-lived.

"You sound like DEA trying to trap someone. You have nothing he needs."

James had mentally prepared for this discussion, even if he didn't really expect it to happen. He quickly types in a reply that he hopes will spark increased curiosity.

"We can offer him something he can never get on his own—legitimacy."

This time, there is a much longer pause.

"Do you want to go home," James says, "and I'll call you if there is a response? Or maybe order some food and wait here?"

"What do you think?" Erica replies.

"Food it is. Will you order?

"Sure. Seafood salads?"

"Great idea."

Erica steps onto the balcony to place the lunch order, while James stares at the computer screen. Several more minutes pass before the one-word response arrives. "Explain."

James's fingers are poised over the keyboard, but he sits motionless, thinking and waiting.

"You've got this," Erica says.

James carefully crafts his message. "All of America, and most of Mexico, thinks he is a ruthless murderer. His interviews did nothing to dispel those thoughts. They were self-serving, and no one believed a thing he said."

"If that doesn't amp up the volume on this nothing will," Erica says, before the immediate response confirms her projection.

Chinga tu madre, pendejo.

James smiles, knowing the response was far from a polite reference to his mother.

"The prey takes the bait," he says to Erica, before entering his retort.

But we can change that. We can tell the story in a way people will believe. We bring credibility. We offer legitimacy.

"Do you really think he cares about legitimacy? Erica says.

"I'm not sure, but I think it is a concept that might at least generate some thought.

Soon, their mystery partner replies. "Why do you think he cares at all?"

"Here goes nothing," James says to Erica, before committing himself to a more substantive reply.

Because he was released from a Mexican prison. But if he is captured now, the Mexican courts have paved the way for his extradition to the United States. He'll be thrown from a plane like Dr. Alvarez, and end up like El Chapo, locked in a tiny room 23 hours a day. He doesn't want to see his wife in custody. His kids. He doesn't want to die in jail alone. He has served his time for all his crimes, except the murder. His only chance is to show that he did not kill Camarena.

Their lunch is delivered while they wait for a response. Erica sets the table on the balcony and adds a cold bottle of white wine. James and Erica bask in the afternoon sun, patiently waiting in an easy silence that has replaced their normal playful banter.

The sun is starting to set when a response finally is

received. James looks at the simple text and shows it to Erica. "How?"

"Loquacious son of a bitch isn't he," Erica says, as James types a response.

Let us do an interview. Anywhere you want. Any conditions you want. We have studied this case for years. We can present people with an interview that will answer questions. We can provide a narrative of innocence and exoneration.

"I must say," Erica says, as James hits enter to send his reply, "if that doesn't get a response, I don't know what would."

They clean the dishes and tidy up from their meal while semi-patiently waiting for a response. Their restraint is soon rewarded.

Call this number. 619-555-4343. Write it down. Use the word Badiraguato. No more communications here. Ever.

With that comment, the conversation thread is deleted, much to James's amazement.

"Good thing we jotted down the number when we did," he says.

The municipality of Badiraguato in Sinaloa includes Caro's hometown of La Noria, James thinks.

"It's either him, or someone doing one hell of a job setting us up."

CHAPTER FORTY-SIX

MONDAY MORNING, Erica and James sit at the small conference table in his office—the marine layer obscuring their view of the ocean—waiting for what seems like a good time in the morning to call.

Finally, around 9:30 a.m, James can wait no more.

"Here goes nothing." Using the speaker so Erica can listen in, James dials 619-555-4343. On the third ring, the call is answered by a male voice.

"Hello."

"I was instructed to call this number and to use the word 'Badiraguato.'"

"Mister Butler, I assume."

"That's right. To whom am I speaking?"

"If you would like to continue the discussion from the weekend, you can meet Attorney David Anderson at his office in San Diego, tomorrow morning at ten a.m."

"Just like that?"

"Just like that."

"Okay. I'll be there." The words are barely out of his mouth when the call is ended.

Erica works furiously on her laptop. "Looking him up now. Here he is. Former federal prosecutor. Partner at Robbins Geller. On his own for the last twelve years or so. Offices in a nice building just off the Gaslamp Quarter. Seems legit. You gonna go?"

"I think I have to," James says. "Don't you?"

"Yes, but that doesn't mean I have to like it. This is moving into different territory."

"I know."

"Do you want to know what really bothers me?" Erica asks.

"Sure, why not," James reluctantly agrees.

"You talked to whoever last weekend, on the dark web, right. Then how did he know who you were?"

"I have no idea..." James looks out over the ocean, pondering his predicament."

The next morning, James takes the easy drive to San Diego. The ninety minutes fly by, and soon James is parking in the garage at the Westin, directly across the street from Anderson's office building. Though the walk is short, today James notices everyone on the street, and can't help looking around far more than normal.

I bet I'd look suspicious as hell to anyone paying attention.

The building is across the street from both the federal courthouse and the federal building, and two blocks from the Metropolitan Correctional Center. Normally, James would have had Bobby someplace close. But since he was meeting with another lawyer in a good part of town, today he decided to go it alone.

Before getting on the elevator, James texts Erica: "Here. I'll check in when I'm done."

James confirms Anderson's office is on the fourteenth floor, with the security guard at the front desk, and takes the middle row of elevators. The elevator doors open, and a directory on the wall points to an accounting firm to the right and the Law Offices of David R. Anderson to the left. James walks through the glass doors to the lobby area sitting adjacent to a large conference room with a remarkable view of the Pacific Ocean, Coronado Island, and the naval base.

James exhales in a low, impressed whistle.

"Spectacular, isn't it," says the receptionist at the desk, to James's right, her name plate identifying her as Jayne Herrera.

"Yes, it is," James replies.

"I never get bored looking at it. You must be Mister Butler."

"Guilty."

"Mister Anderson is expecting you. Would you like anything to drink?"

"No, ma'am. Thank you. I'm fine."

Jayne leads James to a corridor of offices, past several offices apparently housing attorneys with voluminous files. At the end of the hall, James enters the large corner office, and James follows.

"Mister Anderson, this is James Butler."

Anderson had been sitting on a sofa at one end of the office, and rises to greet James as Jayne leaves the office, closing the door behind her.

Anderson is older than James expected—probably in his mid-sixties. His tailored suit fits with the office décor—tasteful, expensive, but not gaudy.

The two men shake hands.

"Good morning, Mister Butler. Please have a seat." Anderson points to one of the plush accent chairs on either side of a sofa.

"Thank you." James looks around the expansive office as he sits.

"Not quite what you expected, is it?"

"I'm not sure what I expected, but I'm pretty sure this was not it."

Anderson takes a seat in the other accent chair.

"A few ground rules first," he says.

"Fine with me," James replies.

"Other than you and me, no names."

"Easy enough. Unwelcome ears?

"Probably not. But one never knows."

"Second," Anderson continues, "I'd like to retain your

legal services and have a check for a retainer in the amount of one thousand dollars made out to your firm's trust account. I'd like to discuss some criminal matters that I have pending."

"I will have it deposited today," James says.

"Now, when would you like to set up this Zoom call?" Anderson asks, dispensing with any preliminary small talk.

"Now we have an issue," James replies forcefully, but politely, adjusting his posture to match his tone. "This is not going to be a Zoom meeting. If I am going to put my reputation on the line, it will be for a personal meeting, not a Zoom call."

"Okay," Anderson says. "If, for the sake of argument, such a meeting could be agreed upon, it will have to be just you."

"It will be me and my paralegal."

"Miss Walsh, I assume."

"You've done your homework."

"I tend to think I'll live a longer, happier life if I leave as little to chance as possible.

"You bring up a point," James says. "On the call Monday, setting up this nice get together, my identity was known, which should not have been possible."

"Rest assured, Mister Butler...nothing nefarious. But there are not a lot of people generally fitting the profile presented. It was not a difficult process of identification. Being incognito is not your forte. Nor Miss Walsh's. Speaking of whom, I'm pretty sure there will be no issues with her accompanying you, as long as there is no one else."

"That's fine." James says. "But I do have one requirement of my own."

"What's that?"

"I won't do it in the mountains, hours away from everything else. We need to be able to get in and get out."

"How exactly do you expect us to accommodate such a request?" Anderson's demeanor is business-like.

"Not my problem." James adjusts his suit jacket in his chair, before sweeping his hand thorough his hair. "And it's not a request. It is a requirement for this to get done."

Anderson sits back a reflects for a moment. "Have you vacationed in Mexico, Mister Butler?"

"I have. I've been to the Yucatán many times, as well as Puerto Vallarta. Many years ago, I took a cruise that stopped in Acapulco, Mazatlán, and Los Cabos."

"Did you like Mazatlán?" Anderson asks.

"I did. I parasailed there, which was fun until I thought I was going to hit a hotel on my way down."

"Mazatlán has a lot to offer," Anderson says. "You should go back. Maybe during Carnival."

Carnival is the biggest annual event of the year in Mazatlán, and the third largest Carnival celebration in the world. The first Carnival in Mazatlán was in 1898, and it has been an annual event since. A tradition of the Mazatlán Carnival is "la batalla naval," the mock naval battle that takes place offshore. Large ships anchored in the water use fireworks to depict ammunition used in naval battles, and light up the sky.

"Isn't that a bit cliché?" James replies. "With a lot of people come lots of eyes."

"Perhaps. But have you ever gone someplace and felt like you could just become anonymous in a crowd?"

"Indeed, I have," James says. "I've also gone in the off-season, when no one seems to care about anyone else. I often check with my traveling companions to see what they prefer, and usually acquiesce to their wishes. But isn't Carnival in the spring? A lot could happen to alter our travel plans between now and the spring."

"You make a valid point," Anderson says. "Me, personally, I like the celebrations around Mexican Independence Day, on September 15th. They are a bit more reverential, and less raucous. But that's only two weeks away. Could you travel that quickly?"

"I know I could use a vacation," James says. "Miss Walsh, too, I expect. Mexican Independence Day sounds wonderful."

SOMEONE HAD TO DIE

As the men talk, James feels the cell phone in his chest pocket vibrating to notify him of an incoming text, which he ignores. Seconds later, he feels another vibration, followed almost immediately by a third.

"Damn it. Do you mind if I look to see who apparently cannot wait to get my attention?"

"Of course not," Anderson says.

James pulls his phone out of the pocket and sees that Steve Williams has texted him three times. He opens the last text and reads the short message: "Someone just called me. Leave now! FBI is on the way."

Looking at Anderson, James stands. "Apparently, I need to leave. The FBI is on the way in."

"There's no need to worry. They come up on occasion. We chat, they leave."

"Sounds nice and chummy. But if it's all the same to you, I'd really prefer to leave before they get here."

"Suit yourself. Follow me." Anderson leaves his office, leading James into the lobby and down a corridor to a set of double doors.

Anderson uses his key card to open the doors, and leads James into a bay for the freight elevator.

"This will take you to the main floor, just off the lobby. You can slip out to the right and take the stairs to the garage."

"Got it," James says, ignoring that he had parked across the street, and not in the building's garage.

As the elevator doors shut, Anderson tries to be reassuring.

"I'll keep them occupied for a bit."

The door shuts, and the freight elevator slowly descends the eighteen floors. When the door opens, James peeks out to his left and can see four people—2 men and two women—in black suits, entering through the main doors. He calmly waits for the group to get on an elevator, before strolling out the revolving door, his head down.

James darts across 1st Avenue, to the parking garage,

running down the two flights of stairs to his level. He quickly surveys the area before unlocking his car. Seeing no one around, he breathes a bit easier.

James slowly drives to the pay kiosk at the exit, scanning for anyone approaching. He inputs the ticket, followed by his credit card, which is inserted incorrectly and spit back out.

Nice job, dumbass.

James reinserts the card. "Come on, come on," he mutters. Finally, the kiosk says, "Your credit card has been accepted."

James reaches for his card, hearing the kiosk say, "If you want a receipt..."

But he speeds off before hearing the remainder of the sentence. No, I don't want a goddamn receipt. I just want to get out of here.

Once on the freeway heading home, James dials Williams's office number, which goes directly to voicemail.

"You've reached Assistant United States Attorney Stephen Williams..."

James hangs up and voice prompts a text message to Williams. "Just checking in with you."

A return message from Williams soon arrives. "Can't talk now. I'll call you about the BBQ later."

Understanding Williams's situation, James dictates a brief response: "Sounds good. I've invited 20 people. Think that's too many?"

James then texts Erica. "Gone. Lots to discuss. Looking forward to our Mexican vacation."

The following day, James is working in his office when Kathy, the firm's regular receptionist, alerts James over the intercom.

"Two FBI agents are coming your way."

Immediately after hearing those words, James looks to see the two male agents from yesterday, at his door.

"Some people wait at the reception area."

"This is not a social call, Mister Butler."

"Damn straight it's not. But come in and have a seat, nevertheless."

The two men enter the office and sit in the two guest chairs in front of James, who returns to the leather chair behind his desk.

"I'm FBI Senior Agent Martin Stewart. And this is my partner, Agent Brian Fox."

"How can I help you, Agent Stewart?"

"Did you visit the office of a San Diego attorney, David Anderson, yesterday?"

"Agent Stewart." James slides his chair closer to his desk. "This meeting will go much better if you don't ask obvious questions, or questions to which you already know the answers. You would not be here if I hadn't been in San Diego yesterday."

"Did you meet with Mister Anderson yesterday?"

"Yes, I did."

"What did you speak about?"

"That information is protected by attorney-client privilege."

"Was anyone else there?"

"That information is protected by attorney-client privilege."

"Did you discuss Rafael Caro Quintero?"

"That information is protected by attorney-client privilege."

"Is that going to be your response to every question, Mister Butler?"

"That would be a wise assumption, Agent Stewart."

Agent Stewart stands to lean over James's desk, and Agent Fox rises next to his partner.

"Perhaps we should bring you into the office for more questioning, where you won't be nearly as comfortable or as smug."

Brian enters the office. "That's a great idea. In fact, when you do that, I'll leave with you and drive to the federal courthouse to get a writ of mandamus from Judge Carney."

Stewart turns. "And you are?"

"Brian Castle. My name is on the wall in the reception area you two so impolitely ignored. Tell you what. On my way to discuss your behavior with Judge Carney, I might also call my old law school classmate. I know him as Danny. You might know him as Deputy Director Daniel Wells. Come to think of it, when I was at US Attorney Reyes's house on Saturday night for his charity auction, he told me not to hesitate to give him a call if he could ever help me out. I think I'll call him after Danny and I talk."

"Your point is made, Mister Castle."

"No, I don't think it is. My point is, don't ever think you can get away with these bush league tactics with anyone in my firm, let alone Mister Butler. If he appeared smug, as I think you called him, it's only because he is exceptionally good and has the unquestioned support of this firm and everyone in it. So if you want to pick a fight, let's go. If not, it's time for you to leave."

"Fine. We'll leave. But Mister Butler, this is not over."

"I'd be disappointed if it was." James flashes a cocky smile as Stewart stares at him before turning to leave with Agent Fox.

Brian shuts the office door behind them.

James stands and smiles at him. "You are so sexy when you're riled up."

"Hell, that was fun. I was almost hoping they'd take you in!"

"Thanks a lot."

"Whatever you are doing is stirring the pot. Keep it up. Just be careful. The universe of people looking to stop you is growing and becoming much more dangerous."

CHAPTER FORTY-SEVEN

THE CITY OF MAZATLÁN IS A BEACH RESORT town in the Mexican state of Sinaloa, located on the Pacific coast across from the southernmost tip of the Baja California Peninsula. Mazatlán was founded in 1531, by an army of Spaniards and indigenous people. By the mid-ninteenth century, Mazatlán was home to a large community of German immigrants, whose influence can be heard in the local music—banda—with some genres having their roots in Bavarian folk music.

Of important note to some, the Pacifico Brewery was established in Mazatlán on March 14, 1900. Today, Mazatlán is the second-largest city in Sinaloa, and is also a popular tourist destination, with its beaches lined with resort hotels.

Over the next two weeks, James had a few very brief email exchanges with Anderson to confirm the trip to Mazatlán on Mexican Independence Day.

James and Erica were surprised to learn that there were no direct flights to Mazatlán from nearby Orange County Airport. James secures a town car service to pick up Erica and then him, and drive them to LAX, thirty-five miles away.

The flight to Mazatlán lasts barely two and a half hours. Soon, the beaches and resorts of Mazatlán are in view as the plane approaches General Rafael Buelna International Airport. James had a reservation at the exclusive Pueblo Bonito Resorts and Spas, which sent a car and driver to the airport to pick up he and Erica.

James and Anderson had agreed that the interview would be in Mazatlán this week, but the precise date or time was yet to be confirmed. So James booked a two-bedroom villa for the next five nights, not wanting to be stuck without a room if the wait drug on.

He and Erica receive their complimentary flute of champagne upon check-in, and unpack in their suite.

"Now what?" Erica asks, after unpacking.

"I think we wait."

"Great. We wait," Erica repeats, deadpan.

"On the positive side, I'm pretty sure we'll eat and drink well."

The next morning, a hungover James is awakened by the hum of a text on his phone.

Joe's Oyster Bar. You'll blend in with the tourists. 8:30 pm. If anything seems amiss, the party is canceled.

James's replies, "Acknowledged."

The rest of the day is a study in patience for James and Erica. They spend much of the day discussing the tenor of the interview and the questions to ask. As with the Félix Gallardo interview, Erica will ask the questions in Spanish to maintain the flow. Plus, James expects Caro will like Erica and be much more comfortable with her.

At 7:45 p.m., the resort's car begins the drive to Joe's Oyster Bar, which sits on the beach in the main tourist area, commonly referred to as the Golden Zone. During the day, Joe's is a beach bar with food, drink, and music, and great views of the three islands offshore from Mazatlán. At 8:00 p.m., Joe's turns into a nightclub with dance music and dancing both inside and in the open beach air.

James and Erica enter just a few moments after 8:00 p.m., and the club already is busy and loud. As planned, they make a slow walk around the club before approaching the bar and ordering two drinks—a Pacifico for James, and a Piña Colada for Erica. As luck would have it, they find a table near the front of the bar and take seats there.

"And now we wait," James says.

"Again." Erica's shoulders sag.

James finishes his beer more quickly than intended, and a waitress takes his order for a second.

"I'm not sure if I should stop drinking, or drink a lot more," James says, after the second Pacifico is placed in front of him.

"I don't think you have the option any longer," Erica says.

James looks up and sees three men walking toward them. None act particularly threatening, though each conveys the clear impression that they are not to be messed with.

The three stop a few feet from the table, and one walks to James and Erica while the other two stay behind.

"Mister Butler. Miss Walsh. My name is Javier. I'll be your escort to the party tonight."

"Thank you," James says. "I just need to pay the tab."

"It's okay. We will take care of it." Javier nods to one of the men behind him, who walks to the bar. "Please follow me."

Javier leads James and Erica to the parking lot at the adjacent Hotel Playa Mazatlán. The lot is well-lit, which gives James and Erica a degree of comfort. In the lot, they are led to a black Ford Expedition.

"Before you get in, we need to check you for weapons," Javier says, as one of the other men starts the Expedition.

"We would expect nothing less," James replies.

Javier and another man pat down James and Erica. Javier pulls out James's cell phone.

"That, I am keeping," James says. "Rules of the party."

"I know," Javier replies. "Just making sure it was a phone."

Erica's hand purse also is searched, and her phone inspected before it is returned to her purse.

"My friends," Javier says. "I am sorry, but I must cover your eyes before we go anywhere."

"That's okay," James replies. "But first I want to know how long the drive is. We had some guidelines."

"Mister Butler, I can assure you we will not be going far, and will not be leaving the city."

"That's helpful," James says.

With that, he and Erica are blindfolded and guided into the Expedition. Javier joins James and Erica in the back seat, with Erica in the middle. The Expedition pulls out of the parking lot and obviously starts down Avenida Playa Gaviotas before turning away from the ocean, at which point James begins to lose perspective on the route being taken. Fifteen or twenty minutes pass before the vehicle starts to traverse what appear to be residential streets, at a slower speed, many stops and a few turns. Finally, the Expedition pulls into a driveway and comes to a stop.

"We will get out here," Javier says. "But please leave your eyes covered until I give you the word."

"Understood," James and Erica say in unison.

James and Erica are helped from the Expedition and escorted to a door. Because they did not climb any steps, James assumes this is a side door and not a front porch.

The door is opened, and they enter, walking carefully. Once inside, Javier shuts the door and removes the blindfolds from James and then Erica.

"Stay here." Javier leaves the room.

Three men remain to watch James and Erica—the two men from Joe's, and a new one who must have been here before they arrived.

James looks around, trying to be innocuous. This appears to be a small house. They are currently in the tiny kitchen, and James can see a hallway to a living room in the front of the house.

Erica reaches over and takes James's hand. He looks to the small kitchen table and points to the chairs.

"Por favor?" he asks the man from the bar, who merely nods.

James and Erica sit and wait.

A few more minutes pass before Javier returns to the kitchen.

"This way, please."

James and Erica stand and follow Javier out the doorway and left, down the hall, past a small bathroom, to a bedroom at the end of the hall. The door is shut as Javier, James, and Erica approach.

Javier whispers instructions to James and Erica.

"Remember, there is a time limit. Please be calm and sensible. Say nothing to upset him. Do not make any sudden moves. Understood?"

"Understood," James replies.

"Agreed," says Erica.

Javier opens the door to the bedroom. A man sits in an easy chair near the far wall of the room. Two wooden side chairs sit in the middle of the room. One torchiere light illuminates the small room. The walls are freshly painted, but completely bare.

James and Erica enter the room, followed by Javier, who closes the door behind them. Javier points to the two chairs, and James and Erica sit.

"How do we know it's him?" Erica whispers.

"It's him. That's Rafael Caro Quintero."

CHAPTER FORTY-EIGHT

CARO LOOKS LIKE the seventy-one-year-old man he is now. But James notes that while he looks old, he doesn't look ill or frail—in stark contrast to Félix Gallardo's appearance.

Caro is dressed casually, but his boots are new and shiny, matched by newer jeans, and a crisp pale-blue shirt. His hair looks to have recently been washed, and even styled.

Caro sits up as James and Erica take their seats, which James attributes to Caro's delight in seeing a beautiful woman. There is a small table next to the chair on which James sits.

"Please put your phones on the table," Javier says. "You can have them back after the interview."

Erica hands James her phone as he removes his phone from his jeans pocket, and places both on the small table. Seeing James's compliance, Javier moves to stand to the right of Caro. Once in place, Javier gives Erica a subtle nod to begin.

Erica speaks with Caro in Spanish, while James tries to understand and waits for Erica's shorthand translations.

"My name is Erica, and this is James. Do you mind if we ask you a few questions?"

"That's why we are here. Ask your questions."

"In Spanish, not English, right?"

"Yes, please," Caro says.

"James does not speak Spanish, so I will translate your responses for him, as needed."

"That's fine. You are much more beautiful to talk to, anyway."

"When I thought about your past and our discussion today, one of the first things I wanted to ask you about was your time in prison. What was prison life like for you?"

"The first couple years were not too unpleasant. The prison conditions were adequate. But then the politics in Mexico City changed, and I was made to be an example. Life got very hard. I never had enough to eat. I was always too hot or too cold. Medicine was rare."

"Given those difficulties, how did it feel to walk out of prison in 2013?"

"Freedom is a beautiful thing. Especially when it has been taken from you for something you did not do."

"How have you been living?"

"My family is kind, and they have helped me. I am very poor and always afraid. I have the clothes on my back and shoes on my feet, but not much more."

"Are you afraid of going back to prison?"

"I trust the Mexican judicial process. A Mexican judge applied the law and said I had served my time. I believe it was fair and just."

"What about being extradited to the US?"

"The United States has had a vendetta against me for nearly forty years. They are convinced I'm guilty of a crime I did not commit. The United States cannot look in the mirror and accept its own flaws. They need someone to blame. I'm the piñata at the US government's fiesta. If they can break me, they all can celebrate. The United States government does not care about justice. They are about power and retribution."

"Did you grow marijuana?"

"Of course. I was poor. My family was poor. Everyone around me was poor. Marijuana was a way for us to put food on the table. To own homes and cars. I'm told marijuana is legal in much of the United States, and likely soon will be legal in Mexico. I did nothing wrong. I was enterprising and successful, and the government didn't like to see a poor boy from Sinaloa become rich and powerful."

"Did you pay off police officials? DFS? Politicians?"

"I did nothing improper. Did some police or DFS work for me in their off hours? Sure. Did I contribute to the campaigns and activities of certain politicians? Of course. But so did hundreds of businessmen across Mexico, and they do so to this day. This is Mexico, *chica*, not the United States. We have our own way of doing things."

"What about Manuel Bartlett Diaz?"

"I know of Señor Bartlett."

"Did Bartlett Diaz work with you?"

"I have never met Señor Bartlett in my life. I have never seen him in person. You don't need to believe everything you read."

"Which is exactly why I am here, asking you these questions. So I don't have to believe what I read. What about the CIA? Did you work with the CIA?"

"Let me be very clear. I never worked with the CIA. I did not know anyone from the CIA. Before I was arrested, I did not know what the CIA was."

"How close were you to Félix Gallardo?"

"I knew Miguel from when we both worked with Aviles, and we moved to Guadalajara around the same time."

"Were you close? Were you friends?"

"No. We were friendly. I had my friends. He had his. Some days, we worked together. Some days—most days—we worked alone."

"You weren't partners?"

"No. Definitely not partners."

"Did he have a financial interest in any of your businesses?"

"Some. As I said, sometimes we did business together."

"Did you work with Juan Ramon Matta Ballesteros?"

"Matta was Félix's friend, not mine. I met him once, at my

home, a few weeks, maybe, before I left Mexico. Matta was a strange and scary man."

"Were you involved in the incident with the two Americans at La Longosta?"

"What incident?"

"Surely, you know the story. Two Americans walked into the La Longosta. You were having a meeting inside, and thought they were DEA agents, and had them killed—ice-picked to death."

"*Loco.* If I was having a meeting there, or anywhere, trust me, *chica*, no one would just walk in. I was a businessman, not an animal. Killing anyone in the La Longosta would be bad for business. I did not kill them. I did not order them killed. I don't know what happened to them."

"Can we talk about Agent Camarena now?"

"Sure. I assumed that was what you wanted to talk about."

"Did you order Camarena kidnapped?"

"I have said this for nearly forty years, and I'll say it until I die—I was not involved in the Camarena matter at all."

"Were you present for his interrogation? Were you there when he died?"

"I just told you. I was not involved."

"But you know, others have placed you there, and even identified your voice on the recordings of the interrogations?"

"I cannot prevent people from lying about me. I cannot prevent people from making false accusations against me."

"Was 881 Lope de Vega your house?"

"I owned many houses. I believe Javier had just helped me acquire that house. We had two parties there that I remember. I did not live there."

"I'd like to give you a chance to explain. Why should anyone believe you were not involved in the Camarena case? When I go back home and tell people to believe you, what will I tell them?"

Caro sits up and puffs out his chest. "I was rich, free, and happy. All of that came to an end when the agent was killed.

For every dollar the agent cost me in confiscated marijuana, I made ten more. For every pound of marijuana destroyed, I planted ten more. There were other sources of income the DEA knew nothing about, and could not have imagined. The Mexican government left us alone. The DFS left us alone. The police left us alone. I had no reason to kill anyone. I had no reason to mess with the life and business I had."

CHAPTER FORTY-NINE

JAMES AND ERICA LET CARO SPEAK, uninterrupted. Moments after Caro concludes, they are startled as all the lights in the house go out, followed by a *Bang!* from the kitchen area. Javier leaves the room and is met by the sounds of muted gunfire and what sounds to James like tasers, even as he notes that he really had no idea what tasers sound like.

James whispers to Erica, "Grab your phone and follow me."

Erica takes the phones off the table, hands James his, and clasps onto James's hand.

"What about Caro?" Erica says.

"Screw him."

James starts to lead Erica out the door, when he is confronted by two men, dressed in black tactical gear, masks, and automatic rifles.

James and Erica back up.

"Against the wall," one yells in Spanish, as the other attends to Caro, zip-tying his hands behind him and taping his mouth.

A third masked gunman enters the room, yelling at James and Erica.

"Vámos! Vámos!" The gunman pushes them toward the door.

James leads the way through the hallway and sees four of Caro's guards on the ground, hands zip-tied behind their backs. James walks toward the front door, but at the kitchen, the gunman yells, "A la izquierda," which James knows means he is to turn left.

Across the kitchen, James reaches a door leading to an alley. He continues that path, followed by Erica and the gunman.

At the alley, a white cargo van is parked, engine running. James can barely see in the window to the driver's seat, but detects the outline of a driver outfitted like the others. The gunman opens the side door to the van.

"Entras," he says, not yelling now.

The van has a bench aligned with each side. James and Erica climb inside as the gunman tells them "Siéntese, por favor," which a whispering Erica translates as "Sit down, please."

Moments later, the other two gunmen approach the van, with Caro in custody with them. Caro is pushed into the van and roughly seated on the bench across from James and Erica. One gunman attaches Caro's bound hands to a handcuff-like device welded to the side of the van, and places a heavy mask over Caro's head. The other gunman sits down and raps on the small widow to the front cabin. Hearing the signal, the driver puts the van into drive and proceeds down the alley.

The van takes a few turns before merging onto what appears to James to be a major street. He starts to take inventory of everything around him and all that he can sense.

Soon, though, his mental processing is disrupted when one of the gunmen removes his mask.

"This thing is too damn hot."

"Speer!" Erica says.

The second gunman's mask is also removed.

"Good morning, Miss Walsh," says Aguilar. "James."

"Son of a bitch," Erica says, vitriol oozing from her words. "Any other surprises?"

The third gunman, who had escorted James and Erica from the house, removes his mask as well.

"I hope I wasn't too rough on you," says Tom, Aguilar's friend from the bar.

"You?" James says. "From the bar, with Aguilar."

"What the literal hell?" Erica shouts.

"I understand you are upset, Miss Walsh," says Aguilar, his tone calm and methodical.

"Upset doesn't begin to cover it."

"I promise to explain in good time. But for now, we have to get out of Mazatlán and out of Mexico. Half the country is going to be looking for our friend here very soon."

"An explanation would be nice," James says. "But for now, please tell me you have a plan."

"Of course we have a plan," Aguilar says. "And the first step is to dump this van."

A few minutes later, the van turns back onto side streets. Abruptly, it turns into an alley before coming to a stop inside a small garage in an industrial section of town. The door to the garage shuts immediately after the Escalade enters.

"Get out," Aguilar says.

James and Erica exit the van to find they have parked next to a black Cadillac Escalade with its rear hatch open. Tom and Speer guide Caro from the van to the rear of the Escalade, keeping him both restrained and gagged. Another man brings Speer a small bag, which he places on the ground next to him.

Speer opens the bag and extracts a syringe and a small vial from a dry ice pack.

"This is etorphine," he says. "A synthetic opioid used to induce unconsciousness. The drug is designed for use by vets on large mammals, like elephants. Though not licensed for use on humans, when administered in smaller doses, it has similar effects to many strong opiates that are used on humans. We have to be careful not to give too much, because an overdose could be fatal." Speer draws the liquid into the syringe, measuring carefully as he talks. "Interestingly, this was the drug of choice by the lead character in the television series *Dexter*."

"I, for one, appreciate the trivia at a time like this," Erica says.

Aguilar cuts a small slit into in the upper right arm of Caro's shirt, before Speer injects the etorphine into Caro's deltoid.

"The difference between television and real life, though," Speer says, "is that rather than getting a near instant reaction, it will probably take our friend here about fifteen minutes to fall into a peaceful sleep, which should last about eight hours, more or less." He removes the tape covering Caro's mouth. "Let's let him breath some. I don't want him dying on us."

Once the tape is removed, an irate Caro begins yelling in a fit of rage. Aguilar turns up the air conditioning in the garage, muffling Caro's words to anyone but those inside.

Caro looks around and continues yelling in Spanish.

"You are all dead! Every single one of you. Dead! I'll have you all filleted, just like I did with your friend."

Erica moves toward Caro and responds to him in Spanish, matching him in intensity and ire.

"Who are you talking about?"

"That pendejo Camarena. That's what this is about."

"So you had Camarena killed?"

"No, my little *chica*. I killed him myself. I watched the life vanish from his eyes. And soon, I'll see you die as well. But not before we have some fun with you."

James starts to move toward Caro, but Speer grabs his arm and whispers, "Let him rant. She is getting more information than we ever could."

"Who ordered you to interrogate Camarena?" Erica says.

"Ordered me? I am Rafael Caro Quintero. I don't take orders."

"Come on. Everyone knows Félix ran things, and you answered to Fonseca."

"Bullshit. I ran my business. I didn't answer to Don Neto

or that skinny bastard who thought he was better than me."

"Then the CIA must have been telling you what to do?"

"The CIA? They had nothing to do with my business. Nothing."

"Then how could you have known who to abduct? Why him? Why Camarena?"

"Do you think we were stupid? There were few DEA agents in Guadalajara. They were tracked. They were followed. They were known. Finding the one who was messing with my business was easy. Torturing him was even easier." Caro's voice fades as he leans against the Escalade. "I will remember each of you, and I'll cut your hearts out myself..." Caro falls to the ground.

"His anger got his blood flowing," Speer says, "and the drugs worked more quickly."

"But we have our answer," Erica says. "We know who killed Agent Camarena."

I hope we live long enough to tell someone, James thinks.

CHAPTER FIFTY

AGUILAR AND SPEER LIFT CARO into the Escalade's cargo bay before Aguilar places a perfectly fitting and sealed cover over the opening, making it nearly impossible to know anyone or anything is beneath it.

Speer shuts the hatch. "He will stay nice and secure here, and we will pump some air inside so he will have a nice sleep."

Aguilar tuns to Erica. "That, Miss Walsh, was the best interrogation I have ever witnessed."

"Thank you. I wish I could say I had it all planned out. It just sort of happened."

"It was perfect."

"Not to interrupt," James says, "but now that he is sleeping securely in the back of the car, what are we going to do?"

"We are going to the airport?" Aguilar replies.

"We are getting on a plane?" James asks.

"No, not the kind you're thinking. We have our own charter service waiting for us."

Speer hops into the driver's seat, with Aguilar assuming a shotgun position. A decidedly befuddled James sits in the rear seat behind Speer, as Erica slides in next to him. Tom takes one look around before climbing into the seat next to Erica as the Escalade leaves the hangar.

The drive to the Aerodromo El Roble airport is a simple ten-minute drive on Highway 512, around 17.5 kilometers from the major Mazatlán International Airport. Upon nearing the airport, Speer takes a road to the right, eschewing the main airport in favor of the freight and charter portions of the airport. Once inside the main gate, he drives down a long line of hangars—many closed for the evening, but some actively loading and unloading cargo. Near the end of the long row is a hangar with its main bay door closed, but lights clearly on inside.

Speer pulls up to the hangar's main door and honks. Moments later, the door opens, he drives in, and the door shuts behind them. In the hangar is a plane, which Speer parks next to before the passengers all exit. He takes a walk around the plane and whistles.

"Some trafficker made a nice purchase," Aguilar says, "for which we now are grateful."

Speer continues to check out the plane like a car enthusiast ogling a vintage Corvette.

"This is a Cessna 441 Conquest," he says. "It's a historic plane."

The Cessna 441 Conquest II is a pressurized, eight- to nine-passenger turboprop powered aircraft designed to fill the gap between Cessna's jets and piston-engined aircraft. The Cessna 441 cruises at 585 kilometers per hour, and has a maximum range of 3,700 kilometers at a speed of 480 kilometers per hour. The plane was also notable for its ability to cruise at 35,000 feet. During its prime, the plane's speed, range, and low costs made it an unparalleled aircraft in its class.

"We are flying this to the United States?" Erica asks.

"No," Aguilar replies. "We are flying this to Mexicali, and then we will drive over the border. If we were to fly this into the US, the odds are too great someone will see us, and we have no idea what our greeting party would look like."

"Okay, then let's go." Erica starts to bounce toward the plane.

"Patience, Erica. Patience," Aguilar says. "We need to time this out right. We want to be driving across the border tomorrow at rush hour, which is around eight a.m. It's about a four-and-a-half-hour flight to Mexicali. So we have planned to leave here around three a.m., which will put us in Mexicali around seven-thirty, and we will have a vehicle waiting to drive over the border. Tom has already filed our flight plans for a three a.m. departure."

"That's more than four hours from now, says an irritated Erica. "What do we do until then?"

Aguilar flashes a smile. "I suggest we rest in the plane. The seats should be perfect for sleeping."

"Sleep? Really?" Erica says.

"Someone needs to be refreshed to drive tomorrow. Tom will sit out here and keep watch."

Tom, Aguilar, and Speer transfer an unconscious Caro to the rear of the plane. His hands remain bound, and Aguilar handcuffs him to the seat.

"He's not going anywhere," he says. "Even if he wakes up."

Erica sits in one of the plane's leather seats.

"Oooooh, this is nice."

"Use the recliner," Speer says.

Erica presses the button on her right armrest, and her seatback slowly descends, until nearly flat.

"You win. Sleep it is." Erica rolls over and closes her eyes, while Speer takes a seat across the aisle and two rows behind her.

Aguilar starts to sit in the row behind Erica, but stops as James starts to leave the plane.

"Don't you want to wait here with us?" Aguilar says.

"Nah. I'm too wired. I'll keep Tom company out here."

James and Tom leave the plane and turn out all the lights in the hangar, save for a small lamp on a desk in the small office on the hangar's right side.

"Think we're safe here?" James asks.

"Probably. But just in case." Tom walks to the office and returns with three rifles. He hands one to James. "Have you ever used one of these before?"

"Never. I haven't shot a gun since I went hunting as a teenager."

"This is an AR-15."

An AR-15-style rifle is a lightweight semi-automatic rifle based on the ArmaLite AR-15 design. In the 2010s, AR-15-style rifles became exceptionally controversial, in part, due to their use in high-profile mass shootings, while concurrently being promoted as "America's rifle," by the National Rifle Association.

"Here is the safety." Tom points to a switch on the gun's handle. "Always leave the safety on until just before you shoot. This is a semi-automatic rifle, which means it will fire a single bullet with each pull of the trigger. But you do not need to do anything to it between shots. These particular guns have been specifically designed to be ultra-user-friendly. They have compensators which counter muzzle climb in case you are firing rapidly, and to allow the user to maintain more on-target shots. We also installed muzzle brakes to reduce gun recoil. And finally, since these might be used at night, these have flash hiders to reduce the muzzle flash from the combustion of gunpowder as bullets eject from the barrel."

"That's probably a lot more than I need to know," James deadpans.

"Probably. But the bottom line is, you can use it competently if the occasion arises."

"Got it," James says.

Tom brings two chairs from the office. "These won't be comfortable, but they will be better than the floor."

"Is it reasonable to assume that I ought not inquire much about *all of this*?" James says.

"You likely can figure it out by yourself," Tom says. "There are a lot of assets in a lot of places that are not on anyone's books."

"Enough said," James replies. "Can we talk about why Caro would be so wanted?"

"Sure," Tom says. "But to do that we have to go back in history some."

"I think we have about four hours, so I'm game," James replies.

"As we discussed before, Tom says, "the relative peace between the different trafficking factions started to erode after the arrest of Félix Gallardo, and really unraveled once his conditions were changed so that he could not continue to oversee operations from prison."

"If he had not been arrested," James says, "do you think he could have maintained the peace?"

"I don't know," Tom replies. "Félix is a bit of an enigma to me, and to those I respect who know more about him than I. I think the calm would have lasted longer. Let's take that as a given."

"But we know the calm didn't last," James says. "And now the drug trade is more fractionalized."

"That's true, and the scope of their operations has changed," Tom says. "Today, the various factions are multi-faceted, and import and distribute cocaine, fentanyl, heroin, marijuana, and methamphetamine in the United States. Broadly speaking, and I mean very broadly, because things change daily, at a minimum, today, five Mexican cartels have the biggest impact in the US: the Sinaloa Cartel, Cartel Jalisco Nueva Generación, the Juárez Cartel, the Gulf Cartel, and the remnants of Los Zetas. There are others, of course, and differing factions within each. This may be more than you care to know, but..."

"As I said, we have the time," James replies. "And I really am interested."

"Okay, then," Tom continues. "The Sinaloa Cartel, also known as the CDS, is one of the oldest and more established drug cartels in Mexico, and controls drug trafficking in several regions, especially in the so-called Golden Triangle, comprised of the Mexican states of Sinaloa, Durango, and Chihuahua. It also has the most expansive international footprint of any of the Mexican cartels, with apparent alliances with the Sicilian mafia and Japanese triads, as well as connections in mainland China.

"Following Félix Gallardo's incarceration and transfer to a maximum-security facility, his nephews, the Arellano Félix brothers, formed the Tijuana Cartel, while the Sinaloa Cartel continued to be run by Héctor Luis Palma Salazar— El Mayo—and El Chapo. Palma Salazar was arrested by the Mexican Army in 1995.

"After several arrests and escapes, El Chapo was arrested in Los Mochis, a port city in Sinaloa, in January 2016, and extradited to the United States. He was convicted on several drug-related charges in 2019, and is serving a life sentence at ADX Florence, known as Supermax.

"Following El Chapo's arrest, control of the Sinaloa Cartel was initially assumed by El Mayo. But his ill health, and the assertion of power and influence by El Chapo's sons, has led to a fractionalization of the cartel, but not a diminution of its power or influence. For a while, it seemed Chapo's kids were seizing control. Then there were reports that Chapo's brother was aligning with El Mayo, presumably to take his place when El Mayo dies.

"Recently, the DEA and the Mexican government have faced a whole new, violent group of cartels and factions. There is the Jalisco New Generation Cartel, or CJNG, based in Guadalajara, and is regarded as one of the most powerful and fastest-growing cartels both in Mexico and the United States.

"The Gulf Cartel, or CDG, may be the oldest organized crime group in Mexico, having been founded as a bootlegging operation during Prohibition. CDG has its principal base in Matamoros, Tamaulipas, directly across the border from Brownsville, Texas. CDG had a violent civil war with the Los Zetas Cartel, its former enforcement arm, which broke off as an independent organization in 2010.

"The Zetas, at one point, were regarded as Mexico's largest and most expansive drug cartel in terms of geographical presence, overtaking their rival—the Sinaloa Cartel—in terms of physical territory. However, in recent times, Los Zetas has become fragmented, and has seen its influence diminish."

"I think I understand the major players," James says. "And I also know there are a number of splinter groups, for lack of a better term. But how does this tie into Caro and our desire to get out of Mexico alive?"

"Like we discussed in the bar back home," Tom says, "after he was released from prison, Caro likely wanted back in power with the Sinaloa Cartel, but that was strenuously opposed by Los Chapitos, who appear to have prevailed in that power struggle."

"Okay," James says. "So getting to Caro would help them get rid of a rival? A seventy-one-year-old former leader who is now wanted and on the run?"

"I understand your point, James, but it could be more than that. Are you familiar with El Cholo?"

"I've read the gruesome news reports."

Carlos Enrique Sánchez, alias El Cholo, was a former key lieutenant with the CJNG, who left the group in 2017 to form the Nuevo Plaza Cartel. El Cholo was abducted by members of CJNG, tortured, and his body mutilated before it was dumped in Jardín Hidalgo, a public square in the center of Tlaquepaque, part of the Guadalajara metropolitan area. Signs were pinned to the body with knives. One of the signs read, EL TRAIDOR EL CHOLO, the traitor El Cholo.

"If you were a cartel leader," Tom says, "wanting more power, notoriety, or prestige, can you think of a better way to announce your dominance and authority to your rivals and the world?"

"If El Chapo's kids wanted to show they were firmly in charge Caro's body, dead or alive, that would do it," James replies.

"Exactly. If the CJNG are willing to butcher one of their former compatriots to make a statement," Tom says, "what kind of a statement could Chapo's make with Caro?"

"Something I'd prefer not to even consider."

"Do you want something to drink?" Tom asks. "I think there are a few beers in the refrigerator in the office."

"A beer sounds pretty good right now." James slides down into his chair while Tom retrieves the beers. "Thank you." He cracks open a cold Pacifico. "When you were talking about the current state of the cartels in Mexico, I noticed you did not mention the Tijuana Cartel."

"Bonus points to you for pronouncing it correctly," Tom says.

"On the west side of Los Angeles, there once was a great Mexican restaurant named Tia Juana's. The best fresh tortillas ever. In any event, the name helped remind me how to pronounce—or not pronounce—the city." James replies.

The Tijuana Cartel was once one of the most significant cartels in Mexico. Inherited by the Arellano-Félix brothers when Félix Rodríguez divided his territory, the Tijuana Cartel was known for its extreme violence and its feud with El Chapo's Sinaloa Cartel. In recent years, the incursion by CDS into Baja California, and the fall of the Arellano-Félix brothers, significantly diminished the power and scope of the cartel.

"It is almost sad how that organization led to the deaths of so many from one family," Tom says. "Brothers and sisters, uncles and aunts. The cartel, as rebranded, is still an influence, but really has taken a backseat, even in its namesake town, to the Sinaloa Cartel. However, some in the agency continue to believe the Toothpicks are still active, particularly in the San Diego area."

James takes note of Tom's reference to *the agency*. James had operated under the assumption that Tom was, or had been, a DEA agent. But no one had confirmed that, and James certainly was not inclined to ask.

"The Toothpicks?" James says.

"Los Palillos, or the Toothpicks, is a group operating within Tijuana Cartel, essentially serving as the armed wing of the cartel in the United States. If there are remnants of the cartel in Tijuana, and of the Toothpicks in California, I thought it best that you steer clear of the area altogether."

"Hence, flying to Mexicali and crossing at Calexico," James says.

"Correct."

"I expect Camarena would be distressed to see where the country has gone," James says. "His death led to more trafficking and more violence."

"I hate to think it was all in vain," Tom says. "The DEA made some changes. The way the agents work is different now. Security is greater. Agents' actions are monitored more closely. There is less individualism. In fact, it's probably fair to say that these days, the DEA does less of the boots-on-the-ground work that Camarena did. It's hard to think that someone had to die to get such changes made, and that so much has been left undone. Mexico is a hard country to change. Drugs and corruption are as much a party of its culture as soccer and mariachis. Not to mention the fact that money corrupts and the cartels have lots of money."

James lets the conversation lull for a moment as he studies Tom.

"You are much *friendlier* now than you were in the bar," James says.

"That was a bit of an act. The intent was to give you information for you to use, without you being overly aware that it was being given to you."

James looks around the hangar. "Apparently, it worked."

"You have big cajones, James. I respect what you've done. Do you mind my asking why?"

"Why what?"

"You're risking your life and career, and that of someone

you obviously care for greatly, but I don't see what's in it for you."

"Is it not enough to want to see justice be done?" James replies.

"Not for most people. It's none of my business. I'm still going to help make sure you get to the US, and that you and Erica are safe. But I'm curious."

A knock on the door startles both Tom and James.

"You go to the back by the plane," Tom whispers. "Take a rifle with you."

James complies and retreats to a hiding spot in the back, where he watches Tom open the door. He can hear Tom speaking in Spanish to the unknown visitor.

Damn it, I really have to learn Spanish.

Finally, Tom closes and locks the door and returns to his chair. James joins him moments later.

"Just a curious security guard. It's all taken care of."

"You sure?"

"I promise."

"Okay, in that case," James says, "I think I'm just going to sit here and rest my eyes for a few minutes."

At 2:30 a.m, Tom rustles James awake, and the two rouse the group on the plane. Aguilar checks on Caro and reports that he remains out like a light. Tom starts his process of getting the plane ready for its flight. At 3:00 a.m., Speer opens the main hangar door, and Tom taxis the plane to the outside. Speer lowers the hangar door and exits out the side door. He checks to be sure it is secured, before jogging to the plane. Once Speer is on board, Tom effectuates the closing of the stairs and begins the taxi to the runway used by charter flights. Without incident or issue, the plane is directed to get in line behind a smaller Cessna, and soon is careening down the runway before taking flight to Mexicali.

Founded on March 14, 1903, Mexicali is situated on

the Mexico–United States border adjacent to its sister city Calexico, California. Mexicali is the capital city of the Mexican State of Baja California, and seat of the Municipality of Mexicali. Mexicali's economy historically has been based on agricultural products, but has gradually added industry, mainly "maquiladoras," or duty-free factories in which parts from the United States are imported, assembled, and then returned to the United States as finished products.

On the flight, Tom advises that he will fly them to the Mexicali international airport—or officially, General Rodolfo Sanchez Taboada International Airport—the northernmost airport in Mexico. MXL is a small international airport, with one runway and one terminal servicing all its flights. A handful of airlines travel regularly to and from MXL, and there are additional charter flights to major cities throughout the year based on demand.

Nearing the airport, Tom communicates with the air traffic control and is assigned a place in line among the landing planes. He is directed to take a circle around the airport before making the approach for landing. James and Erica look out the window, observing the sister cities, separated by an invisible and arbitrary line in the desert.

Soon, though, the plane starts its approach, and Tom guides it in for a perfectly smooth landing. Tom taxis to an open hangar. Once inside, he pulls to a stop and opens the plane door. James and Erica descend the steps to another large and non-descript hangar, notable only by the presence of a black Escalade, apparently identical to the one left behind in Mazatlán.

Tom, Speer, and Aguilar also exit the plane and stretch their legs, stiff from the flight.

"What is this place?" James asks.

"This is another place that does not exist," Tom replies. "Actually, this is a hangar regularly used by the DEA and some other agencies. It's a convenient location, for the obvious reasons."

An unidentified man closes the hangar door before handing Tom a set of keys, which Tom tosses to Speer. The man goes into a room in the back of the hangar and closes the door.

"Let's get our travel companion." Aguilar walks onto the plane, Tom and Speer following close.

Aguilar has his small pouch with him, and he prepares another syringe.

"One more injection, and he should be no trouble for the rest of the journey."

"Unless you overdose him and he dies," Speer says.

"Nah, probably won't happen."

Aguilar injects Caro in the same location as before and returns the syringe to its pouch, which he then stuffs into the waist of his pants. Tom, Speer, and Aguilar unchain Caro and carry him to the Escalade, which was distinguished by a similar secured and hidden cargo bay. The men literally toss Caro into the bay, seal it up, and shut the hatch. Aguilar opens the Escalade's front passenger door.

"Now all we have to do is get past border patrol," he says.

The United States Border Patrol is the law enforcement arm of the Customs and Border Protection, within the Department of Homeland Security. The first Border Patrol Station at Calexico was established in 1939, with only six officers assigned for duty. Today, the Calexico Border Patrol Station is responsible for patrolling 37.1 linear miles of the border, and 731 square miles of Imperial County in the Sonoran Desert. The Calexico West port of entry is open and permits automobile traffic into and out of the United States twenty-four hours a day, seven days a week.

Speer climbs into the driver's seat, and James and Erica begin to take their established seats in the back. James looks back to see that Tom is not getting in.

"Are you coming?"

"No, this is the end of the line for me. If anything goes wrong, we can't have an active-duty agent involved."

James exits the Escalade and walks over to Tom, extending his hand. The men shake without uttering a word, before James returns to the Escalade and Speer drives off.

The drive takes less than five minutes, and the four approach the border crossing into Calexico.

"Ironic, isn't it?" Speer says to no one in particular.

"What's that?" Erica asks.

"Caro's days as a free man come to an end as we travel from Kiki's birthplace to his hometown."

Erica thinks for a moment. "I'm not sure that's technically irony, but it sure is poetic justice."

CHAPTER FIFTY-ONE

THE ESCALADE SLOWLY MAKES ITS WAY into the line for the security checkpoint at a little after 8:00 a.m. Every morning, hundreds of Mexicali residents lawfully cross the border to work in Calexico, only to return to Mexico in the evening. The line is long but moves efficiently.

"Remember, this is just like driving through the checkpoint in Tijuana after a day of drinking," Aguilar tells the group. "Everyone be calm and quiet, and this will go quickly and smoothly."

Within a few minutes, Speer pulls the Escalade to the border booth and rolls down the window to greet the agent.

"Good morning."

"Are you all US citizens?"

"Yes, we are."

"Where are you headed?"

"Back home to Los Angeles. Have to get back to work, you know?"

"Drive safely."

Speer rolls up the window and slowly drives through the maze that is the border crossing, while all four occupants breathe a heavy sigh of relief.

"Piece of cake," James says.

A few miles past the border crossing, James makes a phone call, placed on speaker so everyone can hear.

"Steve. It's James."

"Holy crap, man. I've been going crazy looking for you."

"Well, I'm happy to report that we are in the US of A, and are on our way to LA."

"Where are you now?"

"I'd rather not say, in case anyone is snooping. But we really need your help."

"Name it."

"We have a very HVA with us, and the plan is to deliver it to you, but we need some security. Substantial security. We can't just pull up in front of the courthouse."

"Do you want to tell me what it is? Or who we is?"

"I think it might be best if I don't."

"Are you being followed? Watched?"

"I don't think so. Hell, I don't really know, but I can't take any chances."

"Okay. When you say HVA...how significant?"

"Bigger than anything either of us have ever been involved with before. You might want to get your boss on alert. Maybe the media, too."

"Really? How long do I have?"

"We are about four hours away. I can text when we are inside of thirty minutes, if that helps."

"I can make that work. Give me a second."

Williams thinks through his options.

"Okay, here's the plan. You know the parking structure across the street from the old federal courthouse on Temple?"

"Yeah, across from the Roybal Building," James says. "Isn't that a public lot, though?"

"It is, but go into the garage and take the ramp down two levels. We will be waiting for you. Trust me."

"With my life. And Erica's, too."

"I've got your back. Both of them. Just give me the thirty-minute heads up."

"Will do." James hangs up.

"Good idea not to mention us," Aguilar says.

"Hell, I'm not even sure what I'd tell him at the moment. What route are we taking to LA?"

"We decided against going across to I-5 because of traffic," Aguilar says. "Instead, we are going north to I-10 at Indio, and we can take that into LA. It's early enough that it shouldn't be too hot for our friend."

James laughs and shakes his head. "We are bringing the most wanted man in the Western Hemisphere to justice, and we are worried about traffic!"

His witticism acts as a tension release for the four, who have a good laugh.

A few more miles down the highway, and the decidedly lighter mood is disturbed by Speer.

"Oh no."

"What?" James asks.

"A patrol car is behind us, with its lights on," Speer says.

Everyone looks behind them to see a car approaching fast, lights flashing.

"Is it the CHP?" Erica asks.

"I can't tell yet." Speer slows the Escalade down and pulls to the shoulder.

"It looks like a border patrol car," Aguilar says.

The patrol car parks a good five yards behind the Escalade, and two men get out. The driver is tall, with longer blond hair, while the passenger is shorter, with black hair and a dark complexion, and he carries a rifle with him.

"Damn it!" Aguilar says. "They aren't real agents."

"Where are your guns?" James asks.

"In the back with Caro," Aguilar replies. "We didn't want them to be seen at the border crossing."

"What do we do now?"

"You and Erica stay quiet and keep your heads down," Aguilar says.

The two men from the patrol car start to approach the Escalade, the blond moving to toward the driver's door, while the dark-haired man stays to the rear, the rifle held loosely at his side. Speer rolls down the driver's window and places his hands on the top of the steering wheel.

"What seems to be the problem here?"

The blond looks through the window, searching around the interior.

"We need you to step out of the car. All of you."

James listens from the back seat, mentally noting that the man speaks with a Mexican accent, but not a thick accent as in Central Mexico, but more of an American-Mexican accent.

There's no way this good.

"Can you tell us what the issue is first?" Speer says. "We passed through the border checkpoint not more than thirty minutes ago. There shouldn't be a problem."

"The only problem we are going to have is if you don't get out of the car right now." The man points his gun at Speer.

"Okay, stay calm. I'll get out."

"No! Everyone out. Now!"

Before anyone can react to the demand, a Honda Pilot SUV pulls up alongside the Escalade, carrying four men—two in front, and two in back. The driver puts the Pilot in park as the front passenger seat occupant rolls down the window.

"Do you need any help?"

Without waiting for an answer, all four men jump out of the Pilot and move to the Escalade.

"Do you have a flat?"

The gunman closest to Speer lowers his gun to respond.

"No, no flat. We have it handled. There is no problem here."

In an instant, with military-style precision, all four men from the Pilot pull Glock 17 pistols out from their jackets. The two men from the back seat surround the dark-haired man at the back of the Escalade, while the front seat occupants point their weapons at the speaker.

"Oh, but you are so wrong. We have a very big problem." The driver points his Glock at the gunman's head while taking his gun from him.

The front seat passenger zip ties the agent's hands and tapes his mouth, as the same is done to the other fake border agent. The two hostages are thrown into the back of the Pilot.

The Pilot's driver returns to the Escalade and says, "All under control. You best be going, or you will be late."

A stunned Speer can only utter the simple question of, "Who are you?"

"Friends. Just friends. And Bobby says hello." He returns to the Pilot and drives off.

"Who is Bobby?" Speer pulls back onto the highway.

"A friend. PI and security guy I use a lot. But how did he..." James looks at Erica.

"I thought it would be good to have someone else looking out for us," she says.

"But you didn't know I'd be going this way," Speer says.

"No, but Bobby has been tracing my cell phone since Mazatlán. I texted him before I fell asleep on the plane. He assured me he had us covered. I guess he was right."

"James, don't lose this lady. She's a keeper." Aguilar displays a wide smile.

A few miles down the road, James leans forward to talk to Aguilar.

"I have to ask. How'd you know they were fake?"

"Two things. The passenger was carrying a rifle in the car, which a border agent would almost never do. And the driver didn't get out of the car like a law enforcement officer would. They have a distinctive style. It was obvious."

Once underway, James texts Bobby. "Thank you, my friend. I owe you. Big time."

The response from Bobby is immediate. "My pleasure Mr. Butler. Always happy to help."

"What has happened to our two intruders?"

"I have two words for you. Plausible deniability."

"Understood. Drinks on me soon."

"Very soon. Safe trip to LA."

On the highway, the car approaches a rest area, and Speer takes the exit before pulling into a parking spot far from any other vehicle.

As he puts the Escalade in park, Erica says, "What are we doing here?"

Speer opens his door and steps out, looking into the back of the Escalade

"I'm getting my gun!"

As he goes to the back to retrieve his and Aguilar's guns, James asks Aguilar, "Who were they?"

"Hard to say," Aguilar replies. "Many of the cartels have influence in the States. Here in this part of California, most of the influence comes from either the Sinaloa Cartel or the CJNG."

"Or the Toothpicks?" James asks.

Aguilar gives James a puzzled look.

"Tom and I had a long time to talk last night."

"The more important question is, how did they know it was us?" Erica says.

"No, the more important question is whether there are going to be more," James says.

"I have to think it is not very likely from here," Aguilar says. "Our friend in back should thank us that whoever they were did not get him"

"Better to be El Chapo than to be El Cholo," Erica says.

CHAPTER FIFTY-TWO

ONCE PAST INDIO, the drive is uneventful, much to the relief of James and Erica. Somewhere near Indio, once they had turned onto I-10, Erica lays her head on James's leg and falls asleep.

"Was this the plan all along," James asks Speer and Aguilar.

"Was what the plan?" Aguilar says.

"To kidnap Caro. To follow us to get to Caro."

"Hell no," Aguilar replies. "We are good, but not that good."

"Then what?" James says. "How did we end up here?"

"I was honest with you when we talked after your meeting with Tim. You had skills and an intelligence that were unique."

"And you had tenacity," Speer says.

"That afternoon," Aguilar continues, "I knew we needed to keep an eye on you. But when you went to Guadalajara, the game changed. That's when Tim and I knew you could get things done. The rest was really just waiting for the right opportunity."

"Opportunity for what?" James asks.

"Frankly, we had no idea," Aguilar replies, "but suspected something would come up if we were patient enough."

"And then we managed to hand you Caro on a silver platter."

"It did all come together pretty well," Aguilar says.

"But how did you know we were meeting with Caro?" James asks.

"I'm a spy, James," says Speer, with a smirk and chuckle. "This is what I do."

"Okay, looking back on how we started down this path, how'd you get the note to us in Félix's prison?"

"Money talks, James," says Speer. "Especially in Mexico."

"By the way," James says, "I have to thank you for the anonymous caller. His first tip on Matta did not give us much to go on. But his second really helped us figure out how to reach out to Caro."

"I have no idea what you are talking about," Aguilar deadpans.

"Come on. Do you really need to play Hide the Ball after all of this?"

"I'm not playing. I really know nothing about any anonymous caller. Do you, Tim?"

"This is the first I have heard of it. Truly. It wasn't us."

"Son of a bitch," James says. "I wonder who, then?"

The men ride in silence as they travel, unimpeded, to Los Angeles. Soon, the car nears the urban sprawl of Los Angeles, and James texts Williams with their ETA before waking Erica.

Speer takes the W. Temple Street exit off of the 101 Freeway, and turns right onto the first side street, about four blocks from the garage. He pulls the car over to the curb, puts it into park, and hands the keys to James.

"This is where we leave you."

All four exit the car, and Erica hugs Aguilar before sitting in the passenger seat and shutting the door. James and Speer shake hands.

"We will have time to catch up," Speer says, "but you need to get to the garage quickly. You know the way, right?"

"I am in familiar territory," James replies. "We will be there in three minutes or less."

"Try not to mention us, and to say as little as possible

about the last twenty-four hours, if you know what I mean."

"Understood," James says. "We will be in touch. Thank you."

He gets in the Escalade, shifts into drive, and pulls away without looking back or giving a second thought to what Speer and Aguilar would do next. As he drives up to the garage, James reaches over to hold Erica's hand, flashing a smile equal parts excitement and relief.

He opens the window, takes a parking ticket, and progresses cautiously as the down ramp descends to the lower floors. On the second lower floor, he stops and looks around. Nothing appears out of the ordinary, but there also is no welcoming party.

Erica and James look at each other but don't speak. He pulls forward to the middle of the floor, puts the car in park, turns off the engine, and places his hands on the steering wheel. Then a SWAT team—some wearing DEA vests, others FBI—emerge and surround the car. Neither James nor Erica moves until, moments that felt like hours later, a smiling Williams emerges.

"They are okay. You can let them get out."

"Are you two okay?" Williams hugs Erica, then James.

"We are, now," Erica says. "I've never been happier to see men with guns in my life!"

"The HVA?" Williams asks.

James leans back into the car to open the back lift that exposes the shielded compartment in the back.

"You might want a couple of those agents to come with us," James says, as they walk to the back.

He lifts the top of the compartment to find a bound and gagged Caro.

Williams looks in. "Holy...is that..."

"Assistant United States Attorney Steve Williams, meet Rafael Caro Quintero."

Williams motions, and two DEA agents remove Caro from the trunk.

"He might be a bit groggy and dehydrated," James says, "if anyone cares."

The agents move Caro to an adjacent FBI Suburban. Soon, two men in suits approach Williams.

"James, this is my boss, United States Attorney Ricardo Reyes, and DEA Special Agent William O'Sullivan, the resident agent in charge."

The men undergo the formality of shaking hands.

O'Sullivan asks, "You work with Brian Castle, right?"

"I do," James replies. "And this is his daughter, Erica Walsh."

"Erica? I met you once at a gala in Newport," O'Sullivan says. "You were your dad's date, but you must have been only about thirteen then."

"I think I was about sixteen, but I remember the evening, and you."

Agent O'Sullivan looks toward Caro. "Are you sure that's who I think it is?"

"Absolutely positive," James says. "There is no doubt."

"Wow. I never thought this day would come."

Reyes looks at O'Sullivan and nods toward Caro. "Why don't you go over there and have the honor of Mirandizing the son of a bitch."

"It will be a pleasure." O'Sullivan strides to Caro and places him under arrest.

Reyes watches the proceeding, before turning to Williams.

"I am going to need a good explanation and a full report on this, but well-done."

"Respectfully, sir, I had little to do with it. Any credit here goes to James."

"And Erica," James chimes.

"We can sort out the credit later," Reyes says. "For now, we have a criminal to arraign, and press to address."

"Yes, sir, we do," Williams replies. "I'll be right behind you."

"Tell Brian he owes me," Reyes says, with a warm smile.

"Yes, sir." James smiles as Reyes walks to O'Sullivan and Caro.

Williams turns back to James and Erica. "I had no idea this is what you were talking about. I just prepared for the worst."

"Maybe I should have said something," James says. "I was just being prudently paranoid."

"Am I to believe that you and Erica were able to locate one of the most notorious fugitives in the Western Hemisphere, bind and gag him, stuff him into the trunk of an Escalade, get out of Mexico, and drive to LA, by yourselves?" Williams flashes a knowing grin at James.

"If you could, it would help."

"I'm tough," Erica says.

"Were you in Mexico?" Williams asks.

"Probably a good assumption," James replies.

"You are aware that there is something referred to as international law?" Williams says.

"Erica and I broke no laws, international or otherwise."

Williams smirks and shakes his head. "You know we are going to have to discuss this more at some point."

"Yes, I am well-aware of that."

"But for now," Williams says, "we are going to walk him across the street, to the courthouse. There's a hidden tunnel right over here we can use. Even though I had no idea what you had going on, I trusted you, and as you suggested, I invited some of the press to come. Fortunately, some came, even without having a clue why they are here."

Williams starts to walk to the back of the garage, but Erica and James embrace and make no move to follow.

Williams looks back at them. "You coming?"

"Nah," James says, through a broad smile. "It's all yours from here. But when you speak of me, speak well."

Once across the street, Williams joins Reyes at a hastily planned press conference.

"Thank you for coming. I am United States Attorney Ricardo Reyes, and this is Assistant United States Attorney Stephen Williams. It is our pleasure to announce that, just a few moments ago, my office, working in close cooperation with agents of the United States Drug Enforcement Administration, led by Resident Agent in Charge William O'Sullivan, took into custody and arrested Rafael Caro Quintero, who will be charged with the murder of DEA Special Agent Enrique Camarena, among many other crimes."

Reyes's words are met by an audible gasp from those gathered in front of him.

"I am going to leave now and allow Mister Williams to provide you with more information, and to answer your questions. I have several calls to make. The first being to Missus Camarena. She deserves to hear from me that her husband's killer is in an American jail."

CHAPTER FIFTY-THREE

SEVERAL WEEKS LATER, on a perfect Saturday afternoon, James pulls up to the valet stand at Tony's restaurant. Crystal-blue skies and an ocean breeze provide a postcard setting. James takes in a deep breath of the salty air and smiles, now content in a way he could never have imagined.

He approaches the front door and reads the sign out front: We will be closed from 2–5 p.m. today for a special event. We apologize for any inconvenience.

James glides past the sign and opens the front door.

Tony embraces him. "Mister Butler, welcome."

"I hope this is not causing you too much trouble."

"Nonsense. It's for a good cause and good people. Besides, I'll bill you."

"I'd expect nothing less."

The two walk out onto the patio, the sound of the crashing waves making its way to their perch.

"You are a bit early, are you not? Tony asks.

"I am," James replies. I thought I'd have a drink and think a little before the guests arrive. If that's okay with you."

"Of course it is. Anything you need."

Tony shows James to the table and pulls a chair out for him.

"Your usual to start?"

"Yes, please, Tony. You have everything ready?"

"Everything is exactly as requested. Only three guests?"

"Four, including Erica."

"Erica is family. Not a guest."

"Very true."

Tony leaves, and James looks out at the ocean. The calming sight of the waves rolling into the shore relaxes him as he thinks about what he will say. James is good with words, always has been. But this is different. This is special. This will be from the heart.

Gloria, the lead waitress, brings James his drink.

"Here you are, Mister Butler."

"Thank you, Gloria. I've told you many times to call me James."

"I know. Would you like anything to eat while you wait, Mister Butler?"

James laughs. "No. Thank you, Gloria."

He takes a drink and resumes his introspection, which is soon interrupted by a call.

"Hello."

"Mister Butler, I will keep this short, but I wanted to congratulate you on a job well-done."

James knows instantly that it is the anonymous source from the two earlier calls.

"I'd like to thank you," he replies. "Your social media tip was helpful."

"I am glad it was. And please do not totally discount the Matta connection. But that is a topic for another time and place."

"Since our investigation is over, wouldn't you like to tell me who you are?"

"Mister Butler, surely you know our investigations are never over. We will speak again."

The phone turns silent as the call terminates.

James sits in the quiet for a few minutes, until he hears the distinctive footsteps of a woman's heals coming up behind him. Assuming it is Gloria with another drink, he does not turn his head to look behind him. The steps stop next to him when he feels a soft kiss on his cheek.

Erica whispers in his ear, "Mister Butler, you look absolutely delicious tonight."

Smiling broadly, James leaps from his seat and embraces Erica, holding her tighter and longer than usual.

"Have a seat. It is so good to see you. And you look amazing."

As Erica finds her seat, Gloria arrives.

"Hello, Erica. Welcome back." She winks at James. "What can I get you?"

Looking at James, Erica says, "We are having champagne later, right?"

"We are."

"In that case, I'll have a patron margarita. And I assume James will have one more of his Old Fashioneds."

"You know what, Gloria?" says James. "The margarita sounds good. Why not make it two. Or even better, a carafe."

"My pleasure. I'll be right back."

"Have you been here long?" Erica asks.

"Only about fifteen minutes. Just thinking a bit about what to say."

"Speak from your heart, and you will be great."

"It's just friends," James says, "but with what we all just went through..."

"Babe, I get it." Erica takes his hand in hers. "You'll be wonderful because you are wonderful."

Their gazes connect in a realization that many things had changed and would never be the same again. James leans in closer to Erica, smiling back as she flashes a coy grin.

"James! Erica!" Williams shouts, spoiling the moment.

"Stephen. Welcome, my friend."

James and Williams embrace, before Williams leans in to place a kiss on Erica's cheek.

"I feel like I interrupted a moment."

"You did," Erica replies. "But there will be others."

"Thank you for inviting me, James. This must be so special to you. To both of you."

"It is," James says. "Which is why it is important to have you here. We couldn't have done any of it without you."

"I didn't do anything. You two, though. Bad asses!"

Gloria returns with the margaritas. "I saw you had company, so I brought an extra glass." She pours three drinks.

The three friends raise their glasses.

"Let me do the toast," Erica says. "To true friends whose faith and trust never waiver. And to the virtues of simply doing the right thing."

"Salúd," they say in unison.

The next few minutes are filled with laughter and stories. James and Erica are freer and more naturally happy than they have ever been.

Tony joins the group, leaning in to whisper to James that his three guests are here.

"Three? There are only supposed to be two."

"Trust me. Three men are walking in now."

James stands and looks across the patio, to the doorway. As he does, he sees Aguilar step through the doorway, followed by Speer, who is talking to Tom as they approach the table.

"Gentlemen, you know Erica, of course," James says. "And this is AUSA Steve Williams, the very worthy and grateful recipient of your thoughtful package. Steve, this is former DEA Agent Joe Aguilar, Tim Speer—connected to a certain unnamed governmental agency—and this...well, this is Tom."

"Frank. The name is Frank Tarranova. After what you went through, it's not Tom any longer."

The men shake hands and sit at the table. James nods to Tony, who departs momentarily before retuning with Gloria, champagne flutes, and a chilled bottle of champagne.

"There is some great food coming your way soon," James says. "But before we start, I asked Tony to find us a special bottle of champagne to make a toast."

Tony shows the bottle to the table. "This, my friends, is a 1982 Dom Perignon that has been stored in ideal conditions.

It is the embodiment of cuvee perfection. Do you want to do the honors, James?"

"No. I believe Erica is an expert."

Without hesitation, she stands and takes the bottle from Tony. After placing a towel around the bottom, she skillfully pops the cork, with only a scant of foam escaping from the bottle. Erica hands it to Gloria, who fills each of the glasses. James distributes the filled glasses to the guests.

All eyes are on James, who takes a confident and solemn breath before speaking.

"This is for Enrique Camarena, and for the small amount of justice he received. Not just because someone new is in prison, but because the truth was revealed. Above all, he deserved that. As I was reflecting on things today, I was struck by the idea that Camarena was not perfect. He was not superman. And contrary to how it seems in the movies and stories, he was not the only agent in Guadalajara. I did not know him, of course, but I've met many who did, and I have no doubt he was a good agent, and a good husband, father, and friend. Camarena was let down not only in life, but in death. Used by others for their own agenda or opportunity for fame, glory, and of course, money. He did not deserve that. The truth will not bring Kiki back, nor ease the pain and suffering of his family and friends. But the truth assures that his death was not in vain. That the principles he fought and died for live on.

"Each one of you gave of yourself in small and large ways, and risked your own safety to do what was right. Each of you helped bring the truth from behind the dark curtains of secrecy, and helped use the truth to cast asunder those who falsely used Camarena's name for their own benefit. People may not know your names, but they will always remember what you have accomplished.

"I would be tragically remiss if I didn't mention Erica separately. You are an incomprehensible combination of beauty, brilliance, and determination that inspires those around you, and fueled me each and every day. None of us would be here if not for your efforts. And none of us there will ever forget you getting in Caro's face, compelling him to tell his secrets.

They all circle close to toast. "To Kiki!"

"Now, before we turn this into a real party," James says, "I have something for all of you. Except you, Steve."

They all chuckle.

"As you all know," James continues, "there was a small reward for the capture of Señor Caro. Thanks to some much-appreciated efforts by Mister Williams, that reward has been paid, and paid quickly. And I have the pleasure of distributing the proceeds."

James reaches into the inside pocket of his sports coat and pulls out some envelopes. Looking at Aguilar and Speer, he hands each an envelope.

"You deserve this, and much more." James then looks at Tom. "I'm so sorry, Tom—I mean, Frank. I had no idea you'd be here."

Speer says, "We have Frank covered."

"Are you sure? I could redo the checks."

"It's all good." Frank hugs James. "We did this for Kiki, not the money. But the money is nice, too."

James looks to Erica. "You'll get your envelope in a minute."

James turns to face the men, and raises his glass again.

"Now, my friends, Tony has a feast prepared for you. The place is ours for the next two hours. The bar is open. Eat, drink, and enjoy this amazing day."

As everyone heads to the bar, James puts a hand on Steve's shoulder.

"Before you go and get shit-faced, I do have something for you." James picks up a small, gift-wrapped box from the table. "Since you are a dedicated public servant and were not permitted to share in the reward money, I wanted to get you something to show our appreciation. I thought about buying you a Porsche, but thought that might be a little suspect. So I got you this instead."

Steve removes the wrapping to reveal a watch box.

"I have no idea what this is, but I'm sure it wasn't cheap."

"Open it."

Steve opens the lid to reveal the watch inside.

"Holy crap! It's amazing."

"I hope you like it. I thought it would fit in with your business attire and not raise any ethical inquiries. Just be sure to get it insured."

Steve laughs. "Yeah, I'll do that right away."

Steve is unaware that he has just been gifted a Patek Philippe Perpetual Calendar Chronograph that retails for a cool $270,000. James special ordered it from Tourneau at South Coast Plaza, experiencing the unique challenges associated with special ordering a watch worth a quarter-million dollars.

"I'm serious," James replies. "You could resell this for a significant down payment on a house. Even in Los Angeles."

"I appreciate it so much, but you know you didn't need to do this."

"Of course I did. You helped keep Erica and me safe. That means more to me than any watch could express. You've looked good on the news."

"It has been a whirlwind. We tell a good story, though it bothers me that neither you nor Erica are getting the credit you deserve."

"We don't need the credit. But as you know, it's hard to keep a good story quiet. Some people have learned the basics. It's been good for business, even if there is more than a wee bit of prurient speculation to go with it."

"Speaking of Erica, don't you have something for her, too?"

"Indeed, I do. I should go give it to her."

"Go do what you need to do. From a friend, go do what you should do."

The two men embrace before James walks over to Erica, engaged in conversation with Aguilar. Without a word, James takes Erica by the hand and walks her to the other end of the patio, where they lean against the railing. The afternoon sun shines on them as the sea breeze flows through Erica's hair.

"That was quite the gift you gave to Steve. And I expect a sizable portion of your share."

"It was money well-spent."

"Where's Bobby?" Erica looks around. "He should be here."

"I invited him, but he thought that in his position, he would be better off staying out of sight. But I suspect he is enjoying his new Ludicrous Mode Tesla."

Erica smiles and shakes her head. "Did you save anything for yourself?"

"I have some, and you know I don't care about the money."

"I know, but you deserve to be rewarded, too. You accomplished something amazing."

"We accomplished something special, together. And before we go any further, I have two things for you." James hands Erica her envelope. "This probably makes you one of the wealthiest paralegals in Orange County. Or anywhere else, for that matter."

Erica doesn't look inside to see the size of the enclosed check, but simply folds the envelope and places it her sweater pocket.

"I still can't believe it," she says. "It was your mission, your quest, and you did it."

"It was a journey you took with me."

They gaze out at the ocean for a moment, taking pleasure in the notable absence of the pressure and tension.

"What's the second thing you said you had for me?" Erica asks.

James leans over, placing his right hand on the nape of Erica's neck to pull her closer and draw her into a sensual kiss.

As their lips slowly part, Erica smiles at James. "Took you long enough,"

She moves closer into James to kiss him in return.

CHAPTER FIFTY-FOUR

"YOU KNOW I LOVE spending *every* minute of the day and night with you, James, and I really don't mind that we are not at work on a Monday. But I'm still a bit independent, and would love to know where the hell we're going."

"We should be at our destination very soon, and I'll explain everything then."

James and Erica have been driving in his car for forty-five minutes, heading northeast from James's condo in the Inland Empire, near Ontario and Rancho Cucamonga, toward San Bernardino.

For a moment, Erica starts to think James was planning on hitting I-25, and they'd be taking an impromptu trip to Vegas. But that guess is rendered moot when he takes exit 47 off the San Bernardino Freeway, onto South Indian Hill Boulevard in Claremont. Two quick turns, and James pulls into the entrance to Oak Park Cemetery. He looks at his phone for directions guiding him to a parking spot several rows into the cemetery. Though crazy with curiosity, Erica remains quiet.

James parks the car, gets out, and moves to the other side to open the door for Erica.

"Would you please join me? I have something I want to show you and explain to you."

"Of course. Lead the way."

James takes Erica's hand and leads her to a path up a small

hill, to a row of headstones shaded by a large sugar maple tree atop the hill.

"Right here." James guides Erica to the second headstone in the row.

The headstone, small and not ornate, reads:

John "Jack" Shepherd
Born February 28, 1966
Died October 21, 2019
A Respected Faculty Member and
Beloved Professor

"This was my birth father."

Erica is stunned. In all their time together, she has never picked up any indication that James either knew or cared about his birth father.

"I met him twice. Once, at my law school graduation in 2006. And once, about two and a half years ago."

"The picture in your home office, of your graduation... that's him?"

"It is. Let's sit for a moment. Apparently, he had gone to significant effort to locate me, and came to the graduation. We talked for a few minutes, but frankly, I was not too interested in him or what he had to say, and likely wasn't too nice."

"Totally understandable, of course," Erica says.

"Then a couple years ago, I got a call from him. He told me he was ill, and asked to see me one more time before he died. I still wasn't interested, but I went."

"Because you are a good man, and it was the right thing to do."

"I met him at his office at Pomona College, where he was a professor of international relations. When I met with him, he was quite frail from cancer, but his mind was sharp. We talked for about an hour. He explained that my birth mother and he had dated in high school, and that they hooked up after graduation. He left Indianapolis to go to college at UCLA the next day. And as he tells it, he and she exchanged a couple of letters, but then they fell out of touch. He said she didn't tell him she was pregnant until well after I had been born in the orphanage."

"I expect he did nothing then to find you," Erica says.

"He said he had guilt over it, but he essentially put it out of his mind and concentrated on school."

"Can't really blame him," Erica says.

"No. I don't, and I didn't. But here is where the story gets interesting. After finishing his undergrad in political science, he went to Boalt Hall at Berkeley, now Berkeley Law, to get his law degree. In the summer of 1990, he was a summer associate at a firm representing a defendant in the first Zuno trial. As he told the story, he was deeply disturbed by the proceedings and what he perceived as their lack of integrity. He also said the playing of the interrogation tapes in the courtroom gave him nightmares for years."

"The apple truly doesn't fall far from the tree," Erica says.

"Apparently, it was so disruptive to his psyche, that rather than joining the firm, after graduating law school, he got his PhD in international law and international relations, from UC Davis. He never practiced law, but instead began to teach, first at Cal State Fullerton, and then at Pomona College, where he received tenure and stayed the rest of his career."

"Did you two discuss the Camarena case?" Erica asks.

"Nothing more substantive than what I've said. But he had a copy of *Desperados* on his bookshelf, which he gave me. And then he talked about his life. He never married, and had no other kids, but apparently was a great teacher and very devoted to his students. What was profound, though, was, as I was about ready to leave, he asked if I could imagine his greatest regrets. Since I didn't even know him, really, I, of course, said I didn't know.

"He said it was the significant people who left his life

as quickly as they had entered. The relationships he had ignored, including me. The books he'd started to research and never finished.

"In a soft voice, he had said to me, 'Maybe I'm not unique in this regard, James, but as I sit here knowing the end is close, I'm not as comforted by the things I've accomplished, as I am haunted by the things left undone.'

"I tried to remind him of his many accomplishments and the student messages he had received since his diagnosis, but deep down, I understood. It was all the things left undone. It resonated with me."

"Which led to Camarena, how?" Erica asks.

"I'm not sure exactly. I went home and read *Desperados*, having had some basic familiarity with the case. Somehow it, too, struck a chord. All the things Camarena could have done in his life, but never had the opportunity to do. There were parallels with what Jack had said. I reached out to a few people I know and started getting information on the case, and compiled some files, even met with a couple witnesses. When *Narcos: Mexico* came out, I pulled out *Desperados* and read—or scanned—it again."

"Let me guess," Erica says. "The dreams started not too long thereafter."

"And the rest, as they say, is history."

James pauses for a moment, reflecting on the enormity of what he had just described, and how it had changed his life forever.

"He died three days after we talked. I attended his funeral. There were dozens of former students and faculty members. It was inspiring. I didn't go to the reception. I didn't want to answer questions about who I was and how I knew him. But I paid my respects and was happy I was able to do so."

Erica leans over to kiss him. "You, James Butler, are a good man."

He starts to stand, extending his hand to help Erica up.

"You, Erica Walsh, are an amazing woman. Thank you for letting me share with you."

James looks at his watch. "We should be going."

He takes Erica's hand, and they head back down the small hill. As they walk, hand-in-hand, away from headstoned rows, Erica looks at James.

"Now what?" she says.

"Now we go to your house so you can pack."

"Pack? Where am I going?"

"We are going to Hawaii. I thought we could both use a little rest and relaxation."

"I love it. When are we going?"

"Today. I've cleared it at the office, and we will head out as soon as you pack. But we have one stop to make."

"A stop? Where?"

"Our mystery friend called with a new tip, and I thought we could make a quick stop to check it out on our way to LAX."

"A tip? On the Camarena case?"

"Not exactly. But I promise it will be interesting."

ABOUT THE AUTHOR

JACK LUELLEN is a Denver, Colorado attorney with over 30 years of experience. In practice, Jack has tried cases to courts and juries and has written hundreds of briefs, motions, and memoranda, to state and federal courts, including federal courts of appeal and the United States Supreme Court. Jack first started working on the Camarena case in 1990 and has continued to investigate it in the years since. Jack is the proud parent of an amazing daughter.

Connect with Jack at:
jackluellen.com
Twitter: @jackluellen
facebook.com: Luellen Writing
Instagram: luellen_writing